Praise for *The Foundlings*

'This is a fun and engaging read that will transport you back to a memorable decade'
Family Tree magazine

'This is one of the best books in an excellent series...Highly recommended'
LostCousins

'Absolutely riveting — the best yet in this series!'
Tacoma-Pierce County Genealogical Society

'A must read for anyone who loves unraveling genealogy mysteries'
Columbia County Historical & Genealogical Society

'Once again, Nathan Dylan Goodwin has given us a fabulous, fast-paced tour through investigative genetic genealogy woven through a mystery hidden in a mystery'
Boulder Genealogical Society

'It flows along at a cracking pace and is lucidly written, with occasional twists and turns in Morton's research and some welcome touches of humour'
Waltham Forest FHS

'Another brilliant book that combines family, mystery and genealogy'
Doncaster FHS

'Goodwin's genealogy crime mysteries, including this one, will keep you in suspense as the stories weave back and forth in time and you come to know the characters and their trials'
Utah Genealogical Association

About the author

Nathan Dylan Goodwin is a writer, genealogist and educator. He was born and raised in Hastings, East Sussex. Having attended school in the town, he then completed a Bachelor of Arts degree in Radio, Film and Television Studies, followed by a Master of Arts degree in Creative Writing at Canterbury Christ Church University. A member of the Society of Authors, he has completed several local history books about Hastings, as well as several works of fiction, including the acclaimed *Forensic Genealogist* series, the *Mrs McDougall Investigates* series and the *Venator Cold Case* series. His other interests include theatre, reading, running, skiing, travelling and, of course, genealogy. He is a qualified teacher, member of the Guild of One-Name Studies and the Society of Genealogists, as well as being a member of the Sussex Family History Group, the Norfolk Family History Society and the Kent Family History Society. He lives in Kent with his husband, son, dog and an assortment of chickens.

NathanDylanGoodwin

@NathanDGoodwin

The Foundlings
by
Nathan Dylan Goodwin

For Géraldine, Martin & James

Prologue

23rd September 1973, Haywards Heath, West Sussex

She was the only person to alight from the train at Haywards Heath; the few other passengers, who had occupied the train carriage with her, were likely taking advantage of the hot September Sunday to escape the capital for a day out beside the sea in Brighton. She took a brief glance around the empty platform, then carefully placed the red and white chequered bag, which she had been clutching in her hand, down onto the ground. She pulled a crumpled packet of Embassy cigarettes from her handbag as she watched the train crawl out of the station, continuing its journey south towards the coast. Lighting a cigarette, she stood for a moment in the silence left by the departing train, then she picked up the bag and walked out onto the main road.

She ambled along The Broadway, taking casual interest in the window displays of the small shops that she passed. It being a Sunday, this main thoroughfare running through the town was deserted; the shop interiors were dark, their awnings retracted and the parking spaces in front of them all but empty. Just the way she wanted it to be.

She stopped outside of Jo's Boutique, admiring a fancy new barmink coat in the window. Much nicer than the grubby black leather jacket that she was now wearing. 'Twenty-five quid? Is that a joke?' she scoffed, drawing on the cigarette and continuing on up the hill towards the town centre.

A young couple, arm in arm, were walking towards her. She looked down at the pavement as they passed, not wanting to make eye contact.

She quickened her step until she reached a row of three shops. She paused, glanced up briefly to the first floor, and then tossed the cigarette butt into the road. Looking around her and finding the street to be deserted, she crossed over, heading for the bright currant-red telephone box outside of the Seeboard showroom opposite.

She hastened towards it, pulling open the door and smelling the familiar musty, metallic odour common to every telephone box into which she had ever stepped.

Placing the red and white bag down onto the floor, the woman turned to leave, heading back towards the train station. Behind her, the heavy door closed slowly and weightily. Seconds later, from inside the bag the baby began to cry, the sound amplified by the acoustics of the telephone box.

She continued walking without so much as a glance back.

Chapter One

Morton Farrier was exasperated. He was standing in a large field of Christmas trees on the Dengate Farm Stall in Rye Foreign with a tangle of brambles wrapped around his boots. His wife, Juliette, was grasping onto a traditional Norway Spruce and staring down at the ground.

'Are you okay?' he asked her, questioning the wisdom of trekking up two small hills in search of the perfect Christmas tree whilst being seven months pregnant.

'Yeah, fine,' she answered, meeting his gaze. 'I just don't want anyone else to take this tree.'

Morton looked all around them. The nearest people were on the opposite bank, fifty yards away. 'I'm not sure that's very likely,' he mumbled, gazing at the chosen tree. They were surrounded by two fields of textbook-perfect Christmas trees of all shapes, sizes and varieties but they had misguidedly conferred the decision as to which tree they would be taking home on their two-and-a-half-year-old daughter, Grace, who had opted for the only one on the entire farm with almost no branches at its centre; it looked plainly ridiculous.

'Chosen?' a male voice asked, emerging from the thicket of trees, startling Grace.

'I think so,' Morton said.

'Yes, we have,' Juliette stated firmly.

The owner of the site, David Dengate, approached with a grin and a small saw. 'This one?' he asked, his tone uncertain.

'This one!' Grace said, jumping up and down.

David looked between Morton and Juliette for a final confirmation.

'That one,' Morton reluctantly agreed.

'Okay,' David said, crouching down so that he was level with Grace. 'You're going to need to stand right back and then use some magic to help me cut down the tree, okay?'

Grace nodded as Juliette took her hand and stepped backwards a few paces.

David knelt down on the ground and began to saw through the

trunk at the base. After just a few seconds, he stood up and frowned. 'I can't do it,' he said to Grace. 'Can you help me?'

She nodded and walked over towards him, pulling Juliette along behind her.

'Okay, I'm going to count to three and you need to give it a really, really big push. One…two…three. Push!'

Grace did as she was instructed and leant against a branch of the tree so that it tumbled down. 'Yay!' she exclaimed.

Juliette clapped enthusiastically.

'Right,' David said, hoisting the tree up onto his shoulder, 'let's get this over to your car, then you can get home and start decorating it.'

'Can't wait,' Morton muttered, receiving an admonishing rap on his arm from Juliette.

'Stop being so bah-humbug,' she whispered as they headed back down the hill behind David and the Christmas tree.

'Sorry,' he said. 'It just doesn't seem worth going over the top this year, since we're going to Aunty Margaret's in a few days.'

'This will be the first Christmas that Grace really understands, so we need to make an effort. Besides, we're not going down to Cornwall for another six days yet.'

'I really need to get on with that research, then,' he said. 'I can't very well drop the bombshells on Aunty Margaret, that I'm going to have to drop, without more information to back it up.'

Two months ago, Morton had discovered that his Aunty Margaret had a half-sister about whom the whole family, she included, had known absolutely nothing. In the process of trying to work out how this new-found family member fitted in, Morton had also stumbled upon the unlikely but horrifying truth that his grandfather—Aunty Margaret's dad—had killed a prostitute, named Candee-Lee Gaddy, whilst holidaying in Reno, Nevada in 1980. But, since discovering these indigestible facts two months ago, Morton had been preoccupied with another genealogical case and had not made any additional progress. And now time was pressing down on him; he needed to be able to tell Aunty Margaret the whole story in less than a week's time.

'Start your research later today,' Juliette suggested. 'Once you've helped us to put up the tree, that is.'

'Grace's tree!' she chanted, skipping between a corridor of tall

Norway Spruces.

'Yes, and what a lovely tree it is,' Juliette responded. 'Isn't it, Morton?'

'Yes, it's the best tree in the world,' he said monosyllabically.

Juliette rolled her eyes.

Two hours later, with Bing Crosby softly crooning his way through a Christmas album, the tree was finished. It was standing, fully decorated in the corner of the lounge in their home on Mermaid Street, Rye. Morton stood back to take it in fully. Maybe it didn't look so strange now that it was covered in decorations, and generous quantities of beads and tinsel covered the large gaps in the centre. 'Ready?' he asked, moving over to the light switch.

Juliette nodded, whilst handing over to Grace a small black box with an inset button. 'Press that when daddy turns off the big lights, okay?'

'Yes.'

Morton plunged the room into darkness and Grace pushed the button, illuminating the tree in a soft white light that cast long atmospheric shadows all around them.

'Wow!' Grace beamed. 'Pretty.'

'It's beautiful,' Juliette said.

'Yes, it is,' Morton was forced to agree.

He moved back into the room, placing his arms around Juliette's waist, around their baby bump and stroked Grace's hair. Although he was looking forward to spending Christmas down in Cornwall with his Aunty Margaret and Uncle Jim, his anticipation was soured somewhat by the shocking news that he would have to impart to them. Standing here with his little family, he wished now that they were staying put, just the three and a half of them with lots of good food, wine and Christmas movies.

'Grace,' Juliette said eventually, 'do you want to help mummy to make a Christmas cake?'

'Yes!' Grace replied.

'Aren't you supposed to make them in October?' Morton asked.

Juliette shrugged. 'It'll just be a glorified fruit cake,' she answered, leading Grace into the kitchen. 'We'll let daddy get on with his family tree work.'

'Christmas tree work?' Grace asked.

Morton laughed and ruffled her hair as he followed them into the kitchen. He headed over to a simmering pan on the hob, where he ladled out two glasses of non-alcoholic mulled wine. He chinked glasses with Juliette and gave her a kiss. 'Cheers,' he said.

'Cheers. Good luck with the case,' she said.

'Good luck with the baking,' he replied, pointing to Grace who was shoving a handful of glacé cherries into her mouth.

'Grace!' Juliette yapped.

Morton smiled as he escaped the room, carrying his drink upstairs to his study on the top floor of the house.

He sat down at his desk and drank some of the mulled wine. It wasn't too bad, he considered, given that it was alcohol-free. In front of him was his sleeping laptop and behind that, his investigation wall where he liked to attach the findings of the case on which he was currently working. At the moment, it was empty.

The beginning of a new genealogical investigation—especially the more complex ones—was always a moment of excited anticipation for him, but this one, being so close to home, brought with it an edge of apprehension. But it was too late to back-pedal now; the Pandora's Box had been well and truly opened. All he could do was to arm himself with as many facts as he possibly could before disclosing everything that he knew to Aunty Margaret.

He took another sip of his drink and then woke his laptop. Having worked on another case for the past two months, the first thing that he needed to do was to refresh his memory about his findings; so, he accessed the short document that he had started and carefully re-read it.

Aunty-Margaret's half-sister, Vanessa Briggs, found in a shoebox outside Woolworths in Sevenoaks shortly after birth. Assistant manager found the baby and phoned for an ambulance. Vanessa discovered the truth about her birth in 2019. Uploaded DNA to GEDmatch and discovered two half-sisters who shared unknown mother:

- *Liza, found in Croydon, South London*
- *Billie, found in Manchester*

Both in cardboard boxes within a red and white chequered bag. Identity of their shared mother unknown. Prostitute?

Morton wrote *UNKNOWN FEMALE* in the centre of a piece of A4 paper which he attached to his investigation wall. Below that, he affixed a post-it note with Vanessa Briggs's date of birth: 13th May 1975. She was Morton's half-aunt, despite her having been born eight months after him. Her father, confirmed by DNA, was Morton's grandfather, Alfred Farrier.

Morton returned to his computer to pull up the birth details of Liza and Billie. Both women had granted him permission to access the basic family trees that they had separately created. He soon found that the two trees were pitiful in substance, containing just their own names, the names of their half-sisters and with *UNKNOWN UNKNOWN* as the name of their shared mother. No grandparents, no cousins, no other siblings, no history and no past. Morton knew the feeling only too well. As a teenager, he had discovered that he had been adopted and it wasn't until six years ago that he had learned that his biological mother was none other than his Aunty Margaret, his adoptive father's younger sister. For him, the journey to discovering his biological past, including finding the identity of his father, had been highly complex and deeply emotional, but he was now in a position of clear understanding as to who he really was. It was because of his own history that he had happily volunteered to work pro bono to try and remove the veil over Vanessa's, Liza's and Billie's shadowed past.

The two women's trees were all but useless to him, providing only their dates of birth. Or at least their approximate dates of birth, since there was no official documentation of when each had occurred. He wrote Liza's name and her assumed date of birth of 28th April 1977 onto a post-it note, did the same for Billie and her date of birth of 19th December 1979, and then attached both to his investigation wall.

Whoever their mother might have been, she certainly hadn't stayed in any one place for too long, which had made Morton wonder if that had been her lifestyle choice or a need to cover up multiple unwanted pregnancies, perhaps.

He copied the three women's birth information onto separate index cards which he stuck to the bottom of his investigation wall as the beginnings of a timeline with which to track their mother's movements in a chronological order.

He sat back at his desk and clicked to view the *DNA* tab within his Ancestry account. Liza and Billie had also given him the status of Collaborator to their DNA results, which meant that he had the maximum access permissions. Owing to his having been engaged with his previous case, he still had yet to analyse their results.

First, he pulled up Liza Bennett's page and was presented with three options: *DNA Story, DNA matches* and *ThruLines*. He clicked to view her DNA Story. A monochromatic map loaded onscreen with seven differently coloured, curved shapes superimposed over the top, each offering a loose and unrefined geographical area identified in Liza's DNA. Ethnicity, or admixture reports as they were sometimes known, were an evolving science with many generalisations and errors; Morton rarely paid them too much heed.

Liza's ethnicity was estimated to be 75% England and Northwestern Europe, 10% Scotland, 10% Ireland and 4% France. Within the English bracket, three sub-communities had also been identified: East of England, East Anglia and South East England. Under *Additional Communities* he found another subgroup: Kansas and Southern Nebraska Settlers. The symbol beside this community – and also that of South East England – showed that this area was a recent feature in Liza's DNA, both having occurred somewhere in the past 50 to 300 years. Morton took a screenshot of the page and printed it out.

Next, he clicked to view the DNA Story for Billie Howard. A fresh map appeared with a different combination of geographical areas highlighted. Billie's ethnicity was estimated to be 61% England and Northwestern Europe, 18% Germanic Europe, 8% Wales and 5% Sweden. Interestingly, one of the sub-communities identified in Billie's DNA was also South East England and, again, was annotated with the symbol indicating that it was recent DNA. Morton was slightly surprised – although he wasn't sure why – to discover that she too had Kansas and Southern Nebraska Settlers in her recent DNA heritage. He took another screenshot, printed it out and then changed the DNA Story to that of his half-aunt, Vanessa Briggs.

Morton scrutinised the results, his eyes quickly moving to the 71% England and Northwestern Europe DNA. Sure enough, just like her two half-sisters, Vanessa's ethnicity included sub-communities of South East England, and Kansas and Southern Nebraska Settlers in her recent DNA.

He reasoned that the results *could* indicate that Vanessa, Liza and Billie's mother's family hailed from the South East of England and the border of Kansas and Nebraska. Alternatively, it could just be a coincidence or perhaps something common to many test-takers. He sent a screenshot to the printer and then attached all three ethnicity estimates to his investigation wall.

Morton drank some of his mulled wine and then turned his focus to *DNA matches*, the more useful and accurate aspect of the test. Specifically, he wanted to focus on those people who were related to all three women. From Vanessa Briggs's list of cousin matches, Morton clicked on Billie Howard, then clicked *Shared Matches* to create a point of triangulation. As he expected, the person at the top of the list, with 1749 centiMorgans of DNA was Liza Bennett, their half-sister. Nine other people were listed below, all of them somehow connected to the three women's maternal family.

The person most closely related to all of them was somebody by the name of Denise Prince who shared a healthy 316 centiMorgans of DNA with Vanessa and slightly less with the two other women. Morton sighed when he saw that Denise had not added a family tree and, when he clicked her name, discovered that she had not logged in to Ancestry for over a year. Even though it felt unlikely that he would get a response, he sent her a message through the website, briefly explaining his quest and asking if she would be able to help. Before he moved on, Morton clicked to look at Denise Prince's ethnicity, finding a sub-community of South East England but nothing whatsoever relating to the USA.

Gerard Bramley, matching with 78 cM of DNA came next in the list. Morton was more hopeful when he saw that Gerard had an unlinked-family-tree icon beside his name. He clicked it, finding that it consisted of just three people, two of whom were listed as *Private*. Only Gerard's mother, Cynthia Chiddicks, was viewable. Morton clicked her name to see if any additional information had been added. Nothing. Not even a birth date or location. What he did find, however, was that Gerard Bramley shared the women's sub-community of Kansas and Southern Nebraska Settlers in his recent DNA.

Morton eked out the last of the mulled wine, wishing that it was the alcoholic version. He also wished that the kitchen weren't three floors below so that he could more easily get a top-up. He was half-tempted to send Juliette a text message asking her to bring him more but guessed that her reaction likely wouldn't be a very favourable one.

Returning to the remaining seven shared matches, Morton was instantly disappointed. The amount of DNA quickly fell into low double-digits, meaning that he could be searching as far back as fifth great-grandparents in order to find an ancestor common to them all. It wasn't impossible but it was a monumental challenge and one that he doubted could be completed in the six days that he had remaining before they left for Cornwall.

One match close to the bottom caught Morton's eye. It was the polar opposite of Gerard Bramley's tree, consisting of 3,694 people and whose privacy settings had been set to public. The person matching all three women was named Henry Cowling, an individual sharing between 29 cM and 34 cM of DNA. Morton viewed Henry Cowling's tree as a pedigree so that it displayed direct maternal and paternal antecedents only, stretching back to all of Henry's thirty-two great-great-great-grandparents.

He spent some time snooping around the tree, finding multiple locations around the world, including the wider UK and areas within south east England. Perhaps, somewhere amongst all those people was the three women's mother. But, without significantly more information to hand, trying to work out how they connected to Henry Cowling's tree was, at this stage, impossible.

Interestingly, he could find no links on the family tree or DNA profile to Kansas or Nebraska and wondered if perhaps Henry Cowling and Gerard Bramley were unrelated. Selecting *Shared Matches* between Gerard Bramley and Vanessa Briggs, he found that neither Henry Cowling nor Denise Prince appeared in the list, meaning that they were very likely to be found on different sides of the three women's maternal family tree.

Morton needed *a lot* more information. And it was going to take a lot of time, he realised as he decided that he would send Juliette a text message after all.

Hi! How's it going down there? Any chance of you bringing me a top-up of mulled wine? Or maybe something stronger? Xx

Returning to the list of shared matches, Morton looked again at Gerard Bramley. He only had his mother's name with which to work; it wasn't much to go on, but Morton hoped that it would be just enough to get started in creating a speculative tree. First, he opened up the FreeBMD website and ran a marriage search for Cynthia Chiddicks. In the field for her spouse, he kept the forename blank and typed Bramley as the surname. Thankfully, there was just one result: Cynthia Chiddicks had married a Leslie Bramley in the Wandsworth registration district in the June quarter of 1948. Next, searching for births with the surname of Bramley and the mother's maiden name of Chiddicks, Morton was able to find that Gerard had been born in 1951.

Satisfied that he had identified the correct family, Morton then added all the information to his tree. What he didn't know at this stage, however, was whether Gerard Bramley was related to Vanessa, Liza and Billie via his maternal or paternal side; both lines would need taking back approximately a further four generations to hit a most recent common ancestor. Hopefully.

His mobile pinged with a reply from Juliette.

Yes, of course, husband dearest! Right away. I can't see any problem with that, being seven months pregnant and in the middle of trying to bake a cake with a tantruming two and a half year old. Would you like anything else? Some canapés? A massage, perhaps?

Oh. Morton toyed with the idea of replying that a massage would be wonderful but didn't think that his humour would be appreciated at the moment. Now he *definitely* didn't want to go back downstairs for more drink. He raised the empty glass to his lips, tipped it back and patiently waited for a reluctant droplet of mulled wine, trapped behind a slice of orange, to travel down to his open mouth.

In the time that it had taken him to put the glass back down on his desk, the little green Ancestry leaf hints had miraculously sprouted from beside Cynthia Chiddicks' and her spouse Leslie Bramley's names. He clicked to view which records the mystical algorithms had suggested might relate to Cynthia. The first, as always, was *Ancestry*

Member Trees. He would take a look at that later, but never trusted other people's research above his own in the first instance. The second hint made him smile: *Australia, City Directories, 1845-1948*, pertaining to a Cynthia Bramley, resident in Queensland in 1917. Not much chance of that one's being correct.

Next came *England & Wales, Civil Registration Death Index, 1916-2007*. Without needing to click the entry, Morton could ascertain the key details.

Birth: 19 July 1929
Death: Oct 1969, Croydon, London, England

It was certainly possible that this was the correct Cynthia; it was also certainly possible that it was not. Opening up the British Newspaper Archive website, Morton selected the year of 1969 with Cynthia's married name. Eighteen results. He slowly scrolled down the list until his eyes stopped on an edition of the *Croydon Advertiser*, dated 27th October. The short précis of the full report looked promising, and Morton clicked to see an image of the original newspaper. He was pleased to find that it was a death notification, knowing that they were often full of useful genealogical information.

BRAMLEY. On 20th October 1969, peacefully but suddenly at her home in Croydon, Cynthia, aged 40 years, dearly loved wife of Leslie and mother of Gerard and Susan.

It was brief, but sufficient in itself to confirm that the death related to the correct Cynthia. Morton added the details to the speculative tree that he was building and then, with the substantiated knowledge of Cynthia's birth date, turned to the 1939 Register. He found her quickly and easily, living in Croydon as a ten-year-old girl with two siblings and her parents, Roger and Maisie Chiddicks. Morton saved the new details to the family tree and then ran a search for a marriage between Roger and Maisie. He soon found a scanned image of their original 1925 marriage certificate within the *London, England, Church of England Marriages and Banns, 1754-1932* record set. The document revealed that Maisie's maiden name had been Gaulden and also provided Morton with the names of both her father and Roger's father.

Switching to the 1911 census, Morton was able to track down Roger and Maisie as young children in their respective families, furnishing him with the forenames of their mothers.

Working his way backwards through time, it didn't take Morton too long to identify the names of Gerard Bramley's eight maternal great-great-grandparents. He still needed to find the mirroring eight on the paternal side and then work out which of those sixteen people might be the common ancestors to Vanessa, Liza and Billie.

Morton thought about Juliette's text message and decided that it was time to call it a day on his research. She obviously would appreciate a hand downstairs. He had made decent enough progress for now, he reasoned, rising from his chair. As he went to close his laptop lid, he noticed that a new hint had appeared for Gerard Bramley's great-great-grandfather, Francis Gaulden, on the 1900 United States Federal Census.

He just couldn't *not* click it.

The page opened up, and Morton cast his eyes down to the relevant section, helpfully highlighted in yellow. Francis Gaulden, born in England in February 1860, was recorded as living with his wife, Mabel, and their two children. Morton was puzzled. Just moments before, he had found Francis, Mabel and their offspring on the 1891 England Census, living in London. If they had all emigrated to the US, as it now appeared, then how had Morton been able to trace Gerard Bramley's line backwards through the British records to reach Francis and Mabel Gaulden? The answer was evident. Gerard's great-grandfather, James Gaulden, had remained in London, making him present there for the 1901 England Census, while his two brothers, Thomas and Edward, had gone with their parents to the US.

Morton looked to the top of the record to see in which part of America they had settled: Atwood, Rawlins County, Kansas. He entered the details into Google Maps, instantly seeing that the town was fewer than ten miles from the Nebraska state border. Bingo.

He smiled, having probably just identified Vanessa, Liza and Billie's great-great-grandparents in Francis and Mabel Gaulden. Given their shared ethnicity, which incorporated Kansas and Southern Nebraska Settlers, it was highly likely that the three half-siblings' great-grandfather was either Thomas or Edward Gaulden.

Morton stared at the map of the Nebraska and Kansas border, wondering if perhaps the three women's mother had been American by birth. Whatever the answer, it would just have to wait until tomorrow. He *really* wanted to continue his research and had to fight against his own urge as he closed down the laptop lid. He picked up his empty glass and headed down to his family.

'Wow, something smells very nice,' Morton said, entering the kitchen. 'How long until we get to eat this cake, then?'

Juliette was sitting opposite Grace at the kitchen table and replied, 'Well, I had been planning on saving it to take down to Cornwall with us but…' She glanced across the table at Grace who was doing some colouring in.

Grace looked at Morton. 'Grace sneeze,' she informed him.

'*Into* the cake mix,' Juliette clarified.

Morton pulled a face. 'Nice.'

'Little sneeze,' Grace added.

'So, I think we'll be keeping that one for ourselves,' Juliette said.

'Yeah, I think that's probably for the best. More mulled wine?' he asked.

'Yes, please,' she answered, placing a hand on her bump as she handed Morton her empty glass. 'I can't wait for an *actual* wine, once this little thing is out of me.'

'Little thing,' Grace parroted.

'We probably should start to think about names,' Morton said, ladling out the drink. 'Rather than keep calling him or her 'the little thing'.'

Juliette laughed. 'The nursery said on Friday that Grace had told them that we were planning on calling it The Little Thing. Honestly, though, Morton, I can't face going through the whole procedure we went through with naming this one.'

'Hmm,' he mumbled, sliding in beside Grace and handing Juliette her wine. Owing to a slight hiccup with the clarity of certain key aspects of foetal anatomy on the twenty-week scan, for the remainder of the pregnancy, Grace had been named Albert. It had then taken the pair of them an age to find an appropriate name for her when her actual sex became known. Morton's reading of the entirety of the *60,001 Best Baby Names* book hadn't helped matters and, in the end, it had been Juliette's own great-grandmother, a fierce suffragette, named Grace Emmerson who had provided the inspiration for her name.

'What about the shortlist we created for Grace?' Morton suggested. 'I might have it somewhere. Obviously, there's still Albert for a boy. What were the girls' names? Eden? Felicity? I think they were on the shortlist.'

Juliette screwed up her nose. 'I think—*without* the help of a baby name book—we should come up with a new list for this one; not Grace's leftovers.'

'Yes,' Grace agreed, which made Morton grin.

'There's still plenty of time,' Juliette said, giving a dismissive wave. 'How did you get on with your work?'

'A good start,' he replied. 'I've *possibly* found one set of Vanessa, Liza and Billie's great-great-grandparents but I need to work on triangulating their results against their DNA cousin matches. Plus, I need to check all the other websites where they've uploaded their DNA.'

'Why do you need another person to triangulate? Doesn't triangulate mean three?' Juliette asked. 'Vanessa, Billie and Liza. Three. No?'

'They only count as one,' he said. 'Anyway, enough work-talk for today. Who here wants to sit down and watch The Polar Express?'

'Me!' Grace said excitedly.

'Me,' Juliette said less excitedly.

The three of them trooped into the warm ambience of the lounge and settled down on the sofa together to watch the movie.

'What about Ebenezer for a boy?' Morton asked.

'Shut up,' Juliette replied.

Chapter Two

23rd September 1973, Haywards Heath, West Sussex

Kathy Steadman was sitting in the dining room of her quiet bungalow, eating a cheese-and-ham sandwich. Despite the light rain, the patio door was open to her compact but well-tended garden. She was arching forwards over the plate to ensure that she didn't spoil her smart suit jacket and skirt. It was a workday for her as a WDS—Woman Detective Sergeant—in Sussex Police, but, with it being a Sunday, she was permitted to go home for her lunch.

She took another bite of the sandwich and tossed a small piece of crust out through the open doorway, and then watched as a tame robin bounced down from the fence to peck at it until it was able to be carried off.

The stillness of the bungalow was suddenly broken by the trilling of the telephone. Kathy set down her sandwich and hurried into the hallway where she duly sat at the telephone seat and picked up the receiver. 'Four three one, one double seven,' she announced.

'Sorry to disturb your lunch break, Sarge,' the male voice said. She recognised it immediately as belonging to the Station Officer at Burgess Hill Police Station, which could mean only one thing: an incident requiring her attention had occurred. She picked up a pen and held it poised over the notepad.

'Go ahead,' she said.

'Abandoned baby. Found just after eleven o'clock this morning in a telephone box in Hayward's Heath. Taken to Cuckfield Hospital.'

'Condition?' Kathy asked, scribbling down what he had told her.

'Well, it was alive when they took it in,' he answered.

'Who found it and what was the precise location?'

'A teenage girl wanted to use the telephone and heard it crying. She used the phone in the box to ring 999. It was the one on The Broadway, right outside Seeboard. The baby was in a cardboard box inside a red and white bag. Witnesses reported seeing a young woman walking away in the direction of Heath Road.'

'Boy or girl?' she asked.

'Haven't had that confirmed yet, Sarge.'

'Anything else?'

'That's all I've got.'

'Right. Get someone to interview the girl who found it and find out from Cuckfield how the baby's doing. We need to know if we're looking at a charge of abandonment of a child or… something more serious. Thanks.'

'Right you are. Will do.'

Kathy replaced the receiver, tore off the top sheet of her notepad, locked the patio door and dashed out of her bungalow. Parked on her driveway was a banana-yellow Ford Escort—one of a pair of unmarked General Patrol vehicles used by CID out of Burgess Hill Police Station. Kathy unlocked the car, jumped in and turned the key in the ignition.

In under fifteen minutes, she had reached The Broadway in Haywards Heath. She slowed the car down, noticing the red telephone box outside the Seeboard showroom. She parked the car right outside the shop and stepped out onto the pavement. The main thoroughfare through the town would, on any weekday, be bustling with cars and pedestrian shoppers but was today nigh on deserted. An old man with a cane and a small terrier was ambling along on the other side of the road, and a young mother holding her son's hand was heading towards her. Other than that, there was no sign of life.

Kathy stepped slowly towards the telephone box, peering in through the small rectangular windows. There was nothing in there now to suggest that a baby had been left inside it fewer than two hours earlier. She looked at the shiny metal-grip door handle, wondering if it would be worth getting it checked for fingerprints. She quickly decided that it would be pointless, given how many people would have touched it both before and probably after the person who had abandoned the child. Tentatively, she opened the door and stepped inside. Nothing appeared out of the ordinary. She lifted the telephone receiver, hearing the familiar gurgling purr of the dial tone. She prodded the brushed silver flap for rejected coins, and then crouched down and inspected the concrete floor, wondering why the child had been specifically left here. A certain degree of protection from the elements? The possibility, as had transpired in the event, that someone might come to use the telephone? The answer didn't only have a bearing on trying to work out who had left the baby, but also on the legal aspects of the case; there were two

17

types of abandonment of a child in law. The most serious type was where an infant was left in the middle of nowhere and highly unlikely to be found. The less serious offence was one where the child would likely be discovered. Did the person think that on a quiet Sunday, when all the shops were shut, that the baby would be found? At this point, Kathy couldn't yet be sure.

She left the telephone box and looked up the street towards Heath Road, the direction in which the witnesses had seen a young female heading.

She opened the door on the Escort, sat in the driver's seat, picked up the VHF radio and called the Sussex Police Operations Room at Lewes who in turn patched her through to the station at Burgess Hill. 'CID car KB350, WDS Steadman here. Have the witnesses been interviewed yet about the abandoned baby in Haywards Heath, over?'

Following a short crackle on the other end, the Station Officer replied, 'Yes, they have. Detective Constable Chivers has just got back in, over.'

'Could you relay a description of the potential suspect to me, please, over?'

'Suspect is female, estimated to be between twenty and thirty years old. Shoulder-length curly brown hair, pulled back under a hairband. Looked 'a bit rough'. Wearing a black leather jacket and flared jeans. That's it, over.'

'Did they see her actually coming out of the telephone box or anywhere near it, over?'

'No, just that she was the only person they'd passed, over.'

'Hmm,' Kathy said. 'And how's the baby, over?'

'The nurse I spoke to said it would be fine. The doctors don't think it was left there very long, over.'

'Thank you. Over and out,' Kathy said, getting back out of the Escort and locking the door this time. She began to head in the direction of Heath Road, her pace slow and deliberate. On either side of the street was a run of two-storey buildings with shops on the ground floor and small flats above, occasionally interrupted by garish monstrosities that had been thrown up quickly to fill a post-war housing gap.

Shortly after she crossed the junction with Heath Road, the shops petered out and the right-hand side of the road became residential whilst on the left there were three- and four-storey office blocks.

She continued walking past the Methodist Church and more houses and blocks of flats. Opposite a long row of council houses, Kathy stopped. The woman who had left the child in the telephone box could live anywhere around here. But was that probable? she wondered. As soon as the local journalists got wind of the story, it would very likely be plastered all over the front page of Friday's *Mid-Sussex Times*, and the absence of a pregnant woman's child would be hard to conceal among friends, family and neighbours in a town of this size. As Kathy was pondering the situation, she spotted a sign that drew her attention: HAYWARDS HEATH RAILWAY STATION. Perhaps the woman didn't come from the town at all.

She strode into the station waiting room, finding that the five red metal benches positioned around the room were empty. She walked over to the small kiosk and peered in through the window. A rotund man, wearing the standard British Rail dark navy uniform and cap, was sitting, legs widely apart, holding a folded newspaper in front of his face, a hand-rolled cigarette dangling out of his mouth from under a walrus moustache.

'Hello?' Kathy said, tapping on the glass partition.

The man apparently couldn't hear her, so she knocked a little more loudly this time.

He looked up with a scowl and managed to mouth around his cigarette that he was on a break.

Kathy pulled out her police warrant card and slapped it onto the glass.

The man reluctantly set down his newspaper, dropped the cigarette onto an over-filled glass ashtray and hobbled over to the kiosk window. He said nothing but stared at her with grey, lifeless eyes.

Kathy guessed his type immediately: chauvinistic, slovenly and with no desire to do anything more in life than the bare minimum. If she was going to get any assistance from this man, she needed to play a hard game. She continued to hold her ID up to the glass as she spoke. 'I'm a Sussex Police officer and I need some information from you. We can do this right now and I'm gone from here in less than five minutes, or I can come back when your shift is over, and it might just take quite a lot longer. Shall I take a seat, while you have a think about it?'

'We can do it now,' the man replied.

Kathy smiled and pulled out her notebook and pencil. 'Great. What's your name?'

'So, I'm under arrest or something?' he asked, suddenly appearing worried.

'Did I say that you were under arrest?' Kathy asked. 'I'd make it very clear if you were, Mister...?'

'Weaver,' he answered. 'Ronald Weaver.'

'What time did you start work here, this morning, Mr Weaver?'

'Seven sharp, ready for the first train down from London.'

'How many trains stopped here prior to eleven o'clock this morning?' she probed.

'London-bound or Brighton-bound?'

'Both.'

'Well, being a Sunday and all, out of season, we've just had the two in either direction,' he said with a sniff.

'Did a train arrive here in the hour before eleven o'clock?'

The man nodded. 'Just after ten-thirty.'

'From which direction?'

'London—on its way to Brighton. Look, what's all this about?'

Kathy ignored his question. 'Did you happen to see the passengers who alighted here from that train?'

'Well, yeah,' he said. 'They have to walk right in front of me'—he pointed past Kathy—'through the waiting room.'

'And can you tell me approximately how many passengers came through from that train?'

'Yes. *Approximately* one,' he answered with a smug grin.

Kathy met his eyes. 'Describe him or her.'

'It was a woman, youngish. Had a black coat on. Red and white bag in her hand—squares or stripes... you know...'

It was her, the woman the witnesses had seen walking away from the telephone box, having left the bag containing the baby behind. 'Did she come back here?'

The man nodded. 'Sat over there for a while until the next train back to London.'

'How long do you estimate the time to have been between her

leaving this waiting room and returning?'

He drew in a long breath. 'Say half hour.'

Kathy scribed all the details, certain that she was the person who had left the baby. 'Any other details you can remember about this woman? Hair colour? Eye colour? Did she speak at all?'

The man made a show of trying to remember, rubbing his chin as he stared upward. 'Her hair was pulled back—maybe in a ponytail or some such thing, brown in colour, bit curly. I didn't see her eyes and didn't hear her speak.'

Kathy quickly reviewed her notes. 'You said her coat was black—any other details about her clothing?'

The man huffed. 'Blue jeans, I think. Looked a bit on the grubby side.'

'The girl or the jeans?'

'Well...both, really,' he replied.

'And she still had the red and white bag when she returned?' Kathy asked, knowing the answer but wanting his confirmation.

'No, she didn't. I just assumed she was delivering it to someone.'

'You're absolutely sure that this woman arrived at around half past ten with a red and white bag, left the station and returned around thirty minutes later with no bag, then took the next train back to London?'

The man nodded. 'Yes.'

'Thank you for your cooperation, Mr Weaver. You'll be pleased to know you can return to your newspaper and that you are *not* under arrest.'

He grunted, mumbled something incoherent in reply and shuffled back to his chair.

Kathy arrived at Cuckfield Hospital, parking in front of the intimidating grand edifice. The three-storey brick building had been constructed in the early Victorian era as a workhouse, and every time that Kathy had had cause to come here, she felt the same unwelcoming cold austerity lingering on from its former function.

She locked the Escort and walked towards the main entrance, an ivy-covered square projection at the centre of the oblong building.

She entered the lobby and was instantly hit by the pervasive stench of disinfectant. Suspended on wires from the ceiling were several direction signs to help visitors navigate the myriad of complicated corridors and staircases that spanned the length of the old building. Kathy had been here often enough to know where she was going, and she turned right along a narrow hallway until she came to a staircase barely wide enough for two people to pass. On the next floor, she turned left, opened a set of double doors, and stepped inside the maternity ward.

'Good afternoon,' Kathy greeted the uniformed matron facing her behind the desk.

'Visiting hours are two o'clock until three o'clock, fathers only; or three o'clock until four o'clock, all other visitors,' she replied, lifting the watch that was hanging upside down from her breast pocket. 'It is now one thirty-three.'

Kathy had encountered her before and she was certain that the nurse knew it, too. Outwardly, she appeared middle-aged, but Kathy suspected her to have been a left-over from the Victorian-era workhouse days. She smiled, pulled out her warrant card and held it up to the matron. 'I'm from Sussex Police and I've come about the baby left in the telephone box this morning. I wish to speak with someone who's been dealing with the child.'

The matron said nothing, stood up and disappeared into the office behind her.

Kathy leant on the long surface of the desk, trying but failing to hear what the matron was saying. Moments later, a young and smiley nurse approached her. 'Hello, I'm Sister Ryan,' she said in a soft southern Irish accent. 'Matron says you're enquiring about the little fella we took in this morning.'

'That's right,' Kathy said, registering for the first time that the child was a boy. 'How's he doing?'

Sister Ryan nodded. 'He's doing just great. Would you like to see him?'

'Yes, please,' Kathy replied.

'Follow me,' Nurse Ryan said, leading the way behind the desk to another set of double doors. They walked down a short corridor with large glass windows overlooking the wards on either side. 'That's the maternity ward,' she said quietly, pointing to the room on their right. 'The new mothers are expected to sleep for an hour after their lunch, so we need to keep it quiet. And this'—she indicated the ward opposite—'is the nursery where all the babies are kept while the mothers get some rest.' She grimaced. 'Poor Baby Bradley Broadway, though, he'll be spending *all* his time in here, since he has no mother.'

'Baby Bradley Broadway?' Kathy repeated with a slight cringe. 'That's his name, is it?'

Nurse Ryan shrugged. 'Not my idea. It was Matron's attempt at alliteration with a reference to where he was discovered,' she said.

'Genius,' Kathy replied. 'Think I'll just stick to Baby Bradley if that's agreeable.'

Nurse Ryan grinned as she opened the door to the nursery to be greeted by the sound of two wailing babies.

The room was different from the starkness found in the rest of the building. Despite the crying children, Kathy could tell that it was much quieter in here, somehow shielded from the general hubbub of hospital life; the smell of disinfectant was gone, overridden by the scent of baby powder and the room held a more general brightness with its white-washed walls. In the centre of the nursery were two rows of five cots, six of which were occupied by new-borns. The cots were open-topped Perspex boxes inset within a metal frame. Hanging from each was a clipboard, headed with the infant's name.

Sister Ryan led the way to a cot on the furthest side with the name BABY BRADLEY BROADWAY at the top of the information sheet on the clipboard. 'Here's the wee man,' she said, leaning over and lifting the little boy out. 'You'll be wanting a hold?'

Kathy shook her head. The boy looked so fragile, cradled with his head in the crook of the nurse's arm, with a little triangle of black hair on his crown. Kathy had never wanted children of her own and, now that she was in her late forties, her experiences with her sister's children at this young age were so many years in the past that she feared she might inadvertently harm the little thing.

'He's doing well,' Sister Ryan soothed, gently rocking the boy. 'All things considered.'

'Has he been examined?' Kathy asked. 'By a doctor, I mean.'

Sister Ryan smiled. 'Yes, and he says he's a healthy wee chap.'

'Did the doctor say how old he thought the baby was?'

'About ten days, give or take,' she answered.

Kathy took out her pocketbook and wrote down what the nurse

had just said. 'And is he wearing what he was found in?' she asked, eyeing the white babygrow and mittens in which he was dressed.

She shook her head. 'He needed changing, him, bless him; so, he's in hospital-issue attire, just now.'

'Do you still have what he arrived in?'

Sister Ryan nodded. 'I thought you might be needing to see it, so it's in a bag over there,' she said, nodding her head to the run of built-in cupboards that took up one complete wall of the nursery. She moved to lay the boy back in his cot but paused and looked at Kathy. 'Now, are you sure you don't want a quick hold?'

'Very,' she said with a smile. 'Just in case he decides to decorate my work suit.'

'Probably sensible,' the nurse said, placing him down, pulling the white blanket up to his chin and then tucking in the sides. She walked over to the cupboards and took out a large plastic bag which she handed to Kathy. 'That's it all.'

Kathy peered inside the bag, the smell of ammonia from the dirty nappy causing her to recoil.

'Oh, come now... It's only wet,' Sister Ryan said with a light laugh.

Kathy pocketed her notebook, then pinched the white towelling nappy between the tips of her thumb and forefinger and withdrew it from the bag. She held it aloft in front of her face, slowly spinning it around. There were no markings of any kind on the outside, but, when she looked inside, she spotted a small label. She held it closer to her face, trying to ignore the unpleasant smell. '*Durrell and Dorset,*' she read.

'That'll be the name of the laundry firm who takes the nappies, washes them, dries them and then returns them,' Sister Ryan explained.

Kathy made a mental note of the information and double-checked that the nappy contained no other clues or details, before offering it to the nurse. 'Can I give you that to pass back to Durrell and Dorset, since there's no other evidence on it.'

Sister Ryan took the nappy and said, 'They're not our laundry company, so I think it'll just end up in the bin.'

'So, where are Durrell and Dorset based, then?'

The nurse shrugged. 'I've never heard of them; I don't think they're local to here. We use Spencer's in Burgess Hill.'

'So, just to be clear,' Kathy said, 'Baby...Bradley was found wearing a nappy that would have been issued in a hospital that sends their laundry out to Durrell and Dorset, but which is *never* used by this hospital?'

'Correct.'

Kathy pulled out her pocketbook and wrote down the new information. Then, she returned her focus to the remaining contents of the paper bag: a white babygrow and a plastic bottle of milk. Kathy took out the babygrow and checked it all over but there were no labels, markings or anything that might offer a clue as to its origin. 'Anything unusual about this garment?'

'No, it's just a standard babygrow,' Sister Ryan replied. 'It could have been bought in a shop or given out at whichever hospital the little fella was born in.'

Kathy held up the paper bag. 'And this bottle? How many people have touched it?'

'Just me, as far as I know.'

Kathy nodded. 'Could you pop into Burgess Hill Police Station in the next few days so that we can take some elimination fingerprints from you, please?'

'Yes, sure.'

'Is there anything unusual about the bottle or anything that might give a clue as to where it came from?'

'No, like the babygrow, it's just the basic type that anyone could pick up in any branch of Mothercare in any town in England.'

'Thank you very much, Sister Ryan,' Kathy said. 'You've been very helpful...unlike some on this ward.'

The nurse smiled. 'You should see how she is with the mammies. All hell broke loose this morning because one of them dared to come over to the nursery to cuddle their little one. Oh, she went off like a firework.' Sister Ryan lowered the tone of her voice and attempted to anglicise it before continuing, "Babies need routine, Mrs Ashdown; you are not simply to pick up your child willy-nilly like a toy, unless it is time for their feeding or changing'.'

Kathy grinned. 'Poor women.' She glanced at Baby Bradley. 'At least the rest of these kids have got a mother to take care of them, though.'

'He'll not be short of love while he's here, I can assure you of that much.'

'Good to hear,' Kathy said, turning back towards the doors. 'I'll let you get back to your duties, Sister Ryan. Thank you very much for your time.'

'You're very welcome. Goodbye.'

Kathy entered Burgess Hill Police Station, carrying the brown paper bag from Cuckfield Hospital.

'Busy for a Sunday,' the Station Officer said, glancing up from a newspaper that he was reading.

'Keeps me on my toes,' she responded with a grin.

She passed behind him and headed up the stairs to the first floor where a corridor led to the suite of Criminal Investigation Department offices. The station had been purpose-built a decade ago, replacing the town's decrepit Victorian structure. Kathy passed the Detective Inspector's office and the larger office shared by the seven Detective Constables, continuing until she reached a smaller room that she occupied along with the station's other Detective Sergeant whom she rarely saw, owing to their intentionally opposing shift patterns.

The office was fairly basic, containing a desk for each of the two DSs and a row of metal filing cabinets on the back wall above which hung a large map demarking the station's jurisdiction.

Kathy approached her desk. On the top of her already-heaving in-tray was the typed report by DC Chivers of his interview of the two witnesses. Beside the tray was a cardboard box upon which was a handwritten note: *WDS Steadman, Please find enclosed Mothercare's new range of baby cots. DC Chivers.*

Kathy placed the note to one side and opened the box. Inside was the red and white chequered canvas bag that had been left in the telephone box. Feeling as though she were playing some warped version of pass-the-parcel, Kathy pulled the bag out of the box, then looked inside the bag, finding a cardboard shoebox. Inside the box was a white blanket.

She sighed, slowly coming to the conclusion that, on balance, the mother's intention had been for the child to survive and to be found. It was ironic to her that, with Baby Bradley being safe and well, her duty was now to try and locate the mother in order to prosecute her, rather than to reunite her with her infant.

Kathy removed the blanket, knowing that to try to get fingerprints from wool was completely impossible. It was white and clean with no distinguishing marks. She placed it on her desk and again peered inside the bag, reluctant to touch the shoebox in case there would be a chance of getting it dusted for fingerprints.

She stood up and left her office, walking along the corridor to the room shared by the DCs. Two of them were sitting in silence at their desks, writing. One of them was Detective Constable Chivers, the other was the man whom she had hoped to find: DC Calver, the station's Scene of Crime Officer responsible for fingerprinting.

'DC Calver,' she said, leaning on the doorframe.

He turned his head towards her and smiled. He closed his eyes and rubbed small circles over his temples with the tips of his fingers. 'Let me guess... Hang on... No. It's coming to me... Fingerprinting for the abandoned baby?'

'Wow. You're really good,' Kathy said, sharing a knowing look with DC Chivers.

DC Calver opened his eyes and grinned. 'In your office?'

Kathy nodded.

'Give me two minutes,' he said, finishing off whatever it was on which he had been working.

Kathy returned to her office and sat at her desk to read the witness report. It was brief, containing not much more information than that which she already knew. She compared it to the notes in her pocketbook, which she had made at the train station: *Female, 20-30 years old, shoulder-length brown hair pulled back under hairband. Rough / grubby looking. Black leather jacket. Denim jeans.* There was little doubt in her mind that the two reports had been of one and the same woman.

'Right, then, Sarge,' DC Calver announced, entering her office, wearing gloves, and with his kit bag in one hand. 'Just to say... From what DC Chivers has told me about what he picked up, I'm not very hopeful, to be honest.' He approached her desk and held up the white blanket. 'This is a definite no-no,' he said, prodding the red and white bag. 'As is this. Let's have a look at the box.'

Kathy watched as he carefully took out the shoebox and rotated it around in front of his face. He didn't look very confident. Then he shook his head.

'I don't think so,' he said finally, blowing air from his cheeks. 'I can try and get a latent print from it if you want, but the cardboard is quite rough and porous. We'd have had more joy if it had been a shiny surface, like a cereal box.'

'I'm not sure you could fit a baby into a cereal box,' she replied, picking up the paper bag from Cuckfield Hospital. 'What about this?'

He took the bag and his eyes widened when he saw the plastic milk bottle inside. 'Perfect.'

DC Calver opened his kit bag and pulled out a jar of anthracene powder and a fingerprint brush. Opening the jar, he dipped the brush into the grey powder, tapping off the excess, and then carefully began to brush it onto the surface of the milk bottle, slowly rotating it as he did so. 'Do you know how many people have handled the bottle?' he asked, continuing to coat the item in the metallic grey powder.

'As far as I'm aware, just the mother of the child and the nurse at Cuckfield Hospital.'

'That's good,' he said as he stopped brushing.

'I've asked the nurse to come in for elimination prints,' Kathy relayed.

'Is this the abandoned baby?' Detective Inspector Redmond asked, striding into the office.

'It is, sir,' Kathy confirmed. 'DC Calver is checking items for fingerprints.'

The Detective Inspector stood beside Kathy's desk. He was a tall and slightly gaunt-looking man in his late-fifties with grey side-parted hair and dark eyes. 'Where was it found?'

'In a telephone box outside the Seeboard showroom in Haywards Heath,' Kathy answered, watching as DC Calver held the bottle aloft with a smile.

'Three decent latent prints,' he declared, showing Kathy.

'Excellent,' she replied, delighted to see how clearly the grey anthracene powder had brought out the ridges and marks on the side of the bottle.

She watched as he removed from his bag a roll of fingerprint tape from which he cut a strip just big enough to cover the marks on the bottle. He carefully stuck the tape over the prints, then removed it and held it aloft. 'That got them!' he declared, pulling a sheet of clear acetate from his bag and sticking the fingerprint tape to it. Finally, he took a marker pen from his kit bag and scribed the case details onto the side of the acetate.

'All done?' Kathy asked.

'All done. I'll get this sent directly off to the Fingerprint Bureau at Lewes,' he said, beginning to pack away his things.

'How long do you think it'll be until we get a result back?' she asked him.

'A few days; faster if I lean on them that the mother's welfare is at stake.'

'Thank you, DC Calver.'

'Isn't this all slightly excessive, WDS Steadman?' the DI asked. 'The child *did* survive, did it not?'

'Yes, sir, but I would like to try finding the child's mother.'

The DI raised his eyebrows and folded his arms. 'Just don't put too much into it; I'd sooner you put your efforts into the more pressing cases.' He turned and left the office.

DC Calver whispered, 'He's in one of *those* moods, I see.'

Kathy shrugged. She had a decent enough working relationship with the DI, but he was certainly a capricious boss whose opinion she rarely tried to second-guess.

'I'll get this done now,' DC Calver said. 'Of course, a successful match depends on this woman's having a criminal record; so, I hope you've got other leads to work on.'

'I've got a wet nappy to follow up,' she replied.

DC Calver smiled as he packed the last of his things into his kit bag. 'Lucky you.'

'Yes, lucky me,' Kathy agreed, drawing a circle around the company name, *Durrell and Dorset*.

With the descriptions from the witnesses and the station clerk, the clue in the child's nappy and the possibility of a fingerprint match, Kathy was feeling confident that she would soon be able to identify the mother of Baby Bradley Broadway.

Chapter Three

Alfred Farrier huffed as he stared out of the window of his blue Austin Mini. The engine had been running for several minutes already. He glowered at the closed front door of his home on Canterbury Road in Folkestone. What the dickens was she doing?

'Stupid girl,' he muttered, hammering the car horn, which he instantly regretted doing when Mrs Dyche from next-door parted the net curtains of her lounge window. He gave her a pleasant wave and the curtain dropped, although he knew that she would continue to maintain an unseen vigil behind the window. She and her husband operated their home as a guesthouse, and it had been there that the American family had arrived in January of this year. Their young son, Jack, was the cause of all of this trouble.

Finally, the door opened and his sixteen-year-old daughter, Margaret, struggled down the driveway with a leather suitcase. Despite its being a still, humid day, she was, by his instruction, wearing her thick winter coat.

'Hurry up, for goodness' sake,' he reproached as she opened the door. 'Do you want the whole world to see you?'

Margaret refused to make eye contact as she dragged the passenger seat forwards, trying to manhandle the suitcase onto the back seats by herself.

Alfred huffed again, reached around and tugged the suitcase behind him. 'Get in,' he yapped.

Silently, she reset the seat and sat down beside him.

'Did you remember to lock up?' he asked, lifting the handbrake and preparing to depart but waiting first for her answer.

'Yes,' she replied, dragging the word out, presumably to make some kind of a point that eluded him. She was hardly in any position to be taking the high ground.

Alfred put the car into gear and then pulled out.

When they were away from the house, she asked, 'Can I take my coat off now? I'm boiling under here.'

'Yes, now that we're away from the house,' he replied.

'Heaven forbid the neighbours should see me,' Margaret

mumbled, barely audibly.

Alfred stamped on the brake pedal, thrusting Margaret forwards so that she almost banged her head on the windscreen. 'Yes, indeed. Heaven forbid the neighbours should see!' he shouted. 'My God, look at you.'

Margaret angled her face sharply away from him; he could tell that she was struggling not to cry.

Alfred inwardly sighed as he continued driving towards the A2. The sooner this dreadful business was over, the better as far as he was concerned. This current purgatory, in which they were all forced to live, was no good for anyone. He wound down his window slightly, imagining that the fresh breeze might help to steady his nerves. From the passenger seat beside him, Margaret was removing her heavy coat. She turned around and placed it on the back seat, her swollen belly now obvious despite the loose-fitting dress that she was wearing.

The drive continued without either of them speaking. On several occasions, he had been minded to comment on some of the places that they were passing but he was too worked up to engage in trivial nonsense and didn't have the desire to try to make her feel any better.

The journey took thirty-five minutes, although the stagnant silence in the car had made it feel significantly longer to Alfred. He heaved a sigh of relief when they entered the small village of Westbere, just four miles north-east of Canterbury. He stopped his Mini outside a charming house embowered by trees and whose cream walls were almost entirely bedecked with a purple-flowering wisteria. He switched off the engine, and said, 'Well, come on then. Out you get.'

Margaret hastily climbed from the car and began to reach in over the tilted passenger seat for her suitcase.

'Oh, I'll get it,' Alfred snapped, walking around to her side of the car. He yanked out the case and nudged the door shut with his foot, then led the way up the stone path that divided the flowering cottage garden, until he reached the front door. He tapped lightly on the brass knocker and took a step back as his eyes came to rest on the slate house name plaque, *SWAN COTTAGE*; his mother's home since 1915. But where *was* she? Knowing her, she was in the back garden, tending to her vegetables or fruit trees. With his impatience rising

31

once again, he banged on the lounge window. 'Hurry up, woman,' he grumbled to himself.

A sound of muted shuffling came from the interior of the house, and Alfred could see his mother's outline through the obscure-glass windows as she approached the front door.

'Alfred,' his mother, Nellie, greeted. She leant to one side to get a view behind him. 'Hello, Margaret.' She threw open her arms to welcome her granddaughter, which irked Alfred all the more.

'I can't stop,' he barked. 'Here's her stuff. Telephone me once it's done.'

With barely a second glance at his daughter, Alfred turned and headed back down the path to his car. He hurriedly started the engine, letting out a long breath as he pulled away from the house, glad to have temporarily handed his problem over to someone else.

He turned the car around and began to head back home. He wound down the window some more, hoping that the fresh air might loosen the clamping sensation that he was feeling around his heart. Then he spotted the signpost for Canterbury, just three miles away, and the idea of finding a pub and having a drink to settle his nerves took hold. A stiff glass of whisky was exactly what he needed right now. He pushed the Mini faster down the A28, reaching the city centre in under ten minutes. He drove down the High Street, the main thoroughfare of the ancient city, taking the first parking space that he came to, just a stone's throw away from the Bell Hotel, a public house that he regularly frequented. It was a tall but narrow building, sandwiched between a cobbler's shop and a clothing boutique. Heavy net curtains hung at the front windows and the upper glazed section of the door, offering a welcome privacy to the dingy interior.

Alfred took a quick look around him at the passing pedestrian- and motor-traffic before he pulled open the door and stepped inside the dimly lit pub onto thread-bare carpet. He approached the bar directly in front of him and waited as the barmaid poured a pint of beer for an old man whose glassy eyes seemed to be attempting to focus on Alfred. The man said something incomprehensible, and Alfred ignored him, hating that he found himself in such company.

Alfred walked past the bar and into the saloon room at the back of the pub, where the only light came from a weak chandelier in the centre of the ceiling, giving some degree of privacy to the booths that lined one wall of the room. He passed through to the rear on his way to the lavatories, doing a double take at the sight of a young woman sitting alone in one of the booths. Her head was resting on the table in the crook of her elbow. In front of her were three empty glasses.

'Anna?' Alfred said, finding himself smiling for the first time in a while.

The woman slowly raised her head and looked in his direction. 'Who?'

'Anna!' Alfred repeated, hurrying to her table. He slid in opposite her. 'Would you care for a drink?'

Anna smiled weakly. 'Vodka.'

Alfred touched her curly brown hair. 'It's so great to see you again, my love. I'll be back in a jiffy,' he said, hurrying over to the bar.

'What'll it be?' the barmaid asked.

'A double whisky for me and a glass of sherry for my wife,' he said, nodding back towards Anna.

'She's your wife?' the barmaid asked.

'Yes, that's right,' he answered. 'Do you have any rooms currently available?'

She nodded as she poured out his drink. 'Plenty.'

'I think we'd like one, please. We're both very tired.'

The barmaid shrugged. 'Yeah. Course you are. Fourteen pounds fifty, then, please.'

Alfred wrote out a cheque, and then carried the drinks and room key back over to Anna. 'Here you go, my love.'

'What's this?' Anna asked, holding up the glass.

'Sherry—your favourite,' he said, raising his glass to hers.

'I asked for vodka.'

'Yes, but you don't drink vodka,' he replied. 'Cheers, Anna.'

Anna drew in a short breath, clinked glasses with him and took a long mouthful. 'Not bad, I suppose.'

'I've got us a room here,' Alfred told her, holding up a set of keys.

Anna said nothing but nodded and drank more.

Alfred reached out and held her hand across the table, gently stroking her fingers with his thumb. He felt instantly calmed to be back with his wife. Although he didn't want to talk about Margaret,

33

he felt it his duty to tell her where he had taken her. 'I've just dropped Margaret off at Mother's house,' he said solemnly. 'She'll stay there until…well…after.'

'Great,' Anna said, taking a sip of drink. 'Remind me who Margaret is, again?'

Alfred chuckled. 'Our daughter.'

'Ah, yeah, that's it. We've got another child, haven't we?'

'Yes, Peter. He and his wife, Maureen, will be adopting the child in due course.'

'Whose child?'

'Margaret's,' he whispered across the table.

'Okay,' Anna said.

Alfred ran his hand over her hair again, finding it slightly greasy to the touch. 'Do you want to go up to the room and perhaps take a bath, while I get us another drink?' He slid the numbered room key across to her.

Anna nodded, finished the last mouthful of her sherry, and then stood up.

Alfred kissed her, relishing the taste of the sherry on her lips. He cursed himself for not having some of her favourite *Femme de Rochas* perfume with him. He watched as she folded her black leather jacket over her arm and headed to the door at the back of the room that led to the lavatories and from where a staircase led to the rooms above. She disappeared behind the door and then walked to the bar to order another round of drinks.

Two hours later, Alfred exited through the front door of the Bell Hotel, alone. He kept his head down and hurried over to his car. He quickly climbed inside and started the engine, pulling out and almost hitting a passing motorcyclist. He knew that he shouldn't be driving but he just had to get away.

The alcohol in his bloodstream heightened his sensitivity, making his driving erratic and his responses to potential hazards over-zealous. Much of his drive passed in a blur, but he managed to reach his destination within thirty minutes.

Alfred turned into Hawkinge Cemetery and Crematorium, moving slowly down the long driveway to a car park that was situated in front of the main buildings. He parked up, switched off the engine, then stepped from his car and ambled down a narrow pathway between hundreds of graves. Part of the way down, he walked onto one of the neat grass strips that ran between each row of memorials. A quarter of the way along, he stopped and fell to his knees, bursting into tears.

'Oh, I'm so sorry,' he wailed. 'So, so sorry. Please forgive me. Please.'

Through his watery vision, Alfred looked at the grey headstone in front of him.

In loving memory of
Anna Farrier
1914-1958
A much loved wife and mother

Chapter Four

16th December 2019, Rye, East Sussex

'Say goodbye to Daddy,' Juliette said, holding Grace's hand and leading her into the kitchen, where Morton was eating a cream cheese bagel for his breakfast.

'Goodbye, my darling,' Morton said, quickly wiping a tideline of melted butter from his upper lip as Grace leant in to kiss him.

'Bye, Daddy,' Grace said.

'Have a lovely day.'

'Don't forget I'm going out with Lucy for lunch today and a bit of shopping in Canterbury, so you'll need to pick Miss Farrier up from nursery,' Juliette reminded him as she guided Grace towards the front door.

'I won't forget,' he said. 'Have a good time and don't spend too much.'

Juliette poked her head around the door and waved her credit card at him. 'Mwahaha. Try and stop me.'

He rolled his eyes and stuffed the last piece of bagel into his mouth. The front door banged shut, and Morton was left with a whole blissful day of research in front of him. He made himself a fresh coffee, and then headed upstairs to his study.

At his desk, he opened his laptop and checked his emails. Of the twelve new messages that had rolled in overnight, one from Ancestry caught his attention.

Denise Prince has sent you a message.

Well, that was a turn-up for the books, Morton thought, having not expected any reply at all, never mind one so soon. He clicked the link in the email to view the message, and a web browser opened up to reveal the messages within his Ancestry account. Denise's was at the top.

I dont no much. Got a dna kit for my birthday but dont really do 'genealogy'

Helpful, Morton thought, unsure why the word genealogy had

been placed in inverted commas, as though it were some kind of nefarious pastime that should not be discussed in polite company. Denise was unlikely to be very helpful at all, but he had nothing to lose in replying and asking for further information. Her message to him had only been sent twenty minutes ago, so she might still be sitting at her computer with any luck. He typed out a hurried response.

Hi Denise. Thanks for your message. It would be really helpful if you could tell me the names of your four grandparents (even just surnames would do!). Then I won't need to bother you again. Thank you so much. Kind regards, Morton

He hit send and hoped that the message might elicit a positive reply. He drank some of his coffee, and then opened the speculative tree that he had created for Gerard Bramley who DNA-matched Vanessa, Billie and Liza. Yesterday, he had discovered a couple who, he believed, might be the common ancestors to all four of them: Francis and Mabel Gaulden. The couple had emigrated with two of their sons to the US at some point in the 1890s, leaving one son behind in London. Morton was feeling confident that either Thomas or Edward Gaulden was the three women's great-grandfather. He hoped today to be able to confirm just that.

Having already located the two brothers in 1900, Morton ran a search in the subsequent census, ten years later. He started with Thomas Gaulden, easily locating him as a twenty-eight-year-old liveryman still residing in the town of Atwood in Rawlins County, Kansas. His location of birth and that of his parents was given simply as England. Thomas was listed as the head of the household, followed by a wife, Cornelia, and three children, Emma, Rose and Benjamin.

Three households below, Morton spotted Francis and Mabel Gaulden whose own entries confirmed that he was following the correct family. Returning to the search function, he typed in the other potential sibling's name, Edward Gaulden, his year of birth and the location of Kansas.

Zero results

He edited the search to remove the location. This time there were three results, but each of them appeared upon first inspection to be incorrect. *Edward Gaulin, born Michigan. Edward Gaughlin, born Ireland. Edna Gaulin, born New York.* Just to be certain that they were not transcription errors, he checked each result in turn, immediately eliminating them as possibilities.

Morton drank some coffee, and then spent a little time playing with spelling variations and adjusting Edward's date of birth; but nothing was forthcoming, leaving him wondering if perhaps the man had died prior to the census being taken.

Opening up a fresh tab in his browser, he accessed the Card Catalogue at Ancestry, searching for records relating to the state of Kansas and finding exactly that which he wanted: *Kansas, U.S., Deaths and Burials, Index, 1885-1930.* He clicked the link and typed Edward Gaulden's name into the search box.

One result

It looked correct, but, when Morton came to view it, he found that it was a typed transcription with no ability to see the original document. He examined the source information at the bottom of the page, noticing that the data had come from FamilySearch. In another browser tab, he opened the FamilySearch website and ran his own search for the same document, finding that a scan of the original was freely available to view.

Name: Edward Gaulden
Gender: Male
Race: White
Birth Date: 1884
Birth Place: England
Death Date: 31 Aug 1905
Death Place: Atwood, Rawlins County
Marital Status: Single
Occupation: Farmer
Cause of Death: Typhoid Fever

Unless Edward had had a child outside of marriage, it appeared to

Morton that his line was a dead-end and he needed to focus on his brother, Thomas Gaulden, and his descendants instead.

He returned to Ancestry, noticing that he had a new message from Denise Prince.

dads side prince and thompson mums side hart and pavey

Morton smiled as he jotted down the four names on his notepad, then, despite the abruptness of her message, sent her an effusive reply thanking her for her time.

Before he continued working on the Gaulden family, he switched back to Henry Cowling's extensive online tree, running a search for each of Denise Prince's grandparents' surnames, and hoping to find one of them on there so that he could short-cut his research. For Prince, Thompson and Pavey there were no results at all. For Hart, there was one matching entry: Jack Hart who had married a woman by the name of Gladys Cowling. Morton had a hunch that he might have found the connection for which he was looking, made all the more certain when he read that, according to the tree, Jack and Gladys had both been born, married and died in Kent which fell into the South East England sub-community of Ancestry's ethnicity estimates. If he was correct, then he needed to work out precisely *how* Denise Prince fitted into Henry Cowling's family, hopefully by finding a link to Jack and Gladys Hart. If he could do that, then he would have another set of shared, most-recent common ancestors for the three women.

With a buzz of excitement, Morton conducted an open search on FreeBMD for all marriages between a Hart and a Pavey. There was just a single result offered: Geoffrey Hart had married a Janice Pavey in the June quarter of 1949. Morton noted the details on his pad, then ran a search for children born to them, finding that they had two daughters, Sophie and Jacqueline.

It took less than two minutes for Morton to establish that Sophie Hart had married a Dennis Prince and that the couple had had a daughter, named Denise. Now that Morton knew how Denise Prince connected to the Hart family, he needed to identify the parents of her maternal grandfather, Geoffrey Hart, to make the final connection to the Jack and Gladys Hart who featured on Henry

Cowling's family tree.

Starting with a search in the *England and Wales, Death Index, 1989-2019* record set, Morton found what he believed to be Geoffrey's death in 2018, but which needed corroborating. Turning to Google, he typed Geoffrey's name and presumed year of death into the search box and hit enter. At the top of a long list of erroneous results was a link to funeral-notices.co.uk, a website which held 4.7 million obituaries from around the UK. He clicked it and read the detail.

HART, Geoffrey. 22.10.1930. Husband of Janice, mother to Sophie and Jacqui, grandfather and great grandfather. Passed away peacefully on 14th February 2018. Funeral on 9th March at 2pm at Barham Crematorium.

With the new knowledge gleaned from the funeral notice, Morton returned to FreeBMD and ran a search for Geoffrey's birth. He grinned when the results loaded.

December 1930
Name: Hart, Geoffrey
Mother's Maiden Name: Cowling
District: Medway
Vol: 2a
Page: 1347

Geoffrey was the son of Jack Hart and Gladys Cowling; Morton had just identified the most recent common ancestors to Vanessa, Billie, Liza and their closest DNA match, Denise Prince. To be completely certain that he had found the correct family, Morton pulled up the 1939 Register and found Geoffrey as a nine-year-old boy, living with his parents, Jack and Gladys. There were two further siblings, Roy and Barbara, in the household, one of whom was very likely to be Vanessa, Billie and Liza's grandparent.

Morton was getting closer.

He was now in possession of two distinct sets of common ancestors for the three women's maternal line: the Gauldens and the Harts. His task now was to bring those two family lines down until he found an overlap, ideally in the form of a recorded marriage.

Just over an hour later, Morton sat back in his chair, satisfied with his work on the Hart family. He had found that, although Barbara Hart had married, there were no signs of her having had any children. Her brother, Roy, however, had married one Peggy Raven in 1951 and five children had followed: Steven, Frank, Rosie, Gemma and Craig.

Given their dates of birth, Morton was fairly sure that one of those two sisters, Rosie or Gemma Hart, must be the biological mother of Vanessa, Billie and Liza, all of which led him to a minor problem: Rosie, Gemma and their other siblings had been born in Kent, South East England whilst Thomas Gaulden's descendants were very much rooted in Kansas, USA. So far, he had found no overlap between the two countries, never mind the two families.

Morton realised then that Roy Hart's wife, Peggy, had to have been the person who had passed the American ancestry to Vanessa, Liza and Billie and who, ultimately, must have descended from Francis and Mabel Gaulden. If Peggy Raven had been of a similar age to Roy, then she would have to have been born at some point around 1932. FreeBMD and the 1939 Register failed to provide a match that Morton could firmly attribute to being her, which gave further credence to the possibility of her having been born in America.

He opened up the 1940 US Census and typed in Peggy Raven's name.

Results 1-3 of 3

Peggy Raven, born abt 1932, Missouri
Peggy K Karson, born abt 1929, Texas
Peggy Revin, born abt 1934, Illinois

The top-most result looked promising, and Morton clicked to view a scan of the original census return. Eight-year-old Peggy was recorded as living with her parents, David and Emma Raven. Morton's eyes fell excitedly to Emma's name before he scrolled across the page and found that she was aged 31 years and that her place of birth had been given as Kansas.

Morton hurriedly switched tabs in his browser to examine the speculative tree for the Gaulden family that he had created, tracing down from Francis and Mabel, through their son, Thomas, and his wife, Cornelia, to their children. And there she was, Emma Gaulden, born in Kansas in 1909.

Morton had found how the two families were connected and set about merging the family trees at the point where they intersected: Peggy Raven and Roy Hart, although he had still yet to establish when and where they had married. Peggy had been recorded as living in Missouri, US in 1940, but by the time of her marriage in 1951, she was living in Kent, England, giving him a very narrow window within which to search for the answer.

Opening up Ancestry's *Incoming Passenger Lists, 1878-1960*, Morton inputted Peggy Raven's details with a ten-year search window around 1945. There were fifty-five results, but Morton could quickly see that most of the suggestions were very loose interpretations of his search parameters. Except for the first result. He was sure that he had found the correct person as he viewed a scan of the original ship's manifest. The top of the sheet revealed that the passengers had travelled on the Queen Mary, a Cunard White Star steamship that had arrived at Southampton on the 16th October 1949. He slowly scrolled down the page until he found Peggy among the typed entries.

Port of Embarkation: New York
Name of Passenger: Peggy Raven
Age of Passenger: 17
Proposed Address in the United Kingdom: 72, High Street, Lydd
Profession, Occupation or Calling: Student
Country of Last Permanent Residence: U.S.A.

Morton quickly did the maths, finding that her age matched the Peggy Raven on his tree perfectly. He carefully scrutinised the record, looking for further clues that might provide additional proof that he had found the correct person. Noticing that her intended address in the UK was 72, High Street, Lydd, Morton ran a search for it in Google Maps. The town was situated on the Romney Marshes, seventeen miles southwest of Folkestone. He wondered then if Lydd fell under the Folkestone registration district in which Roy and Peggy had married and where their children's births had been registered.

Opening up the UKBMD website for the geographical coverage of registration districts, Morton scrolled down the 884-page document until he reached Lydd, finding that it did indeed fall under the umbrella of the Folkestone registration district between 1941 and 1974.

Although it was not definitive proof, it was enough for Morton at this stage. Besides which, Peggy's precise date of arrival in the UK and how she had come to meet Roy Hart were questions only on the very periphery of his enquiries.

His next step was to confirm that the speculative tree, which he had created, corroborated with the amounts of DNA that Vanessa Briggs shared with her closest cousin matches. Using The Shared cM Project tool on the DNA Painter website, Morton verified that his research to this point had been correct: Vanessa Briggs was Denise Prince's second cousin, matching with 316 cM of DNA; she was Gerard Bramley's third cousin once removed with 78 cM; and was Henry Cowling's fifth cousin with 31 cM.

Morton sat back in his chair, satisfied with his day's work so far. He was very confident that Gemma or Rosie Hart was the birth mother of Vanessa, Liza and Billie. But which one?

Luckily for Morton, the surname Hart was sufficiently unusual such that, when he conducted a marriage search for the two sisters, he could do so without any date or specific location restrictions. For Rosie, there were no matches whatsoever. For Gemma, there was one about which Morton was cautiously confident. She had married in the Thanet district of Kent in the March quarter of 1974 to a man named Paul Kelly. Morton noted down the details on his pad and then switched his enquiry to search for children born to the couple, instead. The results almost certainly ruled Gemma out, for there was a succession of births registered in 1975, 1977, 1980 and 1981 to her and her husband; the first two having occurred within a few months of Vanessa's and Liza's births.

Morton wrote ROSIE HART in large letters on his notepad and drew a thick circle around her name. He was now fairly sure that she was the three women's birth mother; but he needed more substantial proof before he could give them her name. Would she even still be alive? he thought, running a death search for her. Despite the way in which she had apparently treated the three women as babies, Morton was pleased to find that her name did not appear in the death indexes. Using the priority twenty-four-hour service from the GRO, Morton placed an order for Roy and Peggy's marriage certificate, Rosie's birth certificate, Gemma's marriage certificate and the birth certificate of Gemma's first child in 1975, each one hopefully adding further corroborating evidence of his working theory.

In the meantime, Morton wanted to see if there was anything else he could find out about Rosie Hart. He turned to the online British Newspaper Archive, selecting a date range of 1950 to 1999, and inputted her name into the search box.

'Wow,' Morton said, looking at the highlighted titles from the five suggested results, some of which appeared from the dates and locations possibly to relate to the correct Rosie Hart.

Robbery with violence charge...
Burglary...
A well-known local prostitute...
Accused of attempted murder...
Dart in the eye...

Morton took a long inward breath, staring at the screen as the reality of his investigation sank in. He didn't yet know the precise content of those newspaper articles, or even if they referred to *his* Rosie Hart, but it did not appear to paint this person in a very favourable light, and the burden of responsibility for relaying all of this information to Vanessa, Billie and Liza was squarely his and his alone. The curious—or nosey as Juliette would say—part of him was eager to discover the content of those articles, but the professional genealogist in him, who would have to compile a factual, scrupulous report about this woman, dreaded whatever they might contain.

He needed a break, and he needed a coffee, so he stood up, stretched, and then headed downstairs to the kitchen.

As he waited for the machine to make his drink, Morton thought about the case and the implications of everything which he had discovered so far. How were Vanessa and her half-sisters going to take the news about their biological mother who, it appeared, might have had a serious criminal background and who had gallivanted around the country, abandoning her babies in shop doorways. Then a thought struck him; something that really ought to have occurred to him much sooner: what if there were other children out there, born to Rosie Hart and who had also been abandoned? Vanessa had discovered Billie and Liza purely by chance on GEDmatch, each of them wishing to discover the identity of their birth parents. What were the chances of there being no others?

Morton sipped his coffee, thinking. No official record or national database existed, which would provide him with such highly confidential information; the only way in which he might learn more would be if similar cases of abandoned babies had made the newspapers. He decided that he would run some searches once he had read each of the five articles which mentioned Rosie Hart.

With some degree of reluctance, he made his way back up to his study and sat down at his computer. He wiggled the mouse to reawaken the screen as his mobile began to ring. It was Juliette.

'Hi.'

'Where are you?' she asked, sounding flustered.

'Err…' Morton was confused and so checked his surroundings. 'In…my…study. Why?'

She sighed. 'Okay. Correction: where *should* you be?'

Morton frowned, looked at his laptop clock, and then realised. Grace. 'Damn! I'm leaving right now…'

He finished the call and closed his laptop, ending his research for the day. Rosie's possible criminal history would just have to wait until tomorrow.

Chapter Five

26th September 1973, Thornton Heath, Croydon

Kathy Steadman was sitting on a hard plastic chair in the waiting room of the Maternity Unit of Mayday Hospital in Thornton Heath, South London. The room was small, and every one of the dozen or so chairs was occupied with a man, several of whom were staring at her. She had inadvertently arrived shortly before fathers' visiting hours.

She sighed and folded her arms, not at all enjoying the blatant but unspoken questioning emanating from the men seated opposite her. Over the last three days she had identified the six London hospitals which were serviced by Durrell and Dorset launderettes, discovering this morning that only one of these – the Mayday Hospital – actually had a maternity unit. She was now waiting to speak to someone regarding patients who had given birth in the last few days.

Finally, one of the double-doors opened, and a middle-aged doctor wearing a long white coat stepped into the waiting room, carrying a clipboard. He surveyed the room, his eyes settling on Kathy before smiling. 'Sussex Police?' he questioned.

Kathy nodded and walked over to him.

'Follow me,' he said, pushing the door wider and stepping into a brightly lit corridor. He waited for the door to swing shut behind Kathy, before raising the clipboard. 'You wanted a list of mothers' names who had given birth approximately two weeks ago?'

'Yes, I believe a baby boy was born here a few days prior to the twenty-third of September.'

The doctor ran his index finger down a typed list of names. 'So...in the last three weeks, there have been eleven babies born here.'

It was a much higher number than Kathy had been expecting. 'How many were boys?'

'Seven,' he answered.

Still too high.

'This would have been a boy who had a small triangle of black hair on the very top of his head, born to a woman in her twenties to early thirties with short dark hair—sometimes wearing a headband.

46

Probably no father present.'

The doctor nodded and pointed at the clipboard, holding it in front of Kathy.

'Unnamed boy born seventeenth of September to Tracy Smith,' Kathy read.

'She was a bit of a character, that one,' he recalled.

'In what way?' Kathy asked.

'Didn't want help. Didn't want to talk to anyone. Didn't have any visitors at all. Then discharged herself three days after giving birth, instead of staying for the usual ten.'

Kathy took out her pocketbook and copied down the details. 'Have you got an address for her?'

'We will have, yes,' he answered. 'Wait here. I'll get it for you.'

Kathy watched him stroll off down the corridor. She looked at the name in her pocketbook. Tracy Smith. It sounded suspiciously fake. If the girl had already known that she wouldn't be keeping the baby, then she would hardly likely have revealed her real identity.

The doctor returned with a small scrap of paper. 'This is all we have on her,' he said, handing it to Kathy.

212a Beaconsfield Road, Croydon

'Thank you, Doctor,' Kathy said. 'That's really helpful.'

'You're welcome. Beaconsfield Road isn't far from here. I hope you find her—she'll probably need assistance.'

Kathy nodded. Once again, she was confronted with the stark realities of her role; her job was to track down Tracy Smith—or whatever her name was—and prosecute her, not help her.

She put the paper into her pocket and headed out of the maternity ward, then down the staircase back to the main entrance. Outside was pleasantly warm and Kathy just stood for a moment, watching the steady comings and goings of patients, visitors, cars and ambulances. Tucked into four designated parking bays, she spotted a row of black cabs and headed over towards them. Two of the drivers were leaning against the side of one of the taxis, chatting and smoking.

'Excuse me. Would you mind pointing me in the direction of Beaconsfield Road, please?'

One of the men took his cigarette out of his mouth and said, 'I can take you there for a quid, love.'

'Thank you, but I've actually got my car here,' Kathy said. 'I just don't know the area that well and need directions.'

'What's it worth, love?' he asked with a smirk.

'It's not 'love'; it's WDS Steadman of Sussex Police,' she corrected, really wishing that she didn't continually find such need to use her rank and position in society in order to engender basic respect.

The other driver tossed down his cigarette butt and said, 'Turn left out of here, down London Road fifty yards, then left up St James's Road, straight on over into Windmill Road, which becomes Northcote Road, then Beaconsfield will be on your left.'

'Thank you,' she said, walking back over to the yellow Ford Escort. She climbed in, started the engine, and then began to follow the taxi driver's directions. Within six minutes, she was indicating to turn into Beaconsfield Road. She parked the car and got out, noting that the nearest house to her was numbered 61. She began to walk down the street, examining the house numbers as she went. Her hunch that the address given by 'Tracy Smith' was false increased in likelihood the further down the road she ventured. On either side of her, the house numbers of the two-storey terraced properties were descending as she proceeded; she reached the other end of the road with there remaining no possibility of finding any house numbered anywhere close to 212.

Kathy sighed as she slowly ambled back towards the car, trying to figure out what on earth had prompted this girl to go to all the effort of boarding a train to Haywards Heath in order to leave her child there, when it appeared as though she was living somewhere in the Croydon area. It just made no sense.

She reached the Escort and got inside. She sat for a while, thinking before driving back to Burgess Hill Police Station.

Kathy entered her office and headed to her desk. In her absence this morning, her in-tray had magically grown in height. She inwardly groaned as she picked down the fresh stack of paperwork. On the top of the pile was a typed report by one of the constables who had interviewed the recent victims of a walk-in theft, believed to have been carried out by the so-called Budgie Burglar for which case she was the investigating officer. She read through the report and agreed that the M.O. was similar; the man would pick a sunny day when people had left their windows open, then would approach the front door, carrying an empty birdcage and try the door handle. If it opened and he went unchallenged, he would help himself to whatever he could lay his hands on, but, if confronted by the resident of the house, he would charmingly tell them that his budgie, Tweetie, had just flown inside their open window. The unsuspecting person would then helpfully head off to check for the budgie and he would promptly scarper, trying his luck elsewhere. For two years he had selected different towns and villages to target in West Sussex, having always evaded capture.

'More work,' she muttered, setting the report to one side and looking at the next document in the pile. It was the witness interview statement with the girl who had found Baby Bradley, typed up by one of the ladies in the office opposite hers. Kathy re-read it to make sure that she hadn't overlooked anything and, once satisfied, placed it to one side on her desk.

The final item in the pile was a handwritten note requesting that she telephone the Fingerprint Bureau at Sussex Police HQ in Lewes. Kathy picked up the black Bakelite phone on her desk and dialled the direct number to the bureau. 'Hello, it's WDS Steadman from Burgess Hill,' she said, when the call was answered.

'One moment, I'll pass you over,' a gruff voice said.

In the background Kathy could hear her name being called out and then what sounded like the receiver being accidentally dropped on the floor.

'Hello? Still there?' a young-sounding male voice asked. 'WDS Steadman?'

Kathy smiled. 'Yes, still here.'

'Ah, marvellous. The finger marks on the milk bottle that came from a...DC Calver... I've been through the catalogue, and I've got a match.'

'You have?' Kathy said, surprised that the manual check of every fingerprint in the county of Sussex had been analysed in quite such a short space of time.

'Yes,' he replied, sounding pleased with himself. 'I'll get a full report in the post to you later today, but I thought—given the circumstances of the crime—you might want it in advance in a nutshell?'

'Absolutely, yes,' Kathy said, hurriedly picking up her pen and holding it poised above her pocketbook. 'Go ahead.'

'So, it's from a robbery with violence at the Flackley Ash Hotel in Peasmarsh in August 1971. She and her brother, Steven, served six months for it.'

'Right...' Kathy meant to urge him on, wanting him to cut to the chase and give her a name.

'Her address at the time of the crime was given as Flat 1, 46 Ashford Road, New Romney in Kent—'

'And her name?' Kathy interjected.

'Oh, yes,' the man said with a giggle. 'Sorry, yes. Her name was Rosie Hart, born nineteen fifty-two.'

Kathy wrote down the name and underlined it. She was now in possession of Baby Bradley's mother's name and address. 'Thank you very much,' she said to the young man.

'You're welcome.'

Kathy hung up the receiver, put her pocketbook away and left her office, walking down the corridor and entering the one shared by the Detective Constables. 'DC Cornwell,' she called.

A young detective looked up from his desk with a questioning look on his face. 'Yes, Sarge?'

'Fancy a day-trip out to New Romney with me?'

DC Chivers wolf-whistled, making the other two DCs laugh.

DC Cornwell nodded and stood from his desk. 'Now?'

'Now,' Kathy confirmed, leading the way out of the office.

As they were passing Detective Inspector Redmond's office, he stepped out, almost colliding with Kathy.

'Sorry, sir—we've just got the mother's name on the Baby Bradley case,' she said over her shoulder as she continued down the corridor. 'Rosie Hart.'

The DI didn't reply.

The only General Patrol vehicle left, when she and DC Cornwell arrived in the car park behind the station, was the red Austin Cambridge estate that drove like a hearse. 'You can drive this great lolloping thing,' Kathy said, climbing into the passenger seat.

'So, this is Baby-Bradley-related, yeah?' he asked, turning the engine over.

'Yes,' she answered, removing her pocketbook, and looking over the notes that she had made on the case so far. 'The Fingerprint Bureau came back with a match to a twenty-two-year-old woman from New Romney, called Rosie Hart.'

'Here we are,' DC Cornwell said, looking across Kathy to the building outside of which he had just pulled up. The road was narrow, and he had mounted the kerb in order to keep a car's width clear between the Austin Cambridge and the two-storey building.

Kathy took a good look at it before getting out. The building projected from the rear of the Rose and Crown pub on the High Street. The top half of the building was covered in Kent peg tiles, the lower half plastered and painted white. A spidery hand-painted sign nailed to the door read *Flat 1, 46.* 'Let's hope she's still resident at this charming abode,' Kathy said, as they both got out of the car. 'Go and check around the back and wait there while I knock.'

DC Cornwell nodded and disappeared around the side of the building. Moments later, he stuck his head around the corner. 'Looks like a bit of a drug den, Sarge.'

'Right,' Kathy said, approaching the front door and banging the brass knocker several times.

'*Someone's* home,' she said quietly to herself, seeing movement behind a crescent pane of obscured glass in the top quarter of the door.

The door opened quickly but was abruptly snagged back on a short brass chain. Through the two-inch gap, Kathy could see an overweight man somewhere in his twenties or thirties with untidy hair and a grey tracksuit. He met her stare but said nothing.

Her reception here was not going to be a welcoming one and she instantly pulled out her warrant card. 'WDS Steadman, Sussex Police,' she said. 'What's your name, please?'

'Why?' the man countered.

'Because I'm asking you for it. That's why,' Kathy said with a polite but self-assured smile.

The man stared at her, unblinking. 'Steve,' he said.

'Steve what?'

'Hart,' he said, dragging out the word and pulling a conceited facial expression which Kathy assumed meant that the name should be familiar.

'Is your sister, Rosie, in?' Kathy asked.

Steve laughed. 'Sorry, you just missed her,' he said, looking at his tattooed wrist as though he were wearing a watch. 'Maybe try coming back—oh, I don't know—two years ago when she was last here.'

'Rosie no longer resides at this address. Is that what you're trying to tell me?' Kathy asked, sensing that he was actually telling the truth.

'I am indeed telling you that Rosie no longer resides at this address,' he said, mocking her tone, cadence and voice.

'Where does she live now?' Kathy pushed.

Steve shrugged. 'Buggered if I know. She's not one to sit still, is our Rosie.'

'What's the last known address that you have for her?'

'Look, what is all this about, actually?' Steve demanded. 'What's she done now?'

Kathy quickly considered his question, wondering if she were to give him the truth, whether he might reciprocate; but if she were to do that, there was a massive risk that he might warn his sister, including *why* she was now being sought by the police. She decided to lie. 'Nothing herself, but we think she's hanging around with someone we need to get in touch with.'

Steve blew out his cheeks. 'Let me guess: Dan Thornley, yeah?'

Kathy intimated in her body language both that she couldn't confirm or deny the validity of that which he had said and that he was right, all despite her never having heard of a Dan Thornley before. 'As I say, she's not in trouble herself,' Kathy reiterated.

Steve sighed. 'I honestly haven't heard from her in months. She left here and went to stay with a friend in Croydon.'

'What's her friend's address?' Kathy asked, pulling out her pocketbook and pen.

'Sixty-one Beaconsfield Road,' he answered.

The same house outside of which Kathy had parked that very morning. This was quickly turning into a wild goose chase.

Chapter Six

29th September 1974, Westbere, Kent

Alfred Farrier was sitting in his blue Austin Mini, gazing at the house. He had been here five minutes already but couldn't yet bring himself to walk up the path and go inside. The tiny car felt oppressive. With a grunt, he wound down the window and gulped in the fresh air. As usual for him, he was wearing a pair of trousers, shirt, tie and a cardigan. He looked at his watch: nine fifty-six. He had told his mother that he would be arriving at ten o'clock prompt and to make sure that Margaret and the baby were ready to go. He was tempted just to beep the horn and be done with it, get them out here and get gone; but, of course, she would need help with her belongings now that there were two of them.

He drummed his fingers on the steering wheel and looked again at his watch. Nine fifty-seven.

A vice-like clamp around his ribcage began to tighten, and he unbuttoned the top of his shirt, pulling in a long draw of outside air. It wouldn't be too much longer until this nightmare would be over; after this afternoon, it was his firm hope that the matter would never be spoken of again.

Nine fifty-eight.

Goodness, but time was dragging. *This* wasn't simply a shameful blight on the Farrier family, it was also a great inconvenience, taking his time and focus away from his men's clothing shops in Folkestone and Sevenoaks. Work was busier than ever, and he was spending more and more time travelling to secure better, unusual or interesting fabrics which his tailor could work into the unique creations for which the shop was becoming renowned.

Nine fifty-nine.

He had a trip booked next month to Cannes in the South of France to attend an international conference of European fashion houses, and from there he was heading up to Florence in the hope of securing new patterns and fabrics for the Italian-style slim-fit suits which were rising in popularity. He would be leaving the Folkestone shop in the hands of his manager, Miss Timmins, who had just taken over from his son, Peter, in anticipation of his imminent move along the coast to Hastings.

Ten o'clock. At last.

Alfred took in a long breath, wound his window up and then buttoned the top of his shirt. He got out of the car, straightened himself and then marched up the front path to the cottage. He rapped the knocker firmly and stood back, his hands knitted together behind his back.

His mother answered the door with a wide smile. 'Alfred, come in,' she said, pulling the door open.

Alfred stood still. 'Is she ready? And the... Are they ready?'

'Not quite. My fault...before you say anything,' she replied. 'I've just made a pot of tea, come in and join us for a few minutes. You must be gasping.'

In truth, the stifling heat of the day had left him sweaty and parched. A sit down with a cup of tea, despite everything, wouldn't be such a bad thing, he supposed. He nodded and stepped into the cool house.

'Margaret and the baby are outside. Go on out to them, and I'll bring the tea over to you, directly,' his mother instructed, closing the front door behind him.

Alfred walked down the hallway and out through the French doors at the end of the kitchen. The garden was his mother's pride and joy, filled with an abundance of English cottage-garden flowers, shrubs and plants. Alfred was much more interested in using his garden to grow vegetables, to serve as a productive and efficient use of space; an idea instilled in him in the early years of the war, when seemingly every available piece of ground, public and private alike, had been cultivated to help feed the nation.

Margaret was sitting where he had been expecting to find her: on one of the white cast-iron chairs which were permanently set out in the shade of the two elder trees at the back of the garden. She was looking down at the baby nestled in her arms. She looked different somehow. Changed. Her clothes and hair were the same as usual, but something was different. She looked up at him and smiled.

'Margaret,' he said, dipping his head as he sat down beside her. He caught a glimpse of the baby sleeping silently in her arms.

'Hi, Dad,' she said. 'How are you?'

'Not too bad,' he answered, grateful for a cool breeze blowing across the garden.

'Can you smell the lilies?' Margaret asked him quietly, gesturing her head over to the patch of orange flowers nearby.

'Yes,' Alfred said, 'one of Granny's favourites.'

'Did you know it was the nickname of the Royal Sussex Regiment; the one that Grandad Len and Grandad Farrier served in?' she asked.

'Yes, but I can't recall why, now,' he said, wishing that his mother would hurry up. He looked at his watch: four minutes past ten.

'Well, it's because, in seventeen something or other, a general noticed that the regiments' tunics were buttoned outwards and he said they looked like orange lilies, and the nickname stuck from then,' Margaret informed him before adding the source of her surprising knowledge, 'Granny told me.'

Alfred raised his eyebrows at Margaret's comment, watching a pair of dragonflies flitting overhead. He stifled a sigh.

'Do you want to hold him?' she asked.

Alfred shook his head.

At last, his mother appeared at the back door and tottered down the path towards them, carrying a tray that would most assuredly be laden with all manner of cakes and biscuits.

'Is he still asleep?' she mouthed, quietly setting the tray down on the table.

Alfred studied Margaret's face as she nodded with a small smile. He sincerely hoped that the difference which he had noticed in her was not some kind of warped maternal jubilance.

His mother separated the stack of three teacups, setting each carefully down onto a saucer and then filling them from the teapot. She added a splash of milk, stirred them, and then handed Alfred his cup, saying, 'I'll leave yours there, Margaret, dear, but I'll take the young lad from you if he hasn't woken.' She turned to face Alfred. 'Fruit cake, buns, Bakewell, cheese scone? Or all of the above?'

'Just a piece of fruitcake, please,' he replied, sipping his tea.

She handed him a small, decorative plate with a chunk of fruit cake on it. 'All made by your daughter's own fair hand, fresh this morning.'

Alfred was stunned. 'Margaret made all this?'

Nellie nodded and grinned. 'She's becoming a fine young woman.'

'She's still a girl,' he corrected, eyeing the baby. 'Drink up,

Margaret. We need to be heading back home; the social worker will be arriving with Peter and Maureen in less than two hours.'

'Granny, will you hold Jack for a moment?' Margaret asked.

'Of course, my dear,' she replied, standing up and taking the baby.

'What did you call it?' Alfred asked.

'Jack,' Margaret answered.

'It isn't yours to name,' he spluttered, thumping the plate down on the table and waking the baby directly. 'It isn't *yours*, Margaret. Right. That's enough. We're going.' He stood up and glowered at his mother. 'Where's her suitcase?'

'In the lounge, packed and ready,' she replied.

He looked at his watch and then he looked at Margaret. 'You've got precisely four minutes to be in that car. Understood?'

She nodded weakly as she took the crying baby back from Alfred's mother and walked crestfallen up the garden path towards the house.

'I don't know what's been going on, here,' Alfred said, 'but it wasn't supposed to be a holiday and she *certainly* wasn't supposed to be developing any attachment to the child.'

'Alfred. Calm down,' his mother said.

'I shall not be told to calm down,' he shouted. 'And to let her give it *that* name…of all things. Honestly!' His mother began to remonstrate, but he stomped up towards the house, having heard just about enough.

Margaret was standing in the hallway beside the front door with her suitcase by her feet and the baby resting against her shoulder. She was staring at the floor, sobbing. He picked up the suitcase, opened the front door and walked to the Mini, tossing the case onto the back seat before leaning across to open the passenger door. He gritted his teeth as he watched the emotional display occurring between his mother and daughter at the house.

He turned the ignition and smacked the horn.

The social worker, Miss Christiansen, was thankfully punctual, arriving at Alfred's house at midday. She was a prim little lady in her fifties with round black glasses, a plaid skirt and a white blouse. Over her shoulder was slung a heavy-looking bag which she dropped down to the floor with great relief when Alfred showed her into the lounge.

Alfred smiled. 'My son and daughter-in-law are in the kitchen—shall I fetch them?'

Miss Christiansen pushed her glasses up onto the bridge of her nose, then pulled a voluminous quantity of paperwork from her bag. 'First, I should like to see—' she paused and looked down at the paper in her lap '—Margaret Farrier.'

Alfred's smile soured, and he walked to the bottom of the stairs and called up to her. 'Margaret, can you come down and speak with Miss Christiansen, please?'

His son, Peter, appeared at the door to the kitchen with an anxious look on his face. 'Everything okay?' he whispered.

Alfred nodded. 'Yes. Yes. Get Maureen to put the kettle on, will you?'

'Good idea,' Peter replied.

Margaret descended the stairs with her head hung low. When she looked up, her face was blotchy, and her eyes were swollen and red. 'What?' she said, almost inaudibly.

'The social worker, Miss Christiansen, wants to speak with you in the lounge,' he said brightly. She skulked past him, and he hissed, 'Well? Look lively, girl.'

He followed her into the room and pushed the door closed behind them.

'That will be *just* Margaret, thank you, Mr Farrier,' Miss Christiansen said.

'Oh, yes. Of course,' Alfred said, now backing out of the room. He walked into the kitchen. Both Peter and Maureen shot him a concerned look. 'It's okay. Just a formality.'

'You don't think she'll change her mind, do you?' Maureen asked, pouring the tea with a shaky hand.

'Over my dead body, she will,' Alfred retorted.

'Goodness gracious me. I really didn't imagine I'd be quite so nervous,' she said.

Peter placed his hand on her shoulder. 'It'll all be fine,' he soothed. 'In a couple of hours' time, you, me and the baby will be in our new home in Hastings to start our lives together as a family.'

She smiled and began to cry.

Alfred looked at the pair of them; both in their mid-twenties with good, sensible heads on their shoulders and with the ability to provide a future for the baby, since they had been unable to have children of their own. There was no doubt in Alfred's mind that the right decision was being made.

'I'll take it through,' Alfred said, when Maureen had finished making the tea. He picked up two cups and carried them down the hallway, pausing outside the lounge door to eavesdrop.

'So, if you do decide that this is what you want and sign this piece of paper, you are legally forgoing all your parental rights forever,' Miss Christiansen was saying. 'Do you understand everything that I have explained to you?'

'Yes,' Margaret said weakly.

Alfred nudged open the door and entered the room, giving Margaret a severe stare as he set down the two drinks on the coffee table between them. 'My daughter-in-law made these,' Alfred said to the social worker, taking in the piece of paper in Margaret's hand. 'She's a very, very good housewife.'

'Thank you,' Miss Christiansen said. 'I was just telling your daughter that she is under no obligation nor any pressure whatsoever to sign the adoption papers, and that it must be something that she goes into willingly and with the full comprehension of the irreversible consequences of the decision to surrender her rights.'

'Oh, she *fully* understands,' Alfred said, trying not to sound impatient. 'Don't you, Margaret?'

She looked at the social worker briefly, then picked up the pen from the table and signed her name.

Miss Christiansen took the piece of paper and held it while she stared searchingly at Margaret. After a time, she said, 'Okay. Mr Farrier, would you now sign to say that you were a witness.'

'With pleasure,' he said, taking the form and adding his name and signature to the bottom.

The social worker reached out and placed her hand on Margaret's knee. 'I need to speak with Peter and Maureen, now. This might be a good time for you to go and say your goodbyes—to the baby, I mean.'

Margaret burst into tears and rushed from the room. Alfred turned to see her taking the stairs two at a time. 'She'll be right as rain in a day or two,' he said.

'With all due respect, Mr Farrier, it will take much longer than that;

your daughter will need a great deal of love, patience and kindness.'

Alfred went to respond but held back; the adoption was not yet finalised. 'I'll just go and fetch my son and daughter-in-law for you,' he muttered through a restrained out-breath.

Much to Alfred's relief, forty-five minutes later, the initial formalities of the adoption had been completed and he showed Miss Christiansen to the door. 'Thank you for coming,' he said, shaking her hand.

The social worker smiled. 'I hope it all works out well for *everyone* involved,' she said pointedly. 'Including for your daughter, I mean. Of course, the final decision rests with the courts, whom you shall hear from in due course.'

She stepped outside and Alfred followed her, pulling the door to behind him. 'One more question before you go,' he said, lowering his voice considerably.

'Yes?'

'The baby—he'll never get to find out the truth, will he?'

Miss Christiansen pursed her lips. 'Right now—under current legislation—that little boy has no legal right to find out the identities of his birth parents; but the Houghton Committee have been looking into the matter for some time now and things may well change in the future, Mr Farrier. So, I don't offer you any firm guarantees that one day that boy won't be able to find out who his birth parents were.'

'Oh, golly,' Alfred said.

'For what it's worth, my personal opinion on the matter is that any child should have an inalienable right to know where he came from,' she said, hauling her heavy bag back up onto her shoulder. Her face looked ready for a confrontation, and Alfred might have given it, but he caught sight of someone over Miss Christiansen's shoulder, who distracted him.

'Good day to you,' he said politely, bringing the interaction with the social worker to a curt close.

She nodded, turned and walked down the path to her car.

Alfred looked at the girl. She was leaning on the lamppost outside his neighbour's house, smoking a cigarette and staring at him. She was wearing flared jeans and a red shirt, her hair pulled back under the usual headband. He slowly walked towards her, taking nervous glances around. 'How the devil did you find me?' he seethed.

She grinned, blowing out a long stream of smoke. 'It's me, Anna,' she snorted. 'I'm your wife. So, of course I know where you live. You don't sound very pleased to see me today. Aren't you going to buy me a sherry?'

'I said, I want to know how you flaming well found me?' he repeated angrily.

'My family have got *a lot* of connections around here, let's just say,' she replied.

'What do you want?'

'Spending money from my old man,' she said with a grin.

'And what do you suppose I am? A bank?' he snapped.

She nodded. 'You seem to be doing alright for yourself. I visited your shop in Sevenoaks the other day to see if you were there. Got chatting to a right nice lady who was telling me all sorts about you. She said you'd got exciting plans to travel round Europe coming up. I reckon you've got a pound or two to spare for your poor, old wife... We also had a quick chat about the flat above the shop; she sure seemed surprised I knew it quite so well.'

'How much?' he asked quietly.

She raised her eyebrows and took a drag on her cigarette.

'Dad?' Peter suddenly called from the house. 'Are you coming back in? We'll be heading off, shortly.'

He turned quickly. 'Yes, yes, won't be a moment!'

The girl began to laugh. 'Blimey! *He's* supposed to be my son? He's my age!'

'How much?' Alfred asked, hastily taking his wallet from his back pocket.

'Couple of hundred should do me...for today,' she answered.

'What?' he stammered. 'You must be mad. I don't have that sort of money lying around.'

'I'll take what you've got for now, then,' she said. 'But I'm thinking of relocating, see, and I'll need money to set me up, help me to find a new husband in a new area.'

Alfred opened his wallet and handed her thirty pounds. 'Look, that's all I have.' He turned and began to march back to the house.

'Then that ain't the last you'll be seeing of Rosie Hart,' she called after him.

He entered the house, slammed the front door shut and then closed his eyes, trying to steady his nerves.

'Who was that?' Peter asked, appearing from the lounge with the baby in his arms.

'Oh, she works for a homeless charity I support,' he answered. 'They do great work but are always after more and more money.'

'That's kind of you,' Maureen said, joining Peter and putting an arm around him.

Alfred shrugged. 'We've all got to do our bit, haven't we?'

'Would you like a hold before we go?' Peter asked, offering up the baby.

Alfred smiled. 'Absolutely,' he said, carefully taking the child. 'My first grandson. Do we have a name for the little mite yet?'

'Morton,' Maureen revealed.

'Oh,' Alfred said. 'Not sure I've heard that name before. That's unusual.'

'Morton was my grandmother, Ethel's maiden name,' she said. 'She pretty well raised me, and I always thought I'd name one of my children after her by way of thanks and to remember her by. So, it has to be either Morton or Ethel, since this will probably be our only one.'

Alfred laughed. '*Morton* Farrier.'

The absolute conviction of the decision's having been right—that Peter and Maureen should adopt the boy—was reflected back in the love and warmth that shone over him from their eyes. Alfred sighed with satisfaction, then spotted Margaret at the top of the stairs, tortured, with tears streaming down her cheeks.

Chapter Seven

Morton arrived in his study with great gusto and enthusiasm for the working day ahead. His minor transgression, yesterday—when he had inadvertently forgotten to pick Grace up from nursery—had been forgiven by Juliette and also by the nursery staff. He had ended up only being forty minutes late which hadn't been the end of the world in his opinion.

He sat at his desk with a fresh cup of coffee and the four unopened certificates which had arrived moments previously. He had a good few hours of research time whilst Juliette was out with Grace and her mum, and Morton was determined to put the time to good use. The clock was ticking, and he had just four days until they were leaving for Christmas in Cornwall.

Morton tore open the first envelope. Inside was Rosie Hart's birth certificate which stated that she had been born on the 21st of July 1952 to Roy Hart and Peggy Hart, formerly Raven. The family address was given as 16, Robin Hood Lane, Lydd, Kent.

The next envelope contained Roy and Peggy's marriage certificate. This one was absolutely crucial in proving his theories so far. He was relieved to discover that Roy's father was listed as Jack Hart and Peggy's father was listed as David Raven; excellent validation of his research to this point.

The third envelope contained Gemma Hart's marriage certificate. Her father was stated to be Roy and one of the witnesses to the event was her sister, Rosie.

In the final envelope, Morton pulled out a birth certificate for a boy who had been born to Gemma Hart and her husband. Vitally, the boy had been born on the 22nd July 1975. Unless Gemma had been a medical or religious miracle, she could not have given birth to Vanessa Briggs two months earlier. Morton was content that this provided sufficient evidence to rule Gemma out as being Vanessa's, Liza's and Billie's mother.

He was now convinced that their biological mother was indeed Rosie Hart.

He set the certificates to one side and turned on his laptop.

On the screen in front of him were the five results from his initial search in the British Newspaper Archive for any reference to Rosie.

Robbery with violence charge...
Burglary...
A well-known local prostitute...
Accused of attempted murder...
Dart in the eye...

Morton switched the way that the articles were being presented from *Relevance* to *Date*, wanting to read them in chronological order and thereby achieve a better understanding of Rosie's erratic movements around the country. The results list rejigged itself with *Burglary* as the top-most story from the *Kent & Sussex Courier* 9th July 1970 edition.

BURGLARY
Rosie Hart, aged 18, of Robin Hood Lane, Lydd, was fined £60 and ordered to pay £37 8s 10d restitution for stealing four barometers, two electric blankets and six leather wallets from the Folkestone branch of Greenwood & Sons, between April 24-27. She pleaded guilty to the charge.

Morton printed out the article, being confident from the age and address that it referenced the correct Rosie Hart. The next story, with the hyperlink of *Robbery with violence charge*, was from the *Hastings & St Leonards Observer*, dated 18th October 1971.

TWO FOR TRIAL
Two siblings, charged jointly with robbery with violence at the Flackley Ash Hotel in Peasmarsh, were committed to the new Crown Court at Lewes, where they appeared before the judge last week. They were Steven Hart, a twenty-year-old van driver from 46 Ashford Road, New Romney and his sister, Rosie, aged 19 of the same abode. The pair are being tried for an attempted robbery at the hotel in June of this year. The brother and sister are accused of trying to steal money and items to the value of £5000 after physically assaulting the receptionist on duty at the time. They deny the charges and were bailed on the sum of £50.

Morton double-checked and confirmed in the family tree that Rosie had had an older brother, called Steven. Although it was a different address from the previous year, he was sure that the article referred to the right person, so he printed out the story and added it to his investigation wall. Chronologically, the next article was from the *Kentish Gazette*, dated 16th March 1975.

'A Well-Known Local Prostitute' - court told

Miss Rosie Hart, of Pound Lane, Canterbury, described in court as 'a well-known local prostitute', was fined £5 at Sevenoaks Magistrates Court on Friday, after she had pleaded guilty to causing wilful damage to a window of a shop at 123 High Street, Sevenoaks on 24th December last year. For the prosecution, it was said that Mr Farrier, the owner of Farrier's Fashion, was working inside the shop when a brick was thrown through the glass window that fronted the pavement, where Miss Hart was standing. Witnesses described her as shouting through the smashed pane: 'You're going to get it right in the mouth, you ————. I'll get my money's worth out of you.' In court, Mr Farrier denied any knowledge of the woman. Miss Hart said that it had been an accident and agreed to pay for the cost of the window.

Wow. He gasped as he stared at the story. Here was his first piece of evidence outside of DNA that linked Rosie Hart to his own grandfather, Alfred Farrier. But the account of the actual incident didn't seem to match up with the description in the court proceedings. Rosie's apparent outburst at the shop, where she had felt so passionately that Alfred had owed her money—to the extent that she had smashed his shop window in broad daylight—contrasted completely with her having told the court that it had been an accident. The semi-opaque reason was obvious to Morton: his grandfather had given Rosie what she had felt that he had owed to her in return for her not explicitly making the obvious link between them both; she being a 'well-known local prostitute'. Before he moved on to the next story, Morton looked again at the date on which it had occurred: 24th December 1974. Would Rosie have been obviously pregnant with Vanessa by that time? Could this have been what she had meant by 'getting her money's worth' out of him?

Morton looked up Vanessa's precise date of birth, then typed the date, 13th May 1975, into an online reverse conception calculator. According to the results, Rosie and Alfred had conceived Vanessa at some point in the week between 14th and 20th August 1974. By the time of the window-smashing incident, Rosie would have been highly likely aware that she had been four months pregnant. Although Morton had no solid proof that Rosie's being pregnant with Alfred's child had been the cause of the outburst, it certainly seemed a very high possibility.

He drank some coffee as he clicked back to the results list, dreading what he would find in the next article that had the very troubling headline of *Dart in the Eye*. It was from an issue of the *Manchester Evening News*, dated 4th September 1979.

DART IN THE EYE
A quiet evening in a popular Manchester pub ended when a young woman plunged a dart into a man's eye, the Crown Court was told on Thursday. Twenty-six-year-old Rosie Hart, of Deeper Street, Levenshulme, denied a charge of causing grievous bodily harm with intent to do so, although she did admit to stabbing sixty-four-year-old Edward Crouch of Oxford Road, Manchester after he refused to give her money that she alleged was owed to her. Mr Crouch, who wore dark glasses to shield the injury to his left eye, described to the court how the attack had come as a complete surprise, having had no prior knowledge of his attacker. He had been having a drink in the King's Head with his wife, Agnes on 5th July this year, when the defendant pushed her way through the crowd as he was on his way to the toilet, punching him in the face. Crouch, curator at the Manchester Art Gallery in the city centre, did not realise that she had a dart in her hand until later; he can now only see blurred lines through the affected eye. The man was rushed to hospital where emergency surgery was carried out, but doctors were not certain if they had been able to save his eye. Hart was found guilty and sentenced to 18 months' imprisonment, suspended for two years, during which time she was ordered to be under the supervision of a probation officer.

Morton did not quite know where to begin with dissecting this story. The first job, he supposed, was to be as certain as he could be that it was relating to the correct Rosie Hart. Her age was right, and there were notable similarities to the previous story, wherein she had sought revenge for money owed to her from a distinctly older man who had denied all knowledge of being acquainted with her. Morton searched through the notes that he had made on Billie Howard. She had been found abandoned in a shop doorway on Mosley Street in Manchester city centre on the 29th December 1979, with an assumed date of birth seven to ten days prior.

Morton put Billie's date of birth into the reverse conception calculator, establishing that she had likely been conceived at some time between the 22nd March and 28th March. Once again, Rosie would have known that she had been pregnant at the time that she had attacked Edward Crouch. If Morton could deduce any kind of a pattern here, then it was possible that Edward Crouch was the father of Billie Howard. Before he turned to the final article in the list, he typed *Mosley Street, Manchester* into Google Maps. It was a long road right in the heart of the city centre. Certainly, it would not have taken long for the baby to have been discovered, which was fortunate given the time of year.

He zoomed in closer to the street, slowly tracing its length as the names of shops and buildings popped up along the way. *Barclays Bank. The Portico Library. Sainsburys Local. Bank of China.* Morton paused and looked at the label over a huge H-shaped building on the road. *Manchester Art Gallery.*

Edward Crouch, whom Rosie Hart had stabbed in the eye, was described in the newspaper article as a curator at the gallery. A coincidence? Or had Rosie, in some kind of symbolic gesture, left the baby in a shop doorway near to the father's place of work?

Morton sat back and drank more coffee, considering his theory. Then he opened WhatsApp on his mobile, locating the group that Vanessa had named *The Foundlings* and sent a message, asking Billie if she knew the exact location on Mosley Street where she had been found.

Vanessa had been left in the doorway of the Sevenoaks branch of Woolworths. Where had the shop been located, precisely? He Googled that very question. The top result provided a black and white photograph and the answer: 124a-126 High Street. Copying and pasting the address into Google Maps, Morton switched to Street View, the position of which was planted firmly in the centre of Sevenoaks High Street. He swivelled the camera angle, easily locating the building as it had been in May 2019, being used as a Poundland store. He adjusted the date-slider in the top left corner back to 2008 when the shop had still been a Woolworths. He then changed the address to 123 High Street, the location of Farrier's Fashion, finding himself in exactly the same spot in the centre of the road. His grandfather's shop had been situated directly opposite Woolworths. It appeared to Morton that this had been a clear gesture aimed at the baby's biological father.

Morton reviewed his notes for Liza Bennett. She had been discovered in a shop doorway on the 7th April 1977 in Croydon, London. Without the supporting evidence from a newspaper article, though, Morton realised that he could not draw a similar working theory as he had with Vanessa and Billie, and searches for the story in the British Newspaper Archive produced no results. It had either not made the newspapers, or the particular paper that had run the story was not yet digitised.

For now, his theory was nothing more than that.

He returned to the final result in the newspaper archive search for Rosie Hart. It was from the 18th November 1980 edition of the *Kent & Sussex Courier*.

ACCUSED OF ATTEMPTED MURDER
Two brothers were remanded in custody for one week at Chichester Crown Court on Friday, charged with the attempted murder of a police officer. The two were Steven Hart (29) and Frank Hart (26) of Hythe Road, Dymchurch. They are charged with the attempted murder of Kathy Steadman at All Saints Church, Haywards Heath on 14th November 1980. A third sibling, Rosie Hart fled the scene and is wanted in connection with the crime. WDS Steadman suffered severe stab wounds and is currently in intensive care. The brothers will appear again before the court on Friday. Neither applied for bail.

Nice family, Morton thought, printing out the article. He had wanted to view the five articles in chronological order to understand better Rosie's geographical movement, but what he had also inadvertently discovered was an escalation in her criminal behaviour.

Morton attached the stories to his investigation wall, then stood back, trying to take it all in. He wondered what the reason might have been as to why her criminality appeared to have stopped in 1980. Had the cases simply not made the newspapers? Had she been apprehended and was still languishing at Her Majesty's pleasure? Had she died?

He quickly double-checked that Rosie had not married or died since 1980, finding no results for either possibility; although, online death indexes only ran as far as 2007 and so it remained possible that she had died in the intervening twelve years.

Morton edited his search for Steven Hart's name, hoping to find mention of a follow-up to the attempted murder court case. He found twelve matches and the list of headlines looked as alarming—perhaps worse even—than Rosie's catalogue of misdemeanours. Morton planned to read each of them carefully, but decided to focus on the final entry which was the sentencing of the two brothers. Frank and Steven Hart had each been handed down a fifteen-year sentence for the attempted murder of WDS Kathy Steadman, but there was still no mention in the article of their elusive sister's whereabouts.

Morton's mobile alerted him with an incoming WhatsApp message on *The Foundlings* group. He picked it up and, when he saw that it was a reply from Billie Howard, read the full message.

Hi Morton. Good to hear from you. Apparently I was found by the owner of a greengrocers on Mosley Street. I think it was called Fraser & Steens (maybe Staines / Sterns / Stiens??) - it's not there anymore but if you look on google maps at Manchester art gallery it was dead opposite the main entrance. Billie x

Opposite Manchester Art Gallery. It appeared that his theory might indeed be correct, at least in the cases of Billie and Vanessa. Rosie Hart seemed to have left her children in close proximity to the putative father's place of work. Was it some kind of statement that she had tried to make? Or had she really imagined, in some warped way, that she would have been handing the child over to their custody?

Morton exhaled loudly, contemplating what a truly horrific report he was going to have to write at the end of his research. He could just picture the three women all gathered around together, eagerly anticipating his findings. What he had to tell them was much worse than all that they could thus far have imagined their mother to have been. And he wasn't done yet.

To do his job properly, he needed to have conducted reasonably exhaustive research into Rosie's life, including the possibility of her having had further children. Not to mention the one thing which all three women were desperate to know: where their birth mother was right now.

As Morton had requested, each of the three women had uploaded their DNA to MyHeritage and FamilyTreeDNA. Given what he now knew about Rosie Hart's life, it was with some degree of trepidation that Morton logged into Vanessa's account at MyHeritage. Thankfully, her two closest matches—and by a very long way—were Billie and Liza. He was heartened to see that the next match, with 105 centiMorgans was a lady by the name of Karen Raven who hailed from the US. He clicked on the family tree that she had included in her profile and found that she was related to the three women via Rosie Hart's mother, Peggy Raven; further proof that his analysis to this point had been correct. He logged out of Vanessa's account and logged in as Billie.

'Oh God,' he muttered when he saw the top results. He covered his eyes with his hands and took in a long breath. He peered out through his splayed fingers to see that sandwiched neatly between Vanessa and Liza was a woman, named Amy Praed, matching with a significant 1782 centiMorgans. The snapshot of her profile said that Amy was from the UK and that she was in her 70s. With some hesitation, Morton clicked *Review Match* and a fresh page with comparative data between the two women appeared side by side onscreen. He scrolled down to *Shared DNA Matches*. Vanessa and Liza were absent from the list, meaning that, as Morton had suspected, Amy Praed must be related to Billie via her unknown biological father. The names in the list meant nothing to Morton, but when he reached the section labelled *Pedigree Charts*, he smiled. Praed was Amy's married name; her maiden name had been Crouch and her father was stated to have been Edward Crouch, born 1915 in Manchester. The very same man who had been stabbed in the eye by Rosie with a dart in 1979.

Morton stared at the screen, wondering how best to tackle this delicate situation. Given that Billie lived in Manchester, a face-to-face explanation was out of the question. He would need to break the news—that she had another half-sister who was almost twice her age—over the phone, which was less than ideal. First, though, he logged out of her account and into Liza's. He braced himself as the DNA matches loaded but he was relieved to find that there was nothing untoward in the list.

Morton finished his coffee and then ran the same checks on the FamilyTreeDNA website, thankfully finding no further close matches or anything which required detailed exploration.

He now needed to spend some time running sufficiently exhaustive searches into the possibility of Rosie's having abandoned other children besides Vanessa, Billie and Liza. He opened up the British Newspaper Archive and selected the time period of 1970 to 1979, then typed *abandoned baby* in the search box.

373 articles

Morton scanned down the first ten results, catching glimpses of the various heart-breaking story outlines: *Father who abandoned baby to get cash cleared of neglect... Inverness woman neglected baby daughter... A baby boy who was abandoned on Friday when he was a few hours old, died yesterday in hospital... Police said today they were concerned after a young woman, admitted to hospital, claimed to have abandoned her five-month-old baby in a derelict house...*

He exhaled. This was not only going to be heavy-going research but also incredibly difficult in many of these cases to prove or disprove any connection to Rosie Hart. He looked at the potential ways in which he might filter down the search somewhat, but there was no way he could reduce the search parameters by geographical area, date or newspaper because she had moved around so much. There was nothing for it but to read each and every article.

Three hours and twenty-one minutes later, Morton stood from his desk with a long stretch. He wandered over to his study window which overlooked the cobbles of Mermaid Street. The road was bustling with Christmas shoppers, despite the dreary drab day. He opened the window, taking in the chilly air laced with the tantalising culinary outputs from the restaurants and tearooms nearby. He gazed absent-mindedly at the crowd as he mulled over that which he had discovered. Although the newspaper search had been gruelling, he had found that many of the stories were identical, being so sensational that they had been replicated almost word for word in multiple regional newspapers around the country. Some of the stories pertained to babies born closely in date to Vanessa, Billie and

Liza and so could logically be discounted. In some, one or both of the parents had been named, and in others the mother had herself come forwards or later been found. In the end, Morton had printed out just one article. It was from the *Mid-Sussex Times Millennium Edition* which featured a snapshot of major news stories from the area in the past thousand years. Owing to the nature of the publication, the story was brief.

September 1973
Baby Bradley found in a phonebox! A ten-day-old baby was discovered abandoned in a telephone box outside the Seeboard showroom inside a red and white chequered bag.

He would have totally overlooked the terse account, had it not been for the mention of the bag. Billie and Liza had been found in cardboard boxes within a red and white chequered bag. Was this another veiled clue, like leaving the child close to the father's place of work? He needed to take a look at the original article to be sure.

Movement and shouting on the street beneath his window drew Morton's attention. He looked down to see Juliette and Grace standing with Morton's brother, Jeremy, and his husband, Guy. He grinned and waved.

'Daydreaming?' Jeremy shouted up.

Morton nodded. 'Are you coming in?'

Guy held up a by-now-very-familiar brown box. Morton smiled and gave a thumbs-up as he closed the window and groaned to himself, 'Oh, God. Not more scones.' Jeremy and Guy had set up a shop on Rye High Street, called Granny's Scones, and were forever delivering samples or unsold leftovers, often with the most atrocious combinations of flavours imaginable. Marmite and lemon, peanut butter and cheddar, pear and gorgonzola, and chicken and chilli were just some of the recent exotic flavours that had been foisted upon him. Despite the strangeness of the ingredients, his problem wasn't actually with the taste; it was with the amount that he was eating.

Morton reached the front door just as it opened and Juliette stepped inside, pecking him on the lips. 'Good day's work?'

He nodded. 'Yeah, I think so,' he answered, smiling as he watched Grace darting up the steps to the doorway.

71

'Daddy!' she greeted, wrapping her arms around his leg.

'We come bearing gifts,' Guy said in his Australian accent, holding aloft the scone box, as if Morton might not already have seen it from his study window.

'Yes, so I saw,' Morton said. 'And what delightful flavour do we have today, pray tell? Beef and strawberry? Anchovy and melon?'

'Cheese,' Guy replied.

'With?' Morton said.

'With nothing. Just cheese.'

Morton raised his eyebrows as he closed the front door behind them. 'Presumably some weird, ten-year, cave-matured, cedar-smoked, Nepalese mountain-goat cheese?'

Guy laughed. 'Cheddar, actually.'

'How…unusual,' Morton observed, trying to walk stiff-legged into the kitchen, with Grace still grappled to his thigh.

'Have you seen this yet?' Jeremy asked him, holding up a copy of the *Guardian* newspaper as he slid into a chair at the kitchen table beside Guy.

Morton shook his head, finally peeling Grace's arms off his leg. 'Is it in there?'

Jeremy nodded. 'Oh, yes! But I think we need to have the official reading over a coffee and a scone…or two.'

'Morton, you sort the drinks and I'll sort the scones,' Juliette directed.

Grace scuttled off to her mini kitchen in the corner of the room, hurriedly placing plastic toy-food into a saucepan. 'Grace make gones,' she said.

'*Sc*ones,' Morton corrected as he began to make drinks, eager to read the *Guardian* serialisation of the case on which he had recently been working that involved a man, living under the assumed name, Maurice Duggan, who had been a spy for MI6. The story—or so the journalist who had interviewed Morton had led him to believe—would be centred around the identification of the man who had killed the spy.

'Read!' he instructed Jeremy as he placed the drinks down on the table and sat beside Juliette who had sliced the scones and who was now in the process of applying an artery-clogging amount of butter to each half.

Jeremy stood from the table, opening the newspaper, and turned the double-page spread to face them with a dramatic flourish. '*Spies, Lies and Murder!*' he intoned, energetically reading the headline.

Morton cringed. Below a photograph of the murder suspect was a picture of him that the journalist had taken 'but probably wouldn't use', sitting at his desk with his chin resting on a clenched fist.

Juliette burst into laughter. 'That photo of you! That's hilarious.' She leant in closer and read the caption: '*Morton Farrier, the self-styled forensic genealogist who solved the mystery.*' She laughed again. 'This is just too brilliant.'

Morton scowled at her, then scowled at Jeremy. 'Just read it.'

Jeremy giggled, turned the article back to face him and began to read in some ridiculous, deep and dramatic voice: '*Alexei Yahontov, a former KGB agent has been named by Scotland Yard as the person most likely to have killed the British double-agent, Maurice Duggan. Yahontov arrived in the country from Russia two days prior to the murder and left the following day. CCTV places him in the village of Ardingly, where Duggan had been living at the time, on the morning of his death. Detectives believe that Duggan's murder—staged to appear as suicide—was in reaction to him being about to publish his shocking life story, revealing disturbing details about his time working as a double-agent...*blah blah blah,' Jeremy said, evidently losing interest in the story and searching for something more interesting. '*Morton Farrier, a forensic genealogist based in Rye, East Sussex, solved the case using a combination of traditional genealogical records and DNA. 'I could never have solved such a complicated case without the use of genetic genealogy',* Morton Farrier said, adding, '*DNA never lies!*''

Juliette, Jeremy and Guy all erupted into raucous laughter.

Grace, holding a small saucepan containing a banana, plastic can of tuna and a miniature tomato ketchup bottle ran over to Morton. 'Grace gone,' she said.

Morton might have made a quip about the contents of her saucepan's being the ingredients for Jeremy and Guy's next Scone of the Day, but when Grace noticed that everyone was laughing at him, she, too, promptly joined in.

Chapter Eight

Kathy Steadman sat down in her armchair beside the open lounge window with a noisy exhalation. The day was unseasonably warm and Kathy, wearing just light-blue cotton trousers with a white blouse, was enjoying the gentle breeze floating in from outside. It was her first Sunday off work in several weeks and she was determined to spend the day doing as little as possible. She picked up the cup and saucer from the table beside her, took a sip of the hot tea and sighed contentedly. She put her feet up on the tasselled pouffe and picked up the book that she was currently reading: *The Odessa File* by Frederick Forsyth. She held the book in front of her, judging the position of the bookmark—a fraction over halfway— against the available time, and resolved that she would try and finish reading it today. Other than that, her plans amounted to splendidly little. She might give her mother a telephone call later and maybe go for a walk; but if she ended up doing neither and not stepping foot outside of her bungalow until tomorrow morning, then that was completely fine by her, too.

She sipped her tea, then set it back down on the table and began to read. She had just finished her second sentence when a sound outside made her pause and listen more closely. It was a whistle, a repeating *whit-whit* kind of sound that might be used to summon an errant dog. She tried to ignore the noise and focus on the book, but it was monotonous and intrusive, and seemingly right outside her bungalow.

With a huff, Kathy put down her book, swung her legs off the footrest and headed over to the window, standing behind the privacy of the net curtains.

Directly outside and staring right at her house was the whistling man. He was holding an empty bird cage. 'Tweetie!' he called.

Kathy grinned. Today was her lucky day. She hurried into the hallway, picked up the telephone receiver and dialled 999. 'This is WDS Kathy Steadman. I need a patrol car sent to my home address immediately; the Budgie Burglar is here.'

Kathy rushed back into her lounge to find the man standing there

74

in the middle of the room, holding the cage aloft with an apologetic smile on his face.

'Goodness me! So sorry,' he exclaimed, then raised the bird cage. 'My daughter's budgie has escaped, and I just saw him fly in through your window here.'

Well, he was certainly convincing, Kathy thought. And charming. He was in his late forties, quite handsome with swept-back dark hair, flared jeans and a bright-green open-necked shirt. Kathy returned his warm smile. 'Oh, really? What does he look like, exactly?'

'*Very* distinctive,' he said. 'Turquoise and white. Goes by the unimaginative name of Tweetie that my daughter gave him. She's devastated, as you might well imagine.'

'Oh, naturally,' Kathy said, spotting that her warrant card was open on the sideboard. 'And you say it flew into *this* house?'

'Yes, but it's obviously gone off again,' he said, shifting uncomfortably and starting to walk out of the lounge. 'I'll just leave you in peace. So sorry to have disturbed you.'

'Oh, it's no bother,' Kathy said, following him out into the hallway and grabbing her warrant card as she went. 'Don't you want me to check the rest of the house, first?'

The man shook his head and nervously began trying to unbolt and unchain the front door. 'Goodness me, it's a bit like Fort Knox in here,' he mumbled, having to put the bird cage down on the door mat to free up his right hand.

'Or…like the home of a police officer,' Kathy said, holding up her warrant card.

The man's shoulders sank as he slowly turned to face her.

Kathy quickly pocketed the badge, unsure of how the Budgie Burglar was going to react to being cornered. From over his shoulder, through the obscure glass window, she could see the unmistakable, orange-striped, white police car pulling up outside her house.

The Budgie Burglar picked up the birdcage and suddenly launched it at Kathy's face.

She cursed herself for not having pre-empted that possible course of action as she raised her left forearm to protect her head. The cage smashed into her arm making her yell out in pain.

The Budgie Burglar rushed towards her, knocking her over, and

75

ran into the lounge where she heard a scuffle followed by a PC placing the man under arrest.

'Are you okay, Sarge?' a WPC asked her, rushing into the hallway.

Kathy stood up, wincing, and clutching her left arm in her right hand. She nodded despite some discomfort. 'Yes, thank you.'

'Do you think you need to go to the hospital?'

'No, I'll be fine. I expect I'll have a nice bruise there, tomorrow morning, though,' Kathy replied, entering the lounge to see the Budgie Burglar being handcuffed. He glowered at Kathy as he was being carted off.

'Poor, poor Tweetie,' she said. 'Now he's just *never* going to be found.'

'Sod off, pig,' he spat.

She grinned and said to the PC, 'I'll come down and book him in. With *great* pleasure.'

At Burgess Hill Police Station, Kathy led the Budgie Burglar to one of the four cells at the back of the station. The cell had concrete walls, a small barred window, narrow bed and a seatless toilet in the corner.

'Can you take off your shoes and your belt, please?' Kathy asked him.

Without speaking, the Budgie Burglar did as she had instructed.

Kathy locked the cell door, returned the keys to the Station Officer, and then headed upstairs to her office.

'Shouldn't you be day-off, today?' her counterpart, DS Gadsby commented, glancing up from his desk. Because of their shift patterns, she rarely saw him.

'Well, I do have a cold cup of tea and an unopened book waiting for me back at home,' she said, sitting down at her desk. 'Not to mention a certain invisible budgerigar to catch.'

DS Gadsby, fully appraised of the case, chuckled. 'At least you've finally caught him.'

'Yes,' Kathy agreed. 'To think of all the hours I've wasted doing house-to-house enquiries and taking statements, when all the time all I had to do was to put my feet up at home and open the window. If only the rest of my cases were as simple.'

With the sudden, unexpected conclusion of the Budgie Burglar case, Kathy now faced a mountain of fresh paperwork, drawing together all of the separate incidents that had occurred over the past two years and bringing them into one evidence-based file. Her relaxing day off would have to wait, but at least the case could now be filed in the Detected Crimes filing cabinets in the typists' office, unlike some of her other cases.

It had been almost a month now since she had achieved anything on the Baby Bradley case. After Steven Hart had given Rosie's address as 61 Beaconsfield Road, Croydon, she had been about to drive straight there, when DI Redmond had blocked her, saying that she had already given too many resources and man-hours to the case. Behind his back, she had requested an immediate visit to the address by the Metropolitan Police instead. Unsurprisingly, Rosie had upped sticks and left the property several months ago and, according to her housemate, had not left a forwarding address or any indication of where she might have gone. The report, sitting in Kathy's in-tray, quoted the housemate as saying, 'One day Rosie just packed her bags and left; that's what Rosie does.'

Yes, Kathy wanted to find Rosie from a legal perspective. She loathed the quantity of unsolved crimes for which she was responsible but there was also a growing part of her that was simply concerned for the girl's welfare, something about which nobody else seemed that bothered. But, right now, she had no new leads and no support from above with which to continue her investigation.

Before she set to work on processing a police report against the Budgie Burglar—or Isaac Jones as he had revealed himself to be called—Kathy picked up her telephone and dialled Cuckfield Hospital. Once answered by the switchboard, she asked to be put through to the Maternity Unit.

'Good morning. This is the Cuckfield Hospital Maternity Ward, Sister Ryan speaking. How can I help you?' came the convoluted introduction.

'Oh, great. Hello, Sister Ryan. This is WDS Kathy Steadman from Burgess Hill Police Station… I'm in charge of the Baby Bradley case.'

'Oh, yes. I remember.'

'I was just wondering if I could ask how the little lad was getting on?'

'Very well, I believe,' she replied. 'He's gone to a nice foster couple from Handcross, who are planning to adopt him.'

'That's good to hear.'

'Have you managed to track down his mammy, now?' Sister Ryan enquired.

'No,' Kathy admitted with a sigh. 'She flits around the country, never staying long in any one place, it seems.' Kathy paused. 'To be honest, without any real progress, she's no longer under active investigation.'

'Oh, goodness. I do hope she's alright, you know.'

'Yes, me too,' Kathy agreed. 'Thank you for your time, though, Sister Ryan. I don't want to keep you. Goodbye.'

The Baby Bradley case might never be solved but the Budgie Burglar case had been. Now Kathy needed to make sure that her file was watertight before handing it over to the Crown Prosecution Service. 'Isaac Jones…' she said, writing his name at the top of the report sheet.

Chapter Nine

Alfred sighed. He was sitting in his armchair, close to the electric fire, sipping whisky from a tumbler and trying to listen to *The Sunday Hour* on Radio 2. His patience was wearing thin. He loosened his necktie and unbuttoned his burgundy cardigan, striving to ignore the incessant sound from Margaret's typewriter that was currently clattering away in the kitchen. She was trying to get her speed up to 110 words per minute in preparation for a job interview next week at a legal firm in the town centre. It wasn't the damned machine that was irking him, so much as Margaret's constant huffing and puffing every time that she made a mistake—which, by all accounts, seemed to be at least every other line.

Alfred finished the whisky and lit his pipe, clamping his lips down as he took in a long draw. He closed his eyes for a moment in an effort to settle his nerves. 'For God's sake,' he muttered upon hearing Margaret winding out yet another sheet of paper and screwing it up with a loud sigh.

He opened his eyes and picked up an envelope from the table beside him. He shook out the contents: a short letter from his daughter-in-law, Maureen, and two photographs of the baby boy. Alfred looked at the first picture, struck again by how much Morton had changed in just over two months. So much hair! He could definitely see a family resemblance in the baby's features. He was minded to put the picture in a frame, but then recalled Margaret's acute antipathy when he had tried to show her the photographs, following their arrival in yesterday's first post. Sliding the photograph back inside the envelope, he then looked at the second picture; a professional portrait shot of the new family. Peter, wearing his best shirt, had his arm around Maureen who was proudly holding little Morton up towards the camera. Whether Margaret liked it or not, this one was going to go up on display. He looked at the tired selection of framed pictures on the mantelpiece, all of which had been there for donkey's years. Time for change.

'Errgh!' Margaret shouted from the kitchen, slamming her fist onto the table.

Alfred tugged the pipe from his mouth. 'Now, then. That's enough, Margaret! For goodness' sake!' There was one simple way to end the racket. 'Give me my wretched watch back, will you? Hand it over.'

Margaret entered the lounge, her cheeks bright red. 'I'm only at just over a hundred words per minute,' she complained, still holding on to his pocket watch.

Alfred extended his hand. 'Now, come on. That's quite enough for tonight.'

With a huff, she passed him the watch. He pushed it into his trouser pocket and then walked over to the fireplace, taking down one of the silver-plated frames. It was a picture of Anna, the one which drew regular comment about how much Margaret resembled her. In fact, ignoring the tell-tale clothing and hair style, the photograph could very easily have been confused for his daughter.

'What are you doing?' she asked.

Alfred held up the new photograph of Peter, Maureen and Morton. 'I'm putting this up.'

'Instead of *Mum*?' Margaret stammered.

At that moment, the doorbell rang, saving Alfred from having to answer her. He unclasped the back board and dug the nail of his little finger under the old photograph of Anna, prising it free, while Margaret went to answer the door. He held the picture in his hands and studied it. He had looked at it hundreds of times—maybe even thousands of times—over the years. It had spent the first year after Anna's death on his bedside table. She was looking directly at him, smiling. It had been taken in 1950, shortly after the doctor had told her that she had fallen pregnant with Peter. He remembered the day well. On the back of the excitement of the doctor's news, they had gone out for a celebratory meal and afterwards, on a whim, had dropped into a photographer's studio to get their pictures taken. His memories were suddenly curtailed by the sound of a familiar voice speaking to Margaret. He dropped his pipe on the floor and dashed towards the front door, finding Margaret staring at him inquisitively and that damnable girl leaning on the door frame, smoking.

'Dad, this girl says she knows you and that you owe her money for some work she did at the shop?' Margaret explained, though clearly not believing what was coming out of her own mouth.

Alfred thrust his balled, free hand into his trouser pocket as his anger rose inside him. 'Thank you, Margaret,' he said to her quietly. 'Go to your room, please, and leave me to deal with the matter.'

Margaret alternated her gaze between him and Rosie, not moving.

'*Now*, thank you, Margaret,' he directed, seeing a smirk appear on Rosie's face.

Margaret snatched the photograph of Anna from his hand, saying, 'Well, I'm having this. I'll tell you that much,' then ran up the stairs.

Alfred watched her go, once again taken aback at the bizarre reverence that she always showed for the mother whom she had never known. He listened for the click of her bedroom door closing. It didn't come and he knew that she would be eavesdropping at the top of the stairs. Now, grabbing Rosie firmly by her upper arm, he roughly shoved her outside and pulled the door closed behind them. 'What the blazes are you doing here, woman?'

Rosie was utterly undaunted, shook herself free and smiled. 'That's no way to treat your poor dead missus, is it?'

'I've had just about enough of all this harassment,' he hissed. Almost every week, she had appeared at the Sevenoaks shop, demanding more money which he had foolishly paid, each time taking her at her word that he would not have to see her again. 'That's it. I'm going to go to the police.'

Rosie laughed, throwing her cigarette stub at him. 'No, you're not. I'll tell you what you're going to do. You're going to go in there, fetch your little chequebook out and write me a cheque for…five hundred quid.'

'Huh!' Alfred retorted. 'I am most certainly *not* going to do that. Now, get off my property,' he snarled, turning and opening the door.

'Margaret!' Rosie sang loudly.

Alfred spun around, slapped the little devil around the face, and then marched inside, slamming the front door behind him. From outside, he heard her laughing. Moments later, he could hear her moving away from the house, singing loudly as she went: 'Alfred Farrier's been a naughty boy; he paid Rosie Hart to be his little toy; he wanted her to be his honey; and now he owes her lots of money; pretending I'm his dead wife; has got naughty Alfie into strife.'

'What's *that* all about?' Margaret asked from the top of the stairs.

'Go to your room!' Alfred screamed. 'And—for once in your life,

81

girl—just bloody well listen to what you've been told to do.'

Alfred stormed into the lounge, slamming the door shut, which was echoed directly above him by Margaret doing the exact same thing.

He picked up the empty photo frame and began to cry.

'My! That *certainly* was a profitable trip to the continent, Mr Farrier,' his assistant, Miss Burk, enthused. It was Christmas Eve and the pair of them were standing together in the dusky light on Sevenoaks High Street, admiring the four mannequins which he had just finished dressing in the shop window of Farrier's Fashion. 'And how dapper you look, yourself, Mr Farrier, if I may say so,' she added, clapping her hands together in front of her.

Alfred smiled and felt his cheeks reddening. He was also attired in one of the latest slim-fit, Italian-style suits, the designs and fabrics for which he had procured on his visit to Cannes and Florence. 'You'll find nothing else like it south of Bond Street; you mark my words,' he declared proudly.

'*Très à la mode,*' she beamed, gazing down the High Street. 'And just look at that lovely Christmas display, too.'

Alfred looked at the small shop fronts on either side of the street, bedecked in twinkling coloured lights. 'They've excelled themselves once again,' he commented, shifting his admiration back to the small multi-coloured lanterns that framed his own shop window and the plastic Christmas tree wrapped in tinsel that appeared to be captivating the attention of the four mannequins on either side of it. 'As have you, Miss Burk.'

She smiled. 'Thank you,' she said, rubbing her hands together and glancing up at the dark sky. 'I think it might snow, you know.'

'Well, let's get inside, then and have a little glass of sherry before we close up for Christmas.'

'Wonderful,' she said, leading the way back inside to the warm embrace of the little shop.

Alfred wove his way around the hanging rails of men's clothing through to the door behind the counter, which led to the back room. It was a cramped, windowless space, with piles of cardboard boxes and full clothing racks. In one corner was a small round table and two chairs, where they took their tea-breaks. Alfred removed a bottle of sherry and two glasses from a cupboard at the back of the room and carried them out to the counter.

'And…' Miss Burk began, flipping the door sign over, '…we are officially closed!' She dropped the catch on the door lock and walked over to where Alfred was pouring the drinks.

'Here we go,' he said, handing one to her. 'Cheers. And a very merry Christmas to you and yours, Miss Burk.'

She chinked her glass against his and replied, 'And the same to you, Mr Farrier. What plans do you have for the next two days?'

'Well, this year, it will just be Margaret and I,' he answered. 'So, a quiet one. Peter and Maureen wanted their first Christmas with little Morton by themselves.'

'Oh, that's very understandable,' she said, sipping her sherry. 'How's Maureen getting along? I should imagine it's a very peculiar contrast between carrying a child for nine months inside of you while your body silently takes care of its every need and its being out in the real world where you're run ragged, constantly looking after the little mite.'

Alfred chuckled. 'Yes, indeed. But she's doing very well; a natural, I should say.'

'And Margaret? How's she enjoying being an aunty? Such a lovely role, that, isn't it?'

'Indifferent, I suppose,' he said.

'Well, she's still only young. Such thoughts of babies and the like are a long way off for her yet, I imagine.'

'What are your plans for tomorrow, Miss Burk?' he asked, deliberately changing the subject before polishing off his sherry.

'It'll be me, mother and my aunt. You know, the one who was widowed earlier this year… So, I'll need to try and keep the spirits up for us all. I've got some party games, cards and—' A rattling of the door handle cut into her sentence. 'Who the dickens can that be?'

Alfred looked at the door, fuming. It was *her*. That smug grin on her face and that dreadful black leather jacket that she always wore. Oh, how he despised her.

'We're closed…for Christmas,' Miss Burk called, moving towards the door.

Silently behind his assistant, Alfred shook his head vehemently and flicked his hand in the air, as though swatting a gnat, all the while mouthing the words, 'Go away!'

Rosie held firm with her inane smile. 'Alfie, darling, you owe me money,' she shouted through the locked door.

Miss Burk fired a quick shocked look at her boss.

'Let me deal with this deranged lunatic,' he barked, marching over to the door. 'If you don't go away, I'll call the police,' he yelled through the glass. He turned sharply to Miss Burk. 'She's one of those scammers that goes around trying to extort money from hard-working folk like us.'

'Oh, yes. She looks just the type,' Miss Burk agreed, nodding.

Rosie's smile dropped and she met his gaze menacingly.

He turned and walked back over to the counter, pouring himself another drink. When he looked up again, the girl had vanished. Good riddance, he thought.

'I'm going to call the police,' Miss Burk declared, hurrying past him into the backroom where the telephone was located.

'No, don't worry. I'll do it later. They're fully aware of her: Rosie Hart, she's called, a most dreadful excuse for a human being.' He blew out a long breath, took a sip of his drink, and then smiled. 'Sorry. So, you were in the middle of saying something about party games and keeping your poor widowed aunt entertained tomorrow?'

A God-almighty noise—of the sort that Alfred had not heard since the war—exploded into the room as the large front windowpane smashed inward. He ducked behind the counter as shards of glass flew through the air.

'Oh, my Godfathers!' Miss Burk shrieked, stepping back into the shop and observing that the spot upon which she had been standing moments before was now littered with fragments of lethal glass.

Alfred looked from the brick lying just a few feet in front of him to the person framed perfectly between the four mannequins: Rosie Hart.

'You're going to get it right in the mouth, you bastard,' she said. 'I'll get my money's worth out of you.'

Alfred glanced at Miss Burk who was standing open-mouthed in terror. When he looked back at where the window had been, the girl had vanished and in her place was a gathering crowd of onlookers. Alfred shuddered from the wintery breeze now blowing freely into his shop.

'This your place, sir?' a wiry little man asked, poking his head inside.

Alfred nodded, moving towards the window.

The man pulled out a notepad and pencil. 'And what's your name?'

'Who are you, exactly?' Alfred countered.

'Daryl Lee,' he said with a smile. 'Kentish Gazette. I was just doing some last-minute shopping over the road, and this happens right in front of me. I think I'd say, it's my lucky day, wouldn't you?'

Alfred suddenly felt weak and reached out a shaking hand to grasp a clothing rail. The story was going to make the local papers. He would be utterly humiliated.

'Do you know the young lady who threw the brick?' the reporter asked.

Oh, he knew her alright. But he needed to think of a way to get rid of her, once and for all.

Alfred arrived home late that night, exhausted. He closed the front door quietly, hoping that, given the hour, Margaret would have taken herself off to bed already. She hadn't. She was sitting in the silent lounge.

'Where have you been?' she asked, leaping up. 'I was worried something might have happened to you.'

'Just some problems at work that I had to deal with,' he muttered, taking off his hat, shoes and coat. 'Did you cook something for me?'

She nodded. 'It's in the oven, but I expect it's as dry as old Harry by now.'

'Thank you,' he said, putting on his moccasins and heading into the kitchen, with Margaret following close behind. Using a tea towel, Alfred carefully took a plate of cottage pie, peas and carrots from the oven and set it down quickly onto the place mat on the Formica table. 'Ouch,' he said, flicking his hand. The meal didn't look especially appetising, he thought, prodding it apart with a fork and watching a great gust of steam erupt from the middle. 'Good news,' he said to his daughter through a wooden smile. 'I've arranged for you to have a little holiday down with Alex and Joan in Cornwall.'

'Pardon?' Margaret said.

'Alex and Joan. My half-brother and his wife. Your aunt and uncle.

And your cousin, Andrew. Remember?' Alfred said mockingly.

'Of course, I do. What do you mean, a holiday?'

'I'm going to drive you down there on Boxing Day for a break. Thought it might do you good after... Well, you know,' he said, eating a forkful of shrivelled peas and promptly regretting it.

'Boxing Day?' Margaret asked, putting her hands on her hips.

Alfred sighed, placed down his cutlery, and said, 'Yes. Boxing Day.'

'But how long for? I've got my job interview next week.'

'Margaret. Let's not beat around the bush about this, shall we? Look. You're simply not up to it; your typing speed is nowhere near good enough, as you well know.'

'But I'd like to try at least,' she insisted, the emotion rising in her voice. 'I don't want a holiday in Cornwall.'

'Okay,' he said, removing his wristwatch. 'Sit down there. And if you can do a hundred and ten words per minute, then you don't have to go to Cornwall and you can attend this waste-of-time interview of yours.'

'But...'

'Your choice,' he said, pushing the plate of dinner away. 'I can't eat that.'

Margaret glowered angrily as she removed the cover of her typewriter and fed in a sheet of paper.

Alfred picked up his watch and followed the second hand round until it reached twelve. 'Go.'

Margaret attacked the keys with such determined ferocity that Alfred feared that she might actually achieve his set goal. The second hand of his watch appeared to be slowing down against the tumult from the keys pounding the ink ribbon, and Alfred began to panic that she might yet be at home when the story of the smashed shop window hit the *Kentish Express*. 'Stop!' he barked, thrusting his hand over the typewriter keys.

Margaret was crying as she threaded the piece of paper out of the machine and handed it to him.

Alfred carefully counted each and every word before declaring, 'One hundred and three with four misspellings. So, that's decided, then.'

Margaret rushed from the room.

Alfred stared at the plate of unappetising food. He had found a way of dealing with Margaret but now he was wondering just how he was going to deal with the root cause of all of his problems: Rosie Hart.

There simply had to be a permanent solution.

Chapter Ten

Rye was heaving with Christmas shoppers and, as a result, someone had presumptuously decided to sit in Morton's usual seat in Granny's Scones. Added to this inconvenience, the place was at full capacity, making it difficult for Morton to concentrate on his work. It would have been so much quieter to have worked from home, but Juliette had encouraged him to support his brother's business; he only now considered that that had probably just been her way of getting him out from under her feet for a few hours.

He watched Jeremy as he chatted away with a young couple at the till. It was good to see his brother so happy and settled. A few years ago, their relationship had been so estranged that Morton would have been deeply unsettled to have had him live and work so close by. He blamed himself for the previous breakdown of their relationship: time, hindsight and maturity had exposed to him that. During the period between Morton's being told at the age of fifteen that he had been adopted and his discovering at the age of thirty-nine that his Aunty Margaret was his biological mother, he had taken on the role of a self-piteous outcast, extraneous to the natural family unit of his adoptive parents and their biological son, Jeremy. Maybe things might have been different, had he been told the truth from an earlier age. Morton felt that he should tell Jeremy that he was sorry, but their family didn't really do soul-searching candour. Water under the bridge, he reasoned, picking up his latte and drinking the last mouthful.

He turned back to his laptop, contemplating what he should do next. He had spent a good deal of time searching in vain for digitised copies of the *Mid-Sussex Times* so that he could read the full story of the baby left in the phone box in Haywards Heath in September 1973. He had discovered that microfilm copies of the newspaper for this period existed at Crawley Library in West Sussex; but he wasn't sure that a two-sentence story necessitated the hundred-mile round trip. What would it achieve by seeing the full article? he wondered. If he did find that the story in the report sounded very much like another of Rosie Hart's abandoned children, then what? If that child had subsequently been adopted and had not taken a DNA test on a commercial genealogy website—which it clearly had not—then there was absolutely nothing that he could do to track down that individual. He weighed the ethics of the decision. Could he really attest that his research had been sufficiently exhaustive, given that there might yet be a possibility of a fourth foundling out there somewhere? He opened up the file that he was compiling as he reflected on what else he might need to do before he could close the case.

The obvious missing information, which perhaps was the most pertinent to Vanessa, Billie and Liza after learning that their mother's name was Rosie Hart, was what had happened to her since giving birth to the three of them. After being wanted in November 1980 for some part in connection with the attempted murder of a police officer, Rosie had disappeared. No marriage, no death, and electoral register searches at FindmyPast had produced no results.

Morton turned to a clean page on his notepad and wrote ROSIE HART AFTER 1980?? at the top. Starting with MyHeritage, he was going to work through open and somewhat laborious searches in every genealogical database to which he had access.

He got as far as typing in her name when Jeremy suddenly cranked up the volume on an album of cheesy Christmas classics which had been playing softly in the background up until now and which Morton had so far been just about able to ignore. *Merry Christmas Everybody* began to blast from a speaker directly above him. Decision made. He closed his laptop lid and put all of his bits and pieces into his shoulder bag and headed down to the till.

'You off already?' Jeremy asked.

'Yeah, I need to shoot off for some research,' he said, handing over a ten-pound note.

'Forget it,' Jeremy said, waving a dismissive hand in front of him. 'You're my brother.'

'It's your livelihood. I insist,' Morton said, putting the money down on the counter between them. 'And…sorry.'

'What for?' Jeremy asked.

'For…not being very brotherly in the past. I don't think I handled Dad telling me that I was adopted very well and probably took it out on you for *not* being adopted.'

'That's okay,' he replied, moving around the counter and pulling Morton into a strong hug. 'Where's this suddenly all coming from?'

Morton shrugged. 'Oh, just thinking a lot about family at the moment.'

'It can't have been easy to hear those words and at that age. And from Dad, of all people. I can't imagine he was very sensitive about it, I'll bet.'

'No. No, he wasn't,' Morton confirmed. 'But still; I didn't have to be—' he searched for the right word, but couldn't find it, '—well, you know. The way I was.'

'It's fine. Really. And I'm always here if you want to talk about that stuff.'

'Thank you,' Morton said, breaking away. 'See you later.'

'Oh, take this with you,' Jeremy said, grabbing two scones from the window display and putting them in a take-away box. 'Guy's flavour of the day; strangely, they haven't been very popular.'

'What are they?' he asked, hiding his trepidation and taking the proffered box.

'Turkey and cranberry,' he replied. 'Christmassy.'

'I'm very surprised they're not popular,' Morton commented, as he headed towards the door.

'Have fun,' Jeremy called after him.

Outside, Rye High Street was heaving with pedestrian traffic all togged-up against the bitter wind. He zipped up his jacket and headed home to collect his car.

Morton arrived in Crawley town centre an hour and a half later, having phoned in advance to book a microfilm reader. The drive had taken much longer than he had anticipated, and now that he was here, searching for a space in the County Mall car park, he was very much of the opinion that spending three hours travelling would not be justified by a short newspaper story in the *Mid-Sussex Times*; a story which may well also be totally unrelated to his investigation. He huffed as he wound his way up yet another level of the car park with every spot that he had passed having been taken. He had chosen this as the place in which to try to park because it was the closest to the library.

He was about to ascend to another floor when he spotted an old man with handfuls of carrier bags, shuffling out of the lift doors across the concourse in front of him. Morton edged the Mini slowly forwards, creeping behind the man as he plodded along behind the line of parked cars.

Morton dropped his forehead onto the steering wheel as the man continued to walk and a small but determined queue of cars began to fall in behind him. One of them beeped their horn and Morton wondered what to do. The man was *still* walking.

Morton huffed again and accelerated past. Just as he did so, the old man stopped beside a car and began loading the bags into the boot.

'Brilliant,' he exclaimed, winding his way around to join the back of the very queue of cars that he had just created.

He sat waiting impatiently for several minutes more, resisting the growing temptation to just drive out of here and head home. He spotted the take-away box on the passenger seat beside him and decided to eat one of the scones while he waited. He drew it from the box between thumb and forefinger, holding it suspiciously in front of his face for several seconds before attempting to eat it. He took the smallest nibble. It wasn't too bad, he had to admit. He ate more, finding that he was actually enjoying it. Like most of the bizarre concoctions that came out of Granny's Scones, they sounded much more horrific than they ultimately were on tasting. He popped the last bite into his mouth and then looked up to see that a car was reversing out of a space right in front of him. He smiled and parked up. Grabbing his bag and hurrying out of the building to street level, Morton found himself standing directly opposite Crawley Library. It was a modern building made out of white stone and glass, with each of the four storeys cantilevered above the level below.

He strode through the automatic glass doors into an airy foyer which opened out to a central void where long cylindrical lights were suspended from the ceiling and from which glimpses of the upper floors could be seen. He made a beeline for the semi-circular help desk to his left and stood impatiently behind a teenage boy with stone-washed jeans miraculously suspended half-way down his thighs. He was evidently a foreign student, doggedly struggling to communicate something to the woman behind the counter. He mimed typing, and Morton wasn't sure whether he wanted a piano or a computer.

The woman pointed to the ceiling and the boy walked away, looking all-the-more confused.

'Hi,' Morton said, stepping forwards to the desk. 'I've got a microfilm booked.'

'Second floor,' the woman said, directing him to the long staircase on the far side of the room.

'Thanks,' he said, then made his way up the stairs to the first floor. On his left were several racks of loanable DVDs and to his right was another set of stairs that ran perpendicular up to the second floor where he found a smiling middle-aged man sitting behind a desk.

'Hi. I've got a microfilm booked,' Morton repeated.

'Ah, yes. Morgan?' he asked, sliding out from behind his desk. 'Follow me.'

'Morton,' he corrected. They headed off a few paces to a recess at the back of the open-plan room. On one side was a row of labelled metal filing cabinets and, on the other, a solitary digital microfilm reader. 'Good thing I phoned ahead what with there being just the one reader, then.'

The man turned up his nose as he switched on the machine. 'We only get about one booking a week, now. Most of the newspapers that we have here have been digitised.'

'Just not for the date that I need,' Morton said.

'What is it you were looking for, exactly, Morgan?'

'Morton. It was the *Mid-Sussex Times* for September 1973.'

'Righteo,' the man said, spinning around and running his finger down an invisible line in front of the first filing cabinet. '*West Sussex County Times...Worthing Gazette...Crawley Observer...* Nope.' He continued on to the next cabinet and stopped at the third drawer down. '*Mid-Sussex Times 1963 to 1980.*' He tugged open the drawer and briefly scanned the contents before removing the boxed microfilm. 'Here you go!'

Morton thanked him, carried the film over to the reader, threaded it onto the machine, then took his notepad from his bag where he had written the scant details of the story. All he knew was that it occurred in September of 1973. He fast-forwarded the film to that month. As he slowly scrolled down through the first pages and took in the range of local stories, he guessed that an abandoned baby would have likely made the front pages. Still, he checked every page, including the classifieds, sports section and an entire page dedicated to farming, just to be completely certain. Twenty minutes later, he moved on to the second edition of the month. Once again, the story had neither made the front pages, nor, he found as his search progressed, had it featured further into the paper. When the headlines of the third edition of September also failed to produce any results, Morton double-checked his notes to be sure. It was definitely the correct month and year. He wound through to the fourth and final edition, dated 27th September, and there it was, on the front page, just as he had suspected. *She found a baby in phone kiosk*, the headline announced.

'Bingo,' Morton declared, clicking the zoom icon to read the story in full.

A ten-day-old baby, lying in the sweltering heat of a sun-drenched telephone kiosk in The Broadway, Haywards Heath, was rescued by a 14-year-old schoolgirl, Samantha Wynn. The baby, believed to have been abandoned in the phone booth on Sunday morning, is now in Cuckfield Hospital. The administrator, Mr Brian Davis, said on Tuesday that the 5lb baby, named by nurses as Baby Bradley Broadway, owing to the location of his discovery, was doing very well. 'We have absolutely no worries about his physical condition,' he said. Samantha, of Copyhold Lane, Haywards Heath, went swimming on Sunday afternoon and then walked up to the call box in The Broadway to contact a friend when she discovered the tiny figure of Baby Bradley inside a box within a red and white chequered bag. Samantha picked up the boy, telephoned the police for help, and cuddled her charge until they arrived. Burgess Hill C.I.D. officers quickly followed up clues which took them to Thornton Heath, Croydon. The investigation, led by WDS Kathy Steadman, moved into action on the afternoon of 23rd September—

Morton stopped reading. WDS Kathy Steadman. She had been the police officer that Steven and Frank Hart had been sentenced to fifteen years for attempting to murder, and in which Rosie had also been implicated. He was not a believer in coincidences at the best of times, but this wasn't one he was even prepared to entertain: Baby Bradley Broadway *had* to have been Rosie Hart's child.

He needed to speak to Kathy Steadman urgently. He opened his

93

laptop and ran an electoral register search on FindmyPast.

192 results

Morton scrolled down the list. A long line of Catharines led to one Cathy, and then three pages of Kates followed by a multitude of Katharines and Katherines. He looked closely at the latter group, identifying three, each with a Sussex-based address. Ordinarily, he might have written to all of them; but, with time running short, he opened up Facebook and ran the same search for her there, despite knowing that, for obvious reasons, most current police officers did not use their real names on social media. As it was, Juliette herself went by the bizarre moniker of Ju Woo.

Moving down the results, one woman caught his attention. Instead of a photograph, her circular profile picture was of a solid black background with a thin blue line running horizontally through the centre; something Morton knew from Juliette to be in honour of police officers killed in the line of duty.

He viewed her full profile, making his way straight down to *Photos* and finding that the vast majority were of a garden—presumably hers—in varying states of bloom throughout the seasons. But there was one picture, which he clicked to enlarge, that had been taken in February 2019 of a short grey-haired lady whom he guessed to have been around the age of eighty. Could it be her? he wondered. The rest of the photos on her profile didn't give him any further clues, and her timeline was so bare of postings that he quickly reached her joining date of 2015. Turning to look under *Friends*, he found thirty-three people, many of whom declared some link or other to the West Sussex area. One of them, Carol Blake, also had a profile picture with a thin blue horizontal line running across it. He clicked her profile and saw that listed under *Intro* was a former position as a WPC at Burgess Hill Police Station.

Now confident that he had indeed located the correct Kathy Steadman, Morton typed out a message to her.

Dear Kathy, I hope you don't mind my contacting you. I am a forensic genealogist, assisting three adoptees to track down their shared birth mother. Using a combination of DNA and traditional genealogical records, I have reached the conclusion that their mother was called Rosie Hart. Part of my research has involved examining historical newspapers, where your name has arisen twice in connection with Rosie and potentially with a fourth abandoned child. I would love to speak with you about the case, if you don't mind. Anything you can give to help these three adoptees would be much appreciated. Kind regards, Morton Farrier

He re-read that which he had written, wondering if he had laid it on a little too thick in the final sentence, but reasoned that tugging on Kathy Steadman's heartstrings was his best shot at getting a reply. He clicked send, then returned to finish reading the newspaper story.

—The address in Croydon, WDS Steadman said, had turned out to be false. 'We have other addresses to visit and we shall be pursuing our inquiries to trace Baby Bradley's mother,' she added. 'We will find this woman.'

And did you find her? Morton wondered, taking a series of close-up photographs of the screen before rewinding the film and switching off the machine. He re-boxed the microfilm and placed it back into the filing cabinet.

'That's me all done,' Morton said to the librarian. 'Thank you very much.'

'Okay, Morgan,' he said with a big smile. 'Enjoy the rest of the day.'

'Morton,' he said, heading back down the stairs to the ground floor.

Chapter Eleven

10th March 1975, Canterbury, Kent

Kathy Steadman stifled a yawn. She was sitting in the back corner at one of twelve occupied desks in a classroom in Canterbury Police Station. She was the only woman in the room and casually gazed around her, wondering if the men were as bored as was she. One man, a DS in plain clothes who was in the opposite corner, was gazing out of the window, so Kathy supposed that she wasn't the only one considering this to be a waste of time. At the front of the room was Inspector Rillington, a white-haired man with a trimmed moustache, who was explaining in painful detail the inner workings of a combustion engine. He wafted a long, pointed stick at a diagram on the blackboard behind him, slicing through the smoky fug of the room, stemming from several of her colleagues who were gaping at the presentation with cigarettes dangling out of their mouths.

'Down here, we have the crankshaft,' he explained monosyllabically. 'Connected to the crankshaft, we have a connecting rod and above that, we have a piston. Behind that we see the camshaft. The piston slides up and down in the cylinder bore, and above that are the valves which are being operated by means of a camshaft and push rods through the...'

Kathy stopped listening and met the eyes of the DS in the other corner. He smiled in a way that suggested a shared disinterest in the droning, dull explanation. He covertly placed his fingers over his open mouth to reiterate the point.

'What's your name, there, at the back?'

Kathy quickly looked forwards again as all eyes promptly turned to fall upon her. 'WDS Steadman, sir.'

Inspector Rillington offered a starchy smile. 'Come up here, please, WDS Steadman.'

Kathy pushed her chair back and walked to the front of the room where the inspector stood, offering the stick in his two open palms, as though he were handing over a magic wand.

'Perhaps,' he said, addressing the rest of the room, 'WDS Steadman can tell us precisely where the inlet valve and exhaust valve are located?'

His invitation was met by a general sniggering among the men. One of them, sitting directly in front of Kathy, tugged a cigarette from his mouth and said, 'Good luck with that. My wife doesn't even know where to put the petrol in.'

Several of the men burst into laughter.

Kathy took the stick and pointed it carefully at the diagram, just above the piston. 'The inlet valve is here, and the exhaust valve is here.' She stood, poker-faced, as if waiting for further instructions.

'Very good,' Inspector Rillington was unexpectedly forced to acknowledge, clearing his throat and receiving the stick back from her. 'You may sit down.' He coughed, placed the stick on his desk, and then said, 'I think it might be time for a tea break, gentlemen. Let's say twenty minutes, shall we?'

It seemed from the abruptness with which everyone in the room stood up and made for the door that Kathy wasn't alone in needing a break.

'Impressive,' the DS, who had fake-yawned, said to her as they left the room.

'What can I say?' Kathy replied, 'I'm a woman of many talents.' She paused and added, 'Actually, my dad was a mechanic, so I grew up with dismembered car engines around the house. It used to drive my mum up the wall.'

'Well, it certainly put Rillington in his place,' he whispered, nodding to the inspector leading the course, who was walking a few steps ahead of them.

'I tell you what; he's full of charisma, isn't he?'

The DS laughed. 'Try working with him on a regular basis. Put it this way; we don't call him Happy Harold for no reason.'

'You're based at this station, then?' Kathy asked.

He nodded and then offered his hand to shake. 'DS Richley. Simon.'

Kathy shook his hand and introduced herself, taking him in fully for the first time. He was tall—a good six foot high—with side-parted dark hair and a bushy beard.

'Do you want to sit down with that lot and have a cup of tea, or would you prefer to have a tour of the station with yours truly?' Simon asked.

Kathy made as if to weigh the options seriously. 'Well, I did *so* want to continue discussing the inner workings of an engine,' she joked.

Simon grinned. 'Come with me, and I'll get us a drink and then show you around,' he said, leading her away from the group into a quiet canteen. 'What can I get you? Tea or coffee?'

'Tea, please,' Kathy answered. 'Milk and one.'

'Coming right up,' he said.

'I thought I was here for a three-day advanced driving course,' Kathy muttered. 'Is it all going to be classroom-based and pointing at diagrams of engines?'

Simon handed her the drink. 'This morning is, but we've got the reaction room to look forward to today, then driving on the skid pan tomorrow and the day after that.'

'The reaction room; that sounds rather ominous,' she said.

'With that sweet, sugary tea pumping through you, you'll be right as rain. Come on; bring it with you. Let's have a wander,' Simon said, leaving the canteen and walking down a long corridor. As they walked, he indicated various points of interest. The station was large and set over three substantial buildings. Simon explained that the course was taking place in the CID building—which faced the busy Old Dover Road—having been built ten years ago. He walked them through the custody centre to the third building which was long, brick-built and with few windows. 'The shooting range,' he said, pointing at a door.

Kathy looked in, watching as a young marksman in training took a shot at a silhouetted human target at the far end of the room, under the guidance of an instructor. The officer's shot was sharp and obliterated the target's right shoulder. 'Ouch,' Kathy commented as they turned to move on.

'And finally,' Simon announced, walking further down the corridor and pulling open a heavy door. 'The mortuary.'

Despite the unpleasant musty odour, Kathy stepped into a dark freezing room no larger than eight square feet. In the centre of the room was a lead-lined mortuary table.

'In case anyone pops their clogs in the middle of the night,' Simon clarified.

'Staff or inmates?'

Simon laughed. 'Either, I suppose.'

Kathy shuddered and backed out into the corridor. 'Hang on. Shouldn't we be getting back? It's been almost twenty minutes.'

'Oh, Christ,' Simon said, looking at his watch. 'Yes, let's go.' He took Kathy's empty mug, leant into the nearest office to set their empties down on a colleague's desk and set off.

He led them back in the direction from which they had just come, this time walking at a much faster pace which Kathy took as an indication of how the inspector running the training course would react to their being late. They passed through the custody centre as a young lad in handcuffs was being led towards the Station Officer by two PCs.

'Well, I don't need to ask your name, now, do I?' Kathy heard the Station Officer say. 'Unless you've changed it, of course?'

'Nah, still the one and only Frank Hart at your service,' he sniffed.

Kathy stopped. 'I'll catch you up,' she said to Simon.

'Er. Okay,' he said. 'What's up?'

'Harts,' she replied, turning back to where the Station Officer was booking in the young man. She took out her warrant card and showed it to the closest of the two PCs. 'Can I have a quick word with this young man, please?'

'Be my guest,' the nearest one said.

Frank Hart looked Kathy up and down with a sneer. He was a scrawny-looking thing in his twenties with thick sideburns and shoulder-length hair, wearing flared jeans and a mustard-yellow jumper. Even though he looked very unlike Steven Hart, Kathy was sure that she could see a resemblance in his nose, eyes and narrow chin. 'What?' he asked.

'Are you any relation to Rosie Hart?' Kathy asked.

'Might be,' he said.

The Station Officer looked at Kathy and declared, 'Ignore Mr Difficult, here. She's his sister.'

Frank pulled a face as though he were just remembering. 'Oh, yeah. That's it. Knew I knew the name from somewhere.'

'Do you know where she's currently living?' Kathy asked.

'*If* I had an address for our Rosie, I wouldn't tell ya. But *if* I did tell ya, by the time you got there, she'd probably have moved out anyway; she don't stick around long. Ants in her pants, that one. That's what we always used to say when we was little.'

Kathy looked at the two PCs and then back to the Station Officer. 'I don't suppose any of you have got an address for her?'

'I can double-check for you,' the Station Officer said. 'Are you here for long, today?'

Kathy nodded. 'I'm attending the advanced driving course, so I'll be here for another two days yet.'

The Station Officer said, 'Okay, swing by later today, and I'll let you know.'

'Thanks,' Kathy said, beginning to hurry back towards the classroom. She stopped and turned around. 'Whereabouts is the reaction room—for the driving thing, I mean?' she asked.

'Keep going, third door on your left,' the Station Officer directed.

She thanked him and dashed towards the room. She pushed open the door with an apologetic look on her face as Inspector Rillington glowered at her.

'Good of you to return, WDS Steadman,' he said. 'I thought perhaps that, since you knew how to locate the inlet and exhaust valves on a car engine, you might have decided that you knew everything there was to know.'

'No, sir,' Kathy returned. She was about to explain herself but opted instead for diplomatic simplicity. 'Sorry, Inspector.'

'Would you like to go next in the chair?' he asked.

'Okay,' Kathy answered, now taking in the scene which was in front of her. All of the other participants were gathered around a strange-looking contraption in the centre of the room. It appeared as though some of the basic driving components of a car—steering wheel, pedals and car seat—had been attached to an oblong chest upon which was fixed a television screen.

Kathy climbed into the seat and held the steering wheel, looking at the inspector for further instruction.

'Now,' the inspector said, 'what I've already explained to these gentlemen is that what we're going to do is to measure your reaction time.' He looked at Kathy. 'Your reaction time is the time it takes for you to see something on the road and to take action. Do you understand?'

Kathy nodded and looked at the television screen in front of her. It had on it a hand-painted fixed image of a road with a forward-facing truck, angled as though heading towards her.

'Now, I want you to build your speed up to thirty miles per hour,' he instructed.

Kathy obeyed, gently squeezing the accelerator and watching the speedometer needle rising up to the specified number.

'Now, watch the screen. And when you see something appear on there, I want you to brake.'

Kathy stared ahead. Seconds later a hand-painted motorbike appeared miraculously in the centre of the image. She slammed on the brake.

The inspector looked down at a dial in front of him. 'Your reaction time is zero point four two of a second.' The inspector, not giving any indication as to whether that was considered a good number or not, faced the men. 'Now, zero point four two of a second at thirty miles an hour equates to eighteen point seven feet. But...bear in mind that this is on a normal, dry road surface. Not bad, WDS Steadman,' he said. 'DS Richley, would you like to take the wheel next?'

Kathy stepped out of the driving seat, and Simon took her place. 'Zero point four to beat, then, eh?' she whispered.

At lunchtime, Kathy sat opposite Simon at their own table, eating the bland, budget lunch of dried-out cheese and tomato sandwiches and a packet of ready salted crisps which was provided as part of the course.

'So, tomorrow, we'll be out on the skid pan,' Simon said. 'There's a disused car park not far from here that we're allowed to pour water and oil all over, then drive through it between cones.'

'Sounds like fun,' Kathy said.

'More fun than today, anyway. That much is certain,' he said in a lowered voice.

Kathy took another bite of the unappetising sandwich, then put the rest down.

'Hello,' a male voice said, appearing at her side. It was the Station Officer. He crouched down, resting his arms on the table. 'I've had a look to see what we've got on Rosie Hart, and it's nothing recent, I'm afraid. Her brothers, on the other hand...'

Kathy smiled. 'Thanks for looking, anyway.'

'Sorry,' he said, standing up and walking away.

'What are you interested in the Harts for?' Simon asked.

'A baby abandoned in Haywards Heath two years ago,' Kathy began to explain. 'Rosie was the mother, but she's been like the Scarlet Pimpernel ever since; I'm always one small step behind her. Are the family well known around here, then?'

Simon laughed. 'You could say that, yeah. They come from the marsh area on the Kent and Sussex border, so it depends on where they decide to go to commit their crimes as to who picks them up. As you saw earlier, Frank has taken to thieving and robbing around here, but we haven't seen Rosie in a good while. They call themselves the Kent Krays, which is frankly hilarious.'

Kathy grinned. 'Yeah, they're not quite the big boys from the East End that they think they are, are they?'

'They'll all get what's coming to them in the end,' Simon warned. 'You mark my words.'

'Hmm,' Kathy said, noncommittally. Truth be told, she wasn't sure what the ending was that she wanted for Rosie. A lifetime behind bars certainly wasn't going to improve her life or the life of that poor little boy whom she had left in the telephone box.

'Do you have plans already, this evening?' Simon asked.

Kathy shook her head.

'Would you like to go out for dinner—with me, I mean—somewhere in the city centre? The Curry Garden is pretty special, if you like that kind of food.'

'Yes. I'd like that very much,' she answered with a warm smile.

Chapter Twelve

'Your train leaves in fifty minutes,' Alfred called. He was standing on the bottom step of the staircase, smoking his pipe. He was wearing his usual trousers, shirt and tie, with a grey cardigan. Despite all that was going on, he felt surprisingly calm inside.

'Almost ready,' Margaret returned.

Part of his calmness, he surmised, stemmed from how willingly Margaret had accepted his instruction that she had to return to his half-brother, Alex, in Cornwall. She had clearly learned that the colossal protest and fuss, which she had made last time, had got her nowhere with him. At last, she was toeing the line.

Alfred looked at his pocket watch. They really needed to get going. 'Margaret!' he yelled.

'I'm coming,' she said, appearing with her suitcase on the upstairs landing. She was wearing a flowing white dress which he knew to be one of her nicer outfits. He also noticed that she was wearing make-up and had styled her hair. He felt slightly absolved to see that she was starting to take life more seriously again. 'Ready,' she said brightly.

'Yes. I see. Good show,' he replied, returning her smile as he reached out and took her suitcase. 'Let's go.'

He walked down to his Mini, placed the suitcase in the back and pivoted the passenger seat backwards into place for Margaret to get in.

He climbed into the driver's side and asked, 'What are you looking forward to about being back in Cornwall?'

'Erm... Well, obviously seeing Uncle Alex and Aunty Joan,' she answered. 'I know we live by the sea in Folkestone, but there's something really different about being by the ocean down there.'

'Mullion is a rather wonderful place,' Alfred agreed, starting the engine and pulling out onto the Canterbury Road. 'A different pace of life, somehow; or so it seems to me anyway.'

'Maybe I'm just more of a countryside person,' Margaret commented, staring out of the window at the bustling town centre. After a short pause, she turned to him and asked, 'So, what's the important business that you've got going on that means I've got to go back to Cornwall so soon?'

Alfred cleared his throat as he turned into Folkestone Station Road, grateful that the three-minute car journey was all but over. 'Just very dull conferences and meetings with foreign suppliers and such like; it just means I won't be at home too much.'

Margaret nodded but didn't press him on the subject.

He pulled up directly outside the train station and, keeping the engine running, swiftly jumped out, causing Margaret to do the same, retrieved her suitcase from the back seat, and then placed it down onto the pavement. 'Well, you have a jolly pleasant time down there.'

'Thanks,' she replied, picking up the suitcase. 'Goodbye.'

'Cheerio,' he said, getting into the car, turning it around on the wide road in one deft manoeuvre and heading back home. He looked in his rear-view mirror to see her entering the station without a backward glance. He emitted a long sigh. With the court case looming tomorrow, he was glad to have one less thing to worry about. He was going to make certain sure that she remained in Cornwall until the case—and more importantly the publicity surrounding it—was over. Daryl Lee from the Kentish Gazette had made it very clear that a known local prostitute's launching a brick through his shop window on Christmas Eve would make for a truly sensational story. As Alfred and Miss Burk had been sweeping up the glass, he had heard the reporter taking down a quote from a passer-by who had heard Rosie shouting that she was going to get her money from him.

Alfred parked the car outside of his house. And there she was, like some devil's child whose evil presence he had unintentionally summoned by mere thought alone. She was sitting on his boundary wall in her familiar leather jacket, her greasy brown hair pulled back under a hair band. The sight of her disgusted him, but he no longer feared her as he once had.

He climbed out of the Mini, locked the door, and then approached the house with a deliberate look of indifference on his face. 'Rosie,' he said matter-of-factly.

'Don't want me to be Anna, today, then, no?' she said, placing emphasis on his deceased wife's name.

Alfred clenched his jaw to prevent himself from automatically biting back. Instead, he simply smiled. 'Would you care to come inside?'

Rosie frowned. 'What do you mean?'

'I mean, would you like to come inside my house?' he repeated, opening the front door. 'I shall most certainly *not* be discussing financial matters on my doorstep.' He entered the house, leaving the front door wide open. He changed out of his shoes and into his slippers, catching sight of Rosie in his peripheral vision, uneasily making her way towards him.

She sniffed haughtily as she entered the hallway. 'I want money,' she announced, closing the front door behind her. 'If you pay me enough, I'll testify that it was an accident.'

Alfred smiled. 'Marvellous. It seems we're thinking along similar lines. Would you like a cup of tea?'

'No,' she said. 'I want money.'

'Straight to business, then,' he said, gesturing towards the lounge. 'Come and have a sit down.'

Rosie eyed him suspiciously as she moved into the room, perching on the edge of the first armchair that she came to.

Alfred followed her in, heading straight to the bureau on the far side of the room. He opened a drawer and withdrew a manilla envelope which he handed to Rosie.

'What's this?' she asked.

'Open it,' Alfred encouraged, taking a seat in his usual armchair. 'You *can* read, I presume?'

'Of course, I can bloody read. Think I'm stupid, or something?' she snapped, pulling out the four sheets of typed and stapled paper. She managed just a few seconds of silent reading, lips mouthing the words all the while, before finally shooting him a baffled look. 'I don't get it.'

Alfred crossed his legs at the knees and leant forwards. 'It's my complete, unabridged account of our interactions over recent months, signed and dated in front of my solicitor,' he declared jubilantly.

Rosie shifted in the chair and sniffed again. 'Why?'

'Because I refuse to be blackmailed by you any longer,' he answered simply. 'Now. If you agree to sign the document at the back of the papers, you will be given a one-off sum of five thousand pounds. In return, you will testify that you've never seen me before and that the brick-throwing stunt was an accident; a misunderstanding. You will also leave the area, never to return.'

'What if I don't sign it...?'

'Then, you will not get a single penny from me again, and I will instruct my solicitors to go to the police and pursue you for blackmailing charges.'

Rosie stared at him, unblinking.

He met her gaze, holding his nerve, certain now that he finally held the upper hand. He sat up straight and took a long breath in, determined not to be the first to speak.

She eventually broke the heavy silence by saying, 'I'm pregnant with your baby.' She sat back in the armchair and folded her arms.

Alfred's breath caught in his throat, and he could feel his cheeks flush crimson as his pulse began to race. 'Well, *I* don't believe you,' he mumbled.

Rosie opened her jacket and pulled her t-shirt tight over a blatant baby bump.

'Prove that it's mine,' he spat.

Rosie sneered. 'I'm telling you, it's yours, but it don't really matter, does it?' she said. 'If I tell people it is, then they'll believe it. What's the name of that journalist from the Kentish Gazette, again? Darren Lee? Anyway, something like that. He gave me his business card, he did,' she said, fumbling in her coat pockets. Retrieving a small piece of card from her breast pocket, she read, '*Daryl* Lee, that's it. I expect he'll be very interested in what I've got to say about a respectable businessman getting young impressionable women up the duff and making them pretend to be his dead wife. Headline news, I should say.'

Alfred felt a light tremble in his hands and clamped them between his thighs. She was certainly pregnant, that much was clear, but whether or not the baby was his was impossible to know. But, as the little scheming harlot had just made abundantly clear, it didn't matter if the child was his or not; the damage that the allegation alone could do to him would be incomprehensible: he would lose everything.

'Now, then. *Here's* what we're gonna do,' Rosie said, mimicking him by crossing her legs and leaning forwards. 'You're going to double that amount of money to ten grand. In return, I'll say to the

106

nice judge, tomorrow, that it was all a big accident. And yes, I'll walk away and never come back. I'll even pay you for a new shop window. Think I'll head up to London, or go up north, or maybe somewhere abroad. Who knows?'

Alfred didn't have ten thousand pounds at his disposal. But, right now, that was the least of his worries; he would have to find the money. He nodded agreement. 'I'll pay you in full *after* the court hearing.'

Rosie smiled broadly. 'Lovely doing business with ya,' she said, leaping up and offering him her hand to shake. When he refused, she added, 'Suit yourself…darling husband. I'll be seeing meself out.'

The front door slammed shut, and Alfred collapsed backwards into the armchair, the blood draining from his face and instantly exhausting him. He cursed his own pathetic weakness at ever having clapped eyes on the nasty venomous vixen. He thought about the court case tomorrow and the fact that he had no choice but to trust that she would indeed keep to her word. But where on earth was he going to find this ten thousand pounds? He looked at the clock: 9.16am. If he went to the bank in Folkestone town centre, he could withdraw the five thousand that he had planned to give to her anyway; but he simply did not have the other half. With significantly more time, he would have been able to release equity from the business or the house, but it was entirely impossible to achieve either by close of business today.

He shut his eyes and tried to clear the darkness clouding in his mind. He felt trapped, vulnerable and frightened as the adrenaline pulsating around his body began steadily to dissipate, and a heavy lethargy took over his muscles.

He kept his eyes shut as his breathing became shallow and his thoughts became more and more obscured in a welcome unfollowable tangle. Moments later, he was asleep.

Alfred woke with a start, sitting bolt upright and looking at the clock. 'Damn it,' he cursed, standing up too quickly and finding his legs buckling under him. He sat back down in his armchair to gather his thoughts and strength. Whilst he had been asleep, the name of a person who could definitely help him out of his financial predicament had entered his head as an obvious solution. But, now that he was awake, the idea of asking them chilled his blood. Was there an alternative, though? It was now almost one o'clock in the afternoon. The banks would be closing in two and a half hours. Time was very quickly running out. He stood up again. The decision was made.

Thirty-five minutes later, Alfred gently tapped on the door and took in a long, nervous breath as he waited. He had just come from the bank which had given him the pre-requested five thousand pounds, but, despite his pleas with the manager, he had not been granted a single penny more. He looked behind him at his little blue Mini, wondering if it were too late to change his mind and hurry away. But the door had already been opened.

'Alfred?'

He turned to see his mother's inquisitive stare.

'That's a nice surprise. I wasn't expecting you today, was I?' she asked.

Alfred shook his head. 'I need to talk to you.'

'Well, come in. Is everything alright? With Margaret? And Peter and little Morton...?'

Alfred nodded his head as he entered the hallway. 'They're all fine. Totally fine.'

'Come through to the kitchen,' she directed. 'I was just making some lunch.'

Alfred followed her to the back of the house and sat down at the round four-person table. He was aware that she was now looking intently at him, but he focussed his attention on the gingham tablecloth, running his thumb along the plaid blue and white pattern.

'Would you like a drink...or something to eat?' she asked softly.

'I've done something stupid,' he blurted out, ignoring her questions, his thumbnail whitening from the pressure that he was applying. 'I sought—' he couldn't find the right word, '—comfort in a woman... A woman who has since been blackmailing me. And now. Well, I need five thousand pounds to pay her off, once and for all.' He said it quickly and the moment the words were out of his mouth, the chains around his heart loosened a little. But he still could not look at her. And there was no way that he was going to mention the possibility that Rosie might also be pregnant with his child.

'Alfie,' she said softly, approaching him and placing her hand on his shoulder. 'What do you mean, 'pay her off, once and for all'? Have you paid her something, already?'

'Yes,' he quietly confirmed.

'How much have you given her?'

He slowly moved his shoulders upwards. 'Thousands.'

'Dear God,' she replied. 'What a wicked woman. Has this got anything to do with your sending Margaret off to stay in Cornwall with Alex, again?'

Alfred nodded. 'She smashed my shop window on Christmas Eve, and it's in court in Sevenoaks, tomorrow. I couldn't bear for Margaret to find out about my...my indiscretion.'

He heard his mother take in a long breath. 'Oh, Alfie,' she said again, using that pitiful tone that he simultaneously despised and yearned for in equal measure, taking him back, as it did, to the uncomplicated safety of his childhood.

At that moment, just as she was about to speak, the telephone shrilled in the hallway and his mother began to shuffle off to answer it.

'Leave it,' he barked.

'What if it's important?' she replied, continuing nevertheless into the hallway and picking up the receiver. 'Nellie Sageman,' she answered brightly.

'*This* is important,' Alfred muttered to himself. He listened to the opening salvo of her half of the call, envious of her zeal and enthusiasm, despite the hardships that life had thrown at her along the way. Alfred held his head in his hands, disconnecting from the one-sided conversation coming from the hallway. He felt lighter for having told someone other than his starchy solicitor about what had occurred, but the space created by relief a moment ago, he now found, was being quickly replaced by profound shame and uncertainty.

He closed his eyes and, with his chin resting in his palms on the table, covered his ears. In the dark silence, he saw himself as others must surely see him: a hollow and ill-tempered man whose light had been extinguished a long time ago. When exactly had he become this person? he wondered. Had it been a sudden change when a large piece of him had died with Anna? Or had it been a more subtle, sorry decline? His childhood—in this very house—had been

109

unremarkable and his memories of the transition through to becoming a young working man could produce no hint at the cause of the juxtaposition with the man who he was today. Key moments of his life spooled through his mind but also seemingly in front of him, as though in a film, then stopped. The war. Three and a half harrowing and torturous years he had spent as a prisoner of war in Thailand, where his incarceration had included work on the Burma-Siam railway, which had nearly killed him. It was a dark, dark period which he had long tried to forget. But it had changed him irrevocably. Anna—his dear, darling Anna—had been the one constant, present throughout his conceited youth and the build-up to war. And she had been present in his broken days following the liberation on VJ Day. Perhaps if he faced what had happened during those bleak years of hell, he might happen upon the moment—or moments—which led to the transition to this man who he now was. Before she had died, Anna had pestered him to 'see someone' about all that the war years had done to him, but a bitter concoction of scepticism, solid self-pride and embarrassment had ensured that it had never happened.

A gentle hand on his shoulder startled him. He uncovered his ears and, through bleary eyes, met his mother's gaze. She put her arms around him and held him tight as he sobbed onto her shoulder in such a way as he hadn't done since he had been a child.

'Sorry,' Alfred said, sitting up and hurriedly dabbing his eyes with a handkerchief. 'Excuse me.' He hurried from the room and into the lavatory where he just stood for a moment with his back to the locked door. Then he splashed his face with cold water and took several deep breaths before returning to the kitchen where his mother was standing over a kettle on the hob.

'I think we could do with a nice cup of tea, don't you?' she said.

Alfred looked at his pocket watch: he had an hour and twenty-five minutes before the banks closed for the day. If they were to leave now, she would have time enough to withdraw the five thousand pounds from her account. 'What about the money?'

'Alfie, I would love to help you, but I just don't have that kind of money to hand.'

'Savings?' he pressed.

'It's all tied up in bonds and shares. What little I keep in my current account won't make the blindest bit of difference to what that little madam is demanding. Besides which, I don't think you should be giving her a single penny more. You said it, yourself, that you've already given her thousands of pounds. Give her this money and she'll only be back again next week for more; and the week after, and so on.'

'But I...' he cut himself short. There was little to be gained by arguing or pushing his point. Alfred sat and resigned himself to the worst: Rosie Hart had won.

'That was Alex on the telephone, by the way,' she said, pouring the boiling water into a teapot. 'He said to let you know that Margaret had arrived safely a few minutes ago. He was going to telephone you later, but won't now, and told me to pass on the message, since you were here.'

Alfred nodded.

'She pretty well dumped her things directly and went to their neighbour's house,' she said with a chuckle.

'Neighbour's house?' Alfred questioned.

'Yes. They've a young lad, there, she's friendly with: Jim Daynes.'

Alfred stood quickly. 'For God's sake!'

'What's wrong, now?'

'What do you think's wrong, now? Do you remember what happened last time she got *friendly* with a young man? There's nothing for it. I'll have to drive down there, right now and bring her back. She can stay here with you, instead.'

'Oh, don't be so preposterous,' she chided. 'You're in court, tomorrow, in Sevenoaks. How on earth do you think you're going to drive to Cornwall and back in that time? And what on earth sort of state would you be in for court, if you did happen to make it, you daft beggar? Listen, she's fine, Alex assured me. He knew you might get upset and said to tell you that they're not ever left alone together. Calm yourself and trust your brother.'

'No wonder she was so keen to get back down there,' Alfred muttered.

'Now, sit down, Alfie,' his mother instructed, carrying over two cups of tea. 'Drink this and forget about what Margaret's up to and concentrate on more pressing problems. Focus on tomorrow.' She sat down opposite him and took his hand in hers. 'What are you going to say to this young whipper-snapper?'

Alfred drew in a long breath. He had not the slightest idea what he was going to say to her, tomorrow.

Chapter Thirteen

19th December 2019, Rye, East Sussex

Morton arrived in his study, feeling anxious. There were just two days left until they were due to travel to Cornwall to stay with his Aunty Margaret and Uncle Jim, and he needed to have this case wrapped up before they went. He sat at his desk and thought about how on earth he was going to tell her about her father's exploits. At least with Aunty Margaret, though, he could apply some degree of sugar-coating; something which he could not do with the news that he had to impart to Vanessa, Liza and Billie about their mother. Happy Christmas, everyone. Perhaps there was some good yet to come from it all: he was about to do that which he had been putting off doing and call Billie to tell her the news that she had a half-sibling on her paternal side. He picked up his mobile, opened *The Foundlings* WhatsApp group and then dialled her number.

She answered immediately. 'Hi, Morton,' she said in her broad Mancunian accent. 'How are you, love?'

'Great, thank you,' he lied. 'And you?'

'Yeah, not bad, ta. So, you found our mum yet?' she asked with a laugh.

Morton tittered. 'Not quite, no,' he lied again. 'Making good progress, though.'

'That's good to hear.'

'Yes,' he agreed. 'Erm, you know I suggested that it would be a good idea to upload your DNA to as many databases as possible?'

'Yeah.'

'And I talked you through all the possible consequences of that decision, including the potential to find close relatives?'

'Yeah.'

'Well, you've got a fairly close DNA match come up on MyHeritage,' he informed her.

'Oh, right. Related to the three of us?'

'No, just you. It's on your paternal side, a lady by the name of Amy Praed.'

'Never heard of her,' Billie said with a laugh. 'And do you know how she's related to me?'

'Yes. I believe she's your half-sister.'

'You...my what?'

'I think she's your half-sister,' Morton repeated, bracing himself for whichever direction this conversation might take at this revelatory moment. He had arrived at this very same point with clients several times before: some had burst into uncontrollable tears; others had been left unable to speak; and one had demanded to see the evidence before he would believe it and, even then, wasn't convinced by it.

She laughed, thankfully. '*Another* sister? Well, the more the merrier; that's what I say. Another lass to go shopping and clubbing with, and what have you.'

'Hmm, maybe,' Morton cautioned. 'She is a *little* older than you, though, however.'

'Oh, right. How old is she, then, love?'

'Well. She's in her seventies.'

Billie laughed again. 'Oh my God, that's right hilarious. A sister...up in her seventies. I think her partying days are probably well over, then. Does she know about me?'

'Not that I'm aware of, no. I haven't made any contact with her; taking that next step, that needs to be your decision. Of course, she might well have seen you pop up in her results by now.'

'Oh, right. Well, I'm happy to speak to her, meet up, whatever,' she said. After a small pause, the penny dropped. 'Am I to take it, that means you know who me dad is, then?'

'Yes, I do,' Morton confirmed. 'He was a man called Edward Crouch and he was born in 1915 in Manchester.'

'Christ alive,' Billie gasped. 'No point me asking if he's still knocking about, then.'

'It's *possible* that he's still alive, but just not *that* likely. To be honest, I haven't done an awful lot of research on Edward, but hopefully you'll get more information from Amy.'

'Yeah...course.'

'Just...go in cautiously and be as prepared as you can be that she might not want to establish contact. It might be an even bigger shock for her than it has been for you.'

'Yeah, I know all that; I've had the counselling. They might not take the news well or might not believe it, not want to see me, blah

blah blah. It's fine, Morton, is all that, really.'

'Okay, well I'll send you the details and leave it up to you.'

'Right you are. Thanks, love,' Billie said casually. 'Now, then. Go and find our mum.' She laughed and Morton was relieved that the process of telling her hadn't been too difficult. He said goodbye and ended the call.

Placing his mobile phone down on the desk in front of him, he noticed that he had a new notification in the Facebook Messenger app. He opened it up and saw that it was from Kathy Steadman.

Morton, I'm curious. Your name is familiar to me. Yes, I did have dealings with Miss Hart in the past—not something I'm terribly inclined to relive, if I'm honest. What do you want to know exactly?

Morton smiled as he turned on his laptop. While he waited for it to start up, he clicked to reply to Kathy on his phone.

Hi Kathy. I expect you've seen my name in the newspapers recently in connection with the Maurice Duggan / Alexei Yahontov case. I totally understand that you might not wish to revisit your old police days but I'm really keen to try to find out as much as I can about Rosie Hart for her three daughters who know nothing about her at all. Would you consider meeting me for a quick chat? Happy to come to you or to meet up in a coffeeshop near to you. Thank you very much, Morton

He hit the blue arrow to the right of his message, and it was gone. He held the phone and waited. Seconds later, *Seen* appeared in small grey letters below that which he had written. She had seen it and hopefully would respond.

While he waited, he flipped his notepad to the page headed ROSIE HART AFTER 1980?? Below the title, not a single word had been written. She had seemingly vanished.

With his computer now awake, Morton wanted to gauge approximately how much time he would need to give to broad searches using just Rosie Hart's name with no further filtering: Ancestry had 1,392 records; MyHeritage had 1,237; FindmyPast 13,318; TheGenealogist 100,935; and FamilySearch 264,063.

Clearly, some refining would be necessary, since he didn't have the lifetime for searching available that these results would have demanded.

Returning to Ancestry, Morton could see that they were dominated by US records. Changing the collection type from *All Collections* to *England* brought the list down to a much more manageable 303 results. He began wading through the list. Some records could be dismissed easily, while others required a full verification to be certain of their irrelevance.

After several minutes more, which Morton took to be a direct correlation with the extent of weighing up required to arrive at her decision, Kathy Steadman replied to his message.

Hi Morton. No, your surname is familiar from back when I was investigating Rosie Hart. Probably just a coincidence. Yes, I suppose a quick chat about it wouldn't hurt. I'm free tomorrow, if you want to come and visit me in Haywards Heath? Let me know a convenient time. Kathy

Morton was not a believer in coincidences. Had Kathy Steadman come across his grandfather in her pursuit of Rosie Hart? Did it imply that his grandfather could also be the father of Baby Bradley? Morton hastily typed out a reply.

Hi Kathy. I'll tell you more tomorrow, but my grandfather was called Alfred Farrier and one of the three adoptees that I'm helping was actually fathered by him. A complicated story! Would ten o'clock tomorrow morning be okay to visit? Kind regards, Morton

He put his mobile back down and returned to his searches. So far, he had found nothing relating to the correct Rosie Hart. Another message came in from Kathy.

It was a very long time ago, but fairly sure Alfred Farrier was the name of someone involved in the case. Yes, 10am is fine…

Her message ended with her address and telephone number. He thanked her, then resumed his painstaking work.

At just gone twelve o'clock, which his stomach was telling him was lunchtime, Morton headed downstairs to the kitchen where kids'

Christmas music was playing softly in the background. 'Wow, what's going on here?' he asked.

Grace, with her hair tied back in a ponytail, had a bright-red apron on which was covered in flour, as were her hands, face and the floor beneath her. On the table was a rectangular slab of dough. 'Cooking,' Grace said.

Juliette rolled her eyes. 'Salt dough,' she explained, bending down and handing Grace a metal shape-cutter. 'Right, now push the cutter in to make an angel.'

Grace did as instructed, and Juliette stood up. 'I thought it might be a nice idea for her to make her own decorations, since we can't take the Christmas cake down. I thought Aunty Margaret and Uncle Jim might like one.'

'Brave,' he said, seeing Grace remove the dough from the cutter and take a bite.

'No! You can't eat it, Grace.'

Grace made that discovery for herself and spat it out onto the table. 'Yuck.'

'I told you not to eat it, Grace. It's full of salt,' Juliette warned, holding up the unfortunate, decapitated angel in front of Morton. 'Do you think Aunty Margaret will like this?'

Morton laughed. 'Absolutely.' He opened the fridge in search of something to eat. 'What would *my* two little angels like for their lunch? I'm wondering.'

'Lunch? It's literally just after twelve,' Juliette scorned. 'I take it you've hit a brick wall in your work, then?'

Morton peered out from around the fridge door. 'And, what do you mean by that?'

'You only stop work when you hit a brick wall or when you're told you've got to.'

'*Do* I?' He closed the fridge, finding nothing appetising contained in it, and settled for a bag of cheese and onion crisps. 'Well, alright. It's not a brick wall per se, rather a monotonous trudge through a gazillion records, trying to find out what happened to Rosie Hart. One good thing, though: I'm seeing the detective who worked on the Baby Bradley case, tomorrow morning.'

'Do you think she might know more?' Juliette asked, leaning over Grace and helping her to push the angel-shaped cutter through the dough.

Morton shrugged and ate a crisp. 'I do hope so. Although, she seemed to have a recollection of my grandfather's involvement with her investigation into Rosie…which is worrying.'

Juliette looked at him. 'Oh, do you think he might be Baby Bradley's father, too?'

'I really do hope not, but it's certainly possible. Whoever Baby Bradley is, he hasn't had his DNA tested at any of the major genealogy companies, so it's practically impossible to track him down.'

'What else do you need to find before we go to Cornwall?'

'Ideally, the answer to the first question that they're all sure to ask me as soon as I've told them her name: 'So, what happened to her?''

'And do you think you can find that out in two days?' she asked.

'I'm really not sure,' he answered, stuffing more crisps into his mouth.

Chapter Fourteen

11th March 1975, Canterbury, Kent

Kathy was standing behind a taped-off cordon in the disused car park of a derelict and forlorn dairy factory outside of Canterbury city centre. It was a grey overcast day with a cold easterly wind whipping across the cracked tarmac. She was surrounded by the other dozen officers who were also taking the advanced driving course. They were watching as two identical, large brown Triumph saloons zipped around a course demarcated by a series of red and white traffic cones. A liberal dousing of oil, water, and a lethal combination of the two had been sloshed over the track at various points.

'Watch the instructor on the skid pan very carefully,' Inspector Rillington told them. 'To keep on the tail of another vehicle, you have to be in the right place, at the right speed, in the right gear, at the right time, *all the time.*'

The officers watched as the two cars played cat and mouse around the track.

'I had a nice evening, last night,' Kathy whispered to Simon who was standing beside her, tugging on his black beard.

He grinned. 'Me too.'

They had gone out for a meal in The Curry Garden and Kathy had been utterly surprised by how well they had got on. She had had several fleeting relationships in the past, but nothing sufficiently serious to get her anywhere near walking down the aisle. It would be easy to do as her former partners had done and blame the job for that fact. Working as a female police officer was gruelling—there was no getting around that—and it had undoubtedly played a part in her availability and exposure to any potential suitors. But it was more complex than that; she could see retrospectively that she had never fully committed to the men in whom she had shown a romantic interest because she hadn't been able to bear the idea of giving up the job that she loved, as was the general expectation upon marrying. 'I'm just not the marrying sort,' had been her reply when Simon had asked last night if she'd ever been married. It was her usual, semi-cryptic repartee that she would use to silence meddling friends and colleagues with intentions of setting her up with potential relationships. His reply had taken her aback: 'Me neither.' Strangely, with that currently immaterial information out in the open, she had loosened up and thoroughly enjoyed his company.

The two Triumphs slowed down and drew up in front of the group of officers. Inspector Rillington turned around to address them. 'Now, it's your turn. This morning, you'll all get to learn how to handle the car under a variety of conditions and at a variety of speeds. This afternoon you'll be taught active pursuit techniques.' He clipped his heels together and surveyed the group. He met Kathy's eyes and said, 'Perhaps the member of the fairer sex among us would like to go first?'

'Good luck,' Simon whispered.

Kathy inwardly groaned. Inspector Rillington was an imbecile, but it was always the same. In training exercises among male officers, she was either picked first in a patronising show of chivalry, or last in some unwarranted and unwelcome expression of special consideration since the task might be beyond her womanly mental or physical capabilities. She offered a wooden smile. 'Thank you, sir.' She strode confidently over to the passenger door of the idling car and climbed in.

'Ready?' the moustachioed young lad in the driving seat asked, his eyebrows dancing up and down excitedly.

Kathy nodded, turning her attention to the two further officers getting into the backseats. Once they were in, the instructor turned to Kathy and said, 'I'll take the course a couple of times to show you how it's done, and then it'll be your turn. Okay?' He turned around and faced the two men in the back. 'Then you'll each get a go, provided this one here hasn't gone and written the car off in the meantime, hey.'

Kathy rolled her eyes and watched as the instructor levered the gearstick into first, then eased out onto the course. 'The key is staying in control at all times,' he said, glimpsing from Kathy to his rear-view mirror. 'The surface, here, as you can see, is perfectly dry and fairly predictable. So, once you get to know the car, you'll soon know how to handle it under these favourable conditions. It can get a lot harder, though, if you look up ahead.'

Kathy made a point of physically shifting in her seat, looking at the wet surface forty yards in front of them.

'Is it water or oil?' the instructor asked, but Kathy wasn't sure if the question was rhetorical or not, so she didn't answer.

'Can't see a sheen on it,' a voice from the back seat piped up. 'So, I guess it's water.'

The instructor grimaced, slowing down the Triumph. 'You can't take guesses. I'm slowing the car down until I can be certain of what's under the wheels. A car on water is one thing; a car on oil is a very different matter. The instructor jabbed the brake pedal on and off. 'It looks like water and feels like water, so I'm going to increase my speed slightly.'

Just up ahead of them was an unbroken line of cones, the course veering sharply off to the right. Even though she was confident that the instructor would take an evasive manoeuvre at the last moment and get them around the bend, Kathy couldn't help but apply her foot to a ghost pedal in the footwell and grip the side of her seat.

'Okay,' the instructor said. 'I'm not going to make this bend using just the steering wheel.' He worked the wheel and reached down for the handbrake, lifting it partway and sending the back of the car sliding around. He quickly lowered the handbrake and steered against the cornering, navigating his way successfully between the line of cones. Then he slammed on the brakes and looked between the three of them with a boastful grin.

'Gordon Bennett,' one of the men in the back muttered.

Kathy exhaled quietly, not wishing her colleagues to know quite how on edge that little stunt had just put her.

'Everyone okay?' the instructor asked.

Kathy nodded.

'Okay,' he said. 'Now we've seen what she can do, let's start with a few simpler moves, shall we?'

'Well, that was fun,' Kathy said with a chuckle as she moved slowly behind a long line of policemen and policewomen queuing for their lunch in the busy canteen.

'I loved it, actually,' Simon replied, shunting his tray over the silver bars that ran the length of the servery.

'Exhilarating, that's the word I was looking for,' Kathy said. 'I'm looking forward to the pursuit driving, this afternoon.'

'Then we're out on the roads of Canterbury tomorrow,' Simon

replied, picking up a clingfilm-wrapped sandwich from the shelves in front of him. He turned his nose up, put it back and picked up another. 'Looks like it's cheese, cheese and egg, cheese and cress, or cheese and tomato.'

'Great selection,' Kathy commented, reaching for a plain cheese. She slid her tray along and noticed then the Station Officer from yesterday sitting close by. She caught his eye, smiled and said hello.

He clicked his fingers as if in thought and then pointed to Kathy. 'You were after Frank Hart's sister, Rosie, weren't you?' he called across to her.

'That's right, yes,' she confirmed. 'Did he finally give up an address for her, then?'

'Not really, but Frank did mention in his interview last night that she was supposed to be up in court today in Sevenoaks. Not sure how true it is, though; he's not the most reliable of witnesses,' he shrugged, 'but thought I'd mention.'

'Thank you,' Kathy replied, thinking quickly. She glanced at Simon. 'I need to use a telephone.'

'Come on,' he said, abandoning his tray and dashing for the canteen door, with Kathy close behind him. He led them down to the front desk. 'Telephone, please,' he said to the officer, 'and the number for Sevenoaks Magistrate's Court, urgently.'

The officer pulled a black Bakelite telephone up from behind the desk and placed it on the counter top. 'I'll just get you that number.'

'Thank you,' Kathy said, watching impatiently as the officer rummaged among a stack of telephone directories. She faced Simon. 'God, if she's there... How long would it take for us to get to Sevenoaks?'

Simon blew a puff of air from his inflated cheeks. 'Maybe well over an hour, I'd say, even if we blue-light it.'

'Come on,' Kathy mumbled under her breath, picking up the receiver in one hand but pressing down on the switch hook in the cradle, releasing it only when the officer placed a thick directory in front of her and jabbed a finger half-way down the page.

'There you go,' he said.

Kathy thanked him, checked the dial tone and rang the number.

'Sevenoaks Magistrate's Court. Mrs Dobbs speaking, how can I help you?' a lady with BBC English answered.

'This is WDS Steadman from Sussex Police. I'm calling about a case that might be being heard in your courts today. It involves a young lady by the name of Rosie Hart. Could you check, please?'

'One moment,' Mrs Dobbs said.

Kathy glanced apprehensively at Simon as she listened to a shuffling of paperwork in the background.

'Hello? Are you still on the line?' Mrs Dobbs said after a few moments.

'Yes. Still here.'

'Good. Yes, I can confirm that one Rosie Hart *is* in court at this very moment as it happens.'

'Thank you so much,' Kathy said, slamming down the receiver. 'I need to get to Sevenoaks right now.' She made a quick dash towards the doors, Simon trailing after her.

'The driving course?' he said.

'Sod the driving course. It'll have to wait,' she replied, running to the car park.

Simon laughed. 'Want company?'

'Sure,' she answered, hurrying towards her car. She unlocked the door, placed the magnetic flashing light onto the roof, leant across to open the door for Simon, and then started the engine.

'You going to be putting what you learnt into practice?' he asked with a grin as she threw the car backwards out of the parking space.

'Hold tight,' she replied, thrusting the car into first gear and speeding out of the car park with the blue light flashing and the car's siren blaring. She was utterly determined to get her hands on Rosie Hart, finally.

'Remember: you have to be in the right place, at the right speed, in the right gear, at the right time, *all the time*,' Simon said robotically.

'Shut up,' Kathy laughed, hurrying out of the city.

The journey to Sevenoaks Magistrate's Court took over the hour as Simon had predicted. Kathy pulled up on double yellow lines outside the court—an ugly, single-storey brick building—on Morewood Close. She left the engine running and dashed from the car, calling back that Simon should stay put and simultaneously barging into an old man who was chatting with a young woman outside the court. 'So sorry,' she called behind her as she entered the building. Despite the utilitarian façade, the inside was modern and appeared purpose-built. She strode across the dark-purple carpeted foyer to a screened reception desk behind which sat a prim middle-aged lady with a sour expression on her face.

'Hello, I phoned earlier. I spoke to Mrs Dobbs. Not sure if that's you, or not,' Kathy said breathlessly, holding up her warrant card and not waiting for her to respond. 'WDS Steadman, Sussex Police. Could you direct me to the courtroom with Rosie Hart's case, please?'

The woman behind the desk pushed a pair of half-moon glasses onto the bridge of her nose and squinted at Kathy's warrant card. Then she pursed her thin lips. 'That case is over, I'm afraid.'

'What?' Kathy stammered. 'When did it finish?'

'About ten minutes ago.'

'Oh, God. And the girl—Rosie Hart—where is she?'

'I have no idea, frankly,' she said, seemingly taking great pleasure in her ignorance.

'Thanks very much,' Kathy replied, moving further into the foyer where several smartly dressed people were standing about in loose groupings. She ran her eyes over the individuals, finding that none of them matched the various witness descriptions of Rosie. Two young women, both of whom might just fit the profile, were standing together chatting. Kathy approached them, flashed up her warrant card and asked, 'Rosie Hart?'

Both girls shook their heads and looked at her uncertainly.

Kathy whipped around and addressed the entire foyer of people. 'Is there a Rosie Hart here?' she bellowed.

Her plea was met with instant silence, followed by a unanimous muted reply of shaking heads and murmurs of negation.

'She left a few minutes ago,' a portly man in a pinstripe suit informed her, pushing out from a small crowd and making his way towards her. In his arms was a great bundle of paperwork and folders. 'And who might you be?'

'WDS Steadman, Sussex Police,' she said, producing her warrant card again.

'Ah,' the man said, nodding. 'I'm Miss Hart's solicitor, Phillip Grogan.'

'Where did she go?'

Phillip sighed dramatically. 'Your guess is as good as mine.'

Kathy was losing her patience. Yet again, Rosie Hart was going to elude her. 'How long ago did she walk through those doors?' Kathy demanded, pointing to the entrance.

'Five minutes, give or take.'

'What was she wearing?'

Phillip Grogan frowned. 'Black leather jacket and carrying a white handbag. Look, as her legal representative, I need to ask what this is in relation to?'

'Damn it,' Kathy said, realising in that moment that Rosie had been the young woman chatting with an old man outside the building, whom she had run into. Kathy ignored Phillip's questions and ran for the door. Outside, there was no sign of either the old man or Rosie. She ran diagonally across the trim lawn to her car where Simon was sitting with his elbow on the open window. 'She's gone,' Kathy blurted. 'Did you see a young woman wearing a black leather jacket, with a white handbag? Also, an old man that she was chatting to outside the entrance?'

Simon shook his head. 'Sorry, no.'

Kathy darted around to the driver's side, jumped into the car, spun it around and headed back to the main London Road. 'Which way?' she said, as much to herself as to Simon. Both of them searched left and right. There was no sign of a person matching Rosie Hart's description. 'Think... She doesn't live in Sevenoaks. How did she get here?'

'Drove?' Simon suggested.

Kathy shook her head. 'I don't think she has a car.'

'Bus? Train?'

Train. 'Do you know which way the train station is?' Kathy asked.

'Left out of here onto London Road, then it's not far along on the right,' Simon directed.

Kathy banged the steering wheel as a long line of slow-moving traffic crawled past behind a tractor.

'Blue-light it,' Simon urged.

Kathy shook her head. 'I can't risk spooking her.' Finally, there was a gap in the traffic and Kathy pulled out. She was as certain as she could be that Rosie would have arrived here by train; it was certainly her best bet. The station was just a few yards down the road and Kathy pulled in outside, again leaving the engine running. She jumped out of the car and rushed inside the building, pausing to check the busy waiting room. No sign of her, so she moved out onto the platform just in time to see a train pulling out.

'Where's that train going?' Kathy yelled at the guard.

'London—you're too late,' he replied. 'Next one's in an hour.'

Kathy exhaled, thrust her hands on her hips and watched the train disappear from view. She tried to contain her frustration as she walked back to the car. 'Gone. *Again*,' she told Simon. 'Off to London. I literally just watched the train leave. If it hadn't been for that bloody tractor, I would have had her this time.' Kathy looked at Simon, mulling over her predicament. 'I'm going to go back to the court and find out what the case was about and who that old man was that she was talking to. I'm sure I saw him handing her something—an envelope maybe.'

'Just playing devil's advocate, here,' Simon began, raising his eyebrows in anticipation of her reaction, 'But you are going to *extraordinary* lengths to catch this woman. What's driving this? A desire to reunite her with the baby? Or to see her behind bars for the abandonment of a child? Or is it…bear with me on this…to not have Rosie Hart outsmart you?'

She absorbed his serious question head-on, but she didn't have an answer.

Kathy pulled up outside of 163 Canterbury Road in Folkestone. It was a cream-coloured 1930s house conjoined with an identical neighbouring property. A bright-blue Mini sat on the driveway beside a narrow rectangle of well-kept lawn in front of the house.

She looked down at the piece of paper upon which the court clerk had written the name and address of the occupant, one Alfred Farrier. Upon returning to Sevenoaks Magistrate's Court, Kathy had learned the details of the case which had taken place where Rosie Hart had been accused of smashing the shop window of Farrier's Fashion. Given that Kathy had personally witnessed Alfred talking to Rosie—possibly handing her something—her claim that the window had been damaged accidentally and that Alfred Farrier had denied having had any knowledge of her made the outcome of the case very peculiar.

Kathy climbed out of her car, walked up the driveway to the house and pressed the doorbell. Moments later, a man answered the door, who took her aback. He appeared to be in his mid-sixties and not as old as she had thought him to have been this morning when she had bumped into him outside of the court. The man frowned, making Kathy wonder if he recognised her, too. 'Yes?'

She held up her warrant card. 'WDS Steadman, Sussex Police. Could I have a quick chat with you, please?'

'In regard to what, exactly?' he asked.

'Rosie Hart,' she replied, noticing a flicker of horror in his eyes.

He sighed, pulled the door open and invited her in.

Kathy followed him into the front room, her eyes drawn to the array of photographs on the mantelpiece. 'Nice little family you've got there,' she commented.

Alfred smiled and picked up a silver-framed photograph of a young couple and a small baby. 'My first grandchild,' he told her. 'Morton.'

'Lovely,' she responded. 'Unusual name.' The photo of the little boy made her think of Baby Bradley; whereas Morton had evidently been loved by his parents from before he had even been born, poor Baby Bradley had been callously abandoned and probably never loved by his birth parents.

'Do take a seat,' Alfred said, gesturing to a pair of armchairs as he returned the photograph to its previous position.

'Thanks,' she said, sitting at the nearest chair.

'So, now then. What can I do to help?' he asked, lowering himself into the armchair opposite her. 'I'd hoped that, after the court case this morning, I wouldn't be hearing *that* name ever again.'

Kathy offered a warm smile, not wanting to knock him off-side before she had even begun. 'I'm sure, Mr Farrier. It must have been a very traumatic experience for you. I'm not here about the window incident, though, actually.'

'Oh?'

'I want to speak with Rosie Hart in connection with a baby that was abandoned in Haywards Heath in September 1973.'

Alfred's eyes widened. '*Her* baby?'

'Possibly,' Kathy answered.

He sucked in his lower lip and muttered, 'And what's this got to do with me, can I ask?'

'I believe you might know where I can find her,' Kathy said.

Alfred threw open his hands and appeared quite surprised by her statement. 'I can assure you, right now, that I haven't an inkling of a clue where that unscrupulous vandal might be found; as I said in court today, I've never seen the woman in my life before she hurled a brick through my shop window.'

'Mr Farrier,' Kathy began, shifting in her seat and searching for diplomacy. 'I have no interest in what past connection you may or may not have had with Rosie Hart. I'm not here to investigate you or to accuse you of anything whatsoever. I simply want to track down Rosie's whereabouts.'

Alfred shook his head. 'No idea, sorry.'

Tact was not working. Time for directness. 'I saw you outside the court, handing something to her: what was that?'

A light flush of crimson rose in Alfred's cheeks. 'It was...a map,' he stammered.

'A map?'

'Yes, she handed it to me... Asking me how to get somewhere.'

'And where was that *somewhere*?' Kathy pushed, not believing a single word.

'The bus station. I took the map from her, took a look at it and then handed it back. That was what you saw, Detective.'

'So, of all the people who were milling about inside and outside of the court just minutes after she'd been found guilty of wilful damage to your property, she chose *you* as the best person to request directions from?'

Alfred nodded and Kathy laughed.

She tried one last time, 'Where can I find her, Mr Farrier?'

'I don't know,' he answered, drawing out each word.

'Thank you for your time,' Kathy said, standing up. 'I'm at Burgess Hill Police Station, should anything come to mind, or should you see her again.'

Alfred rose and followed her out to the front door. 'I hope not to see that girl again for as long as I live. Goodbye.'

'Bye,' Kathy said, leaving the house and walking down the driveway to her car. She got inside and let out a deep sigh. It was time to head back to her lodgings in Canterbury in preparation for the final day of her advanced driving course. She started the engine and pulled out, wondering whether she should telephone Simon to see if he wanted to meet up tonight for a drink. She had to admit that she liked him an awful lot more than she had liked anyone in a very long time.

The following day, Kathy entered Burgess Hill Police Station with an inner glow. Last night, she and Simon had gone out for dinner, and afterwards he had asked if they might see one another again to which question she had readily agreed. She smiled at the manner of his asking. 'I know you're not the marrying sort...but I wondered if we might see each other again...like dating?' he had said.

'*Like* dating?' she had replied with a wry smile.

'Well, actual dating but without marriage at the end of it,' he had clarified.

'Yes, I would like that very much,' she had agreed.

'The boss wants to see you,' the Station Officer greeted her, flinging her back to the present moment.

Kathy grimaced, knowing full well why he would have wanted to see her. She and Simon had returned to Canterbury Police Station this morning for the third and final part of the advanced driving course, only to be turned away by a delighted Inspector Rillington. 'Attendance is compulsory for *all* three days and not just when you decide you fancy joining in,' he had admonished them. Word had obviously already reached DI Redmond.

She ascended the stairs to his office and knocked on his door.

'Come in,' he yapped.

Kathy entered the office and closed the door behind her.

DI Redmond looked up and glowered at her. 'Sit down, WDS Steadman.'

Kathy did as she had been instructed, sitting in the plastic chair directly in front of him. She met his cold dark eyes and observed that he was tapping the desk with the fingers of his left hand as if contemplating what to do with her.

'How was the driving course?' he asked.

'The first day and a half were very good, thank you, sir,' she answered.

'And after that?'

'I had to leave the course, sir—'

'*Had to*, WDS Steadman? On whose authority?'

'I had good intel that Rosie Hart was in court in Sevenoaks, and I thought I might be able to apprehend her there, sir.'

DI Redmond hung his head in dismay, then slammed his fist onto the desk. 'Rosie *bloody* Hart! What is it with you and that woman?'

'I just want to find her, sir.'

'Well, you'll be needing to reimburse the station for all the money we wasted putting you on that driving course, and you'll be pleased to know that the officer in charge isn't particularly keen to have you rebook; he said you 'lacked focus'.'

'Sorry, sir.'

'Hmm. Let me make one thing very clear to you, WDS Steadman: you are to cease all active enquiries into the Baby Bradley case and, particularly, into that Rosie Hart woman. You have a veritable tower block of cases on your desk. I suggest that you give some of those the obsessiveness that you've demonstrated in trying—repeatedly in vain, I might add—to track down this damnable woman.'

'Yes, sir.'

'Am I *completely* understood, WDS Steadman?'

'Yes, sir.'

'Not another moment is to be wasted on that case without my say-so. Go,' he said, running a hand over his slick grey hair.

Kathy stood up and left the inspector's office, hurrying along the corridor to her own which she was thankful to find empty. She sat at her desk and exhaled. Then, she sifted through the pile of assorted paperwork, amalgamating everything to do with Baby Bradley into one cardboard file which she carried into the typists' office and placed in a drawer in the metal filing cabinet marked UNDETECTED CRIMES.

And that was that: case over.

Chapter Fifteen

14th May 1975, Sevenoaks, Kent

Alfred strode along Sevenoaks High Street in a dapper brown suit and trilby hat, carrying his briefcase. As usual at this time of the morning, very few cars were passing along the High Street and the pavements had yet to see the flurry of early-morning shoppers. As he walked, he whistled a tuneless oscillation that signified a degree of calmness in his mind. He arrived at Farrier's Fashion a good forty-five minutes prior to the shop's opening at nine o'clock and unlocked the door. Although it had been two months since the court case, it had only been in the last two weeks that his nerves had finally settled and he had been able to wonder truly if he had seen the back of Rosie Hart, once and for all. As he had expected, she had not taken the news well that she was only going to get half of the agreed ten thousand pounds, but he had stood his ground and, despite his tight chest and shortness of breath, had told her that it was five thousand pounds or nothing at all. She had taken the money but left with a parting warning shot: 'I'll be back for the rest.' Alfred had tried to convince himself that if she had been coming back for more money, then she would surely have done so by now. He was still working to gather the remaining five thousand pounds, believing—probably naïvely—that if she had the full amount of money, then she would finally disappear from his life forever.

Alfred made his way to the backroom of the shop where he hung up his hat, placed his briefcase below the small table and filled the kettle. Miss Burk would arrive at any moment, and he liked to have a cup of tea and a plate of biscuits ready and waiting for her arrival. Even though this was something that he did every time that he was working at this branch, she always feigned amazement. He smiled at the routine as he set two cups and saucers down and took a pint of milk from the small refrigerator. 'Oh, well, what a lovely surprise this is!' she would declare when she arrived.

The bell above the shop door tinkled. Perfect timing, Alfred thought, as the kettle rattled to its conclusion.

'Mr Farrier?' Miss Burk called. 'Mr Farrier!' She sounded distressed.

Alfred hurried into the shop, to see Miss Burk appearing really quite flustered. 'Whatever's the matter, Miss Burk?'

'Woolworths!' she cried, breathlessly.

Alfred bound over to the window and looked across the street at a gathering of half-a-dozen people around the entrance to the shop, expecting to see it engulfed in flames. 'Woolworths? What's happened?'

'Mr Colby, the assistant manager, went to open up just now and found a baby!' Miss Burk declared with great histrionics. 'A *baby*, of all things!' She joined him in staring out of the window. 'It was found in a shoebox in a bag.'

As Alfred watched the commotion opposite, a sudden realisation dawned on him. When he had last seen Rosie Hart at the court case, she had quite a bump; and the baby, he reasoned, would have been due at any point now. Would she have done this? Just dumped it opposite his shop? Then he remembered what that detective woman had told him, that she had wanted to speak with Rosie about an abandoned baby in Haywards Heath two years ago. The clustering certainty of his suspicions took his breath away. 'I need to sit down,' he muttered, hurrying to the backroom and slumping down at the table.

'Are you alright, Mr Farrier?' Miss Burk asked. 'You've gone ever so pale. Let me finish getting us that tea.'

'Is the baby…is it…alive?' he managed to say, despite his throat's feeling swollen.

'I think so, yes,' she said, pouring the kettle into the waiting teapot. 'Poor little mite. Who'd *ever* do such a wicked thing, I ask you?'

A cold heartless and evil floozy, Alfred wanted to say. Instead, he murmured his agreement.

'Here you go, Mr Farrier,' she said, placing a strong tea down in front of him.

'Thank you,' he replied, barely audibly as his right hand attempted to lift the cup but without betraying his shaking. Miss Burk noticed, however, and Alfred rushed up his left hand to assist the other in clasping the cup, still spilling some of the contents over the side.

'It really has affected you, hasn't it?' she asked. 'Perhaps you ought to go off home for a little lie-down?'

He shook his head. 'I'll be right as rain after this tea.'

'It's the sort of terrible thing you hear about happening in London, not somewhere like *Sevenoaks* for pity's sake; it just doesn't bear thinking about, does it?'

Alfred sipped more drink, then asked, 'Was there any clue about who might have left it there? Or why?'

Miss Burk shrugged. 'Oh, I really didn't like to pry. Mr Colby said that they'd taken the baby into the shop to keep it safe and warm until the ambulance arrived.'

'Was it a boy or a girl, do you know?'

'I'm not sure anyone had looked, actually, truth be told.'

They sat in a thoughtful silence, drinking their tea. Once he had finished, Alfred stood up, feeling fractionally restored. 'I'm just going to go and see if they need anything,' he said, heading through the shop.

An ambulance was now parked outside of Woolworths, but the previous gathering of people had gone. Alfred crossed over the road and entered the shop. He knew that Mr Colby's office was on the far side of the store, but even without that knowledge, the sound of animated voices would have guided him to the correct place.

Alfred found the small office veritably rammed with people, some of whom he recognised as being other local shopkeepers. The town policeman, PC Jolly, was standing beside the ambulance driver, his attention, like the rest of the people there, focussed on something— presumably the baby—on Mr Colby's desk.

'Mr Farrier,' Mr Colby said with a nod of his head. 'You've heard, then?'

PC Jolly spun around and glared at him. 'Ah! Mr Farrier! Do you know anything about this?' he asked, pointing at the Clark's shoebox on the desk.

'Er...' Alfred stammered. 'Why would I?'

'Because your shop has a direct line of vision to where this little waif was found,' he clarified.

Alfred inwardly sighed. 'I see. No, I was out in the backroom. I didn't know anything about it until Miss Burk arrived. Is it okay?'

'It should be,' PC Jolly answered. 'No thanks to the person or people who dumped her here.'

'Her?' Alfred repeated, craning his neck over to get a better look.

'It's a girl,' Mr Colby said.

Despite everything, the baby seemed quite content to Alfred. She was wrapped in a white woollen blanket and gazing up at the strip lights overhead, oblivious to the crowd of people mustered around her. Alfred stared at her, all the while thinking that he could see more than a passing resemblance to little Morton. No, it was his mind playing tricks on him; at that age pretty well all babies looked the same.

'Nothing with her? No note or anything?' Alfred asked casually.

PC Jolly shook his head.

'I just don't know why *here* of all places,' Mr Colby said, igniting a conversation of incredulity from the assembled onlookers. 'I don't know what this will do for trade, really I don't.'

Alfred quietly backed out of the office, through the store and out onto the High Street, where he found himself gasping for air. He leant on the side of the ambulance to get himself together and gather his thoughts. The scheming minx had left nothing attributable to him with the little girl, thank goodness. She had done it to make a point; letting him know that she was still looming in the shadows. Even though the dates vaguely matched up, he didn't really believe that he was the father of that little girl lying in a shoe box on Mr Colby's desk in Woolworths. It was all too ridiculous to even contemplate.

He took in a long breath and then crossed the street to his shop, finding Miss Burk gazing out of the front window. 'I think I *will* go home and have that lie-down, Miss Burk. Can you hold the fort, here?'

'Absolutely,' she said. 'You really have come over all queer, haven't you?'

He nodded gravely.

'The baby will be okay, won't it?' she asked.

'I think so, yes,' he mumbled, walking through to collect his trilby hat and briefcase. 'Thank you, Miss Burk,' he said, leaving the shop, bound for home.

'For God's sake,' Alfred muttered on hearing the typewriter as he stepped into his house, clattering nineteen to the dozen in the kitchen. He kicked off his shoes, hung his hat on the stand and then marched towards the dreadful racket. 'Stop,' he barked.

Margaret jumped with fright. 'Oh!' She raised a hand to her chest and exhaled. 'You scared the living daylights out of me. I wasn't expecting you back until tonight.'

'Well, I'm home now,' he replied. 'I don't feel well, and the last thing I want to hear is *that* blasted thing thundering through the house,' he said gesturing to the typewriter.

'Can I just finish the letter of application I'm writing for a job—?'

'No, you cannot,' he snapped. 'I'm going for a lie-down, and I'll not suffer being disturbed.'

Alfred climbed the stairs, realising how harsh he had just been with her. This morning's event had undoubtedly put him under a heavy cloud, but he was also finding more and more of late that, with regard to Margaret, his default position was one of agitation and general intolerance.

Closing his bedroom door, he loosened his tie and collapsed onto the bed.

When it came to Margaret, he couldn't help himself or his heated outbursts. He shut his eyes and tried to find a way to unravel the knotted ball of emotions and reveal the reasons behind his behaviour towards her. The most complicated, and that which was central to all of the other errant threads, was fundamentally that she reminded him of Anna; an unavoidable fact that only grew and matured in tandem with her own growth and maturity. The commonality between them—both physically and in their personalities—was cruel, for another part of his subconscious mind also could not help but attribute his wife's death in childbirth to Margaret. On a daily basis he was reminded of Anna's death by a person who ostensibly acted and looked exactly as she had done. Woven into these profound psychological strands was also the simple fact that he didn't want her to get a job and leave their home; he wouldn't manage living alone. Margaret did all the household chores that Anna would have done, which brought him full circle back to resenting the fact that she had lived on when Anna had not.

Alfred's complicated thoughts began to fray at the edges as sleep lured him in. Once again, he had not found a solution or a way through to disentanglement. He was pushing Margaret away and there seemed to be nothing that he could do to stop it.

The following morning, Alfred was standing behind the till in the

Sevenoaks branch of Farrier's Fashion, gazing out of the window across to Woolworths, directly opposite. There was now no sign of the considerable commotion that had been created yesterday by the discovery of the baby in the shop doorway. In fact, his expectation that it would be the talk of the town until more interesting gossip came to the fore had been unfounded. He had passed Mr Colby, the assistant manager at Woolworths, on his way in to work this morning and he had greeted Alfred with a comment about the warm weather and wished him a good day. He had made no mention at all of the child. When Miss Burk had arrived first thing, and she and Alfred had sat down together for their early cup of tea, she hadn't mentioned the baby either. Of course, that could simply have been her attempt to avoid upsetting him again, as she had seen how it had, yesterday. It seemed as though everyone had forgotten the news. But not so for Alfred. The little girl's face was indelibly imprinted on his dreams last night. He had woken in a cold sweat, having dreamed that PC Jolly had, then and there, named him as the father and handed the girl over to him. He had fed her, soothed her and had done something that he had never had to do before in real life: changed her nappy. When he'd fallen back to sleep, the dream evolved into one in which Peter and Maureen raised her as Morton's little sister. Then he had seen Anna, clear as day, repeatedly demanding, 'What have you done, Alfred? *What have you done?*'

'Miss Burk,' he suddenly said.

She glanced up from where she was hanging some new patterned shirts that had just arrived from the continent. 'Yes, Mr Farrier?'

'Could you hold the fort for an hour or two? I've got a few errands to run,' he said.

'Certainly,' she replied with a smile.

'Thank you,' he said, collecting his trilby and leaving the shop. He took a long hard look at the entrance doors to Woolworths, though quite what he was expecting to see, he wasn't sure.

Alfred strode purposefully up the High Street, the shops on either side gradually petering out, being replaced by the treelined Dartford Road. On his left, he passed the memorial of a life-sized soldier, the colour of the Statue of Liberty, standing atop a white stone plinth upon which were engraved the names of the town's war dead. Alfred kept walking, thinking how close his own name had come to being added to the small memorial in the village of Westbere from where he had embarked on his service in the Second World War. Death had come so very close to him on several occasions. Fate's revenge for cheating death, he considered, had been the mess that his post-war life had become. What next? he wondered.

Twenty-five minutes after leaving his shop, Alfred arrived at Sevenoaks Hospital. He didn't know what coming here would achieve, but, once the idea had entered his mind this morning, he had felt compelled to come. He had always thought that the building appeared confused, the original structure from the 1860s being hidden among a great succession of oblong brick additions that protruded from almost every aspect of the original building, as though the need for a new extension each time outweighed any architectural or aesthetic considerations. He entered the lobby and made his way over to the reception desk where a young lady with long black hair and excessive make-up was sitting, monitoring his arrival. She feigned a smile.

'Hello,' he said amiably, removing his hat. 'I've come to visit a girl—a baby—who was brought in yesterday morning.'

'What's the name?' the lady asked, picking up a clipboard in readiness.

'I'm not sure,' he answered. 'She hasn't been named as yet.'

She nodded and ran a bright-red fingernail down the list of names in front of her. 'Baby Wooly?'

'That will be her,' he said.

'Yeah, we don't have a maternity unit here, so she's just up on the regular female ward. But you will need to be a relative to see her. Are you the grandfather?'

'Er, yes. That's right,' he lied.

'Okay, it's the Stanhope ward,' she said, gesturing to the signage dangling above her head.

Alfred thanked her and followed the signs to the ward, the stench of disinfectant increasing as he progressed further through the hospital. At the nurses' station inside the double-doors he smiled and said, 'Hello, I'm the grandfather of Baby Wooly. May I see her, please?'

The nurse appeared slightly taken aback but then stood up and said, 'Of course. Follow me.'

'How is she?' Alfred asked, following her into the ward containing a dozen beds, half of which were occupied by adult women. Incongruous to the rest of the ward was the little cot standing where a bed should have been, and to where the nurse was leading him. 'Good. All things considered.'

They reached the cot and Alfred leant over. She was sleeping soundly. Again, he was reminded of the strong resemblance to little Morton. 'What will happen to her?' he asked.

The nurse frowned and Alfred detected a change in her demeanour. 'You're her grandparent, correct?'

Alfred nodded, knowing that he had been rumbled. It was time to leave. He smiled. 'Thank you so much for letting me see her. I'll be off now.'

'Here, wait a minute,' the nurse said, reaching for his elbow. 'Is your child a birth parent of this baby?'

He shook his head. 'No, but I really must be going.'

'Wait!' the nurse called as he marched briskly down the ward. 'Matron!' she shouted. 'Matron!'

Alfred reached the end of the ward and was within a few feet of the exit doors when his way was abruptly blocked by a middle-aged nurse—Matron, he assumed—with a sour scowl on her face.

'He said he was the baby's grandfather!' the nurse called.

'I'm not,' Alfred said to the Matron. 'I was nearby yesterday when it was found, and I just wanted to check that she was doing okay...and I knew I wouldn't be allowed unless I said that I was some relation or other. I can assure you, Matron, that I am *not* that baby's grandfather.' He placed his trilby on his head and began to move past her. 'Good day.'

'What's your name?' the Matron demanded.

'Mr Colby,' he replied, without turning back.

He walked as fast as he could towards the exit, hoping to goodness that there were no security guards employed at the hospital. He left the building without being accosted further and emitted a huge sigh of relief as he considered what a stupid thing it had been that he had just done. But one other thing that this visit had achieved was to knock his preceding conviction severely that the child could not be his.

138

Chapter Sixteen

20th December 2019, Haywards Heath

Morton arrived at Lowfield Road and pulled up outside a neat little detached bungalow with two windows either side of a maroon front door. Beside a short driveway was a trimmed lawn bordered with well-kept shrubbery. With his bag slung over his shoulder, he got out of the car and headed up the drive, noticing that the windowsill in one of the rooms facing the street was lined with Christmas cards. He rang the doorbell and a moment or two later there was a blur of brightly coloured movement behind the obscure glass. The door opened and an older lady, wearing a red cardigan and purple trousers, smiled. 'Morton?'

He nodded. 'Hi there. Thank you for seeing me.'

The door widened and Kathy beckoned him inside. 'Come through. Come through,' she said. 'Though I'm not too sure I'll be of much use to you.'

'Well, anything you can tell me about Rosie Hart would be great,' he replied, following her into a warm lounge.

'Do you know, I've said that very same phrase, oh, at least a hundred times over my career. Anything to drink before we start that line of interrogation?' she asked with a grin. 'I'm having a coffee.'

'A coffee would be just lovely, thank you,' he answered. 'Milk, no sugar.'

'Make yourself comfortable,' she said, pointing at an old-fashioned, navy, velvet sofa.

Morton sat down and took out his notepad and pen. The pad was open to the page headed ROSIE HART AFTER 1980?? that was still resolutely blank. His trawling of the multitude of records suggested by all of the genealogy websites to which he subscribed amounted to very little tangible evidence, even once he had filtered down the results to the UK only. He was placing an awful lot of hope on Kathy Steadman having some answers for him.

He leant back in the chair and looked around. Aside from the sofa on which he was sitting, there were two matching armchairs, a small television, three bookcases and a dresser. In one corner, beside the window, was a cage containing a bright-green and yellow budgerigar with its eyes closed, balancing on one leg. Show off, Morton thought, casting his eyes to the windowsill and noticing with horror that the cards on display were not related to Christmas—in fact, now that he thought about it, there was nothing festive in the room at all—they were sympathy cards.

When Kathy returned carrying two mugs of coffee, Morton didn't know whether to offer his own condolences for the loss of a person whom he knew nothing about. Spouse? Child? Parent? Sibling?

'Here you go,' she said, placing a mug down onto a coffee table beside him.

'Thank you,' he responded, deciding not to mention the possible elephant in the room. He took her in more fully, estimating her to be in her mid-eighties and appearing in good health with a kind, grandmotherly demeanour. She had shoulder-length white hair and a subtle hint of make-up around her eyes.

She sank down into one of the armchairs with a suffering sigh and held her mug between both hands as she looked at him. 'So, you're trying to find Rosie Hart because you think she might be the mother of three women that she abandoned when they were babies—have I got that much right?'

'Yes, that's correct,' Morton confirmed.

'But how do you know that Rosie Hart *was* their mother?'

'DNA,' he answered.

Kathy's face showed uncertainty. 'It's all come on a long way since my day. We hadn't even really heard of DNA back when I was trying to catch her.' She tutted. 'I can't pretend I fully understand how it all works. But you're sure she was definitely their mother?'

'Yes, undoubtedly.'

'I know you've come to ask me questions, but I'm fascinated. Where did she leave the poor young ones?'

'The first—that I know about, at least—was my half-aunt, Vanessa. She was found outside Woolworths on Sevenoaks High Street in 1975—opposite my grandfather's shop, Farrier's Fashion. Then there was—'

'That's it!' Kathy interjected, punching the air. 'I knew I knew the name, Alfred Farrier. So, *Rosie Hart* left a baby opposite his shop in 1975?' she clarified.

'Yes,' Morton said. 'My grandfather was the baby's father.'

'Well, I never did. I interviewed your grandfather. Went to his home in Dover—or Folkestone, I'm thinking it might have been—to speak to him.'

'Yes, it would have been Folkestone,' he confirmed. 'What did you need to speak with him about? Did you think that Baby Bradley was his?'

'Oh, no. Not at all. It was about where I could find that wretched Rosie. I rushed over to a court hearing in Sevenoaks where she was standing accused of damaging your grandfather's shop. I got there too late and thought perhaps your grandfather might know where she was. So, I went to his house to ask him. He claimed not to know.'

'Did he tell you anything at all?' Morton asked, making notes on his pad.

Kathy shook her head vehemently. 'I can't recall the details now, but I remember coming away none the wiser. I seem to think that he pretended like he'd never known her. But you're saying that he fathered a child with her?'

'That's right, yes,' Morton said. 'And what happened after you saw my grandfather—with regard to the investigation into Rosie, I mean?'

'Nothing. We had no new leads, no idea where she was, and my boss, DI Redmond, put a complete stop on me putting any more time into the case.' Kathy shrugged and went to sip her coffee, but then lowered it again and asked, 'And she did it the *twice* more, you say? Sorry, we've gone off-track.'

'Yes, the next time was 1977 in Croydon, and then 1979 in Manchester.'

'It really beggars belief, doesn't it?' she said.

'Well, she certainly does seem to have made a habit of it,' Morton agreed. 'So, could you tell me about the Baby Bradley case? How did you know that Rosie was the mother?'

'Old-fashioned detective work gave us some good leads, but then the conclusive proof was her fingerprints on a bottle of milk that was found with the baby.'

'But did you never find her?'

'No, she found me,' Kathy said rather ominously.

'Before we come to that part,' he began, 'did you ever have any inkling about who the father of Baby Bradley might have been?'

'No idea at all,' she said. 'Remember these were the days before DNA. We really only had blood groups and the mother's word. I take it that you think your grandfather could be in the frame, then?'

'No, I don't actually,' he replied. 'Well, of course it's *possible*, but I have this unproven theory that she left the babies somewhere close to where the father lived or worked. Do you recall what would have been opposite the Seeboard showroom in Haywards Heath at the time?'

Kathy's eyes widened as she exhaled. 'Goodness. I think just shops with flats above, actually. I've no idea, now, which shops they were. Sorry.'

Morton made a note to try and establish which shops had been there and who might have been living in the flats above at the time. 'So, you said that Rosie found *you*, rather than the other way around,' he said. 'I take it that's…well…you know…the attempted murder in 1980?'

'Yes, that's right,' she muttered solemnly. A short silence was broken by a startling, elaborate chorus from the budgie in the corner, which had apparently woken from its one-legged slumber. Kathy set down her mug of coffee, and said, 'Sorry. He'll be wanting his treat,' she said, ambling over to his cage. She bent down and took a single strip of millet from the cupboard below. 'Here you go, Isaac Jones,' she said, pegging it up above his perch.

'Isaac Jones?' Morton queried, finding it an odd name for a budgie.

'My sister bought him for me last week; she thought I needed the company after Simon, my partner, died. God knows why she thought a budgie might help. I suppose he has…in some strange, small way.'

'Sorry to hear that,' Morton said, glancing again at the sympathy cards.

'Thank you. I met him back in 1975; we were training together— actually, he was with me when I raced off up to Sevenoaks Court in search of you-know-who.' She smiled at the memory. 'Dragged him off with me without giving him a choice, poor fellow. Still, there we are,' she said, sitting back down and drinking more of her drink. 'Where was I, now?'

'The attempted murder,' Morton reminded her, his pen poised in preparation.

Chapter Seventeen

14th November 1980, Haywards Heath, West Sussex

'Wow, this is a treat,' Kathy said, sitting at the dining room table and looking hungrily at the roast dinner in front of her.

'It's a treat to have you home for Sunday lunch,' Simon replied. 'Wine?'

Kathy grimaced. 'I'd better not. Save me a glass for this evening, though.'

'Well, tuck in,' he said, 'You've only got an hour.'

Kathy picked up her cutlery, needing no further encouragement, and began to devour the food. Simon was an excellent cook and Kathy had been more than happy to relinquish the role of head chef when he had moved in over four years ago. Having resigned herself to a life dominated by her career, it had come as quite a surprise to find how quickly she had taken to living as one half of a very happy couple. When the inevitable questions came about their living together unmarried, they would both laugh and chorus in unison, 'We're just not the marrying sort.'

'I'm going to tackle that laurel in the back corner of the garden later,' Simon said. 'If you don't mind, that is...'

Kathy scowled at him. 'It's your house, too,' she said, parroting herself for the umpteenth time. 'Dig it out completely if you like; it's going wild down there. Lovely beef.'

'Not bad,' he agreed, cutting into the tender meat.

'I was going to suggest that—' Kathy began. She cut herself short, as the telephone began to ring in the hallway. She groaned.

'I'll go,' Simon said, finishing his mouthful as he stood up, and hurried into the hallway. 'Four three one, one double seven... Yes, one moment. Kathy?'

Kathy closed her eyes and slumped forwards, the warm calmness that she had been feeling moments before quickly cooling; she knew that it had to be work on the telephone. She rose from her chair and hurried into the hallway, where Simon had his hand held over the mouthpiece.

'The station,' he whispered.

Kathy rolled her eyes and took the telephone from him. 'WDS

Steadman.'

'We've had a call from a member of the public about a young lady acting suspiciously with a red and white bag out of which they believed they heard a baby crying.'

'What?' Kathy stammered. 'Give me the details—quickly.'

'The call's just come in. She was spotted entering the churchyard of All Saints in Lindfield.'

'Lindfield?' she questioned.

'Correct.'

'I can be there in five minutes,' Kathy replied, slamming down the phone and running for the front door. 'Save my dinner,' she shouted down the hallway. 'And the wine.'

She jumped into the CID Ford Escort, started the engine, and sped towards Lindfield, her heart racing at the possibility of catching Rosie Hart in the act of another abandonment. Lindfield was technically its own village but the gradual north-easterly expansion of Haywards Heath had all but obliterated the boundary lines.

It being a Sunday afternoon, the traffic was mercifully light, and Kathy had reached Lindfield in under five minutes. All Saints Church was on the far side of the village, being among the last few properties before the long swathes of fields, forests and farmland of the High Weald.

She drove past the small quaint shops and rows of historic houses on the High Street as the grey church spire came into view on the right-hand side. The low stone wall that encompassed the church directly bordered the carriageway and, as far as she could recall, there was no car park. Kathy swung the Escort onto the red stone pavement that terminated at the pathway to the church and leapt out of the car, not bothering to lock it. She pelted into the churchyard at full speed, scanning left and right as she ran towards the vestibule. The door to the church was shut, so Kathy slowed her pace and followed the brick path that wound its way around the building, through shrubs and ancient graves.

'Damn it,' Kathy muttered, sensing that she was once again too late. She reduced her pace to a fast walk, nearing the back of the church. Then, she spotted her. A female figure wearing a black leather jacket—carrying a red and white chequered bag identical to that in which Baby Bradley had been found—was standing in the far corner of the churchyard, with her back to her.

Kathy strode calmly past a row of oblong tombs, then left the path, cutting diagonally towards Rosie who placed the bag down and turned.

At last, they came face to face.

Kathy held up her warrant card and said, 'WDS Steadman, Sussex Police. You are not obliged to say anything unless you wish to do so, but what you say may be put in writing and given in evidence; Rosie Hart, I am arresting you for the abandonment of a child.' She had waited a very long time to say that and she couldn't help but smile.

A wide grin spread across Rosie's face; her striking ambivalence startled Kathy. It was almost as if she had been anticipating her arrival. 'This baby?' Rosie asked, picking up the bag. She tipped it fully upside-down, and Kathy lunged forwards in horror only to watch a naked doll tumble out onto the grass.

Rosie laughed loudly and Kathy knew that she had been set up.

She heard movement from behind her and whirled around to see Steve and Frank Hart walking towards her. The seriousness of her situation quickly became apparent as she caught sight of the baseball bat that Steve was holding by his side, just as Frank opened out a flick-knife.

'And, so, we meet again,' Frank said.

'Nice to see you again, WDS Steadman,' Steve added with a laugh. 'Seems you've got a bit of a thing for our family. We're honoured; we really are. Your first time meeting our Rosie, though.'

Kathy stepped backwards away from the two brothers and went to turn around.

Suddenly, a searing, unbearable pain shot through her head from the back of her skull, sending her plummeting forwards onto a horizontal gravestone and into unconsciousness.

Chapter Eighteen

20th November 1980, Folkestone, Kent

'For goodness' sake,' Alfred yelled. He was peering under the bonnet of his Austin Mini, as if the reason why the car was refusing to start might suddenly present itself.

'Having trouble, Mr Farrier?'

Alfred raised his head and saw his neighbour, Mr Dyche, looking in his direction. Alfred wiped his hands on a rag, and answered, 'Ruddy heap's refusing to turn over.'

'Hmm,' Mr Dyche said, strolling towards him, his hands slung in his pockets. He stood beside Alfred and peered under the bonnet, returning his glasses to the bridge of his nose. 'Have you tried the distributor cap? We've had a lot of rain lately and it might have got damp in it—that's what used to happen with my little Millie.'

'No, I haven't,' Alfred admitted, leaning in and unfastening the cap. He ran the rag around the inside and then replaced it.

'Isn't it time you upgraded your old motor?' Mr Dyche asked. 'You'd get a decent price for this little one, what with the way you've looked after it. You want to get yourself something like that.' He angled his body towards the shiny new W-reg Vauxhall Astra parked on his drive.

Alfred ignored the gloating and walked around to the open driver's door. He had been toying with the idea of trading in his Mini for some time now; years, actually. The issue was financial. Although he had the money in reserve for this very purpose, he couldn't bring himself to go through with the purchase, just in case, as had happened two years ago, Rosie Hart showed up again to demand more money from him.

'Go on, then,' Mr Dyche called. 'Turn her over.'

Alfred turned the key in the ignition, pulled out the choke and, after a throaty start, the Mini fired up.

'There you go!' Mr Dyche yelled triumphantly. 'I thought that would be the trouble.'

Alfred climbed out of the car and thanked his neighbour as he shut the bonnet.

'So, how's your Margaret getting on?' Mr Dyche asked him.

Alfred offered a thin smile. 'Oh, very well, thank you.'

'Good. Good,' Mr Dyche muttered.

'Anyway. Must dash,' Alfred said, hurrying as quickly as he could back to the driver's side. 'Thanks for the advice. Much obliged.'

'You're welcome,' Mr Dyche said, quickly adding, 'Irene and I do miss our regular coffee mornings, you know.'

'Yes, we must do them again soon,' Alfred agreed, slamming his door. He had not had any social visitors inside the house since Margaret had upped and left, and he wasn't about to change that policy anytime soon. He began to pull off from the drive but, just before he reached the road, a Ford Escort drew up in front of him. Alfred stopped the Mini, applied the handbrake, and then switched off the engine. He acknowledged the man behind the wheel of the Escort with a nod of his head and got out of the car.

'Well, now, that was a jolly short trip!' Mr Dyche joked from his doorstep.

Alfred smiled. 'Visitors,' he answered, watching as the man stepped out of the vehicle and walked towards him. 'Hello!' Alfred greeted cheerfully, more for Mr Dyche's benefit—who was continuing to observe proceedings—than for any genuine sentiment towards the fellow heading up his drive. Despite the warm weather, the man was wearing a long dark mackintosh with the collar turned upwards and a trilby hat pulled down to shield his dark eyes. 'Do come in!' Alfred continued in a sprightly tone as he led the way up to the house and unlocked the front door, issuing a final farewell nod to Mr Dyche's curious gaze.

The visitor closed the front door behind him and removed his hat, thereby revealing his concrete-coloured hair.

'Come through,' Alfred encouraged, pointing at the open lounge door. The man walked in and sat in the same armchair in which he had sat on his first visit here just over one month ago. He had arrived in a cloak-and-dagger fashion, much like today, refusing to reveal his identity. During his short visit, he had given very little away about himself, except to say that Rosie Hart was a 'mutual dilemma' for them both and for which dilemma he claimed to have conceived of a solution. In the days since his visit, Alfred had taken this oblique reference to mean that the tall shifty-looking man, now sitting opposite him, had had similar involvements with the girl as had he.

'It's done,' the man said, giving Alfred a hard stare.

'Detective Steadman?' Alfred questioned quietly.

'Yes,' he confirmed. 'She's taken care of.'

Alfred's breath caught in his throat. It was one thing to have spoken about it in abstract but to hear that the officer, who had sat exactly where the man was now sitting, had been 'taken care of'—a brutal euphemism that he did not care to unpick—made him feel nauseous. He looked up at the man, wondering why he had returned; he had made it clear that his first visit would also be his last…unless a problem arose.

'You needn't worry. I'll keep to our agreement,' Alfred confirmed gruffly. The man had said that he would deal with Detective Steadman and the girl, and all Alfred would need to do would be to provide him with an alibi, should the necessity arise.

'That's not why I'm here,' he replied. 'She knows.'

'Who she? Knows what?' Alfred asked.

'Rosie Hart has somehow gotten wind of our plan.'

'What? How on earth did *that* happen?' Alfred stammered. '*I* certainly haven't breathed a single word to anybody.'

'And neither have I,' the man retorted sharply, appearing to resent the insinuation.

'How, then?'

'It's not just us,' the man revealed. 'There are other men in our predicament. And now she knows of our plan, she's after revenge…as well as money.'

'My God,' Alfred stammered. 'What's she doing?'

'Blackmailing, lying, extorting, using violence. *Extreme* violence… I think she might even have killed someone.'

'What?' he demanded, leaping to his feet.

'Calm down. I don't know it for certain. He fell and drowned, so it could just have been an accident.'

'Well, the sooner you enact the second part of the plan, the better,' Alfred snapped.

'It's all in hand, but…'

'But what?'

'I don't know where she is. That's why I'm here; to warn you.'

Alfred's head sank into his hands. After a few seconds, he looked up. 'So, she could be out there, somewhere, intent now not only on financial gain but also wanting some sort of revenge? Well, that's just marvellous, isn't it? What in God's name is she doing with all the money?'

'Drugs, from what I can gather,' the man answered flatly.

Alfred sighed deeply. 'What exactly would you advise that I do about there being a psychotic, drug-addicted whore bent on revenge somewhere out there?'

Bizarrely, the man found what he had said amusing. 'Lie low, whilst I track her down.'

'Hmm,' Alfred mumbled. 'Well, actually, I'm going away next week and won't even be in the country for some time.'

'There you are, then,' the man said, rising from his chair with some haste and making for the door. He pulled his coat on, tugged his hat down over his eyes and opened the front door. 'You need to get yourself a cleaner,' he commented, drawing his left shoe back and forth over a small clump of dirt on the carpet.

'Will I see you again?' Alfred asked, disregarding his comment.

The man turned to him and said, 'Let's hope not,' and then hurried away from the house.

Alfred closed the door and stood fixed to the spot as the man's words replayed through his mind. Rosie Hart was out there, somewhere, intent on revenge and extorting more money. The decision not to upgrade his car had been the correct one. He clenched his jaw, desperately hoping that the man would quickly locate her and obliterate her from his life. He felt none of the detached concern for Rosie that he had felt for Detective Steadman and whatever had befallen her. Not for the first time, he found himself wishing upon Rosie some of the types of barbarity and inhumanity that he had suffered during the dark days of his internment in Singapore and Thailand. The spot of dirt on the carpet at which he was staring gradually softened into a watery blur at the same time as his thoughts crystallised and he could, for the first time, see a linear progression from the shell of a man who had returned to England in October 1945 to the person that he was today.

Alfred took out his handkerchief, wiped his eyes and blew his nose, mentally repackaging and stowing the past, and returned himself to the present time: to the filthy and untidy house; to the list of jobs that needed seeing to before his trip overseas next week; to his worries over Rosie Hart's location and nefarious intentions.

He looked around him, not knowing where to begin with the housework. He had been living alone for four years now, after Margaret had abandoned him. The bitterness of her departure still hung in the air, evidenced not only in the state of the house but in his own deteriorating health. He had not cooked himself a single hot dinner in all that time, living on a bland diet supplemented by the occasional pub meal.

A cup of tea, that was what he needed to freshen his thoughts. He shuffled into the kitchen and set the kettle to boil as he wondered how Margaret was getting on. Everything that he knew about her life over the past four years had been second-hand information, passed on to him by his son, Peter, or his half-brother, Alex; nothing at all from Margaret herself. If he were brutally honest, he couldn't blame her for leaving. He had seen it coming, like a head-on car crash in slow-motion of which he had had plenty of time to steer clear, to forge a new, safer path. But he just hadn't been able to take it. Letters had arrived from America from the boy who had put Margaret in the family way. Alfred had snatched them up each time, of course, and had never shown them to Margaret; yet, he had treated her as though she had been blameable for their arrival. Then there had been her reaction to the invitations that he had been regularly extending to Peter, Maureen and little Morton. Perhaps, he now considered, it had been foolish of him to have expected her to prepare the house and dinner for their visits and to join in the pretence, playing the part of Morton's doting aunt.

Alfred poured the hot water into the teapot, fully immersed in the recent past. He remembered the blasted letters arriving addressed to Margaret and postmarked in Cornwall, which he had blindly assumed innocuous, when, in fact, they had turned out to be the very thing that had established a new life for her down there: a job offer from a tearoom and an offer of engagement from a young man with whom she had been liaising during the periods where Alfred had banished her down there. It had been a maddening mess of his own making and, rather than apologise to her when he had discovered her duplicity, he had smashed her wretched typewriter on the kitchen floor and cast her out of the house at that very moment. He had not seen hide nor hair of her since.

He poured the stewed tea into a dirty teacup, added some on-the-turn milk, and then carried it into the lounge, where he stood behind the net curtains, gazing outside with anonymity. He spotted a young lady strolling past and, for the briefest of moments, was filled with cold dread that it was Rosie Hart. It wasn't her; but she *was* out there, somewhere, watching and waiting.

Staring absent-mindedly at his Mini, Alfred tried to imagine the day that he could stand here and look out of this very window without a concern, perhaps eyeing his new car. But Rosie Hart needed taking care of first, just like whatever had happened to Detective Steadman.

Chapter Nineteen

20th December 2019, Haywards Heath, West Sussex

'Rosie Hart standing in front of me, grinning like the proverbial cat, and her two brothers—armed—walking towards me from behind is the last thing I could remember,' Kathy said, releasing a heavy breath.

'How awful,' Morton said, lowering his coffee and meeting her gaze in a moment of concerned silence.

'Then I was repeatedly stabbed. My chest still looks like a flesh-coloured knife rack to this day,' she said with a wry smile. 'Lucky to be alive, I was told by the multiple doctors who performed the pneumonectomy.'

'What's that?' Morton asked, dreading the answer.

'Lung removal,' she said cheerfully. 'I've only got my right lung left; my left lung wasn't right.' Despite the subject matter, she grinned at a phrase she must have repeated dozens of times over the years.

'God,' Morton blurted out.

'Could have been worse,' she said. 'I've managed with one lung but don't think I would have fared so well with neither of them. I was probably saved because the Harts were stopped in the act by the vicar entering Lindfield church to get ready for a service. They chose a Sunday, thinking that it would be the quietest time of the week, but they hadn't checked or reckoned on the fact that the church might have been in use. On a Sunday!'

'Did they ever work out which of the Hart siblings actually stabbed you? You said that it was Frank holding the knife.'

'The two brothers never gave that information up in court, but the vicar testified that he saw Rosie standing over me with the knife in her hands,' Kathy answered. 'As reliable witnesses go, he was pretty trustworthy.'

'But she was never found?'

Kathy shook her head. 'We thought she must have gone abroad. If she'd stayed local, we'd have found her eventually, I'm sure of it.'

Morton made some notes on his pad. What he was hearing from Kathy Steadman painted yet more darkness onto Rosie Hart's character, all of which he would need to communicate to Vanessa, Billie and Liza. But, still, he had learned nothing about her whereabouts after the attack in November 1980. 'Was an alert not put out for her arrest at the airports and ports?'

'I don't think so,' Kathy said.

'Why's that?'

'Maybe I just wasn't important enough for that level of response,' she answered.

Another thing was bothering him, which he raised: 'Obviously luring you into the churchyard was a trap,' Morton began, 'but how did they know that *you* specifically would be the officer called out and that you'd go alone?'

Kathy raised her eyebrows and took a moment to answer. 'Unless it was a major incident, we would rarely send two officers out together on a Sunday because we only ran a skeleton staff. You have to remember that this wasn't central London, it was sleepy, leafy West Sussex where not much happened.' She smiled and then added, 'We were even allowed to go home for lunch on a Sunday as a special treat, which was exactly where I was when the call came in.'

'Would that have been common knowledge, though?' Morton pushed.

'There's another unanswered question,' she replied cryptically. 'Knowing that we ran a reduced service out of Burgess Hill on a Sunday was hardly a state secret and anyone with a bit of time on their hands could have worked it out. But precise shift patterns and my proximity to the church on that exact day? That would have taken some working out.'

'Inside help?' Morton wondered.

'No good comes of dwelling on it, though the thought has crossed my mind on and off over the years,' Kathy admitted. 'But I can't think who or why. The police officer in me can't find a motive or a suspect. The most likely scenario is simple, determined observation. They watch my house and the station for a couple of weeks and understand my movements.' She shrugged her shoulders. 'It wouldn't take a genius with a bit of patience to figure it all out.'

'But what about the timing? You were investigating her back in the mid-1970s and the attack was, what, 1980? And you had nothing to do with her in the intervening years?'

'Yes, you're right. And I don't have an answer for that, either,' she said.

'Odd,' he commented, writing more, and pausing while Isaac Jones sang a warbling melody that was at first pleasing but, when it failed to end, became an irritation.

Morton leant forward and raised his voice over the noise, 'Is there anything else you can remember that might help me to locate her now? Do you think her family might cooperate? The brothers or sister, perhaps?'

Right on cue, Isaac Jones stopped singing.

'You'll get nothing whatsoever from the family; thick as thieves they are. Obviously, after the attack, I couldn't go back to policing, so I haven't really kept tabs on them all, but I've got a feeling one of the brothers might have died in prison. God only knows about the rest of them.' Kathy drew in a breath and met Morton's eyes. 'As much as it doesn't give those three women closure, perhaps it's best not to find out more? Leave things as they are? I don't imagine for a second you're going to find a Damascene change of personality along the way and see some television-style emotional reunion between them all, I really don't.'

Morton nodded. The idea of reuniting Rosie with her three abandoned children was preposterous and one that hadn't entered his thinking previously about what would happen if he were to track her down. Perhaps Kathy was right, and it was better to close the case now; he had certainly conducted exhaustive research into what had happened to her. People disappear all the time after all, and God knows Rosie had very good reason to conceal her identity. To all intents and purposes, he had fulfilled the unwritten brief to identify Vanessa, Billie and Liza's birth mother.

He finished the last of his coffee. 'Well, thank you very much for taking the time to see me. I'll leave you in peace,' he said, rising from his chair.

'I hope it wasn't a wasted trip for you,' she said, standing up.

'No. Not at all. Thank you,' Morton said, actually feeling unsure if the trip *had* been a good use of what little time he had remaining before they went to Cornwall. He stowed his notepad and pen in his bag and made to leave. As he reached the front door, he turned and asked her, 'Is the telephone box still there?'

Kathy laughed. 'The one on The Broadway? You're a bit late if you're thinking of stopping by and collecting some DNA.'

Morton smiled. 'No. I just thought that, while I was in the area, I might go along and take some pictures to add to my file.'

'I'm pretty sure that, like most telephone boxes, it's long gone. Just like the Seeboard showroom itself,' she replied.

'What's there now, do you know?'

'After Seeboard left, it became an upmarket stationers' shop—the only place I could get a hold of multicoloured four-ring binders locally—then that closed down a few years ago and it's been empty and boarded up since. I think there are plans afoot to demolish it.'

'I might just take a look on my way home, before it gets knocked down. Thanks again. Goodbye,' he said, opening the front door.

'You can't miss it. It's on the corner of Church Road and The Broadway, almost opposite The Star pub. Good luck! Cheerio,' she said.

Morton walked quickly down the drive, a chilly wind eddying around him.

'Let me know if you find her!' Kathy called after him.

He turned and replied, 'Will do!'

'But don't give her my address, whatever you do!' Kathy added, making Morton turn and laugh.

Back inside his Mini, he started the engine, wondering what to do next. He typed *Church Road* into his SatNav. It was less than four minutes' drive away. He thought for a moment longer, then decided that, since he was so close, it would be stupid to ignore it and began the drive into Haywards Heath town centre.

He found the building with ease, but parking close to it was not so simple; it was perched on a complicated four-way junction and surrounded by double yellow lines. Turning past the building up Church Road, he continued a short distance and then tucked the car into a vacant parking bay on the right-hand side. He climbed out and walked back down to the corner, studying the ugly off-white edifice that had formerly been used as the Seeboard showroom as he went. It was three-storeys high and appeared to be one of those functional but aesthetically unappealing buildings which were thrown up in the 1950s and 1960s in response to post-war housing shortages.

He turned onto The Broadway and took a photograph of what

would have been the front of the Seeboard showroom, now covered in black hoarding. In front of it was an empty bus stop, but, as Kathy had said, there was no sign of a telephone box. He continued along the pavement until he spotted a perfect square of dark-grey tarmac, set unobtrusively against the much-lighter-grey pavement, close to the edge of the road. He stood within its invisible walls, gauging the square to be the perfect size for a telephone box. Morton was fairly confident that it had been here on this very spot forty-six years ago that Rosie Hart had left Baby Bradley in a red and white chequered bag.

Morton gazed around himself, taking photographs, and wondering who that abandoned infant might have become. Somewhere out there was a forty-six-year-old man who could be completely oblivious to the opening pages of his life's story.

Opposite him were three shops: a barber's, a newsagent's and an HSS Hire shop. Above the premises was a single storey that appeared from the household objects visible through the front-facing windows to be residential accommodation.

As he studied the buildings—mentally noting that the shops were numbered three, five and seven—he considered whether it might be worth taking a look at the electoral registers for 1973 to find out the names of the occupants, although he quickly realised that if the purported father had only been a worker in whatever shop had been running there at the time, then they would not appear in the registers at all.

Morton looked at his watch. Was it worth taking such a long shot? The electoral registers were held at West Sussex Record Office in Chichester, about an hour's drive in the *wrong* direction. In fact, Haywards Heath, where he was now standing, was pretty well half-way between his home and the archives.

It wasn't worth the long shot, he reasoned, beginning to walk back to his car.

He reached the Mini and climbed in, grateful to be out of the cold. Just as he started the engine, a thought occurred to him: he remembered that, during his research into the Duggan Case, he had needed to examine electoral registers for the West Sussex parish of Ardingly—about five miles away—and he was certain that there had been a boundary change around 1974 and, for the period prior to that, the electoral registers for this part of Mid-Sussex were actually held at *East* Sussex Record Office.

Taking out his mobile phone, Morton pulled up the website for the office, accessed *Research Guides* and scrolled down to *Guide to Electoral Registers*. He clicked the hyperlink and a 99-page Word document opened up. Thankfully, the mammoth file was arranged alphabetically by location. Morton read the relevant part for Haywards Heath.

Cuckfield Rural
1970-1974 Mid-Sussex [Then in West Sussex]
C/C 70/348

It confirmed that the registers were in fact held with East Sussex Record Office at The Keep in Falmer, just a few miles south of his current location. Now, that *was* worth the long-shot.

Morton programmed The Keep into his SatNav and then proceeded to drive the sixteen miles to the archive.

He parked outside the building which had been purpose-built back in 2013. He got out of his car, slung his bag over his shoulder and marched through the automatic double doors to the small reception area.

'Hi,' Morton said to the young receptionist. 'I haven't got an appointment, but I was wondering if you had any spaces in the Reference Room. It shouldn't really take me too long to find what I'm looking for.'

'Yep, we're very quiet, today,' she confirmed. 'You can choose where to sit; as long as it's not on somebody's lap, that is.'

Morton offered a polite chuckle, then entered the cloakroom area. He had had the strict rules rammed down his throat often enough to know that only his laptop, notepad and pencil were permitted in the archives, and those needed to be inside one of the transparent plastic bags hanging beside the lockers. Everything else, Morton stuffed inside locker number ten, and then he crossed the foyer into the Reading Room. Just inside was a cylindrical metal post, the top of which he tapped with his reader's card. A green LED light flashed up beside the glass door and he entered the Reference Room.

The spacious room, containing five long lines of continuous desk space, was deathly silent; the receptionist had been correct about it being quiet with only two researchers in the entire place.

Looking over at the help desk, Morton felt his soul being crushed under the glare of hell's chief archivist, Miss Deidre Latimer. She met his glower with one of her own and folded her arms to complete the picture of the hostile dragon that she was. He gave her a forced, false smile and muttered his greeting as he switched his attention to where he might sit. Ordinarily, it wouldn't have mattered where he positioned himself, but he couldn't stand the idea of sitting with his back to her. He chose a spot near to the tall, floor-to-ceiling bookshelves at the far side of the room and sat down, glancing back to see if she was watching him. She was. He didn't bother smiling this time. He had no real idea as to why she hated him so much, but her dislike of him went back as far as the early days of his research in the old former record office in Lewes. Only once—just after Grace's birth—had she shown a vague hint of her actually being human, when she had asked to see a photo of Grace and had managed to speak in full sentences to him without her usual unveiled sarcasm.

Morton opened his laptop and, rather than have to beg Miss Latimer for the WIFI password, used his mobile as a hotspot to access The Keep's website. Having logged in on his account, he copied the reference details into the search box, and then placed an order for the Cuckfield Rural electoral registers for 1973. The status of the order was given as *Waiting*, but Morton hoped, given how quiet the archive was, that the wait wouldn't be too long.

He took his pad from the polythene bag and read the notes that he had made at Kathy Steadman's house.

KS repeatedly stabbed. Chest 'like a flesh-coloured knife rack'. Vicar witnessed Rosie with knife over KS

He stared at those words, wondering yet again how he was going to tell the three women what a monster their mother had evidently been. He continued reading the notes.

KS presumed Rosie 'gone abroad'

Morton paused for a moment, staring blankly at the table in front of him. Owing to the size of the results list in his previous searches, he had concentrated his efforts in finding what had happened to Rosie after the attack in November 1980 to the UK. But what if she *had* absconded overseas? He closed his eyes for a moment, placed his elbows on the desk and his head in his hands, thinking. Where might she have gone? As he had discovered in his research into the Duggan Case, it was relatively easy to flee England for mainland Europe, undetected. A private plane to Le Touquet, or a boat taking an unofficial stop in Saint-Malo, and she could be gone forever, untraceable. From what he had learned about Rosie Hart, though, having access to a private plane or chartering a fancy boat trip didn't quite fit. If, as Kathy had said, an all-ports alert had not been put out for her, then she could just as easily have boarded a ferry or a plane and left without any official intervention. The thought of her possibly having friends or family abroad settled in his mind for a brief moment, and then, slapping him like a frying pan around the face, came the three women's ethnicity reports.

He hurriedly returned his focus to the laptop, noticing that the status of the electoral registers had switched to *In Transit*, which meant that they were on their way up from the basement holdings and would soon be in Miss Latimer's claws. He opened a fresh tab in his internet browser and logged in to access Vanessa Briggs's DNA. He clicked to view her Ethnicity Estimate, then brought up Kansas and Southern Nebraska Settlers from the Communities sub-group and read the general description.

You, and all the members of this community, are linked through shared ancestors. You probably have family who lived in this area for years—and may still do.

Morton stopped reading. '*You may still do…*' Might Rosie Hart have fled the country and returned to her US relatives? Was it such a stretch of possibilities to imagine that she might have gone to stay with her maternal grandparents or cousins out in the Midwest, at least temporarily while the heat died down after Kathy Steadman's attack?

'Mr Farrier?'

It was Miss Latimer, and the tone was sharp and reprimanding. He

159

looked over towards the help desk and saw that, in her hand, she was holding a blue ledger. 'I take it you want your document?' she called over, drawing the attention of the other two researchers.

He nodded, swallowed hard and walked over to the desk.

'I thought you might have been under some illusion that we offered waitress service, here,' Miss Latimer said, pulling a moue with her mouth and placing the register on the desk between them.

He never did have the right response in the moment. Should he meet her reply with his own sarcasm? Or play along, as though it were taken as a joke rather than as the passive-aggressive jibe that was so obviously intended? Or perhaps call her out on it and risk appearing pathetic? Instead, he laughed, picked up the blue book and replied using her Christian name, which was something he knew that she abhorred. 'Not at all, Deidre. I wasn't under some *illusion*; just busy working, was all.'

'Another undercover spy ring?' she derided. 'I noticed your name as a tiny footnote in the Alexei Yahontov and Maurice Duggan story.'

He was stuck for a quick repartee, so found himself thanking her as he walked away with the register.

'You did well not to get kidnapped again,' she called after him. 'Or poisoned by Russian spies.'

He ignored the comments, sat down at his desk, and then opened the book to the first page, learning that the register was arranged alphabetically by street name across the entire district. He flicked through until he reached The Broadway and began to methodically draw his index finger down the list of street numbers, until he found that for which he was searching.

Flat 3 (first floor)
JACOBSON, *Clive*
JACOBSON, *Clare*
PARKER, *James*
ABERDAM, *Aureliusz*

Flat 5 (first floor)
STEVENS, *Paul*
STEVENS, *Susan*

Flat 7 (first floor)
REDMOND, Derek

The list held more male names than Morton had been hoping to see. Then there were the unknown quantities of men who undoubtedly would have worked in the three shops below the flats, or even in the Seeboard showroom itself. He pulled out his mobile and, after taking a quick glance over at the help desk and seeing that Miss Latimer was engrossed in seemingly cordial conversation with someone else, quickly took a photograph of the page.

Even though the visit here had not provided him with anything which he could add to the case file, Morton was not overly disappointed, having known before he had even stepped through the doors that checking the electoral registers to add possible weight to an unproven theory was highly likely not to yield any results. Besides, he was now much more intrigued by the idea that Rosie Hart might have fled England for America. But time, he noticed, glancing at his laptop clock, was quickly running out; it would be better to call it a day now and get home for dinner with Juliette and Grace, and then try to do some more work, later tonight.

Morton closed the electoral register book, folded down his laptop, crammed his belongings inside the plastic bag and headed back over to the counter, grateful to see that Miss Latimer was still conversing with the other researcher. He cautiously placed the ledger onto the desk and stepped away.

Without even looking at him, Miss Latimer raised a hand and clicked her fingers at him, then said to the person in front of her, 'Would you excuse me for one moment? Do bear with me.' She looked at Morton and smiled. 'Could I see your copying pass, please?'

'I don't have one,' he replied.

'Oh,' she stammered. 'And yet...you took a photograph of that document,' she said, pointing to the electoral register.

'I took...*one* picture,' he said.

'Then you'll need to purchase a copying pass, won't you?'

'How much are they?' he asked, knowing fine well the answer.

'Fifteen pounds.'

'Fifteen pounds for *one* photograph? I'd rather delete it than pay that,' he retorted.

'If you could just do that in front of me, then, on this occasion, I will agree to forgo charging you for the copying pass...as a gesture of goodwill,' she said with another sickly-sweet smile.

Morton huffed as he withdrew his iPhone from his pocket, opened up his camera roll and showed Miss Latimer the useless photograph that he had taken. Then he hit the trashcan icon in the bottom corner and clicked *Delete Photo.* 'Happy?' he couldn't help but say.

'Ecstatic,' she replied.

'Now, there's a first,' he muttered as he strutted towards the exit with his head held high in indignation. He reached the doors without them opening for him and remembered at that moment that, for security reasons, the person on duty behind the desk had to push a button to release them. He huffed, taking in his own reflection in the glass and seeing Miss Latimer's amused facial expression behind him. He counted to three and then turned to face her. She feigned being engrossed in conversation once more. 'Deidre, I'd like to leave, please,' he called loudly.

Without looking at him, she pressed a button concealed below the desk and the doors opened.

'Merry Christmas,' he called back as he strutted towards the locker area, fuming. The photo was worthless to the case, but that was beside the point. The woman was infuriating. He went to his locker, shoved his things into his bag and hurried from the building. He climbed into his Mini and sighed deeply. Home time.

Morton entered the front door of his house, slightly startled. In the hallway in front of him, an eclectic abundance of Grace's toys was strewn about. To his left, in the lounge, the sofas had been shifted into the centre of the room and covered with blankets, duvets and throws, presumably in some attempt at creating a den. In the kitchen to his right, three suitcases were open on the floor and Grace, dressed as Olaf from *Frozen*, was busy removing the toys and clothes from the smallest case and tossing them onto the floor. Juliette was nowhere to be seen.

'Erm,' Morton began, moving into the kitchen. 'Should you be doing that, Gracie?'

Grace smiled. 'Help Mummy.'

For a moment, Morton panicked, his brain telling him that Juliette required his help. A multitude of horrific scenarios played out in the seconds before he heard her walking down the stairs. She entered the kitchen and threw her arms around him. 'Save me,' she whispered dramatically.

Morton laughed. 'From the packing, the daughter or the pregnancy?'

'All of the above. Just all of it,' she answered, clinging on to him for dear life.

'Sit down and I'll make you a drink,' he directed.

Juliette slumped down at the kitchen table, placing her hands on top of her belly. She spotted that Grace was busy unpacking her suitcase. 'Oh, darling, please don't do that. That's all in there to take to Aunty Margaret's house for Christmas. Go and play in your camp that we made.'

'Okay,' Grace said, taking a small pile of books out of the suitcase and tottering from the room with them.

'It's been like this all day: two steps forward, one step back, sometimes three...'

'I'm here to help. Just tell me what you need me to do,' Morton said. '*And...* I've found a boy's name I really like. I came across it in my research today.'

Juliette's head sank forwards as she emitted a lengthy groan. 'Oh, God. I'm not sure I can cope with another layer of absurdity right now,' she huffed.

'You haven't heard it yet,' Morton responded, slightly offended as he boiled the kettle.

'From your research? So, it's an historical name... Let me guess. Aethelred the Unready? Winston? Julius? Napoleon? Aristotle?'

'Very funny.'

'Go on, then. Hit me with it.'

'Isaac,' Morton said.

Juliette's mouth turned down in consideration as she nodded her head. 'I...like it, actually.'

'I *really* like it,' Morton said, withholding the unneeded information that they might well be about to name their child after a budgerigar.

'Isaac Farrier,' Juliette said. 'Yeah. Nice. But we still need a girl's name.'

'Yes. I haven't made any progress yet on that front,' Morton conceded.

'There's still time. All done with Vanessa's case?' she asked, sounding hopeful.

Morton shook his head and grimaced. 'I've got a *tiny* bit more to check,' he said, squashing an inch of air between his thumb and forefinger.

Juliette rolled her eyes. 'We're literally going to Cornwall, tomorrow morning. Are you going to be doing research on the drive down there, too?'

'Now, that's not a bad idea, actually,' he answered. 'I'll help you pack when Grace is in bed.'

'Thanks.'

'Then I'll do a bit more to get this case closed. I probably shouldn't have wasted today, visiting this detective who was trying to find Rosie in the early 1970s. I didn't really get much out of her. She was stabbed by Rosie and had to retire from the police force, plus her boss had already closed the case…'

Juliette was gazing at the dishevelled suitcases, not really listening or noticing that his sentence had trailed off.

'Kathy's boss…'

Morton rushed into the hallway, opened his bag and took out his pad, scanning down the pages of notes that he had made earlier today at Kathy's house. There it was.

KS boss, DI Redmond shut down search for Rosie

DI Redmond. He was pretty certain that a Redmond had been one of the occupants of the flats opposite the Seeboard showroom, but he could not now recall his first name. 'Damn it,' he said, cursing himself for having deleted the photograph that he had taken. Stupidly, he had not thought to jot down the information. He thought hard, trying to retrieve the man's Christian name, but it just would not come.

'Damn it!' Grace mimicked from the lounge. 'Damn it!'

Morton sighed. 'Don't say that, Grace.'

Juliette appeared in the kitchen doorway with a scowl on her face. 'Any reason our two-and-a-half-year-old daughter is swearing like a builder?'

'Sorry,' Morton said.

'What's the matter?'

'Short version: I didn't want to spend fifteen pounds on a copying pass at The Keep, so I took one photo on my mobile—just one— and then was made to delete it in front of the demon archivist.'

Juliette grinned and extended her hand. 'Phone.'

Morton obliged and placed his phone in her hand. 'I deleted it. She made me,' he repeated.

Juliette tapped the screen a few times and then handed it back with the photograph of the electoral registers open in front of him.

'How did you do that?'

'It was in your recently deleted folder.'

'Wow. Thanks very much. Morton Farrier, one. Deidre Latimer, nil. Ha,' he said.

'Er, no. *Juliette* Farrier, one. Deidre Latimer, nil,' she corrected.

'Fair enough,' he agreed, splaying his fingers across the screen and looking at the list of residents.

Flat 7 (first floor)
REDMOND, Derek

Morton immediately phoned Kathy Steadman.

'Hello?' she answered.

'Hi, Kathy. It's Morton Farrier again. Sorry to trouble you so soon. Are you free to talk?'

'Hi. Sure…'

'Great. I went to East Sussex Record Office after seeing you this morning and I looked at the electoral registers for the flats opposite where Baby Bradley was found. Can I ask what the first name of your boss, DI Redmond, was?'

Kathy cleared her throat and said, 'Yes, it was Derek. Derek Redmond.'

'Damn it!' Grace shouted from the lounge.

165

Chapter Twenty

19th December 1980, Haywards Heath, West Sussex

Tears welled in Kathy Steadman's eyes as she opened the passenger door, swung her legs around and stood up to face her little bungalow for the first time in more than six weeks.

'Wait!' Simon instructed her, rushing around from the driver's side and threading his arm solidly through Kathy's.

'Simon… I'm okay,' she tried to reassure him.

'You've had a lung removed, Kathy,' he retorted.

She shrugged. 'Well, we clearly don't *need* two of them.' She walked slowly towards her home, in truth very grateful for Simon's assistance and comforted to know that he would be there to nurse her back to full health. She was still on the path to recovery and had gone against the doctor's advice in leaving hospital ready for Christmas. They had assured her that, in time, she should make a full recovery and be able to lead a normal life. Except, it wouldn't be completely normal: her career in the police force was over. The job which she had loved, and which she had believed she would hold right through until retirement, had been cruelly snatched away from her. She had spent many wakeful nights in hospital, wondering what she might do with her life instead of policing, but nothing that had come to mind interested her in the slightest; she had wanted to become a police officer for as long as she could remember. What she definitely did *not* want was that the home in front of her, which she had missed so desperately, would eventually turn into a prison. She had bitten Simon's head off when he had half-jokingly suggested that she could become a housewife. Not that it mattered right now, she was finding just walking a few feet to be exhausting enough, as her single lung struggled to provide sufficient oxygen to her sleepy leg muscles.

'You okay?' Simon asked.

Kathy looked at him and nodded, drawing to a stop just a few feet from the front door. She raised a finger. 'One minute.'

'Take as long as you need.'

She drew in a breath and then moved forwards to the bungalow, waiting while Simon unlocked it.

166

'Do you need me to carry you over the threshold, Miss Steadman? Is that it?'

Kathy chuckled, then raised a quick hand to her chest. 'Don't make me laugh. I'll walk, thanks.' She stepped inside, overwhelmingly grateful for the sights, sounds and scents of familiarity. She blinked tears away as she shuffled into the lounge and sat down in her armchair. 'I cannot even begin to tell you how it feels...how relieved I am to be back here.'

Simon kissed her forehead. 'And I can't even begin to tell you how relieved I am to have you back here. You rest. I'm just going to go and finish getting the dinner ready. Do you need anything?'

Kathy smiled and shook her head. 'I have *everything* I need, right here, thank you, Simon.'

He kissed her again—on the lips this time—and then pointed at a stack of post on the small table beside her. 'Fan mail.'

She watched him leave the room, then sat awhile in the warm stillness of her bungalow, slowly moving her gaze from the Christmas tree, which Simon had put up, to the family photographs, paintings and little ornaments around the room, appreciating them anew. On the mantelpiece was the first photograph of her and Simon together, taken on the morning of the advanced driving course in Canterbury, minutes after they had first met. As luck had had it—or fate, as Simon always liked to say—they had been photographed standing side-by-side, so it had been easy to crop the rest of the trainees out of the image. She stared at it, her memories of that day slowly bleeding into the life that they had forged together in the last five years. How close she had come to losing it all. 'She narrowly missed your heart,' the first doctor, whom she had seen after regaining consciousness, had told her; to which Kathy had managed to reply, 'And I narrowly missed Rosie Hart.' He had mistaken her attempt at humour as deliriousness caused by the general anaesthetic.

From the kitchen, Kathy could hear Simon muttering to himself over the clatter of pots and Radio Two playing at a low volume. She picked up the two-inch pile of post from beside her and set it down on her lap, ripping into the topmost envelope to find that it was a get-well-soon card from her next-door neighbour. She continued working through the pile, finding an assortment of similar well wishes and Christmas cards, many of which, she noticed by the post mark, had been sent in very recent days, the senders presumably awaiting news of her condition before committing to the cost of a stamp. Partway through the pile was a note, in Simon's handwriting, of calls that had come in during her absence. She glanced at the headings at the top of the paper—*Date. Time. Name. Notes.*—and grinned at his gentle meticulousness. The list of names expressing concern and offering their best wishes was familiar, until she reached a telephone call that Simon had taken on the 6th December from WDS Lewen at Burgess Hill. Under *Notes*, he had written *ring back at your convenience.* She had never heard of a WDS Lewen at Burgess Hill.

'Simon?' she called.

'Yes!' he replied, rushing through to her as though she might have just gasped her last breath. 'Are you okay?'

'Calm down. I'm fine,' she reassured him, then held up the piece of notepaper. 'WDS Lewen? Are you sure that was the name?'

Simon nodded and rolled his eyes. 'I think I was a bit short with her at first, but she apologised when I explained the situation. She said she hadn't realised how serious it was.'

'But who is she?' Kathy pushed.

Simon shrugged. 'No idea. But dinner is served, Ma'am. So, please accompany me to the dining suite.' He leant forwards, offering her his hand, then helped her out of the chair.

'I hope you're not expecting a tip,' she said, following the wonderful smell of home-cooked food into the dining room. She chuckled lightly when her eyes fell onto a roast dinner and glass of red wine waiting on the table.

'Well, you did say to save your dinner and wine,' he said, helping her into the chair.

'I did. I did,' she agreed.

Simon sat opposite her and raised his wine glass. 'To new beginnings.'

She echoed his toast and sipped her wine. 'Bliss. The first I've had in weeks.'

'Now, if the phone goes this time, please let's just ignore it,' he instructed.

'Believe me, I'm not getting down from this table until this delicious-looking dinner is gone,' Kathy replied, picking up her cutlery and beginning to tuck in. She was grateful for the first-class care that she had received in the hospital but, in her mind, there was nothing like being back in her own place, with her own things, and having a home-cooked meal.

As they chatted through a leisurely and relaxed dinner, Kathy began to feel a sense of normality returning, something she had questioned as ever being possible again in the days immediately following her emergency surgery. Towards the end of the meal, she raised her concerns about what the future might hold for her.

'What about a civilian police job?' Simon suggested.

'A secretary, you mean?' she scorned.

'No,' Simon countered. 'More and more police work is shifting over to civilians now. At Crawley we hardly have any police officers doing jobs like fingerprinting or photography anymore.'

Kathy did not look impressed at the suggestion but also did not want to dismiss the idea out of hand. 'Well, I've got to go back into Burgess Hill at some point to clear my desk. I'll ask DI Redmond if he's got any advice or ideas.'

Simon smiled and reached across the table for her hand. 'There's really no rush, Kathy. Much better to get your health back first.'

'I know,' she said, rising from the table and putting Simon's empty plate onto hers.

'I'll do that,' Simon insisted, taking them from her. 'You go and sit down.'

'I was literally *just* sitting down,' she responded, perhaps a little too sharply.

'Listen, Kathy. You've just had major surgery. I'm not trying to wrap you up in cotton wool, here. In a week or two, you're very welcome to clear the table, but, right now, I want you to rest.'

Kathy exhaled and muttered, 'Fine,' as she ambled from the room, back into the lounge. She observed the stack of post still waiting to be opened, but her eyes settled on the call log that Simon had made. She picked up the piece of paper, double-checking that the name was WDS Lewen, and crept off into the hallway and eased the door closed, hoping that Simon wouldn't hear her. She sat down at the telephone seat, picked up the phone and dialled Burgess Hill Police Station.

'WDS Steadman, here,' she instinctively said when the call was answered. Officially, she still was WDS Steadman, but hearing the

169

words coming from her mouth sounded as though she were somehow deluded about the seriousness of her injuries, as though she were on a short holiday break. 'I'd like to speak to WDS Lewen, please,' she added hastily.

'Putting you through, now.'

'WDS Lewen,' a young, waspish voice answered.

'WDS Steadman, here,' Kathy asserted. 'You wanted to speak with me?'

'Ah, yes. Thanks for calling back. I hope you're recovering well?' she said, giving Kathy no time to answer. 'I'm tasked with going through your undetected crimes—quite a number of them—seeing what a pair of fresh eyes can do. I've been working alongside DC Cornwell, and he mentioned a case involving an abandoned baby in a telephone box in Haywards Heath? This would have been September 1973. Baby Bradley, the newspapers named it.' The intonation rose at the end of her last three sentences, as though Kathy might have forgotten the case, or no longer have all her wits about her, and needed a bullet point reminder.

'I know the case very well,' Kathy stated. 'The mother of the child was the person who stabbed me.'

'Oh, really? I thought two of the Hart brothers were in prison for that?'

'It doesn't matter,' Kathy dismissed, not sure where this conversation was headed, but not liking the woman's tone at all. 'What did you want to speak with me about, exactly?'

'What you did with the Baby Bradley files?'

'What do you mean? They're in the undetected crimes filing cabinets in the typists' office,' she answered.

'Not that I can see, they're not. How was it filed, then? Clearly not under Baby Bradley?' WDS Lewen said.

Kathy could not remember how she had filed the case, but she didn't like to admit it to this young upstart. 'I'll come in; I need to get my things anyway.'

'Okay. When would you like to do that? I'll just grab my diary.'

'Now,' Kathy said. 'I can be with you in fifteen minutes.'

'Oh, right,' WDS Lewen said. 'Fine. Goodbye.'

Kathy held the receiver to her ear, ignoring the flat continuous dial tone, despising the way that Rosie Hart continued to haunt her life, and questioning why—of all the many cases that she had ever worked—was this the only one for which the files had seemingly been misplaced. She told herself that it was just a coincidence, that, when she got to the station, she would be able to locate the file immediately and place it smugly into the young officer's hands. But her gut instinct told her otherwise, that something was amiss. Despite WDS Lewen's passive-aggressive comment that Kathy had left quite a number of undetected crimes, there were in fact so few that it would only take someone a matter of minutes to work through the entirety of them and locate any supposedly incorrectly filed case.

She finally placed the receiver down and ambled into the kitchen. 'I need to pop in to the station,' she said, leaning on the doorframe.

'Okay. When do you want to go?' Simon asked, turning from the sink.

'Now,' she replied. 'Please.'

Kathy was determined to enter the station unaided. Simon had acquiesced, reluctantly driven her in and was now waiting on double yellow lines directly outside the front of the building. She walked slowly up the stairs, pausing every few steps to catch her breath, feeling grateful that she had managed to get to the first floor without encountering anyone.

The first office that she came to was DI Redmond's. The door was closed, and she peered in through the small square pane of glass, finding the room empty. In some strange way, she was actually relieved that the conversation about the unlikely possibility of her taking on a civilian role within Sussex Police would have to be postponed.

She took a moment and then continued along the corridor to the DS's office that used to be hers. She entered uncertainly, as though she were somewhere rather unfamiliar. To a certain extent, she was. Her desk—her *former* desk—had been moved to a new position under the window and everything on it belonged to someone else, presumably the short-haired youth sitting in Kathy's old chair.

'WDS Lewen?' Kathy guessed, trying for nonchalance.

The youth with short black hair whipped around but neither stood nor smiled. 'Yes?'

'WDS Steadman.'

Still no smile, just a flicker of a nod of recognition as she turned and crossed her legs at the ankle, tapping one end of a biro on the desk beside her. 'Did you have any further thoughts about where the Baby Bradley case files might have got to? DI Redmond said to leave it and presume them lost… Maybe you took them home for bedtime reading before you were attacked…or…'

'No. The files never left the building,' Kathy insisted. 'Not with me, at least. I left everything in the undetected crimes filing cabinet.'

WDS Lewen motioned her open hands towards the door in a be-my-guest kind of gesture.

'Why are you especially interested in this case, anyway?' Kathy asked.

'Oh, I'm not. Not especially. I'm your replacement and I just want to be sure that nothing's been overlooked in all of the undetected crimes under your supervision, that's all. When DC Cornwell mentioned it in passing, I went to take a look and couldn't find it.'

Kathy raised her eyebrows, trying not to read too much into how quickly she had been supplanted. The original phone call from WDS Lewen had been made on the 6th December—way before anyone at the station could even have been informed of her prognosis. 'Is DI Redmond around, today?'

'Should be, but hasn't come in,' she replied.

'Right,' Kathy mumbled, turning and walking across the corridor to the typists' office which she was pleased to find devoid of people. She paused for a moment in front of the four-drawer metal filing cabinet marked UNDETECTED CRIMES, confirming her memory with herself, and then pulling open the third drawer down which contained those cases that she had failed to close successfully. She fingered through the cardboard dividers, checking the small plastic nameplates as she went. She moved past familiar cases until she hit the back of the drawer.

'It's not there,' WDS Lewen observed, standing behind her with her arms folded.

'Well, it *was*,' Kathy said, beginning a lengthier reverse trawl, checking the contents of each separated file as she went. 'It must have got mixed up.'

WDS Lewen huffed. 'Listen. Really. If you did take it home, it's fine. Just bring—'

'No. *You* listen. I *didn't* take it out of this office,' Kathy insisted, becoming exasperated and feeling slightly dizzy from all the exertion. But there was no sign of the file. She pushed the drawer shut and placed a hand on the one above.

'Don't bother. One of the typists has been through the whole thing with a fine-tooth comb—several times, in fact,' WDS Lewen commented.

In that moment, Kathy saw herself from a distance. It was not quite an out-of-body experience, but it was enough of a disconnection from reality to see the scenario in a true clarity. 'It doesn't matter, does it?' she said, as much to herself as to WDS Lewen. 'It's all over...' Rosie Hart had won.

'Hmm,' came the nondescript grunt from the doorway.

'Goodbye,' Kathy said, pushing past her and heading for the stairs.

'Don't forget your things,' WDS Lewen called after her, disappearing briefly back into the DS's office and returning with a small cardboard box which she handed over to Kathy, apparently glad to get it out of her way. 'From your desk.'

Kathy took the box without acknowledgement and left the building. Numbly, she walked out of the front door to where Simon sat in the car, waiting for her. He smiled as he leant across and pushed open the passenger door for her.

'Okay?' he asked.

Kathy nodded. 'Let's go home.'

Chapter Twenty-One

19th December 1980, Reno, Nevada, USA

'Welcome to Reno,' the taxi driver sang, raising his hands from the steering wheel and inviting Alfred to see what was being revealed through the windscreen.

'Wow,' Alfred gasped, leaning forward from the spongey back seat and resting his elbow on the driver's headrest. In front of him, converting night to day, was an endless flood of illumination from the grand buildings that they were passing; hotel and casino lights flickered, flashed and rotated as far as his eyes could see, and, directly in front of them, suspended above the street, was the famous Reno Arch, with *THE BIGGEST LITTLE CITY IN THE WORLD* lit up underneath the name; it was like nothing he had ever seen before in his entire life.

'First time, here, I'm guessing?' the driver chuckled.

'Yes,' Alfred confirmed, struggling to take it all in. 'What a place.' His eyes fixed momentarily on a double-life-size Marilyn Monroe-esque figure standing in front of a mirrored wall above the Sahara Hotel, her arms flung open above her and her dress frozen mid-flutter. Then came the Silver Spur casino, its name flashing in western-style lettering. Building after building caught Alfred's flitting attention as they continued along North Virginia Street.

'You here for business or pleasure, sir?' the driver asked.

'Both, I hope,' Alfred answered. 'I'm here for the Master Tailors' Conference—I'm in the fashion business, you see—but I'd like to do some sightseeing while I'm here.'

'Well, let me tell ya. Whatever you're into, we got it all, right here.'

Alfred wasn't sure how to take that comment, so kept quiet and continued to be transfixed by the dazzling lights in every direction that he looked. Even the smaller businesses, which they were passing, announced their trade in glitzy brilliance. He tried to imagine Farrier's Fashion illuminated in such big bright letters on Sevenoaks or Folkestone High Street; the image of his shop standing out so resolutely against the drab façades of the neighbouring properties was sufficiently absurd to make him grin. Even in central London, this opulent street would look distinctly out of place.

'If you're wondering why it's gone dark for a second,' the driver said, 'it's because we're driving out over the Truckee River. Normal service will resume right…' he dragged out the word, '…now! With your hotel, in fact, sir.'

Over on the right-hand side was a tall slender hotel, topped with the words *Pick Hobson's Riverside* in neon red lettering from which appeared to fall long ropes of tumbling white light down each side of the building.

The driver pulled over in front of the hotel and skipped around to open the rear passenger door. 'Here we are, sir: Pick Hobson's Riverside hotel and casino. You're gonna have a blast.'

Alfred stepped out of the taxi in his long brown mackintosh and trilby hat, and stared up, mesmerised as the driver moved to the rear of the car, opened the boot and hauled out his suitcase. 'Thank you,' Alfred said, handing him a five-dollar bill. 'Keep the change.'

'Thank you, sir. Have a great stay in Reno.'

Alfred picked up his suitcase but remained standing in situ as the taxi pulled away, slowly absorbing his other-worldly surroundings. The pavements were busy with casually dressed men and women, dipping in and out of the series of glass entrance doors to the hotel. Directly above them was the hotel name, again in red lights, and below that, some of the highlights on offer inside. *Entertainment: The Toni Ingram Show. Snack Bar. Buffets. 24-Hour Dining. Shop. Casino.*

This place had it all.

For the first time in a very long while, Alfred found that he was smiling. The burden of the past few years and the multiple mistakes that he had made were all gone, albeit perhaps but temporarily. With a lightness in his step, he entered the hotel and, once again, felt as though he had just slipped into a different dimension. Just beyond the marbled lobby area, under subdued lighting, Alfred could see row after row of silver one-armed bandits and, to his surprise, saw that almost every single machine was occupied. Further back, in a section bathed in bright white light, were a series of croupier tables and in the far distance—much further than seemed possible from the dimensions outside of the hotel—were long runs of slot machines. A thin cloud of grey cigarette smoke hung in the air above him, as though itself suspended from the low ceiling.

Alfred strode over to the reception desk—a very long, black,

175

marble counter staffed by six beautiful young women in a smart blue and red uniform that made them appear to him as though they might be air hostesses.

'Good evening, sir,' the nearest one said with a wide smile that revealed perfect teeth through crimson lipstick. 'Are you checking in with us?'

'That's right,' Alfred replied stiffly, removing his trilby. 'Mr Farrier.' He looked at the name badge pinned to her chest: CINDY, it said in red lettering.

'Is that a British accent?' Cindy asked.

'Yes, well detected.'

'I *love* it,' she enthused. 'I've always wanted to go to London. How awesome.' She looked down at a clipboard. 'You're staying with us for four days in room…two fifty-four. Oh!'—she looked up at him enthusiastically—'which is on the *sixth* floor, with an *amazing* view over the Truckee River. You'll *love* it. I'll just get you your room key.'

'Splendid,' he answered, watching as she headed out through an open door behind her, reappearing moments later dangling a single key on a plastic fob with *Pick Hobson's* on one side and his room number on the other.

'Here you go, Mr Farrier,' Cindy said, dropping it into his open hand. 'Is there anything else I can do for you? Perhaps a dinner reservation for tonight in our restaurant or a ticket for The Toni Ingram Show? It's supposed to be *amazing*.'

'I'm a little tired, so perhaps tomorrow night.'

'Absolutely, sir. This desk is staffed twenty-four hours a day. So, anything you need, just come right on over and ask.'

'Thank you.'

Cindy leant forward and pointed further into the bowels of the casino. 'You'll find the elevators over on the left there, and beyond that is the bar and restaurant. Enjoy your stay, Mr Farrier.'

Alfred thanked her again, placed his trilby back upon his head and walked in the direction of the six lifts. The doors to one of them opened just as he was approaching and an exotic, glamorous young woman with bleach-blonde hair and a short leather skirt stepped out, giving him a wink. Alfred doffed his hat in acknowledgement and then took the lift to the sixth floor. The corridor was narrow with subdued lighting and he had to strain his eyes to see the tiny red numbers painted on each door. His room was the penultimate of the floor. He unlocked the door and stepped into a surprisingly spacious room with an overwhelming stench of cheap air freshener. The large window, with its curtains open, drew him into the room. The view out over the shimmering city was just breath-taking: fantastically illuminated skyscrapers reaching out all the way to the black silhouetted mountain range of the High Sierra foothills in the far distance; it truly was a magnificent sight to behold.

Alfred suddenly felt terribly alone, wishing that he could have someone standing beside him with whom to appreciate it all. He shuddered, aware of the chill and low hum coming from the air conditioning unit below the window. He bent down to switch it off and tried to shake the feeling of utter isolation that seemed to have been amplified again by the new stillness of the room. It was the staggering sights that he was witnessing all by himself that was serving to underline his desperate loneliness, he realised. If the Master Tailors' Conference had been held in some drab English city, he would hardly have been gazing out of his hotel room window pining for company.

He tugged the curtains closed, reanimating an unpleasant amalgamation of stale smoke and synthetic cleaning product in the room. Alfred collected his suitcase from beside the door, placed it down on the double bed and sprung the brass clasps open. Inside was his brown wash bag and a selection of neatly folded clothes which he began to remove and hang up in the small wardrobe opposite the foot of the bed. When the suitcase had been emptied and stowed away, Alfred sat down on the bed with a sigh. He was tired—exhausted, actually—and looked at the appealing left-hand pillow. Odd that after twenty-two years of sleeping alone, he had always remained on the same side of the bed. Back home in Folkestone, he still had the same double bed in which Anna had died and, if he thought hard enough, could still picture her sleeping beside him. But not here. Her side of this bed, paradoxically, belonged to a thousand people and to none, all at once.

He picked up his navy-blue cotton pyjamas, which he had laid out on the bed, and began to unbutton his shirt. In the silence of the room, he caught the low thrum of distant city life and questioned himself. What was he thinking? It was Saturday night in Reno and he was about to pack himself off to bed for what would probably be a sleepless night due to his being over-tired. One whisky in the bar would probably be enough to settle him for sleep, he reasoned, as he convinced himself to stand up and make for the door. Without another thought, he retraced his steps back along the dim corridor and rode a lift down to the ground floor.

Alfred stood for a moment in the centre of it all, slowly surveying his surroundings. Despite its being close to eleven o'clock at night, the place was alive with blatant hedonism—smoking, gambling and drinking from bottles—the type of vices that he would have openly condemned back in England.

Over to his left was a pink neon light that announced the location of the bar. He walked towards it and took a seat at one of a dozen stools fixed in front of the long marble bar top. Alfred cast his eyes over the glass shelves containing an array of unfamiliar drink bottles, overwhelmed by the sheer volume. In the mirrored tiles opposite him, he traced his gaze from his own weary face to the barman serving a customer at the far end, then back towards his own reflection. Partway along, his eyes met with someone staring back at him. A young woman. She smiled, raised a glass, then shook it from side to side, presumably as a demonstration of its wanting emptiness.

Alfred switched his focus from the mirrors to the real person. He considered her to be in her early twenties with strawberry-coloured hair cut above the shoulders and a straight fringe ending just above her eyebrows. She was wearing heavy make-up, a loose-fitting shirt and a short black leather skirt. He smiled.

'What'll it be, buddy?' the barman asked, heading towards Alfred and running the back of his hand across his sweaty brow.

'Double-whisky for me, please and a large sherry for the young lady, there,' he said, nodding towards the woman seated a few bar stools along.

'Sherry?' the barman queried, turning to face the young woman and raising his voice to ask, 'You wanna have a sherry? This guy's buying.'

She shrugged. 'Hell, if he's buying... Sure,' she answered, stepping off her stool and tottering towards Alfred in remarkably high heels. She sat down beside him and stared in his eyes. 'What's your name, honey?'

Alfred cleared his throat and told her his name.

'Cute! Like Alfred the butler from Batman, huh? I loved that show when I was a kid. You look a little like him, too. He was always my favourite character, quietly running the show in the background but without the need to chase around Gotham City in spandex, declaring how amazing he was.'

'If you say so,' Alfred replied, not having the faintest clue what she was talking about but enjoying her big smile and warm features.

'Double-whisky and a sherry,' the barman declared, setting the drinks down in front of them.

'Thank you,' Alfred said, pulling his room key from his pocket. 'Could you put it to my room, please. Number—' he had forgotten and waited for the plastic fob to stop spinning and hold steady in front of his eyes '—two hundred and fifty-four.'

'No problem,' the barman said, scuttling away.

'Cheers, Alfred,' the young lady said.

'Cheers,' he responded, tapping his glass into hers.

'You're British, right?'

Alfred nodded.

'Oh my gosh. So just like Alfred from Batman!' She declared, gently smoothing the lapel of his jacket. 'Nice suit, Alfred. I'm guessing you're here for the tailoring conference?'

Clever girl, Alfred thought. 'Yes, well deduced,' he said, taking a large swig of his whisky.

'First time in Reno?'

'Yes.'

'You picked a good place to stay. The *whole* city started here,' she explained, opening her free hand and gesturing to the casino or perhaps to the wider city itself. 'Reno, as we now know it, started *right here* in 1859, in this *very* hotel. It started out as a hotel for gold-seekers passing east from California in the gold rush.'

Alfred raised his eyebrows. Maybe she wasn't so clever, after all. 'I think you'll find they went west *to* California for the gold rush; but let's not split hairs. I take your point that this was a place of great historical importance, though.' He looked around him, with a superior nod.

The young lady shook her head. 'No, actually, it was the reverse; it was called The Rush to Washoe. Folks shot east *out of* California to find their fortunes in gold and silver under the slopes of Mount Davidson.'

'My most humble apologies, my dear. I believe I stand corrected.'

She shrugged. 'Oh, but let's not split hairs.'

Alfred saw her grin and he couldn't help but laugh. 'You remind me a lot of someone.'

'Someone back home?'

Alfred took a moment to answer. 'Someone from the past. Long ago,' he said eventually. 'Anna.'

Unexpectedly, she touched his face, running the softest hands that he had ever felt slowly across his cheek. He closed his eyes and was drawn backwards in time. The touch lasted for just a few short seconds but the memories that it evoked bridged across to the years which he had spent with Anna.

'Do you want another?' a hard-edged voice demanded.

Alfred opened his eyes. The barman was standing in front of him, holding Alfred's empty glass. 'Yes, please.' He turned to her. 'And another for Anna...for my lovely friend, here.'

The barman moved off with a nod and Alfred caught himself in the mirrored tiles across the bar. An old, self-soured man stared back.

'I can be Anna,' the young lady said, placing a hand gently on his thigh.

A complex myriad of contradictions fired like battle cannons through the sphere of his thoughts, each continuously ricocheting and colliding with another: the anguish of the recent past; the anxieties and pain caused by Rosie Hart; the estrangement from Margaret; but most of all, the desperate loneliness of the last twenty-two years.

The noise in his head subsided. Despite himself and all that had gone on with Rosie and the fact that it would only be a fleeting respite, the bottomless longing for companionship won the battle.

'I think I'd like that,' he said softly, placing a hand down onto hers.

'Do you want these charged to the room again?' the barman asked, placing the two drinks down.

'Yes, please,' Alfred confirmed.

'Shall we take them up?' she said to Alfred, stretching across for her drink.

The barman took her wrist and whispered, 'Be careful, Candee-Lee. The management aren't going to be too happy if they see you escorting this gentleman to his room. Remember last time?'

'It's okay, Jonny,' she reassured him. 'Mickey's on tonight and he won't make any trouble.'

The barman raised his eyebrows, shrugged and sauntered out to the tables to collect empty glasses.

'Unusual name,' Alfred commented, standing from the barstool.

'Candee-Lee Gaddy and Alfred Pennyworth,' she said, threading her arm through his.

'Alfred Pennyworth?' he questioned as they moved through the bar, arm-in-arm, towards the lifts.

'Sorry, just another Batman reference.'

Chapter Twenty-Two

21st December 2019, Cadgwith, Cornwall

Morton eased off the accelerator as barbed tendrils of gorse from the high hedges on either side of the single track began to brush against both wing mirrors of the car. They passed a five-bar gate that opened onto a wide grassy field beyond which he could see the rooftops of the beautiful cottages dotted on the hills surrounding Cadgwith Cove. 'Get ready!' he said, trying to muster some enthusiasm from the last vestiges of his energy.

'Thank God for that,' Juliette muttered from the passenger seat beside him as she shifted uncomfortably. 'I really can't take much more of this.'

'What?' Grace asked, leaning as far forwards as her car seat would allow. The journey had been painful for all of them, but most of all for Grace. Boredom, travel sickness and the need for regular stops at every service station that they had passed had dominated the excruciating ten-hour journey.

'Look at the houses, Grace; they're called thatched cottages because the roofs are made from reeds,' Morton said with forced cheerfulness. 'And look—the sea!'

'Oh,' Grace said, sitting back in her chair having clearly expected much more.

Juliette exhaled and drummed her feet in the footwell. 'The baby's doing a tap-dance on my full bladder.'

'Nearly there,' Morton said, slowing the car almost to a full stop as he turned sharply between two small white-washed cottages. The short track was a dead-end containing a path to just three houses which overlooked the shingle beached cove, one of which belonged to his Aunty Margaret and Uncle Jim.

Morton tucked the car onto a short pea-beach driveway, the Mini's front bumper coming to a stop just inches from a number-plate-style plaque that said *SEA VIEW*. With vivid clarity, he recalled parking on this very spot on this very day exactly five years ago; he remembered the consuming feelings of anxiety and apprehension at what he had come here to learn. The information that he had gleaned from his Aunty Margaret about his biological father had been scant but sufficient enough to eventually establish his identity. How much had changed in those five years, he considered. Here he was, arriving with some degree of trepidation once again, but this time a very different man—

'No time for maudling and reminiscing,' Juliette said, correctly intuiting his disquiet as she hurriedly removed her seatbelt and jumped from the car.

He watched as she attempted a lolloping run to the cottage, then turned to see that Grace was pulling the tell-tale tearful grimace that they had learned from this journey to be a thirty-second warning of imminent vomiting. He leapt out of the car, opened the rear passenger door and fumbled with urgent fingers and thumbs around Grace's seatbelt clasps.

'Sick,' Grace warned just as the contents of her stomach erupted down her dress and over Morton's shirt.

'Great,' Morton mumbled. 'Feeling better now?'

Grace nodded unconvincingly.

He stepped back out of the car and unbuttoned his new fancy Christmas shirt, standing topless as a biting Atlantic wind whipped across the hilltop. He reached back inside the Mini, unfastening Grace's seatbelt, hauled her out of the car, and then helped her to stand out of the Christmassy dress that he had chosen for her. Admittedly, Juliette had warned him that it would not be the best clothing in which for her to travel, but he had wanted them to arrive looking smart. Now, standing in a white vest and knickers, she looked like some kind of a street urchin, and he was certain that, when she had less pressing matters on her mind, Juliette would remind him of her earlier sage advice.

'I cold,' Grace moaned.

'I freezing,' Morton countered, reaching for Grace's coat and then helping her into it. He searched for something for himself but all he could see was Juliette's cardigan. Her small pink woollen cardigan, to be precise. 'Brilliant,' he said, squeezing himself into the ridiculously tight top that left his chest and midriff completely exposed.

Grace looked up and laughed.

'Well, you don't look much better,' he said, taking her hand and walking the short distance to the cottage where Morton found the front door ajar. Inside, Juliette was in mid-conversation with Aunty

183

Margaret. They both glanced across at him and Grace. 'So, no, it—' Juliette stopped talking and, with comic precision, she and Aunty Margaret both did a double-take in his direction. Juliette looked at Aunty Margaret and then gestured to the door and said, 'Presenting...my husband and daughter.'

Aunty Margaret cackled with laughter as she rushed over to embrace the two of them. 'What on earth happened?' she exclaimed, pulling away from him and shifting her eyes between them.

'Sick,' Grace replied.

'Oh, my little dear! Are you feeling better now?' Aunty Margaret asked, gently caressing her hair.

'Yes, I better now,' Grace confirmed.

Morton rubbed his bare forearms, grateful to see that the open fire was roaring. He took in the spacious lounge, finding that very little had changed in the intervening five years. In fact, the decor had not altered at all and even the Christmas tree was in exactly the same position. The cottage was typical of those built in the area in the fifteenth century, with low ceilings, thick stone walls and exposed oak beams, giving it a warm, cosy feel.

'Your Uncle Jim is out on the boat. Hopefully, he'll bring us something decent back for our dinner tonight. In the meantime, I think a nice hot drink is what you all need to warm your cockles,' Aunty Margaret said. 'What'll it be?'

'Oh, tea for me, please,' Juliette said.

'Coffee, please,' Morton answered. 'I'll just go and get the suitcases in.'

Juliette hugged Grace to her side, and said, 'Then we'll put you in something nice and snuggly, little Miss Farrier.'

'You're in the same room as last time,' Aunty Margaret called from the kitchen as Morton stepped back out into the cold air, hurrying down to the car where he took out the three suitcases and Grace's Peppa Pig backpack which he just managed to squeeze over his arm. He locked the car and was about to begin the short walk back to the cottage when he spotted, to his abject horror, a large walking group heading down the track towards him. 'The day just gets better,' he muttered, glancing down at himself as he dragged the three suitcases behind him, with the Peppa Pig backpack dangling on his chest over the pink cardigan.

'Don't ask,' he said to the first walker who passed him, looking him up and down.

'Suits you,' she replied with a laugh.

He gave up offering any explanation to the next half-a-dozen walkers, simply saying, 'Good afternoon,' absorbing their various reactions and continuing towards the cottage.

'Think I've just terrified a local ramblers' group,' Morton told Juliette once he was safely back inside the house. He handed Grace her backpack, and said, 'Here are your toys, Gracie.'

'Thank you,' she said, unzipping it and pouring all the contents out onto the oak floor.

'I'll take the cases upstairs and extricate myself from this,' he said, looking down at the cardigan.

Juliette shrugged. 'You can keep it if you like.'

'Well, one of the walkers just told me that it suited me. So, maybe I will.'

Morton dragged the luggage up the narrow staircase, passing an old photograph of his grandfather that he had not seen before. He paused to look at it. It was a natural, black-and-white shot of him smiling outside one of his shops. Morton still could not quite believe that he had killed somebody, and in such an horrific and barbaric way. It just didn't equate to the grandfather whom he himself had known growing up. He strongly suspected that when he told Aunty Margaret, she would feel exactly the same way.

In the bedroom, he quickly changed into a fresh shirt and then went back downstairs, finding Aunty Margaret in the kitchen, loading a startling quantity of home-made cakes and scones onto a large tray. 'Need a hand?' he asked.

'No, you go and take a seat.'

'Having spent the best—no, *worst*—part of ten hours sitting down, I think I'm okay standing for a while,' he answered, taking her in fully. She had had white curly hair for as long as he could recall, but despite this, she still looked good for her sixty-one years.

'Well, you take the cakes, then and I'll bring the drinks,' she said.

Morton carried the tray through to the lounge, finding Juliette, sitting on the battered green sofa, with Grace at her feet, trying to put a turquoise ballgown on her Ken doll. She held it up to Morton and said, 'Like Daddy.'

'Thanks, Grace. I'll take that as a compliment,' he replied, setting the tray down on the coffee table and sitting in beside Juliette. 'Has the baby's dance routine ended?'

Juliette shook her head and placed his left hand firmly on a spot on her belly.

Morton grinned as he felt the strange swimming sensation beneath his palm and fingers. It was an experience like no other for him and instantly calmed the disquiet at the back of his mind about how he was going to broach the subject of his Aunty Margaret's having a new half-sister and a killer-father. Maybe he should just blurt it all out, just like that, with no sugar-coating. Merry Christmas, everyone.

Aunty Margaret entered the room with the drinks, then sat down in an armchair opposite them with a sigh. 'It's so lovely to have you all down here for Christmas. I've so been looking forward to it. You can't know how much.'

'Us too,' Morton agreed.

'It's great to be down here again,' Juliette said, looking around the room. 'How long have you been here for, now?'

'In this place, or Cornwall?' Aunty Margaret questioned.

'Both?'

She blew air from her cheeks and looked to the ceiling for the answer. 'Goodness... We've lived here for thirty-odd years, and I moved down here when I was eighteen in December 1976. So—' she paused a moment, '—forty-three years ago. Goodness!'

'Why Cornwall?' Juliette asked.

Morton studied Aunty Margaret carefully, keen to hear her answer, having always believed that she had left her home in Folkestone in need of a fresh start, somewhere miles away from the life that she had had and miles away from him, the child whom she had given up.

'Well, I came down here a few times and stayed with my aunt and uncle, and got to know and love the place, then a job and a young man came up and the rest is...well...history!'

'Where did your uncle and aunt live?' Morton questioned, feeling as though he should know the answer, yet didn't.

'Mullion Cove; a nice little place,' she answered, glancing at the grandfather clock behind her and adding, 'It's only a fifteen-minute drive away, if you fancy seeing it later?'

'Definitely,' Morton agreed.

'I think,' Juliette began, 'Grace and I will leave you to it, if that's okay? I think she's spent quite enough time in cars for one day.'

Morton gave her an appreciative look, thinking that she had probably declined the invitation in order to give him time to talk about the delicate family situation that needed to be addressed.

'Let's have our coffee and cake, and then we'll drive over there—it's just on the other side of the Lizard.'

'Perfect,' Morton said, offering a smile that entirely contradicted his anxious mind.

'Beautiful, even in the depths of winter,' Aunty Margaret enthused.

'It really, really is,' Morton concurred, mesmerised by the giant Atlantic waves that were crashing against the two stone piers that formed Mullion Harbour. They were standing beside a small fishing vessel at the terminus of the Nansmellyon Road, a single track which descended down to the cove.

'You'd not believe it now,' Margaret began, 'but kids do harbour-jumping off the end of those walls in the summertime,' she said, pointing at the stone projections that were now being lashed and battered by the tall waves.

'Rather them than me,' Morton said, shivering.

'And in this little café, here,' she said, turning to the end building in a run of pebble-dashed houses on their right, 'you can get the best local ice-creams topped off with the best Cornish clotted cream. You need to come down in summer, next time,' she laughed. 'You always come in winter.'

'We will,' he promised absent-mindedly, as he rehearsed what he had planned to say to her. But now didn't feel like the right time to bring it up, somehow.

'Let's have a wander up the hill,' she said, leading the way between two holiday properties on the right-hand side of the path that led down to the harbour arm. 'You can take this towpath all the way around the Lizard to our place, you know,' she told him, pointing to a sign for the South West Coast Path, 'if you're feeling adventurous while you're here.'

'Yeah, I'm not sure Juliette and Grace would be up for that, somehow.'

They began to ascend the narrow dirt track that cut across the steep hill, their conversation being kept to innocuous trivia and certainly nothing that afforded Morton the ability to segue into the news that he had to impart. He followed her up the steep incline, having to raise his voice on occasion to counter the wind gusting over the cove. As they appeared at the top of the hill, directly in front of the Mullion Harbour Hotel, she said breathlessly, 'Almost there.' She turned around to look back over the harbour. 'That's the path over yonder that eventually leads back around to Cadgwith.' She pointed to the wavering brown track that wound its way up a grassy slope on the opposite side of the harbour.

Morton gazed at the stunning view of the coves and rugged headlands of the Lizard Peninsular, then looked to where she was pointing. In a repeat of his earlier horror, Morton spotted the group of walkers who had passed him when he was scantily clad in a pink cardie outside Aunty Margaret's cottage earlier on. They were marching down the hill into the cove towards the harbour where he and Aunty Margaret had been standing just a few minutes ago. 'Where are we headed?' he asked, keen not to have to bump into them again, if at all possible.

'Just behind this hotel,' she answered, moving on, thankfully.

After a short walk, she stopped still in front of a row of terraced, white-washed cottages and folded her arms. 'There, that one,' she said. 'Coastguard Cottages—second on the right—that was where Uncle Alex and Aunt Joan lived. That little dormer window right at the top there, that was the room I stayed in. The house next door—number seven—on the end of the row; that was where your Uncle Jim lived. That's how we met.'

'So, you'd met him before you actually made the move down here?' Morton asked, staring at the cottages.

'That's right. Yes… Your grandfather parcelled me off down here a few times to get me out of the house.'

Morton shot a quizzical look at Aunty Margaret. There had been something in her tone which suggested that there was more to this story. 'Oh?' he encouraged.

She faced him and said, 'There was a court case going on that involved him, and he thought sending me down here would mean that I didn't get to hear of it. But, of course, my friends back in Folkestone showed me the newspaper story as soon as I got home, anyway.'

'What was the court case?' he asked, knowing the answer fine well but wanting to hear her interpretation of the event.

She raised her eyebrows. 'Oh, some young girl, or other, smashed the windows of his shop in Sevenoaks.'

And with that, Morton had just found his way in. All the fretting that he had done about how to raise the subject, and Aunty Margaret had inadvertently just handed him the perfect lead in on a plate. 'Rosie Hart,' he said simply.

Aunty Margaret stared at him, looking a little puzzled. 'Yes, I think that *was* her name, actually. How did you know that?'

'Long story. *Very* long story.'

'Oh, I'm not in any sort of a hurry,' Aunty Margaret laughed. 'As long as we're back before dark, that is.'

The words that he had rehearsed for this moment jumbled in his head, and he couldn't find a way to say it with any subtlety. He decided to come right out with it directly. 'I found something out about Rosie Hart, involving your dad.'

'That sounds ominous.'

'I think,' Morton began, 'that… No, I *know* that your dad had a child with her.'

'What?' Aunty Margaret stammered. 'A child? As in a baby? His baby? *By* him, I mean.'

Morton nodded.

Aunty Margaret shook her head. 'With this girl?'

'Yes. With Rosie Hart.'

'No,' she said vehemently.

'DNA,' he replied, trying to fast-track the inevitable you-must-have-made-a-mistake conversation. 'Vanessa is her name… She's your half-sister.'

Aunty Margaret slapped her left hand to her chest.

When Morton saw the look of shock on her face and the way that the blood had drained from her cheeks, he was worried that she might keel over out there in the cold. He realised then that the ethical dilemma which he had been facing—about whether or not to tell her that her father had killed a prostitute in Reno in 1980—had just been resolved: he could never see himself being able to tell her that piece of the story. What was there to be gained by telling her,

189

anyway? he questioned. It would simply have to remain yet another Farrier family secret.

'A half-sister...' she repeated, staring at the cottages with her mind clearly elsewhere. She faced Morton. 'Is she my age?'

Morton grimaced. 'More my age, actually.'

'Wow,' she said, drawing in a long breath. 'So...Dad would have been in his sixties—when he fathered her?'

'Yes, that's right.'

'Are you *really* sure, Morton? There can't have been any sort of mix-up at the testing laboratory? You hear of these things...'

'I'm sure.'

After a long silence, she met his eyes. 'It's certainly a lot to take in... Have you met her, this Vanessa girl?'

Morton nodded. 'She's very nice. She's an illustrator from Westerham in Kent.'

Aunty Margaret frowned. 'Let me get this straight. Vanessa's mother was Rosie Hart, the girl who smashed up my dad's shop?'

'Yes.'

'I remember suspecting there was more to that story; else why would he have sent me off out of the picture like he did? It was a bit of an overreaction for someone vandalising his shop, and I think—if I remember correctly—that the story implied that Rosie was some kind of a...well...prostitute? Golly. You do have to wonder about all this DNA business and the skeletons it throws up...'

'It certainly can be upsetting and divisive, providing heartache to some but providing solace to others,' Morton said, fully aware of the potential consequences, risks and benefits of DNA testing.

Aunty Margaret folded her arms and asked, 'When was Vanessa born, exactly?'

'Thirteenth of May 1975.'

'May seventy-five. May seventy-five,' she parroted while calculating something on her fingers. She looked up at him, shocked. 'Conceived in August 1974. Why, that mean old... Just at the very moment that he was shipping me off to my granny's house because of what people would think about what *I'd* done... And there he was...doing *this*.'

Morton shook his head. 'I know. I know...'

Aunty Margaret scoffed. 'The sheer hypocrisy is *staggering*,' she vented. 'While I was sitting on that very lawn over there'—she nodded to the garden of number seven Coastguard Cottages—'he was out galivanting with some young floozy, and then had the audacity to preach to me about the error of my ways!' She shook her head. 'And the effects that his critical judgement had on my entire, whole life, Morton... I can't...'

Morton's insides folded over when he saw that she was crying. He began earnestly to question that it had been right to tell her anything at all. Had he been blindly naïve to imagine that she would be overjoyed at being told that she had a half-sister? Clearly, he had underestimated the psychological impact of discovering her father's actions.

'I can't even tell you how unbearable he made my life, Morton,' she sobbed. 'I know he struggled after mum died, I really do. And trying to raise two kids alone can't have been easy—especially for a man on his own in those days—but... I forgave him for an awful lot a long time ago, but this news just changes everything. Even though his behaviour and his actions towards me were positively Victorian, I could at least understand that he was judging everything against his strict moral compass...which you're now telling me was a complete and utter, total lie. So why did he treat me as he did, then?'

Morton met her angry gaze, uncertain whether the question was rhetorical or if she actually expected him to be able to provide an answer. He pulled her into a full embrace and held her whilst she cried onto his shoulder. He looked over at the Coastguard Cottages, imagining his Aunty Margaret there as a young woman, just six months after having given birth to him, and her falling in love with Uncle Jim. Meanwhile, three hundred miles away, Rosie Hart was up in court, seven months pregnant, accused of vandalising the shop belonging to the man who had impregnated her. It was madness.

Aunty Margaret broke away. 'I think we should be getting back,' she said, gathering herself and dabbing her eyes with a tissue. Without waiting for him to answer or speak, she walked off with a striding pace, leaving Morton with the distinct impression that she wanted to be left alone. But he had no choice except to follow one step behind her, like a naughty child in tow.

They reached the front of the Mullion Harbour Hotel in complete silence. Just to add to his woes, the gaggle of walkers from earlier were heading directly towards him, and there was nowhere he could go and nothing that he could do except to smile and hope that they didn't recognise him.

'I preferred what you had on earlier,' the first in the line quipped.

'Thanks,' he replied, trying a false smile.

'Probably more appropriate attire for the windswept Cornish coast,' another added with a titter.

'Yes,' he agreed.

'Pink's more your colour,' an elderly man chortled.

'Thank you,' he replied, following Aunty Margaret down the sharp descent into the harbour.

When the walkers were out of earshot, Morton called after her, 'I am sorry. Would you rather I hadn't told you?'

Without turning around, she merely nodded, and he was crushed.

The journey back to Sea View was painful, particularly when Morton and Aunty Margaret had got back into the car and had lost the protection from acute awkwardness afforded by the ability to distance naturally on the narrow walk down the hillside. On the drive back to Cadgwith, Morton had tried light-hearted conversation but had only been met with short, mumbled responses. For the most part, she had stared out of the passenger window in stony silence.

'Nephew!' his Uncle Jim greeted him in his thick Cornish accent when they arrived back at the cottage, pulling him into his usual trademark bear hug. He was a big man with a ruddy complexion and wild hair. He had evidently just got home, as he was still wearing his wax jacket and thigh-high yellow boots. 'You took a trip to Coastguard Cottages, hey? Where my eyes first fell upon on that beautiful beast over there.' He moved over to try and kiss Aunty Margaret, but she brushed past him and headed straight for the stairs.

'I've got a headache and need a lie-down,' she mumbled.

Uncle Jim frowned. 'Oh,' he said, calling after her, 'But I've got lobster!'

When Aunty Margaret failed to respond, Juliette stared at Morton and screwed up her face. 'I can cook them,' she offered. 'Not that I've ever cooked lobster before.'

'Oh, it's a piece of cake,' Uncle Jim responded. 'It's the

dismembering and shell-cracking that's the tricky part. Come into the kitchen and I'll show you how it's done.'

Uncle Jim moved towards the kitchen and Juliette opened her hands towards Morton, mouthing, 'What happened?'

'Tell you later,' he glumly whispered back.

Morton slumped down onto the sofa beside Grace who was watching a cartoon on the television. He kissed her on the cheek and started to ask what she'd been up to when Juliette shrieked from the kitchen, 'God! They're still alive!'

'Course they are,' Uncle Jim cried with a deep belly laugh. 'You don't want to be cooking dead ones; you'll end up in casualty.'

Juliette arrived back in the lounge, sitting down beside Morton. 'You're cooking. There are literally three live lobsters walking around the kitchen.'

'Brilliant,' he responded.

'I expect you weren't very subtle about it, I'll bet,' Juliette chastised in hushed tones.

'Well… I was *sort of* subtle,' Morton answered, barely audibly, trying hard not to wake Grace who was asleep in a travel cot at the foot of the bed in which they were lying, but also very conscious of the fact that Aunty Margaret and Uncle Jim were in the next bedroom. 'I just didn't foresee her having *that* reaction. I mean, I didn't know how bad things had been for her as a teenager. How could I have known?'

'What are you going to do about it, now?' she whispered. 'It's day one of our holiday, here, and we're all in bed and it's not even nine o'clock at night.'

Morton shrugged. 'What *can* I do?'

'Apologise,' she suggested quietly.

'I've got the feeling she doesn't want to talk about it *at all*,' he replied. 'I mean, she's stayed in her room all evening. Maybe…we should just go home in the morning?'

'What?' Juliette hissed, a little too loudly, making Grace stir in the cot.

Morton shrugged, then waited for Grace to settle again before daring to continue. 'I don't think it was actually the revelation that she had a half-sister that was the issue,' he tried to explain. 'It was

193

more about what that meant for her relationship with her dad. Strangely, I think she could cope with the idea of him being a harsh authoritarian with strict moral codes which she had broken, but finding out about the things he was getting up to amounted to unacceptable hypocrisy.' He lowered his voice even further and leant closer to Juliette. 'And that's even *without* mentioning what happened in Reno.'

Juliette sighed. 'You Farriers are so damned complicated,' she mumbled, lifting her book from the bedside table. 'I might as well read, then, since I'm a prisoner in my own bedroom.'

Morton nodded and picked up his laptop and notepad. 'And I'm going to see if I can find out what happened to Rosie Hart.'

'Well, I tell you something,' Juliette muttered. 'If she's not dead already, then I'm going to flipping well kill her myself; she's ruined enough people's lives already.' She opened her book and started to read but quickly put it down on the bed, and added, 'And I tell you something else for free: she's *not* going to ruin my Christmas.'

Morton smiled thinly and sighed as he started up his laptop. He looked down at his notepad, having done nothing more since Kathy's revelation yesterday that her boss at Burgess Hill had been named Derek Redmond, coincidentally also the name of the occupier of one of the flats opposite to where Baby Bradley had been left. The telephone conversation with Kathy had lasted quite some time, with both of them reaching the same conclusion: that DI Derek Redmond was very likely the father of Baby Bradley and was also very likely to have been the person who had tipped-off the Hart siblings about Kathy's shift patterns, knowing that, with her off the case, he would more likely evade any potential damage to his career or even prosecution. Kathy had been rightly shocked when she had realised that her former boss had probably been in cahoots with the Harts to have her killed. When Morton had suggested that Derek Redmond should now face criminal charges, she had informed him that he was long-since deceased.

Morton turned several pages in his notepad, returning to the blank page headed ROSIE HART AFTER 1980?? His searches within the UK had failed to turn up any likely results and, given what Kathy Steadman had said about the police wondering if she had left the country after the attempted murder, he set his focus on her possibly having absconded to the US.

The first and most logical place to start, he reasoned, was with Rosie Hart's maternal grandparents, David and Emma Raven. Morton opened up the family tree on Ancestry, which he had created for them, and clicked to view the most recent document chronologically that he had accessed pertaining to the couple: the US 1940 Census. Despite both having been born in Kansas, they were recorded as living in the neighbouring state of Missouri.

Ancestry had attributed thirteen hints to David Raven's name, all of which Morton now examined. He scrolled down and clicked on the second offering: *Missouri, U.S., Death Certificates, 1910-1962.* A scanned copy of an original death certificate loaded in front of him.

Place of death: De Paul Hospital, St Louis.
Usual residence: 2044a E. Adelaide Av, St Louis
Date of death: August 5, 1960
Date of birth: 10-21-1908
Birthplace: Atwood, Rawlins County, Kansas
Name of Husband or Wife: Emma Raven
Cause of death: Coronary thrombosis

Morton jotted down the key information, certain that this was the correct person, then saved the document to David Raven's profile. Returning to the hints list, Morton clicked on *U.S., Find a Grave Index, 1960s-Current,* discovering that David Raven had been buried in Bellefontaine Cemetery in St Louis. The entry also included an image of a flat rectangular memorial which Morton clicked to enlarge. It was simple in its description, giving just David's full name and years of birth and death. Of most interest to Morton, however, was the addition of the name of his wife, Emma, and her date of death in 1984, which meant that she would definitely still have been alive when Rosie Hart had first disappeared.

Switching his attention to Emma Raven, Morton clicked to look at the nine suggested hints on her Ancestry profile. He moved down past known information until he reached *U.S., Public Records Index, 1950-1993, Volume 1* which he discovered was a database collated from various sources, including telephone directories, marketing lists, changes of address forms, public record filings and land records.

Name: Emma Raven
Birth date: 21 Nov 1909
Phone Number: 773-0842
Address: 2857 Missouri Ave, Saint Louis, MO
Residence Date: 1979-1984

He now had firm evidence that Rosie Hart's maternal grandmother had been alive and living in St Louis after the attempted murder in November 1980. But was Rosie living with her? he wondered, running a search for Rosie herself in the same database.

Results 1-50 of 8,587

Morton edited his search to include her precise date of birth and the results list plummeted by 8,587 to precisely zero. He removed the day and month from the search and allowed a five-year window on either side of 1980, but, when he scrutinised the results list, found it to be far too broad and with little ability to be absolutely certain that he had the correct person. One thing was clear: Rosie had not been recorded as living with her grandmother during this critical time, but Morton knew that that did not necessarily mean that she hadn't stayed there outside of official documentation.

He realised, emitting a long, low groan, that he needed to start his search for Rosie Hart in America after 1980 from scratch; there were no obvious short-cuts that he could take. He would start with Ancestry, but if that yielded nothing, then he would repeat the search at MyHeritage, FindMyPast, FamilySearch, TheGenealogist, Genealogy Bank and Newspapers.com.

'What's up?' Juliette asked, glancing across at him.

'Nothing,' he muttered, reluctantly clicking *Search All Records* on Ancestry and amending the database collection to the United States only. He entered Rosie's name, year of birth and the location of St Louis, Missouri for places that she might have lived, then hit the search button.

Results 1-50 of 71,066

Brilliant. He took a cursory glance down the results, finding that they contained references to any and all events that had happened at any point since 1952. Morton edited the search filter for records dated between 1980 and 2000, then began the laborious task of wading through 11,103 suggestions, many of which he quickly realised could immediately be discounted.

More than an hour and a half later, Juliette shut her book and then stretched. 'That's me done,' she yawned. 'Are you carrying on?'

He nodded. 'I want to finish this search tonight,' he whispered. 'I've checked over three thousand results so far.'

'How many to go?'

'Eight thousand and something.'

'Jesus. Night,' she said, leaning over and kissing him on the lips, then switching off her bedside light.

'Night,' he said, resuming his work.

The next batch of results were easily dismissed, relating to page after page of links to high school yearbooks. 'Next,' he whispered to himself as he clicked on to the following page to see more of the same.

Another hour of searching passed and Morton's eyes began to feel heavy. He yawned and rolled his head around, wondering if perhaps he should go and make a drink and continue working downstairs. Another yawn and he decided to push on, finding that the results were now dominated by Social Security references, something Rosie Hart, as a British citizen, would highly likely not have claimed, had she ended up in the US. The penultimate result on the page made Morton lean in closer to the screen. *Nevada, U.S., Death Index, 1980-2012.* His eyes widened to combat the tiredness as he clicked the link.

Name: Rosie Hart
Birth Date: 21 July 1952
Birth Place: England
Death Date: 20 Dec 1980
Death Place: Reno, Washoe, Nevada, USA

Morton's addled brain could not quite process what he was seeing.

Was it her? He flipped back in his notepad and checked the details taken from Rosie's birth certificate. The birthdate was correct. The birth location, although very broad, was correct. But something about the date of death was bothering him. It was familiar. But why? Then it hit him. 'Oh my God,' he said, far, far too loudly.

Juliette gasped and shot up in bed. 'What? What's happened?'

Then Grace began to cry.

Seconds later, Uncle Jim called out, 'Everything okay in there?'

'Er, yes. Fine, sorry,' Morton shouted over Grace's wailing. 'Just a nightmare.'

'Righteo,' Uncle Jim replied.

'What *is* the matter?' Juliette demanded, sliding out of bed to comfort Grace. 'You've woken everyone up, now. It had better be something good.'

'Rosie Hart died…the exact same day as my grandfather murdered Candee-Lee Gaddy…in exactly the same location,' he whispered in reply.

Juliette nodded as she cuddled Grace to her chest. 'Okay. Fine. Yeah. That *was* something good enough to wake everyone,' she was forced to concur.

Chapter Twenty-Three

22nd December 1980, Haywards Heath, West Sussex

Kathy finished fixing the Christmas cards, which had arrived in the first post, to the back of the lounge door. She walked at the slow pace that the last few days of being at home had taught her was optimal for gaining strength but without tiring her out. She entered the spare bedroom, pulled open the cupboard and took out the domed parcel wrapped in greaseproof paper tied with string. She carried it carefully into the kitchen where she untied the knots and then removed the paper to reveal the Christmas pudding that she had made back in early November. It looked perfect. Given what had happened, she was thankful now that she had taken advantage of a day off work to make the pudding, rather than wait until the traditional Stir-up Sunday at the end of November. With warm reflection, Kathy recalled the numerous occasions when, always on the Sunday before Advent, she and her younger sister had helped their mother to make the Christmas pudding, and would stir the mixture together while their mother would take on the role of a witch, and cackle, 'Stir-up, we beseech thee!' They would make a wish and drop a sixpence each into the mixture and then store the pudding in the larder until Christmas day.

Kathy smiled at the returning memories as she heard Simon's key turning in the door.

'Miss Steadman!' he called dramatically. 'I come bearing great tidings!'

Kathy rolled her eyes playfully and met Simon in the hallway, finding him standing with his eyes closed, his lips pursed, and holding a piece of mistletoe aloft in the air above him.

She smiled and kissed him on the lips. 'Fresh mistletoe,' she commented sarcastically. 'That *is* good news.'

Simon reopened his eyes. '*That* wasn't the good news.'

'Go on,' she encouraged.

'The sergeant at Crawley responsible for advanced driver training; he is retiring early next year,' he said.

'And that's good news because...?'

'Because there'll be a vacancy; one that you'll be perfect for.'

'Oh,' Kathy said, taken aback. She stared at him, considering the proposition. It wasn't a *bad* idea, just one that had never entered her head prior to this moment. 'But what about my situation? Can one be a single-lunged, advanced driving instructor?'

Simon nodded enthusiastically. 'One can indeed, for *I* have checked. The Chief Inspector would like to see you at your convenience in the new year.'

Kathy nodded, quickly warming to the idea. She had spent a good deal of time worrying about what the future might hold for her. This job might just be the perfect solution, but she had plenty of questions. 'And would that be—'

The doorbell sounded, cutting her off.

Simon turned and stepped the few paces back to the front door. He gave a wooden smile of unfamiliarity to the visitor.

'Hi, is Kathy...erm WDS Steadman in, please?'

Kathy recognised the young male voice and approached the door. 'DC Cornwell—this is a surprise,' she said, coming to the conclusion that he had probably been sent to deliver further well-wishes from the station. 'Come on in.'

'Thank you,' he said, entering the bungalow.

When Kathy saw that he had come empty-handed, she suddenly had the idea that he might be here at WDS Lewen's bidding and that it might have something to do with finding Rosie Hart. Perhaps there had been a breakthrough at long last.

'Come in. This is Simon, my partner,' she introduced as they trooped into the lounge.

'Nice to meet you,' DC Cornwell said.

'Likewise,' Simon responded. 'Can I get you a drink? Tea? Coffee? Christmas tipple?'

DC Cornwell smiled. 'I'm fine, thanks. I won't stay long.'

'Take a seat,' Kathy gestured, sitting in her usual armchair. Turning to Simon, she said, 'I'll have a tea, please.'

'Right you are,' he said, disappearing from the room.

'Well, this is an unexpected pleasure,' Kathy said.

DC Cornwell had the fixed expression which Kathy recognised immediately as the one that officers inadvertently held just before they delivered terrible news. It was a look that somehow managed to combine acute graveness with authoritative reassurance. He looked down at his shiny black shoes, then back up to Kathy. 'It's DI Redmond; he's dead.'

'What? Golly,' Kathy gasped. 'What happened?'

'He fell from a window in a block of flats,' he revealed.

'Oh, my goodness,' Kathy said.

'I was just on my way home and thought you'd like to know before it becomes public knowledge. The powers that be are trying to minimise the gory details that get released, but you know what the journalists are like if they smell something's off.'

Kathy shot him a look. '*Is* something off, then?'

DC Cornwell shifted uncomfortably. 'The flat he fell from was actually a squat used by drug addicts, prostitutes and the like,' he said, looking back at the floor.

'Ah.'

'So, he was clearly there conducting an undercover operation.'

Kathy couldn't help but smile at her colleague's attempt at diplomacy. 'Is that the official line? An undercover operation that nobody knew about?'

He nodded.

'Oh dear,' she responded, unable to help herself from thinking about DI Redmond's unfavourable attitude towards her expending time and resources on finding Rosie Hart. 'I don't suppose WDS Lewen has had any joy with finding Rosie? Or the missing Baby Bradley files?'

DC Cornwell shook his head. 'Not that I'm aware of, no. Sorry.'

Kathy sat back in her chair. 'I think it's probably safe to say that Rosie Hart has got off scot-free with the abandonment of a child and the attempted murder of a police officer. She must be out there somewhere right now, laughing her socks off.'

Chapter Twenty-Four

22nd December 1980, Reno, Nevada, USA

Alfred woke up in his hotel bed with an internal warmth, slowly emerging from within a dream that he didn't wish to end. He fought to keep his eyes closed, trying desperately to grasp at the frayed and quickly fading narrative in which he had been so immersed just moments before. The firm detail of the dream, which had seconds ago seemed so real and concrete, slipped further into obscurity, and he frantically reached around his mind to hold on to more. But it was as useless as trying to grasp a handful of water. The heart of the dream, which had been a hybrid of fantasy and flashback, was now lost and all that remained were the nonsensical bare bones: he had been living in his current house in Folkestone, but perhaps some thirty years ago, when Anna had still been alive. Except it hadn't been Anna in the dream. Like some strange Hollywood adaption of his life, the woman wearing Anna's clothes, who had all of her mannerisms and who was raising their children, had actually been Candee-Lee Gaddy, the woman whom he had met here three nights ago.

He opened his eyes and sighed deeply. He hoped to see Candee-Lee again tonight. Their evening together on his first day in Reno had been magical and, although it had ultimately boiled down to a business transaction of sorts, there had been something there that Alfred had not experienced with another woman since Anna. She had left him in the very early hours of the morning with a lingering kiss. 'Same time tomorrow, Alfred Pennyworth?' she had said.

'Absolutely,' he had replied. 'I'll see you in the bar. Perhaps we could go out somewhere for dinner?'

'Perfect,' she had said, kissing him again.

But she had not turned up. Alfred had spent the entire evening drinking whisky alone at the bar, waiting and looking up in anticipation every time someone had approached.

'You looking for Candee-Lee?' Jonny, the barman from Saturday night, had eventually asked him.

Alfred had nodded, hoping that perhaps she had left a message with him.

Jonny had screwed up his face. 'She's probably out working. Try some of the bars on East Fourth Street; that's another one of her hangouts.'

His words had been a devastating blow to Alfred. The reality of his relationship with Candee-Lee had struck him squarely between his drunken eyes and he had taken himself off to bed feeling the foolish old man that he really was.

But today was a new day, Alfred thought, pulling open the curtains to see a crisp blue sky over Reno. Today was the final day of the Master Tailors' Conference and this evening he planned to go out looking for Candee-Lee, absolutely determined to find her. Whatever their relationship was, or might have been in his dreams, was irrelevant: he just wanted to spend one more evening in her company and talk about gambling, gold-seekers and Gotham City.

Alfred drew himself a bath, brushed his teeth, dressed in his smartest suit and tie, and ran a comb of Brylcreem through his hair. He pulled on his shoes and spotted the postcard on the sideboard that he had written to Margaret. He picked it up and re-read his message, wondering whether or not to send it. His words had been as close to conciliatory as he could manage, verging on an apologetic tone and expressing his hopes that she was keeping well. Yes, he determined, he *would* send the postcard.

Picking up his room key, Alfred strode out into the corridor and took the lift down to the ground floor.

'Good morning,' he greeted the beautiful young woman behind the reception desk.

'Well, good morning to you too, sir,' she replied with a broad smile. 'Did you sleep well?'

'Very well, thank you.' He placed the postcard down onto the desk. 'Would you be able to post this for me, please?'

'Absolutely, no problem. Is it for England?'

'That's right—to my daughter,' Alfred replied cheerfully.

'Sure thing. One moment,' she said, disappearing through the door behind her.

Alfred gazed absent-mindedly around him, thinking about what he would eat for breakfast. Despite the strange mix of flavours, the eggs, bacon and maple syrup that he had had yesterday morning had been surprisingly tasty. But then he wanted to try—

Alfred's thoughts disintegrated. His eyes took in the opening paragraph of today's *Reno Evening Gazette*, folded over on display with a selection of other newspapers on the reception desk. Alfred picked up the paper and read the story.

Woman found murdered in Reno is identified
A woman found murdered in Governors Bowl Park in Reno Saturday afternoon has been identified as Candee-Lee Gaddy, 23, whose last known address was in K Street, police said last night. Relatives of the woman were notified yesterday after identification was established from fingerprints taken at Saint Mary's Regional Medical Center. Deputy Coroner Lin Anderson said that an autopsy performed at the hospital revealed that Ms. Gaddy had died from multiple stab wounds. Last night, police were trying to establish when Ms. Gaddy was last seen before she was killed. They said they would try to find witnesses from the East Fourth Street bars where she had reportedly worked. Homicide Detective Henry Gale said two young boys playing in the park found the partially clothed body about 3pm Saturday.

She was dead.

'Okay, that's all taken care of and you've also got some post of your own... Sir? Sir? Are you okay?'

Alfred looked up and met the receptionist's concerned stare.

'Is everything okay?' she repeated, handing him a sealed envelope with his name and room number handwritten on the front.

Alfred nodded. 'Could I take this paper, please?'

'Sure. They're complimentary for our guests.'

He walked briskly to the lifts with the newspaper and envelope under his arm and hurried back to the confines of his bedroom. There, he closed the door and sank down onto the bed. Candee-Lee Gaddy was dead. According to the newspaper article, she had died not long after their rendezvous had ended. Alfred looked again at the story. Stabbed, multiple times. Who could have done such an horrific thing?

It took a moment for Alfred to steady his breathing, then he tore open the envelope which he had just been given. Inside was a note, written on paper headed with *Pick Hobson's Riverside* that simply said: *See you soon, Anna.*

Alfred gasped, instantly joining the horrific dots between Candee-

Lee's death and the note which could only have come from one person. She was here, in this city, out for revenge. The implications for him—as one of the last people to have seen Candee-Lee that night and with several witnesses—were crystal clear.

'Goodness me,' he breathed, splaying out his arms and lying back on the bed, sending the newspaper falling to the floor.

He bent down to pick it up, opening it fully on the front page for the first time.

'My God,' he stammered when he saw the story directly above the one concerning Candee-Lee's death.

Chapter Twenty-Five

22nd December 2019, Cadgwith, Cornwall

Morton woke with a sharp jolt. He reached out for Juliette but found her side of the bed to be cold. He sat up and stretched. Daylight was fighting to get in behind the thick curtains. He picked up his mobile phone from the bedside table and looked at the time: twenty past nine. He yawned and collapsed back onto the pillow, having endured a shocking night's sleep. As it often did when he was doing genealogy, time ran at double speed and he was shocked to find that the discovery with which he had woken the whole house last night had occurred at just after one o'clock in the morning. It was at that point that Juliette had insisted that he switch off his laptop and go to sleep. He had duly obeyed the first part of her command, but sleep had not arrived for several more hours, as his mind tried to dissect that which he had discovered. How could Rosie Hart have died on the *exact same day* and in the *exact same place* as Candee-Lee Gaddy? His mind had lurched from one unlikely and illogical theory to another, until just one remained: that his grandfather had murdered both the women. Whilst the household had slept peacefully, Morton had lain in bed feeling as though he had locked-in syndrome and, alone with his thoughts, had rehearsed compiling and presenting the case file for Vanessa, Billie and Liza about their mother. It was always going to be an horrendous document to compose, but now it appeared as though it would come with the added codicil that *his* own grandfather had killed their biological mother. Brilliant.

DNA was helping to solve a myriad of complex crimes, identify human remains and reunite adoptees with their biological families, but it was also presenting a raft of ethical dilemmas for unsuspecting individuals for which there was precious little training or preparation. This case, Morton thought, was an exemplary example.

He opened the curtains of the small bedroom window, half-wishing that he had never volunteered to take on this case in the first place. But he had; and now it was his duty to apply the fifth principle of the Genealogical Proof Standard and write up a coherent, soundly reasoned conclusion.

He stared out over the picturesque cove, watching a fishing boat being winched up the stony beach. He wondered if that was his Uncle Jim's boat and what culinary delights he might have procured for their evening meal tonight. A wash of dread came over him as he thought about the awkwardness of last night's dinner, making Morton reluctant to leave the bedroom. He picked up his mobile and sent Juliette a text message.

Are you downstairs? Is Aunty Margaret okay? xx

Juliette replied almost instantly.

You've surfaced then?? Everything's normal. We've gone to Helston for a girls' day out - thought you might need some sleep / work time? Currently eating a full English Breakfast pasty from a shop to rival your brother's for weird pasty flavours. Xx

A full English Breakfast pasty??? he typed back, adding the green-faced pre-vomit emoji.

Everything's normal, he read again. That was Farrier-family speak for resolutely sweeping uncomfortable topics under the carpet, never to be discussed. He could well imagine Aunty Margaret not mentioning the revelation of having a half-sister ever again, which made life very awkward for him. Vanessa had already asked him on *The Foundlings* WhatsApp group how she had taken the news and when she might get to meet her half-sister. Morton had not replied to her yet, hoping for some seismic shift in Aunty Margaret's feelings on the matter.

Morton padded downstairs in his pyjamas, carrying his laptop. A light crackle from the dying open fire in the lounge was all that could be heard in the still cottage. He made himself a coffee, sat down beside the Christmas tree and opened his laptop.

Onscreen in front of him was the reference to Rosie Hart's death on the Ancestry website, just as he had left it last night. It was a typed index with no ability to access the original death certificate which Morton was desperate to see. He scrolled down to the source information at the bottom of the page, finding that it had come from the Nevada Department of Health and Human Services. He copied and pasted the name into Google. The fourth result in the list was what he was looking for: the ability to purchase a death certificate. According to the National Center for Health Statistics, he needed to send $25 to the Office of Vital Records in Carson City, Nevada. Morton noted the full address, then read the final paragraph.

The applicant MUST include a copy of a photo ID with the request and proof of relationship to verify direct and tangible interest.

Damn. *Direct and tangible interest…* Was it direct and tangible enough to believe that his grandfather had killed the decedent? Were Nevada death certificates anywhere else online? he wondered, opening a new tab on the FamilySearch website and using their Wiki page to search for death certificates in Washoe County that might appear anywhere on the internet.

'Aha,' he said, sipping his coffee as he clicked on *Nevada County Birth and Death Records, 1871-1992*. He typed Rosie's details into the search box and was instantly disappointed to see no results.

Morton edited the search parameters several times but failed to find her. He returned to the main listing page for Washoe County and then clicked *How to Use this Collection* beside the vital record link.

This collection consists of county birth and death registers and certificates from county courthouses throughout Nevada. This collection does not include Carson, Carson City, Churchill, Clark, Elko, Lake, Lincoln, Mineral, Pershing and Washoe counties.

It appeared as though Morton would not be able to access Rosie Hart's death certificate after all. Where else might he find details of her death? If his suspicion was correct and she had been murdered by his grandfather, then the story would likely have made the newspapers. He opened up Newspapers.com and typed *Rosie Hart* and *Reno* into the search box. The top result was for the *Reno Evening Gazette*, dated Monday 22nd December 1980; a date and a newspaper title that he was already horribly familiar with. 'Here we go. Oh, God,' he muttered in dreaded anticipation of whatever he was about to read. He hovered the mouse over the link for several seconds before finally clicking.

Run Over By Bus
A British woman visiting the city was killed after she was run over by a bus at a downtown intersection on Saturday. Multiple witnesses saw Rosie Hart stepping into the road looking the wrong way at the junction of Fourth West and North Sierra and was crushed by the back wheels of the bus. The twenty-eight-year-old woman had only arrived in the city the day before and was taking a short vacation before visiting her grandmother in St Louis. According to Washoe County Coroner, Harry Hicks, the incident occurred about 2.30pm. His investigation of the accident indicated the bus driver was not at fault since he had a green light at the intersection and apparently did not see the woman until it was too late.

'Wow,' Morton gasped after he had read through the story twice. He zoomed out and was shocked to see that directly below this story was that of the murder of Candee-Lee Gaddy. The irony that he had looked at this very page two months ago was not lost on him. Adding to the paradox was that sandwiched between the two stories was the only photograph of Rosie Hart that he had come across in his research. She was nothing like the image of her that he had held in his mind. She was young, pretty and with a warm smile; it was little wonder that the older men had fallen at her feet.

He saved the story and took a separate screenshot of Rosie's photo to add to the report that he needed to write.

'Sorry, Grandad,' he said, briefly glancing up to the beamed ceiling, offering an apology for his accusations of double murder. He set the laptop down on the sofa beside him, picked up his coffee and tried to make sense of the case. Unless his grandfather had been driving the bus, then he wasn't guilty of killing Rosie Hart, but it surely couldn't have been a coincidence that she had been in Reno at the exact same time as him.

Nothing made sense.

Whilst he had been packing to come down here, Morton had deliberated about carefully unpicking the timeline from his investigation wall and bringing it with him, but quickly convinced himself of the absurdity of the idea. Now, he wished that he had done just that, deciding that he needed to create a digital version instead to try and get his head around what had occurred.

Opening up a new Word document, he began to add the key

information of the case in chronological order. After half an hour, he had created the timeline. Morton focussed his attention on the final events, a loose theory forming in his mind.

14th Nov 1980 - Kathy stabbed
20th Dec 1980 - Candee-Lee Gaddy stabbed to death
20th Dec 1980 - Rosie Hart hit by a bus

He recalled how horrific Kathy Steadman's injuries had been and that she had been considered lucky to have survived. Clearly, Rosie Hart was very capable of murder. Was it too much to consider that she might also have killed Candee-Lee Gaddy? She was certainly in the right place at the right time, but what would her motive have been? Pure revenge against the father of one of her children? Why him, though, and not the others?

He did not have any leads regarding Liza's potential biological father, but he did for Billie and Baby Bradley: when and how had Derek Redmond and Edward Crouch died? he wondered.

Morton picked up his mobile and opened *The Foundlings* WhatsApp group. He looked at the last message from Vanessa and thought for a moment. He couldn't very well ask Billie if she knew about the circumstances of her biological father's death without first answering Vanessa's question which was still lingering unanswered, about how Aunty Margaret had taken the news of her having a half-sister. He clicked on Billie's name and sent her a direct message instead. Then, he sent one to Kathy via Facebook Messenger, asking her if she knew when Derek Redmond had died and anything else that she knew about his death.

The more he thought about it, the more he hoped that his theory might be correct and that his grandfather could be exonerated for the murder of Candee-Lee Gaddy. But the Reno police had closed the case. His grandfather's DNA had been found at the scene; any circumstantial evidence that Morton *might* be able to procure would go nowhere against that.

Placing his laptop back on his thighs, he scrolled up the front page of the *Reno Evening Gazette* to the story of Candee-Lee's murder and searched for the name of the homicide detective who had investigated it. Henry Gale.

Morton typed the detective's name into Google and began to search various stories for the man, finding that he had retired from active duty in 2003, going on to form his own private investigator firm out of Las Vegas. He found that *Henry Gale PI* had his own website and sent him an email outlining the case and asking him if any other evidence might have been kept from the murder which could now be DNA-tested. It was a long shot, but, as he had already proven with this case, it was one well worth his taking.

With the balls firmly in other people's courts, Morton placed his laptop to the side, stretched and yawned. He needed a break. It was coming up to lunchtime and he was still sitting in his pyjamas, but he also still needed to write the concluding report for Vanessa, Billie and Liza, and preferably before everyone returned from their trip to Helston.

He stood up, wandered over to the window and peered out over the cove. Despite the cosy warmth inside the cottage, getting out for some fresh air appealed to him. He had the vague idea that there was a wooden bench not far from the house with views overlooking Cadgwith; perhaps he could sit there and type up his findings.

Having hurried upstairs to wash and dress, Morton pulled on his winter coat, placed his laptop and notepad in his bag and stepped out of the cottage. The air was surprisingly motionless, with an absence of the usual Atlantic winds that tended to whirl around the cove in wintertime. He took in a few long breaths, unable to stop his thoughts from returning to the hope of being able to exonerate his grandfather from murder. He suddenly felt guilty for the way in which he had so readily allowed the revelations to tarnish the fond memories that he had of the man. He sighed and began to walk slowly up the narrow grass South West Coast Path, which ran close to the cliff edge, until he reached a wooden bench with a perfect view over the cove. He sat down, took out his laptop, finding a reply waiting from Kathy.

Hi Morton. I dread to ask why you want to know when Derek Redmond died! I'm not sure of the exact date, but it wasn't too long after my 'incident'. I seem to recall I'd not been home from hospital very long when one of the officers from the station came and told me. I'll try and get you the exact date. I believe he fell from a block of flats in Crawley. Best, Kathy

211

The exact date would be useful, but even knowing that he had died just prior to Rosie Hart absconded to America was significant. He replied to Kathy asking for any further information about Derek Redmond's fall, explicitly asking if there might have been anything suspicious about his death. Then, he began to write the report into what he had discovered about Vanessa, Billie and Liza's biological mother. As he typed Rosie's name and added her photograph, he realised that this was probably going to be the hardest report that he had ever had to write.

'Daddy!' Grace's voice shrieked as she and Juliette emerged hand-in-hand from the coast path. She ran up and hugged him.

'Hi, darling,' he responded, pulling her up onto his lap and kissing her on the head. 'Have you had a nice morning?'

Grace nodded. 'Yes. We went play park.'

'Oh, did you? Lovely.'

'Hi,' Juliette said, leaning over with her hand on her bump to kiss him on the lips.

'How did you know I was here?' he asked, glancing down the track, unable to see the house from this secluded spot.

Juliette held up her mobile phone. 'Find My Friends.'

Morton rolled his eyes. 'Stalker.'

'Yep. All done?' she asked hopefully.

'Almost,' he answered. 'I can't quite send the report to the women just yet, though, as I'm waiting on a final couple of bits, including—' he cupped his hands over Grace's ears, '—that my grandfather might *not* have murdered a prostitute after all.'

Grace shook his hands from her head and glowered at him.

'What?' Juliette stammered. 'Who did, then?'

'Take a guess…'

Juliette's eyes widened. 'No! No way! How on earth did you find *that* out? Wait. Are you joking? Is that why she was in Reno when she died?'

'It's just a theory at the moment,' he said, 'but one that I need to firm up, either way.'

'Good job you didn't say anything about it yet to Aunty Margaret, for goodness' sake.'

'Absolutely,' he agreed. 'How is she?' He looked at Juliette and nodded back in the direction of the cottage.

'Totally fine—normal. She's back at the house, baking. I think she wants us all to play some board games together this evening.'

'Sounds good to me. Any mention of Vanessa or…?'

'No. Nothing.'

Morton took in a deep breath. 'Right, give me thirty seconds and we can head back together.' Having concluded the report with the suggestion that the three sisters add themselves to the UK Adoption Contact Register in case there were other half-siblings out there who could be matched to them, he attached the requisite form, CR part 2, and then saved and closed the file. 'Done!' he declared, stowing his laptop and notepad, and, taking Grace by the hand, led the way back to the coast path. When he got there, he paused and, instead of turning left back to the cottage, turned right.

'Where are we going?' Juliette asked.

'Just there,' he said, pointing ahead of them.

'Ahh, yes,' Juliette said with a smile, guessing where they were headed. 'Five years ago.'

Morton continued until he reached an old, dilapidated coastguard hut that sat perched on the very edge of the clifftop. It was surrounded by a low stone wall above which were stunning views across the rugged coastline. He put his arm around Juliette and said to Grace, 'On Christmas Day five years ago, Daddy asked Mummy to marry him right on this very spot.'

Grace looked between the two of them indifferently, apparently not sure of the reaction that was required of her.

'Best decision of your life?' he asked her as his mobile pinged with an incoming message.

She screwed up her face. 'Better than the decision to eat a full English breakfast pasty, this morning,' she replied, rubbing her tummy. 'And I don't think the baby is too keen, either.'

Morton smiled, staring out to sea and reflecting on how much his life had changed in the intervening five years. He had been a very different person back then, having only recently discovered that Aunty Margaret had in fact been his biological mother and not simply his father's sister. And it was whilst walking on these very cliffs that she had revealed the tiny snippets of information that had allowed Morton to track down his biological father. It was astonishing to him, standing here, how much the previous uncertainty about his biological parents had left him with a lasting, permeant sense of feeling adrift. He had never wanted to marry or have children, suffering as he did from a severe disconnect between him and the surname a future spouse or child would receive from him. But now, he felt calmly and completely anchored to his family and to their shared past.

He kissed Grace and Juliette in turn.

'I bored,' Grace said, pulling on Morton's hand.

'Come on, then. Let's get back to the house.'

They walked the short distance down the coast path and entered the cottage.

'You must be freezing!' Aunty Margaret said. 'Dinner's in the oven, the fire's restocked and I've dug some old board games out of the cupboard that we can all sit and play together later.'

'Sounds great,' Morton said, standing in front of the fire and warming his hands. 'Did you have a good day?'

'Oh, yes,' Margaret answered. 'Just perfect. I can't get your Uncle Jim to go shopping for love nor money; so, to have a day out with these two gorgeous ladies was pure bliss, don't you know.'

Morton smiled. 'That's good. And I got most of my work done, too.' He remembered then that he had received a text message whilst up at the old coastguard hut and took out his mobile phone to take a quick, surreptitious look. One WhatsApp notification from Billie and one Messenger notification from Kathy. 'I'm just going to pop my stuff upstairs,' he said, not wishing to read the messages in front of everyone.

'Bring me down that *Guardian* article you were in,' Aunty Margaret said. 'Juliette's been telling me all about it.'

'I think it's down here, actually,' Juliette said, heading over to her handbag.

'It's embarrassing. *Please*, read it before I get back down,' Morton muttered, picking up his bag and heading to the bedroom and closing the door. Sitting on the bed, he looked first at the message from Billie.

Hi Morton. Hope you're getting along ok. I've asked my older and wiser sister, Amy about my dad's death. She said it were a bit tragic actually. Apparently he

214

fell into the canal in Manchester on his way home from the pub and drowned. It was the 16th November 1980. Sad all round! Hope you have a great Christmas x

Fell into the canal and drowned? Or was pushed into the canal and drowned? he questioned, switching apps to read Kathy's message.

Me again. Derek Redmond died 17 December 1980. The official verdict was accidental death but no witnesses came forward who actually saw him fall. Please don't tell me this has something to do with you know who? Best, Kathy

'Morton?' Juliette called up from downstairs. 'Have you got lost, or something?'

'Just coming,' he shouted down as he hurriedly opened his laptop. He brought up the digital timeline that he had created and added the new information.

14th Nov 1980 - Kathy stabbed
16th Nov 1980 - Edward Crouch drowned
17th Dec 1980 - Derek Redmond fell to his death
20th Dec 1980 - Candee-Lee Gaddy stabbed to death
20th Dec 1980 - Rosie Hart hit by bus

It certainly appeared on paper to be plausible and possible that Rosie Hart had gone on a revenge rampage against the men whom she deemed to have slighted her. Could she reasonably have been in Crawley, West Sussex when Derek Redmond had died on the 17th December and then been in Reno three days later when Candee-Lee Gaddy had died? Didn't the article regarding Rosie's death mention her arrival? He looked back at the screenshot that he had taken. *The twenty-eight-year-old woman had only arrived in the city the day before...* And after all, Crawley was just a stone's throw from Gatwick Airport. Yes, it was possible for Rosie Hart to have committed all of these crimes, he thought. But he had nothing more than thin circumstantial evidence with which to prove his case.

'Daddy!' Grace yelled up the stairs.

'Coming,' he repeated, staring at the chronology of events. He made a snap decision: because the evidence against Rosie was so weak, he would send his concluding report to Vanessa, Liza and Billie right now, leaving out his unfounded suspicions about Edward Crouch, Derek Redmond and Candee-Lee's deaths. There was enough in the report to get their heads around without adding unsubstantiated claims about their biological mother's also having been a sadistic murderer.

He took in a quick breath and typed out a message to the three women.

Dear Vanessa, Billie and Liza
I hope you are all keeping well and are ready for Christmas. Barring one or two elements, I have concluded my research into your biological mother. The process was not an easy one. I know that the three of you had your suspicions about your mother's lifestyle, which have been confirmed in my research. Attached are two PDF documents. The first contains just your birth mother's name, photograph, short biography of her life and a family tree. The second contains sourced and detailed information about her life. I do need to offer a cautionary word here: in the second document, I have not attempted to water down or gloss over some of the unpleasant aspects of the case. I know from earlier conversations between us that you were all very keen to find answers, no matter how bad they might be. The facts of the case, however, are much worse than I had warned you to prepare for and unfortunately do not make for happy reading. For the first time ever in my career, I would advise you to only open the first document to learn your biological mother's name, brief details of her life and to see her photograph. It is, of course, your choice but my advice is that the second file makes for distressing and unpleasant reading.
I wish the three of you a very Happy Christmas and New Year.
Kind regards,
Morton

He sent the message and then sat in stony silence for several seconds until Grace shouted, 'Daddy! Daddy! Daddy!'

Morton closed the laptop lid, stood up and headed out into the hallway where he passed the old black and white photograph of his grandfather. He paused and looked him in the eyes. 'Sorry,' he said sincerely.

Downstairs, Morton found Aunty Margaret reading the *Guardian* newspaper article about him and the Duggan Case. She saw him enter the room and read aloud, "*I could never have solved such a complicated case without the use of genetic genealogy*', Morton Farrier said, adding, '*DNA never lies!*''

Morton rolled his eyes. 'Quite true,' he agreed. Then he thought for a moment and added, 'But just sometimes it answers the wrong question.'

Chapter Twenty-Six

25ᵗʰ December 1980, Folkestone, Kent

Alfred was standing behind the net curtains, looking out of his lounge window. For the first time in several years, he could do so in the certain knowledge that Rosie Hart was not about to skulk up the drive, demanding money from him. The relief was both palpable and immense. Once he had recovered from the shock of seeing the news of her death in the very city in which he had been staying, the picture of what Rosie must have done crystallised, and he knew without a shadow of a doubt that she had killed Candee-Lee. It was a very clear attempt at double-revenge: someone he cared about had been murdered and he would undoubtedly have been squarely in the frame, had Rosie not been squashed under a bus and, therefore, been unable to tip the police off with his name. As soon as Alfred had read the story in the *Reno Evening Gazette* and read Rosie's chilling note, he had packed up his belongings and taken the first flight home.

Things were going to be different now, Alfred had resolved. Very different. The first change had been the house. Since his arrival back home two days ago, he had spent several hours cleaning and tidying so that the place now looked semi-respectable. Then, there was Margaret. On the plane home, he had finally accepted that his relationship with her was probably broken forever and that the irrevocable damage had been largely of his own making. He had thought long and hard about how to make things up to her and, yesterday, he had taken the typewriter, which he had smashed, into town to be repaired. The shop proprietor had told him that a brand new one would cost him far less money, but the machine had originally belonged to Anna, and he hoped that Margaret would appreciate the sentiment and effort that he had gone to in its restoration. He was even considering driving it all the way down to Cornwall himself, once it had been repaired. It was a small gesture but one that he hoped that she would be able to see was as close as he could ever get to apologising.

He watched through the window as an orange Ford Cortina pulled up in front of his house. He smiled and turned around to find that his mother was sitting in the armchair with her head tipped backwards and her mouth open, sound asleep. 'They're here,' he said quietly.

'Hmm?' she said, looking all around like a startled pigeon.

'Peter, Maureen and the boys,' Alfred said. 'They're here.'

'Righteo,' she said, rising from the chair with the sudden vitality of a much younger woman. Alfred hoped that he would be quite so agile when he would be in his nineties. She followed him through to the hallway and stood at his side as he pulled open the front door.

'Happy Christmas!' he greeted as the four trooped up the driveway.

'Happy Christmas, Grandad,' six-year-old Morton called, running up and hugging him. 'Happy Christmas, Great Granny!'

'Did Father Christmas bring you lots of nice things?' Nellie asked the boys, leaning down.

'I got the Mousetrap game, sports car Top Trumps and some Famous Five books,' Morton replied.

'Did he say a mousetrap?' Nellie questioned Alfred.

'It's a board game, Granny,' Peter explained.

'Oh, I see.'

'And I got these,' four-year-old Jeremy said, thrusting two Action Men into the air. 'They're both called Dave.'

Alfred chuckled, glanced up at Peter and Maureen, and then said, 'Come in before you catch a cold. I'll get the kettle on.' He stepped back inside and held the front door open while they entered the house. 'You all go and sit down.'

'I'll give you a hand,' Peter offered, following him into the kitchen while everyone else moved into the lounge. 'How was your Christmas dinner?'

'Oh, it wasn't too bad for my first go,' Alfred answered. 'Actually, the turkey was dry, the sprouts undercooked, the potatoes burned and the gravy like ditch water. Honestly, I don't know how these women do it, I tell you.'

Peter laughed as Morton came running into the kitchen.

'Grandad,' he said, dragging out the word in the way that he did whenever he wanted something.

'Yes,' Alfred replied, copying him by lengthening his answer in return.

'Can you help me with the family tree, please?'

Peter rolled his eyes. 'He's got this All About Me project to do for school over the Christmas holidays and he's very taken with the family tree part of it. Asking me all sorts of questions which always lead to more questions. I said to ask you about names, places and dates.'

'I need to do a family tree and stick photos all over it,' Morton clarified.

'Right,' Alfred said. 'Just let me get everyone a cup of tea and then we'll see what we can do, shall we? You should also speak to your great-granny: wait till you hear all that she can remember. Just make sure you speak up when you're talking; her hearing isn't what it used to be.'

'Thanks, Grandad,' Morton said, skipping back into the lounge and relaying the news to anyone who would listen.

'You don't need to do too much,' Peter said dismissively of the nuisance as he boiled the kettle. 'Just give him your parents' names and birth dates; that'll do him.'

'Okey-dokey,' Alfred answered, feeding five tea bags into the ceramic teapot.

'I'll finish up in here,' Peter offered. 'You go and sit down with everyone.'

'Thanks. I'll go fetch a piece of paper and a pencil for this family tree business,' Alfred said, heading into the lounge and hearing that his mother was mid-way through regaling Morton with family information while Jeremy played with his Action Men in the centre of the room.

'My husband was called Charlie Farrier—he was your *great-*grandfather—and he was born in 1890 in Lambeth,' she told Morton.

'Where's Lambeth?' he asked.

'London,' she answered. 'And he died not too long before you were born, actually, in July 1974.'

Alfred was rummaging in his bureau when he stopped and looked at his mother. 'No, he didn't,' he corrected. 'He died in the First World War.' He pulled out a piece of paper and added, '*Len* died in 1974, but he's not your direct blood line, Morton, so you don't need to worry about him, lovely man though he was.'

Morton looked confused but determined, nonetheless.

'Great-Granny married again,' Maureen explained. 'After your great-grandad died.'

Alfred could see that his mother appeared confused. Then her eyes widened. 'Oh, I am daft. Just ignore me,' she said, slumping back in her chair and folding her arms.

Alfred sat down with the paper on his lap. 'Are we starting with you?' he asked Morton.

'Yes, please.'

'Okay,' Alfred said, jotting down Morton's name from the top of which he drew a short vertical line. As he went to write the names of Morton's parents, he glanced across and could see that Maureen was looking uncomfortable, perhaps worrying about the name that he might write down for Morton's mother. 'Peter...and Maureen,' he found himself saying loudly as he wrote, just to be safe. 'Then there's me, your dad's dad, born just before the First World War in 1914.'

'Did you fight in the war?' Jeremy asked keenly.

'Not in the First World War, no,' Alfred replied. 'I would have been your age! In the Second World War I did, though.'

Jeremy gasped.

'What did you do?' Morton asked him.

Alfred took in a long breath. 'I'll save that for another day. Let's concentrate and fill this in for now, shall we? And then I'll see what photographs I've got to go with it for you.'

'Thanks, Grandad,' Morton said, looking over his shoulder at the growing tree.

'This is the First World War, Dave,' Jeremy said, pointing the gun from one Action Man to the other. 'Okay. Let's get in the helicopter, Dave.'

Alfred watched for a moment impassively as Jeremy whooshed an Action Man around in one of his mother's fluffy slippers which was playing the part of the anachronistic First World War helicopter. He was aware that in his peripheral vision both his mother and Maureen were observing him, probably wondering how he would react to the question about his war service, since he had never uttered a word about it to anyone. He stared at his and Anna's name on the rudimentary Farrier family tree in front of him. If, as he suspected was the case, the war years were to blame for some of his later difficulties, then perhaps it was time to revisit those terrible years. But he knew that he would never be able to speak the words, not to his family, his friends or even to his doctor. But, he considered, looking at the paper and pencil before him, maybe he could write things down. Or, better still, type them up when Anna's old machine came back repaired and restored. Maybe.

'Grandad, are you still awake?' Morton asked.

Alfred smiled. 'Yes. Sorry, I'm here. Now, where was I? My mother and father. Well, my mother can tell you her own details,' he said, looking at her to find that she was fast asleep again. 'Or not.'

Peter entered the room, carrying the tray of drinks. 'Here we are,' he said, setting it down on the coffee table. 'Shall I switch the television on? The Queen will be on in three minutes, then it's *20,000 Leagues Under the Sea*—you'll enjoy that film, boys. It's about a giant sea monster.'

'But I want to do my family tree,' Morton complained. 'I don't want to watch a stupid film.'

'We can do that,' Alfred said. 'Let's you and I go out into the kitchen when that's on. I've got a photo somewhere of *my* grandad Farrier, an old agricultural labourer with a big bushy beard. Would you like me to see if I can find it?'

'Yes, please,' Morton answered. 'What's an agricultural labourer?'

'A farm hand,' he answered, leading the boy into the kitchen and feeling grateful to be able to nurture a bond with his first grandchild. He ruffled the boy's hair and thought of Margaret separated from her child but still utterly convinced that the right decision—however painful—had been made. Then his thoughts inexplicably jumped onto Rosie Hart. What if she had been telling the truth about her baby being his? That little girl, left outside Woolworths in Sevenoaks would now be five years old. He wondered what had happened to her. He had made gentle enquiries with PC Jolly and Mr Colby from Woolworths about what had become of the child but neither of them had known anything. Even if she had been his daughter, there was nothing that he could do for her now. All he could do was to focus his energies and time on the people on the family tree in his hand, replete with its omissions and half-truths that he hoped Morton would never find out.

Chapter Twenty-Seven

25th December 2019, Cadgwith, Cornwall

Morton was woken by the floorboards creaking in the hallway. Judging by the depth of darkness in the room, it was still early. Outside the bedroom door, he could hear Uncle Jim's best attempt at moving around the cottage stealthily, huffing and puffing, banging doors and muttering to himself. Morton rolled over, picked up his mobile from the bedside table and squinted at the time: 7.06am on Christmas morning. Among the raft of notifications on his screen was an email alert from Henry Gale, the detective turned PI from Las Vegas. He opened his phone to read the message.

Morton, Interesting to hear from you. Yes, I was on the Gaddy murder case back in 1980. I was relieved to hear that they'd finally closed the case by identifying Alfred Farrier as the perpetrator but if what you said in your email is true, then this casts a big doubt over that certainty. You asked if any other evidence had been collected from the crime scene? We found the murder weapon—a blade without a handle and what might be interesting to you is that other than Gaddy's blood, we found another sample near where the handle should have been where someone cut themselves whilst holding it. Obviously, that didn't necessarily occur at the time of the murder, but the semen and blood sample were <u>not</u> from the same person. To be honest, Morton, I don't rate your chances at getting this case reopened but it's probably worth contacting Reno Police Department and telling them everything you've told me and maybe they'll run the blade through the same tests as the semen sample. You can drop my name in as the original investigating officer in case that helps. Good luck, buddy. HG

Morton was at once heartened that the detective working on the case had agreed with him that his grandfather's conviction was at best ambiguous and at worst completely wrongful. The fact that there had been blood on the knife that hadn't matched Candee-Lee Gaddy or his grandfather was striking, and Morton was very surprised that the Reno Police Department had not pursued the blood over the semen, especially given that the two samples had not matched each other. If Venator, the Investigative Genetic Genealogy company which had solved the crime, had not been headed up by a very distant ex-girlfriend of Morton's, then he might have contacted them for further details; but it was all very awkward, worsened by the fact that he was ostensibly trying to exonerate his own grandfather. He quickly decided that, as a private company outside of law enforcement, they would have pursued whatever DNA samples had been provided by the Reno Police Department, anyway. It was they who Morton needed to contact, not Venator.

He sat up in bed, effortlessly trying not to disturb Juliette or make a sound that might stir Grace. From the next bedroom, he could hear Aunty Margaret shuffling about and he wondered actually whether he should wake his sleeping wife and daughter. He could just imagine Aunty Margaret and Uncle Jim sitting downstairs by the Christmas tree patiently waiting for them to appear. For the last three days, she had been her usual bubbly and bright self. No mention had been made of the revelations about her having a half-sister and Morton had been forced to message Vanessa and explain the situation. He had considered a watered-down version of the truth or even an outright lie—perhaps that he had not yet had a chance to tell her—but settled on the simple truth that Aunty Margaret was having a difficult time processing the information. Vanessa had said that she didn't mind and that she was busy dealing with the information about her biological mother, anyway. The three half-sisters had all opened his first report, the one containing Rosie Hart's name, photograph, short biography and family tree, but, so far, none of them had opened the second report detailing her criminal background. Billie wanted to read it, Liza did not and Vanessa was undecided. They had arranged a face-to-face meet-up after Christmas to try and agree on a unanimous decision: they either all should read it, or nobody would. Morton thought that it was a laudable endeavour, but whether they could actually all agree on a single course of action was another matter entirely.

He opened up a web browser and ran a Google search for the Reno Police Department. Their website was top of the results list, and, under *Contact*, Morton found an email address which he clicked. He typed out a more formal, carefully constructed message than that which he had sent to Henry Gale, adding the former detective's name as a supporter of his request to have the case re-examined and the knife DNA-tested. When he had finished composing the email,

Morton read it through and then sent it. He closed his mobile, swung his feet around to the floor and then tip-toed towards the door, thinking that he would leave Juliette and Grace sleeping for longer while he went downstairs and chatted with Aunty Margaret and Uncle Jim. However, in the event, a one-man band stomping across a carpet of bubble wrap would have made less noise getting across the old, exposed floorboards than Morton did. Both his wife and daughter were wide awake before he had even laid his hand down on the door latch.

'Father Christmas has been,' Morton whispered, hoping to smother Juliette's inevitable annoyance.

She groaned. 'No, he hasn't. I asked for a lie-in.'

'Father Christmas!' Grace chanted, leaping up and stretching her arms out towards him. Morton picked her out of the travel cot, gave her a kiss and said, 'Happy Christmas, Graciekins. Shall we go and see if he left any presents for you under the tree?'

'Yes!' she said, spinning her head and looking at Juliette. 'Mummy, Mummy!'

Another groan from Juliette, then she took in a long breath, stretched in the bed, sat up and said flatly, 'Happy Christmas.'

The three of them trooped down the stairs, finding Aunty Margaret and Uncle Jim in the lounge, illuminated by the tiny fairy lights on the Christmas tree and the bright flames from the newly revived open fire. They were sitting in their dressing gowns, each holding a cup and saucer, and listening to their hi-fi system, playing Christmas carols softly in the background.

'Good morning and happy Christmas!' Aunty Margaret beamed.

'Saint Nicholas has visited!' Uncle Jim barked, pointing at the pile of wrapped gifts around the base of the tree.

'Presents!' Grace cried.

Morton fake-gasped. 'Actually, I'm sure they're probably all for me.'

'No,' Grace countered, squirming to get down from his arms.

She rushed over to the gifts and knelt down in front of them, utterly mesmerised.

'Well, let's see what Father Christmas got you, then,' Juliette said, reaching for a present with Christmas-themed Peppa Pig wrapping paper and handing it to her.

Grace tore into it and pulled out a painting set. 'Wow!' she said, studying the contents of the box.

'You can paint your own horses,' Juliette enthused. 'Do you want to get another present and we'll see who it's for?'

Grace put down the painting set, picked up another present from the pile and began to tear the wrapping.

'No, wait,' Juliette said, reaching for the gift. 'It might not be for you. To *Jim*,' she read, passing it over to him.

Uncle Jim held it aloft for a moment. 'Whatever could this be?' he said, opening the package to reveal two pairs of white long johns. 'Perfect! Me others are riddled with more holes than a sieve. Thank you, Margaret—I mean, thank you, Santa.'

'Take another one, Grace,' Juliette said, 'and I'll read the label to see who it's for.'

Grace picked up a small, wrapped box and passed it to Juliette. 'To Margaret.'

'Ooo!' Margaret uttered, taking the present and tearing it open. She burst into laughter as she held up a deep-blue bottle of perfume. 'Midnight Fantasy from Britney Spears!' She looked across at Uncle Jim, elbowed him and said, 'My midnight fantasy is you not snoring beside me like some washed-up old seal. Britney Spears, honestly. I'm sixty-one years old, for heaven's sake!'

Grace giggled at the analogy as she selected—probably deliberately, Morton guessed—the largest gift under the tree, which she was unable to pick up owing to its weight and obscure dimensions. 'This one,' she said to Juliette.

'How did the seven-months-pregnant woman get the job of chief present distributor?' Aunty Margaret begged, directing the question at Morton and Uncle Jim. 'One of you men get down there.'

'Sorry, yes,' Morton said, kneeling on the floor beside the tree. He looked at the label of the present Grace had chosen. 'Oh, there's a surprise: it's for Grace Matilda Farrier.'

Grace grinned as Morton carefully slid it in front of her. She gasped when a set of handlebars appeared from the torn wrapping paper. 'A bike!'

'Your first bike,' Juliette enthused.

Grace finished unwrapping the present and was about to climb on when Morton said, 'We'll take it outside later, shall we? You can't really ride it indoors.' Seeing her disappointment, he added, 'Come and choose another present.'

Grace obliged, picking up a thin parcel which she handed to Morton.

'Uncle Jim, another one,' Morton said, passing it over.

'I am a lucky devil,' he said, ripping it open and then smiling. '*Cadgwith Then and Now*,' he read out the book's title. 'Wow, I didn't know such a thing existed. Thank you, Morton and Juliette.'

'It's old photos of the village with new images to show how the same part looks in the modern day, with a bit of history written in between,' Morton explained.

'He's so old, he'll probably appear in both sets of photos,' Aunty Margaret quipped with a laugh.

'Thank you, dear wife,' he countered.

'Give Grace another one,' Juliette said, pointing, 'then open that envelope down there.'

Morton found another gift for Grace, which she tore into in seconds.

'A piano!' she said, holding up a boxed mini keyboard.

'Shall I open it for you?'

'Yes, please,' Grace said.

Morton took the keyboard out of the box, switched it on and handed it back to her. 'That'll please the neighbours,' he said, picking up the envelope addressed to him as Grace began to play a tuneless song with garbled lyrics.

'A Big Y-700,' Morton exclaimed, pulling out a sheet of A4 paper from the envelope. 'Excellent. Thank you very much.'

'A big why? What?' Aunty Margaret asked.

'Who?' Uncle Jim chipped in. 'When?'

'Big Y-700. It's an upgrade on my paternal Y-DNA test,' Morton explained.

'It says it's intended for expert users with an interest in advancing science,' Juliette added. 'I thought—since I got you your first ever DNA kit when we stayed here for Christmas five years ago—that I had to get something DNA-related.'

Morton smiled, recalling how, back in 2014 autosomal DNA tests were not available in the UK and she had had to get an Ancestry kit shipped to a friend in the USA, who had then in turn posted it on to

Juliette.

'Is there still *more* to learn from your DNA?' Aunty Margaret asked. 'You found your dad, after all.'

Morton smiled. 'There's *always* more to learn with DNA.'

'Oh, it's all beyond me,' Aunty Margaret began. 'There's something else family tree related for you in that box there; but first your good wife needs to open something.'

'I've got just the thing,' Morton said, rummaging among the pile of gifts for an envelope with her name on the front. 'Here it is,' he said, handing it to her.

'Is that a big why as well?' Uncle Jim asked, watching as she took out a sheet of paper.

'No, only men can take a Y-test,' Morton answered, not really certain if Uncle Jim was being serious or not.

'Oh, fab,' she said. 'A weekend of spa treatments for two at Flackley Ash Hotel. Thank you very much.'

'I thought it might be a nice pre-baby escape,' Morton said, having had the idea from reading the newspaper article about Rosie and Steven Hart trying to steal from them back in 1971.

'The calm before the storm,' Aunty Margaret added, elevating her volume to match Grace's song which was a curious, heavy metal, shouty version of Twinkle Twinkle Little Star.

'Grace!' Morton said, reaching over for the volume button and turning it down.

'I could really do with it right now, actually,' Juliette muttered, looking longingly at her voucher.

'Shall I open this one, now?' Morton asked Aunty Margaret, referring to the parcel at which she had previously pointed.

'Yes, although, don't get your hopes up too high. You might not like it—give it to a charity shop if you don't.'

Morton took off the wrapping paper, revealing an unmarked cardboard box. Opening the flaps at the top, he peered inside. 'A typewriter,' he said, carefully removing it. It was an old vintage Imperial Model T with *Made in Leicester, England* written on the bottom of it. On the side was a small, faded gold label with *Anna Farrier, 163 Canterbury Road, Folkestone, Kent* typed on it.

'It belonged to my mother, your grandmother,' Aunty Margaret explained. 'Thought you might like it.'

'It's…wonderful. Thank you very much,' Morton said, obviously moved. 'I really love it.'

'More presents,' Grace said, turning away from the keyboard and facing Morton.

'Yes,' he agreed, eyeing the remaining stack. 'There's plenty more presents.'

'We could be here a while,' Uncle Jim muttered, gazing into his empty teacup.

Almost forty minutes later, including a short interlude for hot drinks, the huge pile of presents had been unwrapped, leaving a state of apparent devastation strewn across the lounge floor. Juliette had just taken Grace upstairs for a bath and Uncle Jim was peeling potatoes in the kitchen, leaving Morton and Aunty Margaret to tidy up.

'I really love the typewriter,' he said, stuffing handfuls of torn wrapping paper into a black bin bag.

'Oh, you're very welcome. I thought you'd appreciate it.'

'Don't tell Juliette, but I think it's my favourite gift.'

Aunty Margaret laughed. 'I won't tell her. It's actually in good working condition—I tried it before I wrapped it up. Not that I expect you to be using it in these days of laptops and what have you.'

'I *am* going to use it,' he said. 'I might even type up some of my genealogical cases on it. Lends them a bit of a real-history feel.'

'You wouldn't guess that it had been completely smashed to pieces, would you?'

'What, *that* machine?' Morton said, pointing to the typewriter.

Aunty Margaret nodded. 'When my dad found out that I was moving down to Cornwall, he smashed it on the kitchen floor in outright anger.'

'Really? But why?'

Aunty Margaret shrugged. 'He was angry that I'd kept my plans from him, but I knew that if I told him, he wouldn't let me leave.'

'But you repaired it?'

'No. I didn't. *He* did. Gave me a hell of a shock, one day; he just turned up out of the blue and handed me the typewriter. It was all very awkward. He was about to turn around and drive straight back to Folkestone, too. Can you imagine? Of course, I invited him in, and he ended up staying a night or two down here. I got the impression he wanted to say something and maybe explain himself, or apologise, or something, but he never could do it.'

'You think driving down here and giving you something that belonged to your mother was like some kind of peace offering?' Morton asked.

'Yes, that's exactly it. He did say he'd actually used that typewriter himself to write down what happened to him during the war, so you'll be the fourth Farrier to use the machine. Maybe you can get Grace to type up a story when she's older and make it five.'

Morton was immediately intrigued by her previous comment. 'Do you know what happened to whatever he typed up about the war?'

'No idea. I've never seen hide nor hair of anything. I guess it went the way of a lot of his paperwork when he died: to the dump. Peter was very quick to get a house clearance firm in and get matters tied up as soon as possible after he died, and, of course, with me being down here, I couldn't really say too much.'

Morton grimaced at the very thought of all that history going to the dump.

'After he brought the typewriter down here, he seemed to have changed; at least he did for the few hours that I saw him. All the anger seemed to have gone out of him.'

'I wonder what happened?' Morton asked, gathering up the last of the rubbish from the floor.

Aunty Margaret tied up the top of her black sack and exhaled. 'Another of life's mysteries. He really was a very, very contradictory person, you know,' she muttered. 'I'm not sure he'll ever be fully understood.' She turned to face him. 'To be honest, trying to answer Vanessa's inevitable first question of 'what was he like?' has kept me awake for hours trawling through fragments of my life, trying to answer that question. What *was* he like? He was a tyrant. He was kind. He was cruel. He was troubled. He was an amazing grandfather. He was a hard worker. He was secretive. He was hypocritical. He was short-tempered. He was difficult. He was generous...'

'He was very complicated,' Morton finished.

'Exactly that,' Aunty Margaret said. 'All this introspection and looking into the past for answers—' she shrugged, '—it hasn't really got me anywhere or closer to working out which of those versions of the man was really him: I think, for whatever reason, he was just a different man to different people at different times in his life.' Aunty Margaret stood still, staring out of the lounge window for a long moment. 'I always wanted a sister, especially when I was growing up. I had Peter, of course, but, being a boy and being eight years older than me, he and I weren't really very close. I suppose I felt more like an only child and not having a mother, either... That didn't help matters. It was a bit of a shock when you told me about Vanessa, you know?'

'I'm sure,' he agreed. 'And I'm genuinely sorry for burdening you with something you'd rather not have known.'

'The truth always comes out in the end, love,' she mused. 'Anyway, having thought about it a great deal and talked it over with Jim, I've decided that I *would* like to meet up with her—assuming she still wants to, that is.'

Morton smiled. 'She'd *love* to meet you. I think you'd get on very well together.'

'Well, you can pass her all my details and we'll take it from there, shall we?'

'I'll text her right now. I'm sure it'll be the best Christmas present she could wish for.'

'Oh, I don't know about that,' she laughed. 'What about Vanessa's mother, this Rosie woman? What was she like?'

Now, there was a question. He thought about all that he had discovered and opted simply to say, 'She was also very, very complicated.'

Epilogue

16th March 2020, The St Pancras Renaissance Hotel, London

Morton was sitting on a plush, olive-coloured velveteen sofa in the opulent grand lobby of The St Pancras Renaissance Hotel, feeling very much out of place and woefully underdressed in a pair of black jeans and a plain-looking white shirt. Sitting opposite him, on a matching sofa were Vanessa, Billie and Liza, all much more appropriately attired for such a five-star venue.

Liza glanced again over at the doorway. 'Shall we wait, or shall I pour?' she asked, eyeing the uncorked bottle of champagne.

Vanessa looked at her watch. 'Give it five more minutes.'

There was a shared look of apprehension on the three women's faces. 'So, how was your trip to St Ives?' Morton asked Vanessa, trying to lighten the mood.

'Amazing,' she started, then turned to face her two half-sisters on either side of her. 'Last week, I went down for an artist's retreat thing and extended it to include a visit to meet my other half-sister, Margaret.'

'Oh, wow. What were that like?' Billie asked in her heavy Mancunian accent.

'We got on *so* well,' she answered. 'On paper, we probably don't have that much in common and what with such a large age gap, but we never once stopped talking. There were no awkward silences or thorny issues. Uncanny, really. I'm hoping to go back down to Cornwall next month for a longer break—lockdown-depending.'

'Oh, that'll all be done and dusted in a few weeks,' Billie commented. 'And that's even if we go into a lockdown at all.'

'I think, looking at what's happening in Europe, it's probably inevitable, now, I have to say,' Liza commented.

'Did you talk about she-who-shall-not-be-named with Margaret?' Billie asked.

Vanessa shook her head. 'Margaret didn't bring her up and I sure as hell didn't want to.'

'Good,' Billie said. 'Her name should never be spoken aloud again.'

'In case we summon up her evil spirit,' Liza chimed in, making her half-sisters laugh.

'I can't *un*read that report,' Billie said, gesticulating wildly with her hands. She was the only one of the three women to have read the entirety of Morton's discoveries into Rosie Hart's life, after they had failed to reach a unanimous agreement. 'I sooo regret reading it. I should have listened to you, Morton. Oh, she were a right vile woman, that one. Just vile.'

'I've literally deleted the entire email, so I'm never tempted to give it a look,' Liza admitted. 'I'm done with her and done with caring. I've got you two and that's all I need.'

'*Three*. Make that three,' Morton corrected, nodding over to the entrance as a smartly dressed man with a wide smile on his face strode towards them. There could be no doubting his identity.

All three half-sisters looked across at him and then expressed varying degrees of shock: Vanessa put her hand to her mouth; Liza gasped; and Billie burst into tears.

'Luke?' Liza, the closest in proximity to the man stammered.

He nodded and pulled her into an embrace which he repeated with equal fervour for Vanessa.

'I just can't believe it,' Vanessa said, clinging on to him and beginning to cry.

'Me neither,' he replied softly.

Finally, the pair broke apart and Billie, with lines of mascara running down her cheeks, reached out and pulled Luke to her. 'My brother...' she stammered.

Instinctively, Vanessa and Liza wrapped their arms around the pair and the four half-siblings were joined together for the first time in their whole lives.

After some time of near-silence, the group broke apart and sat down on the sofa.

'Hi, I'm Morton,' he introduced, meeting the man's gaze.

'Luke,' he replied, shaking Morton's hand. He was a handsome forty-six-year-old with short brown hair and dark eyes, wearing a smart navy-coloured suit that made Morton feel even further under-dressed. 'It's great to meet you at last. I've heard a lot about you from these three.'

'*Now* can I pour?' Liza laughed. 'I *really* need a drink!'

Luke looked mock-offended. 'Oh, is meeting me for the first time that bad?'

'God, no. I'm just a bag of nerves, is all,' she said, extending her arm to show her quivering hand.

'Go on, then,' Vanessa encouraged. 'Pour away. I could do with it, too.' She faced Luke and dabbed her eyes. 'It's so good to meet you at last.'

'Yes, it's amazing to meet you all in person,' he agreed.

'Allow me,' Morton said, seeing Liza's shaky hand move towards the chilled bottle.

Luke sighed. 'It's felt like forever that I'd been on that Adoption Contact Register, desperately waiting for someone to appear. Then you three turn up all at once; it's…blown me away.'

'I'm an emotional wreck, me,' Billie admitted, dabbing her eyes with a tissue. 'Hey. Has all me make up run all over?'

Vanessa looked at her and then shook her head. 'You're fine.'

'*Six* glasses?' Luke questioned, looking at the flutes that Morton was gradually filling.

'We're expecting one more guest,' Morton answered, glancing at the doorway. 'And, right on cue, here she comes, now.'

'Not another half-sibling?' Luke whispered to Liza who quickly shook her head.

'Hello again,' Morton greeted, turning to Luke and saying, 'Luke, this is Kathy Steadman. Kathy, this is Baby Bradley Broadway.'

Kathy opened her arms and pulled him into a long hug. 'Look at you! My goodness. It's a stupid thing to say, but I'm going to say it anyway: you've grown a lot since I last saw you!'

Luke laughed. 'I hear you spent quite a lot of time trying to find my birth mother and got injured in the process? Thank you—so sincerely—for all your efforts and all it cost you,' he said, then turned to his half-sisters. 'But actually, from what I've been hearing about her, perhaps it was a good thing that we were never reunited with her.'

'Quite,' Kathy agreed, taking a seat beside Morton as he handed out the flutes of champagne. 'She certainly was a piece of work.'

'But we're not going to talk about her,' Billie stated.

'Not even use her name,' Liza added.

'Oh, believe you me,' Kathy began, 'when Morton, here, first got in touch with me, her name was the last thing I wanted to hear or discuss. But…he was very persuasive, and I wanted to help you.'

'Thank you, both,' Vanessa said, glancing between Morton and Kathy. 'We really appreciate all your efforts.'

'We got there in the end,' Morton said, raising his glass above the table. 'To family.'

'To family,' they all echoed, chinking glasses and then retaking their seats.

'You look so like Liza,' Billie said to Luke.

'Do you think so? I think we've all got the same nose,' he said, running a finger over the bridge of his.

Kathy looked at the four half-siblings, chatting and laughing together for the first time in their lives. She leant across to Morton and said quietly, 'I'm just glad they're all so happy and have done so well despite their—how shall I put this?—inauspicious beginnings. Just look at their joy.'

'Yes, life could easily have gone so very differently for them,' Morton agreed.

Kathy lowered her voice to a whisper. 'And you say that she died in Reno? And might have killed someone there?'

Morton nodded. 'I'm pretty sure she did, but I've got no firm evidence…*yet*.'

Kathy chuckled. 'Well, from what I've seen of your research, I'm sure you'll find the answers in the end.'

'I hope so,' he answered. He had exchanged several emails back and forth with the Reno Police Department who were so far unwilling to reopen their investigation, their main sticking point being that he could not provide any substantial evidence that the person whose blood was on the knife was any more likely to have killed her than his grandfather. He had vowed to persist and every year on his grandfather's birthday to try once again to get the case re-examined. *She* would not win.

'And what about Derek Redmond and Edward Crouch?' Kathy whispered.

'Well, I've handed everything over to West Sussex Police and Manchester Police who have both said that they'll take a look into the two deaths, but neither have officially re-opened the investigations yet.' He shrugged. 'I haven't said anything to them yet, either,' he nodded over to the four half-siblings who were all laughing about something. 'I will, if and when the cases *are* re-opened.'

'I guess if the three deaths do end up being confirmed to have been caused by her, then it makes her a serial killer?' Kathy said quietly.

'I hadn't thought about that,' Morton muttered. 'But yes, it would. Wow.'

The pair fell silent as Morton pondered that which Kathy had just said. Even ignoring the circumstantial evidence, Rosie Hart was the most calculatingly evil person that he had ever had to investigate; never had he been more relieved to close a case file than he had been with this one.

When a lull in the conversation across the table finally appeared, Kathy leant across to Luke and asked, 'So, tell me about your life; has everything worked out for you?'

'Yeah, very well, actually,' he answered. 'I was lucky enough to have amazing parents who did everything to ensure I had a loving, fun and supportive childhood. I went to university and studied law, and I now run my own practice in North London. I've got a wonderful wife and two daughters. So, yes, my life worked out very well, thank you.'

'And did you know, growing up, that you were Baby Bradley?' she asked.

Luke smiled. 'Yes. I'd always known that I was adopted and, when I was around the age of ten or eleven, I became more inquisitive, and they showed me the newspaper article and even took me to the phone box to see the exact location.'

'But presumably they couldn't tell you anything about your birth parents?'

'No, and as soon as I was eighteen, I accessed my adoption file. But, of course, there was nothing in there about my biological family because nobody knew who they were…until now.'

'Are you going to read the file that I compiled on her?' Morton asked him. When they had all matched one another on the Adoption Contact Register, Vanessa, Billie and Liza had explained about Morton's investigation and had shared both reports with him.

Luke grimaced and folded his arms. 'I'm not sure. Part of me—probably the lawyer part—wants to know every detail, no matter

236

how grim. But the other part of me—probably the human being—doesn't want this monster in my life or to detract in any way from my real parents. They were the ones who raised me, loved me and looked after me.'

'Ignore the lawyer, most people do,' Billie joked. 'Honestly, I can't tell you how much you don't want to read it.'

Luke smiled at Billie, then addressed Morton, 'And you think that my biological father might have been Derek Redmond who was your—' he flicked his eyes to Kathy, '—boss at Burgess Hill?'

'Yes, I do. But you'll need to take a DNA test to be absolutely certain.'

'Again,' Luke said, 'I'm not sure. He didn't sound like a very nice person, either. It sounds weird but I didn't actually join the Adoption Contact Register in the hope of finding family, I already had that. I just wanted answers and, between all of you, I've kind of got them, along with three fantastic sisters. I'll probably just leave things as they are, to be honest.'

'You sound very level-headed,' Kathy commented.

Luke smiled. 'What about you after the attack? Could you work again?'

Kathy raised her eyebrows. 'I needed a lot of recovery time, obviously, but then became a police driving instructor which I really loved. I did that for fifteen-odd years, then set up my own driving school until retirement.'

'Glad to hear that she-who-shall-not-be-named didn't end your career,' Liza commented.

'Oh, goodness me, no,' Kathy said, sipping her champagne. 'I tell you something, she did a lot of bad things in her life, but, sitting here looking at you—so happy and well-adjusted—she did at least four things right. So, cheers to you four for your strength and resilience.' She raised her glass across the table and toasted the four foundlings.

'Cheers,' they all echoed.

Vanessa, Billie, Liza and Luke all began chatting again, and Kathy turned to Morton and asked, 'And how are your little ones?'

'Great, thanks,' he replied. 'It was my daughter, Grace's third birthday yesterday and my little boy, Isaac, is almost four weeks old, now.'

'Isaac?' Kathy queried.

Morton nodded, knowing what was coming next.

'That's the name of my budgie!'

He grinned. 'Yes, I know. It's where I got the name from.'

'But didn't your wife mind your son being named after a burglar?'

'What?' Morton said, a little too loudly and drawing the attention of the four half-siblings opposite.

'My budgie was named after the Budgie Burglar, Isaac Jones,' she said.

'You've gone and named your son after a burglar?' Vanessa said, trying to keep a straight face.

Morton exhaled. '*Please*, nobody can ever mention this to my wife. *Not Ever.*'

Morton's absolute seriousness was lost on his fellow acquaintances who all burst into laughter.

Historical Information & Acknowledgements

This story emanated from a few loose threads that had been left dangling from *The Sterling Affair* (Morton #8), notably the parentage of Morton's newly found half-aunt, Vanessa Briggs, which positioned the past narrative element of this story in the 1970s. Knowing that there would be some police procedural work involved in this story, I set about finding a detective who had worked in Sussex during this time who could assist me with this information. So, my first thanks go to Malcolm Buckingham, Peter Poulter and Geoff Childs who made enquiries and social media posts on my behalf, which eventually led me to Dave Scales, a retired detective who had worked in Sussex during the 1970s. I was fortunate enough to be able to interview him in person between lockdowns in August 2020 and was delighted not only to receive assistance with the general police procedural work during the 1970s that I had been seeking, but also to learn about a baby abandonment case that he had worked on during this period. Some details fictionalised in this book came from this real case, as outlined below.

On a quiet Sunday morning in August 1978, a fourteen-year-old-girl, Samantha Wynn, went to use the public telephone box on The Broadway in Haywards Heath, situated just outside the Seeboard showroom, when she found a six-day-old baby girl in a cardboard box on the floor. She dialled 999 and comforted the child until the police arrived. The infant was taken to Cuckfield Hospital where she was deemed to be in good health. DS Dave Scales, who had been at home on his lunchbreak from the Burgess Hill Police Station, was put in charge of the investigation. Part of his work included enquiries at Haywards Heath train station and, because of an unusual label in the baby's nappy, followed a lead back to a London hospital, which culminated in the identification of the birth parents. The child, dubbed 'Baby Susie' by the nurses who looked after her, was later adopted by her biological mother's family.

Dave Scales also kindly provided me with the real-life story of the Budgie Burglar, although he wasn't called Isaac Jones.

I'm grateful to Jane Colquhoun for putting me in touch with Roger Wray who in turn put me in touch with Neal Rylatt, an expert on fingerprinting techniques during this period. Thank you very much for all your help and detailed explanations.

My gratitude also goes to Dave Oates for information regarding Canterbury Police Station and to Jan Saunders who provided additional policing advice.

Grateful thanks to my mother, Jane Goodwin, for helping with my questions about the archaic nature of maternity hospitals around the time of my birth in 1976.

Thanks to David Dengate for appearing as himself in the book. If you're in the area of Rye Foreign, pop into the Dengate Farm Stall for seasonal fresh fruit, vegetables and, of course, Christmas trees!

I'm very grateful to many other people who answered various questions on social media, particularly to all those who sent me screenshots of their US Ancestry ethnicity reports, which helped inform this aspect of the book.

Thanks to my good friend, Faye Booker for agreeing to be on the cover of this book (not realising quite how unpleasant the character was before she had agreed to model) and to Patrick Dengate for once again creating a fantastic cover.

I'm indebted to my group of early readers: Mags Gaulden, Connie Parrot, Natalie Levinson, Helen Smith, Dr Karen Cummings, Cheryl Hudson Passey, Elizabeth O'Neal and Laura Wilkinson Hedgecock. You've all been fantastic highlighting typos, missing words, offering ways of improving the story and suggesting new research avenues for Morton, such as the UKBMD register of parishes and registration districts (thanks, Karen!). Thanks also to Peter Calver, who read the story prior to publication and who suggested some changes, including not referring to Aunty Margaret as being old at the age of sixty-one!

Once again, I am very grateful to those groups, bloggers, writers and individuals who champion me and my writing. In particular, Peter Calver at LostCousins; The Genealogy Guys (Drew Smith & George Morgan); DearMyrtle (Pat Richley-Erickson); Scott Fisher at Extreme Genes; Bobbi King and Dick Eastman; Sunny Morton; Lisa Louise Cooke at Genealogy Gems Podcast; Amy Lay and Penny Bonawitz at Genealogy Happy Hour; Andrew Chapman; Karen Clare and Helen Tovey at *Family History* magazine; Sarah Williams at *Who Do You Think You Are?* magazine; Randy Seaver; Jill Ball; Shauna Hicks; Cheryl Hudson Passey; Linda Stufflebean; Sharn White;

Elizabeth O'Neal; Wendy Mathias; James Plyant; Denise Levenick and all of the Family History societies around the world, too numerous to name individually, which have run such kind reviews of the series.

My final thanks must go to my husband, Robert Bristow for all of his 'behind the scenes' efforts, not only with this book but with all of them.

Further Information

Website & Newsletter: www.nathandylangoodwin.com
Twitter: @NathanDGoodwin
Facebook: www.facebook.com/NathanDylanGoodwin
Pinterest: www.pinterest.com/NathanDylanGoodwin
Instagram: www.instagram.com/NathanDylanGoodwin
LinkedIn: www.linkedin.com/in/NathanDylanGoodwin

Morton in Lockdown!

**Want to know what Morton got up to during lockdown?
Want to solve a mini case with him?
Then have a read of *Morton in Lockdown*, an exclusive
interactive web-based story available from
www.nathandylangoodwin.com**

(Here's a sneak preview from Part One. Can you think like Morton
Farrier and reach Part Six?)

Part One

Monday 20th April 2020, Rye, East Sussex

Morton Farrier was bored. It wasn't a word he would ever normally use to describe himself. 'Only boring people get bored,' his mother used to say when, as a child, he would complain to her that he had nothing to do. Maybe he *was* boring. The world was currently upside-down where normality had been suspended indefinitely; perhaps in the course of things he had become less interesting.

The problem was that all of his genealogical cases had ground to a halt on the 24th March, the day after the prime minister had ordered a nationwide lockdown, in line with many other countries around the world. Since the lockdown included every archive, library, church and museum in the country, if his research could not be undertaken online then it had been put on indefinite hold.

He was standing in his study, right at the top of his house on Mermaid Street in Rye, gazing out of the window. Ordinarily, on a warm and sunny day like today, the streets of Rye would have been packed with tourists and holidaymakers. Instead, it resembled a scene from *The Walking Dead* with empty streets and only the occasional person darting out for essentials with a look of fear on their faces, lest they should find themselves confronted with another human being. Strange times. 'Unprecedented', as every news outlet was keen to say about each daily twist and turn. Once this was over, the word *unprecedented* needed to be removed from the dictionary or become universally agreed to be a swear-word. And *furlough* for that matter. He was sure that he had never heard the word in his life before all of this started.

He sighed. There was literally nothing to do. Life had stopped. The view of Rye from his window might as well have been a fake movie backdrop for all the life it was currently displaying. He would think twice next time before moaning about the noisy summer crowds who would gather on the cobbles outside his home, taking photos of all the quirkily named properties. *'The House with Two Front Doors!'* they would chime, standing without thought on his front steps to have their photos taken. Some even felt that it was okay to knock on both of the doors to see which one got answered.

'Morton!' came a shout from downstairs. It was Juliette, his wife.

'Yes?' he replied.

'Can you come down and give me a hand, please?' she called.

He drew in a breath and headed down to the ground floor, where he found Juliette in the kitchen, shoving a baking tray into the oven. Their three-year-old daughter, Grace was sitting up to the table colouring a picture of a lion bright pink and green.

'That's lovely, Grace,' Morton said, crouching down beside her.

'Yes it is,' she agreed, adding pink eyes.

He turned to face Juliette. 'What did you want me for?' he asked.

She stared at him, her face flushed, and tugged a piece of paper free from a *Boston* magnet on the fridge. 'We need these bits from the shop. I know you don't want to go out, but we need them. Also,' she said, 'do you hear those noises?'

Morton listened. The baby was murmuring from the lounge and the phone had just started to ring with Juliette's mother's nightly call. He nodded.

'Would you like to deal with any of them?' she asked.

'No,' clearly wasn't an option. Nor had it been a rhetorical question.

Your Choice!
Morton goes to the shop
Morton answers the phone
Morton goes to the baby

**Visit www.nathandylangoodwin.com/morton-in-lockdown
   to choose your story path**

244

Hiding the Past
(The Forensic Genealogist #1)

Peter Coldrick had no past; that was the conclusion drawn by years of personal and professional research. Then he employed the services of one Morton Farrier, Forensic Genealogist – a stubborn, determined man who uses whatever means necessary to uncover the past. With the Coldrick Case, Morton faces his toughest and most dangerous assignment yet, where all of his investigative and genealogical skills are put to the test. However, others are also interested in the Coldrick family, people who will stop at nothing, including murder, to hide the past. As Morton begins to unearth his client's mysterious past, he is forced to confront his own family's dark history, a history which he knows little about.

'Flicking between the present and stories and extracts from the past, the pace never lets up in an excellent addition to this unique genre of literature'
Your Family Tree magazine

'At times amusing and shocking, this is a fast-moving modern crime mystery with genealogical twists. The blend of well fleshed-out characters, complete with flaws and foibles, will keep you guessing until the end'
Family Tree magazine

'Once I started reading *Hiding the Past* I had great difficulty putting it down - not only did I want to know what happened next, I actually cared'
LostCousins

The Lost Ancestor
(The Forensic Genealogist #2)

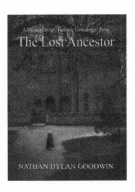

From acclaimed author, Nathan Dylan Goodwin comes this exciting new genealogical crime mystery, featuring the redoubtable forensic genealogist, Morton Farrier. When Morton is called upon by Ray Mercer to investigate the 1911 disappearance of his great aunt, a housemaid working in a large Edwardian country house, he has no idea of the perilous journey into the past that he is about to make. Morton must use his not inconsiderable genealogical skills to solve the mystery of Mary Mercer's disappearance, in the face of the dangers posed by those others who are determined to end his investigation at any cost.

'If you enjoy a novel with a keen eye for historical detail, solid writing, believable settings and a sturdy protagonist, *The Lost Ancestor* is a safe bet. Here British author Nathan Dylan Goodwin spins a riveting genealogical crime mystery with a pulsing, realistic storyline'
Your Family Tree magazine

'Finely paced and full of realistic genealogical terms and tricks, this is an enjoyable whodunit with engaging research twists that keep you guessing until the end. If you enjoy genealogical fiction and Ruth Rendell mysteries, you'll find this a pleasing page-turner'
Family Tree magazine

The Orange Lilies
(The Forensic Genealogist #3)

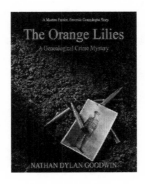

Morton Farrier has spent his entire career as a forensic genealogist solving other people's family history secrets, all the while knowing so little of his very own family's mysterious past. However, this poignant Christmastime novella sees Morton's skills put to use much closer to home, as he must confront his own past, present and future through events both present-day and one hundred years ago. It seems that not every soldier saw a truce on the Western Front that 1914 Christmas…

'The Orange Lilies sees Morton for once investigating his own tree (and about time too!). Moving smoothly between Christmas 1914 and Christmas 2014, the author weaves an intriguing tale with more than a few twists - several times I thought I'd figured it all out, but each time there was a surprise waiting in the next chapter… Thoroughly recommended - and I can't wait for the next novel'
LostCousins

'Morton confronts a long-standing mystery in his own family—one that leads him just a little closer to the truth about his personal origins. This Christmas-time tale flashes back to Christmas 1914, to a turning point in his relatives' lives. Don't miss it!'
Lisa Louise Cooke

The America Ground
(The Forensic Genealogist #4)

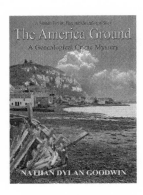

Morton Farrier, the esteemed English forensic genealogist, had cleared a space in his busy schedule to track down his own elusive father finally. But he is then presented with a case that challenges his research skills in his quest to find the killer of a woman murdered more than one hundred and eighty years ago. Thoughts of his own family history are quickly and violently pushed to one side as Morton rushes to complete his investigation before other sinister elements succeed in derailing the case.

'As in the earlier novels, each chapter slips smoothly from past to present, revealing murderous events as the likeable Morton uncovers evidence in the present, while trying to solve the mystery of his own paternity. Packed once more with glorious detail of records familiar to family historians, *The America Ground* is a delightfully pacey read'
Family Tree magazine

'Like most genealogical mysteries this book has several threads, cleverly woven together by the author - and there are plenty of surprises for the reader as the story approaches its conclusion. A jolly good read!'
LostCousins

The Spyglass File
(The Forensic Genealogist #5)

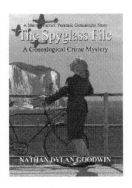

Morton Farrier was no longer at the top of his game. His forensic genealogy career was faltering and he was refusing to accept any new cases, preferring instead to concentrate on locating his own elusive biological father. Yet, when a particular case presents itself, that of finding the family of a woman abandoned in the midst of the Battle of Britain, Morton is compelled to help her to unravel her past. Using all of his genealogical skills, he soon discovers that the case is connected to The Spyglass File—a secretive document which throws up links which threaten to disturb the wrongdoings of others, who would rather its contents, as well as their actions, remain hidden forever.

'If you like a good mystery, and the detective work of genealogy, this is another mystery novel from Nathan which will have you whizzing through the pages with time slipping by unnoticed'
Your Family History magazine

'The first page was so overwhelming that I had to stop for breath...Well, the rest of the book certainly lived up to that impressive start, with twists and turns that kept me guessing right to the end... As the story neared its conclusion I found myself conflicted, for much as I wanted to know how Morton's assignment panned out, I was enjoying it so much that I really didn't want this book to end!'
LostCousins

The Missing Man
(The Forensic Genealogist #6)

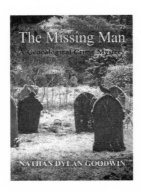

It was to be the most important case of Morton Farrier's career in forensic genealogy so far. A case that had eluded him for many years: finding his own father. Harley 'Jack' Jacklin disappeared just six days after a fatal fire at his Cape Cod home on Christmas Eve in 1976, leaving no trace behind. Now his son, Morton must travel to the East Coast of America to unravel the family's dark secrets in order to discover what really happened to him.

'One of the hallmarks of genealogical mystery novels is the way that they weave together multiple threads and this book is no exception, cleverly skipping across the generations - and there's also a pleasing symmetry that helps to endear us to one of the key characters...If you've read the other books in this series you won't need me to tell you to rush out and buy this one'
LostCousins

'Nathan Dylan Goodwin has delivered another page-turning mystery laden with forensic genealogical clues that will keep any family historian glued to the book until the mystery is solved'
Eastman's Online Genealogy Newsletter

The Wicked Trade
(The Forensic Genealogist #7)

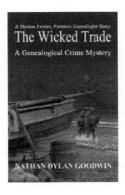

When Morton Farrier is presented with a case revolving around a mysterious letter written by disreputable criminal, Ann Fothergill in 1827, he quickly finds himself delving into a shadowy Georgian underworld of smuggling and murder on the Kent and Sussex border. Morton must use his skills as a forensic genealogist to untangle Ann's association with the notorious Aldington Gang and also with the brutal killing of Quartermaster Richard Morgan. As his research continues, Morton suspects that his client's family might have more troubling and dangerous expectations of his findings.

'Once again the author has carefully built the story around real places, real people, and historical facts - and whilst the tale itself is fictional, it's so well written that you'd be forgiven for thinking it was true'
LostCousins

'I can thoroughly recommend this book, which is a superior example of its genre. It is an ideal purchase for anyone with an interest in reading thrillers and in family history studies. I look forward to the next instalment of Morton Farrier's quest!'
Waltham Forest FHS

The Sterling Affair
(The Forensic Genealogist #8)

When an unannounced stranger comes calling at Morton Farrier's front door, he finds himself faced with the most intriguing and confounding case of his career to-date as a forensic genealogist. He agrees to accept the contract to identify a man who had been secretly living under the name of his new client's long-deceased brother. Morton must use his range of resources and research skills to help him deconstruct this mysterious man's life, ultimately leading him back into the murky world of 1950s international affairs of state. Meanwhile, Morton is faced with his own alarmingly close DNA match which itself comes with far-reaching implications for the Farriers.

'If you love a whodunnit, *The Sterling Affair* is sure to grab your curiosity, and if you enjoy family history, you'll relish the read all the more'
Family History magazine

'The events of the book are as much of a roller-coaster ride for Morton as they are for the reader. If you're an avid reader of Nathan Dylan Goodwin's books, you won't need to be convinced to buy this latest instalment in the Forensic Genealogist series - but if you're not, now's the time to start, because *The Sterling Affair* is a real cracker!'
LostCousins

The Foundlings
(The Forensic Genealogist #9)

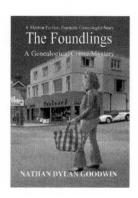

Forensic genealogist, Morton Farrier, agrees to take on a case to identify the biological mother of three foundlings, abandoned in shop doorways as new-born babies in the 1970s. He has just one thing with which to begin his investigation: the three women's DNA, one of whom is his half-aunt. With just six days of research time available to him, his investigation uncovers some shocking revelations and troubling links to his own grandfather; and Morton finds that, for the first time in his career, he is advising his clients not to read his concluding report.

'This is a fun and engaging read that will transport you back to a memorable decade'
Family Tree magazine

'This is one of the best books in an excellent series...Highly recommended'
LostCousins

'Absolutely riveting — the best yet in this series!'
Tacoma-Pierce County Genealogical Society

'A must read for anyone who loves unraveling genealogy mysteries'
Columbia County Historical & Genealogical Society

Manufactured by Amazon.ca
Bolton, ON

29669667R00152